A Breath of Scandal

CONNIE MASON

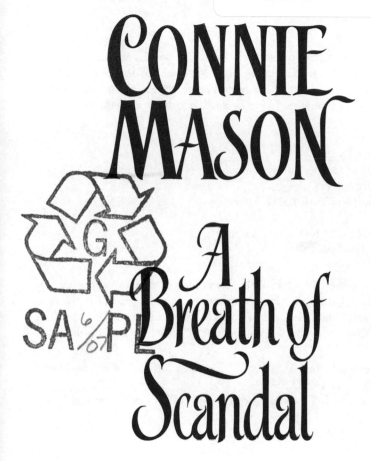

A Breath of Scandal

An Avon Romantic Treasure

AVON BOOKS
An Imprint of HarperCollinsPublishers

AVON BOOKS
An Imprint of HarperCollins*Publishers*
10 East 53rd Street
New York, New York 10022-5299

Chapter 1

French Coast
1765

Julian jammed his woolen cap down low over his forehead, slipped from behind a stand of trees lining the desolate stretch of beach, and joined the ragtag group of peasants who were rolling barrels of prime brandy and carrying chests of French lace from the gaping mouth of a cave. Beneath a moonless sky, darkness and mist swallowed the beach and sea beyond as peasants and smugglers alike worked diligently to pile their contraband on the shore.

Julian had huddled out of sight in the chilly predawn, waiting for the ship anchored just beyond the breakers to send its jolly boats to pick up the contraband. Wearing a beard to disguise his identity, Julian had joined a group of peasants who had been promised top wages for a night's work. More than they could earn in a year.

"There's the signal for the boats," a man standing beside Julian said in country French that Julian understood perfectly. "We'll be paid well for this night's work." Julian merely grunted.

A man in a billowing cloak that swirled around his tall form suddenly appeared on the mist-shrouded beach. He lifted his arm and waved a glowing lantern back and forth. An answering light appeared from the ship's bow. Julian knew it was the signal he'd been waiting for and tensed. When the first jolly boat arrived, the man in the cloak pulled his collar up high so that none would recognize his face. Intuition told Julian that this was the man called the Jackal, the smuggler Whitehall had been trying to run down for years. The man who had been responsible for the death of Julian's fiancée.

The hackles rose on the back of Julian's neck. He wanted this man so badly he broke out in a cold sweat just thinking about it. He wouldn't rest until he saw the Jackal swinging at the end of a rope. And now that he was on the verge of identifying the Jackal, anticipation soared through him. Julian Thornton, Earl of Mansfield, had his suspicions, but no solid proof to take back to William Randall and Whitehall. Of one thing Julian was certain: The Jackal was someone of importance, for his information was always on target, as if he knew ahead of time when and where Randall's agents would strike.

His body tense, his head tucked low, Julian rolled a barrel down the sandy beach to the waiting longboat. The moment he'd learned when the shipment was to be sent and where it was to land, he'd sent the information by a swift messenger to Randall. This time the smugglers were in for a surprise. Agents would be waiting for them to arrive on a deserted stretch of coast in Cornwall. Julian was sure of his information, for he'd gotten it directly from a sailor aboard the ship carrying the contraband. Money worked every time.

The shrouded figure in the billowing cloak kept careful watch of the contraband being loaded into the jolly boats. Julian passed beneath his intense scrutiny, head tucked down, eyes averted. As much as he wanted to identify the Jackal, he didn't look up for fear of being recognized. But Julian knew he would have his day once the smugglers had been taken into custody.

After the boats were loaded, he dared a glance over his shoulder and saw the Jackal conversing with one of the smugglers.

The smuggler singled Julian out and motioned to him. "Ye there! Come here."

Julian pretended not to hear as he waited on the beach with the peasants to be paid for his night's work.

"Ye there! Step forward!"

Julian froze. He sensed danger and tried to diffuse it by pretending to be one of the villagers.

"Me, monsieur?" Julian asked in the broad, country dialect he'd heard spoken in the village.

"Aye, ye," the smuggler said in rough, barely understandable French. "Do ye speak English?"

"Ah, non, monsieur. I am but a poor farmer who needs the coin to feed my family. I speak only country dialect."

"Stupid Frog," the smuggler muttered in English. "Get aboard the jolly boat."

Julian began to sweat beneath his thick sweater and knitted scarf. "I must return to my home," he replied. "My wife awaits me."

"The Jackal wants ye taken aboard," the smuggler said.

"The Jackal?"

The smuggler pointed to the cloaked figure striding away from them. "Aye, the Jackal. 'Tis what we call him."

"What does he want with me?" Julian asked, beginning to feel like a trapped rabbit. Had the Jackal recognized him?

The smuggler grinned, revealing a mouthful of rotted teeth. "He thinks ye be a government agent." He shuddered. "Ye better pray ye ain't."

"You are mistaken, monsieur, I am no spy," Julian said obsequiously. "Can I go home to my wife now?"

"Get in the boat," the sailor ordered, pushing a pistol into Julian's back.

"Why doesn't the Jackal confront me himself if he thinks I am a spy?" Julian challenged.

"No one questions the Jackal," the sailor said. "No one sees his face except a privileged few, and you ain't one of them. He'll send one of his men to question ye."

Julian felt the cold fingers of death brush his face. He'd been so careful to cover his tracks. So meticulous about his secret identity. Not even his brother, Sinjun, knew the precise nature of his work, or the name by which he was known.

They called him Scorpion. His identity was known only to William Randall. His work for Whitehall had taken him to the continent, to Italy, and to various destinations throughout the British Isles, wherever he was needed.

He was sure this time he would succeed. He'd come so close. Where had he gone wrong? Who had penetrated his careful web of secrecy? Who wanted him dead?

Julian cursed his bad luck when the smuggler searched him and found his pistol.

"I'll take that," the smuggler said, stuffing the weapon inside his belt. Then he prodded Julian toward the boat. Julian knew that once he was in the boat he was as good as dead. He had to act now. Before he reached the boat, Julian broke and ran for cover.

It was not to be. A shot pierced through the night, finding a target in Julian's shoulder. Julian spun around and hit the wet sand. He fought to master the pain and continue his flight, but two brawny smugglers were upon him almost instantly. They dragged him down the beach and tossed him into the boat.

Immediately the boat was pushed out into the water. Julian heard the slap of oars, felt the boat rock. The buzzing in his head intensified, muffling the world around him. Then he knew no more.

Julian awoke to the creak and groan of wooden beams, the soft slap of water against the hull, and the clink of metal rings on yardarms. He heard canvas whipping in the wind and felt the deck heaving. He tried to rise but grinding pain in his shoulder curtailed his valiant efforts. A groan slipped past his lips.

A shadow loomed before him. "So yer awake, are ye?"

Julian stared mutely at the hulking figure.

"The Jackal says yer a spy. We'll find out soon enough when we unload on the beach near Dumfries."

It took a moment for the ship's destination to register in Julian's head. "Dumfries! That's in Scotland. I thought . . ."

"Aye, I know what ye thought. The Jackal changed our destination. He learned that agents were waiting for us in Cornwall. We're to head up Solway Firth, unload our cargo on the beach when we see the signal, and wait for the wagons that will transport it to London and Edinburgh."

Pain made concentrating difficult, but Julian saw no logic in the sailor telling him these things. Unless, of course, the Jackal had no intention of letting Julian live.

Julian shifted on the narrow bunk, stifling a groan as pain radiated through his body in wave after wave of raw agony. Gingerly he touched his shoulder, surprised to find a crude bandage over his wound.

"I did that," the sailor bragged. "I ain't a doctor, but I've patched many a sailor in my time."

"Why did you bother?" Julian asked wearily.

"The Jackal wants ye kept alive for questioning. He's curious about the man called Scorpion. And he wants to make sure yer the agent who's been a thorn in his side for so long. Soon as ye give up yer information, he'll have ye killed."

It would be a cold day in hell before he'd give anything of value to the Jackal, Julian swore. "How long before we reach Solway Firth?"

"Four days. Ye been out like a light fer longer than that."

"I'm thirsty."

The sailor plunged a dipper into a bucket of water and handed it to Julian. Julian managed to drink half of it before the effort became too much and he handed the dipper back to the sailor.

"I'll bring ye something to eat if there's anything left after everyone's had their fill." The sailor headed out the door. "And don't think ye can escape 'cause there's nowhere ye can go. Nothing but miles of water out there."

Julian stared at the closed door so long that it began to swim before his eyes. He had four days. Four days in which to plan his escape. Silently he pondered his chances for survival. He was wounded, weak from loss of blood, feverish, and could expect no help.

He was as good as dead.

Four days later Julian was still weak, still feverish, and had yet to devise a viable plan of escape. He dragged himself from the filthy bunk to the porthole and peered out into the darkness. The ship was anchored in the firth, a few hundred yards from shore. His view of the activity taking place on deck was obstructed, but he heard sounds indicating that the contraband was being lowered to jolly boats waiting in the water below.

Julian returned to the bunk to conserve his strength for the ordeal he knew he'd soon have to face. The wait was long and agonizing, but when the door to his prison was flung open, it was almost anticlimactic.

A sailor appeared in the doorway. "Can ye walk?"

"Well enough," Julian said grimly as he rose stiffly and shuffled forward.

The narrow corridor and ladder leading up to the deck was almost beyond his capability, but somehow he managed. Then cool, damp air hit him like a jolt of adrenaline when he most needed it.

Julian made a move toward the railing and felt the barrel of a pistol pressing into the middle of his back.

"Stay here till they're ready to take ye to shore," the smuggler warned.

Julian glanced wildly around him. Every able-bodied man was engaged in some activity or other as they moved about the deck with grim purpose. It was now or never, Julian thought as he girded himself to make a last-ditch effort to escape. Accepting death meekly didn't appeal to him. He might still die in the attempt, but time had run out. And should he never be identified as Scorpion, the Jackal would pose no threat to his family.

There was Emma, his beautiful sister, who had grown up too fast and was already a handful. And Sinjun, who had finally found a woman he loved enough to give up his decadent ways. Sinjun's son would do the earldom proud, especially since Julian planned to produce no heirs. After Diana's death, Julian had vowed never to marry. No other woman or child of his would die on his account.

Julian inched closer to the railing, pretending an interest in the activities below. His guard followed, glancing down to see what had caught Julian's attention. Taking a deep breath, Julian gripped the railing and vaulted over, launching himself up and away from the boats below. He fell. Down . . . down . . . into the dark, churning sea.

He was dimly aware that the railing was suddenly crowded with sailors. Gunshots broke the silence of the night; bullets struck the sea around him, spraying water into his face. Then a bullet plowed into him, and pain explode in his brain. His arms went numb, his body sank, and water closed over his head.

Chapter 2

Scottish coast

Colorful Gypsy skirts stirred by brisk sea breezes whipped wildly about Lara's long, bare legs as she stood on a cliff above the firth, watching the tide roll out. How she would miss the untamed land of her birth when she returned to London to take up residence with her father.

Lara sighed heavily. She hated balls, routs, and stuffy dinner parties, but her father wanted her to have a season in London. At twenty, she should have had her season behind her, but she had resisted. Raised by her Gypsy mother in a Romany camp until the age of thirteen, Lara hadn't even known of her father's existence. Her mother had revealed his name as she lay dying from a lung disease. It had come as quite a shock to Lara to learn that her father was an English nobleman who never knew she existed.

Not knowing her father had never mattered to Lara, for she loved her life with the Rom, and worshipped her grandmother Ramona and grandfather Pietro. But Serena, Lara's mother, had insisted that

Ramona and Pietro take Lara to her father upon her death. To her father's credit, he had welcomed her with open arms.

The one thing that saved Lara from being miserable in her new life was her father's generous and loving nature. He had allowed her to return to Scotland and the Romany camp each summer to be with her grandparents. But Lara feared this summer would be the last, and she felt as if a large part of her life was about to end.

Lara glanced down at the pounding surf. The outgoing tide had exposed an inviting crescent of beach that spoke to the untamed Gypsy in her. With the exuberance of a wild child of nature, she flew down the narrow path leading to the beach, her dark eyes glowing with the pleasure of being young, lighthearted, and free of strictures for a few more weeks.

Lara ran along the beach, her bare feet leaving small prints in the wet sand. She lifted her face to the warm sun and laughed aloud from the pure joy of being alive on this fine day.

"Lara! Ramona is looking for you. 'Tis time to move on."

Lara looked over her shoulder and grinned at Rondo, the playmate of her youth, now a handsome man of twenty-three, looking down at her from the cliff above.

"Must we leave?" Lara complained. " 'Tis so beautiful here."

"Pietro wants to reach Lockerbie in time for the big fair. Our horses should sell well there."

Lara nodded, then turned for one last look at the beach and sea beyond, absorbing the untamed beauty of sand and water and towering cliffs into her pores. Her inquisitive gaze settled on a bundle of rags that had washed up on the beach. Her curiosity piqued, she started forward.

"Lara, where are you going?"

"There's something on the beach."

Rondo sounded impatient. "Leave it. 'Tis probably nothing of importance."

But it *was* something. Lara felt it in her bones, heard fate calling to her. She dropped down on her knees beside the bundle, tentatively reaching out to touch something that looked more solid than mere rags. She encountered flesh and bone and let out a startled gasp.

A human body!

She turned the body over. It was a man, one precariously close to death. She found a weak pulse. His face was ashen, his lips blue and bloodless.

"Rondo, come quickly! 'Tis a man!"

Rondo scrambled down the path. "Is he alive?"

"I think so."

He pushed her aside. "Let me have a look."

For some unexplained reason Lara was loath to leave the man's side. Something within her whispered that this man needed her. She watched with bated breath as Rondo felt for a pulse and placed his ear against the lifeless chest.

"Aye, he's alive, just barely."

"Do something. We can't let him die."

"I don't see why not. He probably came from one of the smuggling ships operating in these waters. He's dressed like a peasant or a common sailor."

"Don't be so hard-hearted, Rondo. Press the water out of his lungs."

Grumbling, Rondo turned the man on his stomach, straddled him, and began pumping in and out.

" 'Tis no use," Rondo said.

"Keep pumping," Lara urged. For some obscure reason it seemed important to keep this man alive.

Rondo renewed his efforts and was rewarded when a gush of water spurted from the man's lungs. He gagged and coughed, but his eyes remained closed and his breathing ragged.

Lara's voice was anxious with worry. "Let's take him to Ramona. She'll know what to do."

"I don't know why it's so important to cart a man who probably won't live out the day up the cliff," Rondo complained. "He's a *gadjo*."

"Rondo, please. He's a human being."

"You know I can refuse you nothing," Rondo said as he hefted the man over his shoulder.

"He's bleeding!" Lara cried when she saw blood dripping down one limp hand onto the wet sand. "Hurry!"

Lara led the way up the path, looking back frequently to make sure Rondo followed. They reached the top, and Lara instructed Rondo to take the wounded *gadjo* to her wagon.

" 'Tis not right," Rondo complained. "You're a maiden."

"Just do as I say, Rondo. I'm going for Ramona."

Pietro intercepted Lara before she reached the gaily painted wagon her grandparents shared. "What is it, little one?"

"I found a wounded man on the beach, Grandfather. Rondo carried him to my wagon. I need Grandmother to heal his wounds."

"What kind of wounds?"

"I don't know. There's blood, but I don't know where it's coming from. Please fetch Grandmother. Tell her to bring her healing tools and herbs."

Pietro must have sensed his granddaughter's urgency, for he hurried off to do her bidding, allowing Lara to hasten back to her wagon.

"How is he?" she asked as she ducked inside.

Rondo had finished his cursory inspection of the unconscious man. "He's seriously wounded, probably shot more than once. Someone wanted him dead . . . badly. The *gadjo* will bring trouble to us, Lara. 'Tis best we let him die."

"What's this about dying?"

Ramona ducked inside the wagon, pushing Rondo aside to look at the man lying on her granddaughter's bed. Her dark face was deeply lined and her hair streaked with gray, yet somehow she appeared ageless. Her ample figure was garbed in clothing every bit as colorful and flamboyant as her granddaughter's.

"Who is he?"

"There's no identification on him," Rondo said. "Look at him. The rough clothes and scuffed boots are those of a peasant."

"Can you save him, Grandmother?" Lara asked anxiously.

Ramona's brown eyes held the wisdom of ages as she looked beyond Lara, to something only she could see.

"He is *gadjo*," she intoned dryly.

"And I am half *gadjo*," Lara reminded her.

Brow furrowed, Ramona studied her granddaughter intently, then returned her gaze to the wounded man.

"I will do what I can. Rondo can remain to help me

remove his clothing, but you must leave. You are still an innocent."

Lara wanted to object but knew Ramona would fight her on this, so she left the wagon without an argument. She joined Pietro outside. His thick, gray brows were knitted together with worry.

"Who is he?"

"We don't know, Grandfather, but he's as near death as a man can get."

Pietro suddenly looked alarmed. " 'Tis not good, Lara. I fear this man will bring trouble to our people. What if his enemies come looking for him?"

"I don't know," Lara said, looking down at her dirty toes. "I haven't thought that far ahead. Rondo thinks he'll die, so that problem will probably never come up."

Pietro held out his arms and Lara walked into them. "Why is this man so important to you, little one?"

Lara had no answer. She bit her lip to keep them from trembling and shook her head, sending a tangle of shiny dark curls cascading over her shoulders.

"Ah, little one. You are so beautiful, so innocent, yet so filled with life." He smoothed a wayward curl from her forehead. "You are fiery and untamed, just like your mother. Spirited and impetuous, too, and sometimes I fear for you. I hope your father finds a mate worthy of you."

"Maybe I'll never marry, Grandfather," Lara ventured. "I will not marry without love."

"I feel confident you will find a man to love, little one."

Lara glanced toward the wagon. "What do you suppose is taking so long?"

"If anyone can heal the wounded *gadjo*, 'tis your grandmother. You must have patience."

Patience, Lara thought, was something she'd never had in abundance. Then suddenly the door opened and Rondo staggered out. He was white as a sheet and looked ready to lose the contents of his stomach.

"Rondo! What is it?"

"Ramona is digging out the bullet in his back now, and the one she removed from his shoulder is festering. 'Tisn't a pretty sight."

"Bullets? More than one?" Lara said.

"Two. He was shot once in the shoulder and again in the back. The infection is serious and still might kill him despite Ramona's healing skills."

"I'm going in," Lara said, striding resolutely toward the wagon.

"Lara, the man's naked," Rondo said, grabbing her arm.

Lara shrugged away. "Someone needs to help Ramona. Obviously you've no stomach for it."

Rondo made another grab at her but Pietro stopped him. "Let her go," the older man said. "No one can stop Lara when her mind is made up. Haven't you learned that yet?"

Lara opened the door and stepped inside the wagon. Her gaze darted to the bed, where Ramona was bent over the inert body of the man she'd found on the beach.

"Hand me that bottle of disinfectant," Ramona said crisply. "If you've come to help, make yourself useful."

Lara found the disinfectant on the nightstand and handed it to Ramona. "How is he?"

"Still alive."

Lara's gaze was drawn to the bed, to the man lying atop the covers. He was naked but for a cloth covering his loins. Lara couldn't look away. This man was no peasant, nor was he a common sailor. He wasn't Scottish, either. He hadn't the Gaelic look about him. Beneath his beard his handsome face was patrician, and his long, lean body was too elegant to come from peasant stock. He appeared to be a man who kept his body in top shape.

His chest was broad, his biceps prominently defined. Lara had no idea what lay beneath the cloth covering his loins, but it had to be as impressive as the rest of him. Yet it was his face to which her gaze kept returning. His lips intrigued her. They were full and sensual, inviting all kinds of wicked thoughts. His lashes were indecently long for a man; his eyebrows were as dark as his hair and elegantly curved. His square chin was entirely masculine. Lara tried to envision the color of his eyes but soon gave up.

"What are you doing?" Lara asked, returning her gaze to Ramona.

"I'm squeezing out the infection. There's little more I can do. The bullet in his back was difficult, and dangerously close to his lungs. Hand me the needle and thread. I'm going to sew him up. Then we wait, and rely on a higher influence to make the decision of life or death."

"I'll sit with him, Grandmother," Lara said, pulling a chair close to the bed.

Ramona finished stitching the wounded man and settled a blanket over him. She searched Lara's face, then nodded acquiescence. "I will return soon."

"Grandmother," Lara implored, "tell Grandfather that we mustn't leave for the fair at Lockerbie until your patient can travel. The roads are rough. Jostling him about in the wagon could kill him."

"I will discuss it with Pietro," Ramona said as she let herself out the door.

Lara sat beside the wounded *gadjo*, waiting for him to open his eyes. Questions about him burned her tongue. There was so much she wanted to know. His name. Where he came from. Who wanted him dead. A small voice within her whispered that there was more to this man than met the eye. She knew Ramona sensed it too, for she seemed to know things no one else knew. Ramona could read a person's palm and predict his destiny, unlike some Gypsies, who merely pretended to have the gift her grandmother possessed.

Lara wasn't aware of the passage of time until Ramona returned to the wagon a few hours later. "How is he?"

"Nothing has changed."

Ramona felt his forehead. "The fever will begin soon. I sent Rondo to fetch cold water from the sea. Go eat with the others, I will sit here with him."

Lara didn't want to leave, but obeyed her grandmother with marked reluctance.

Lara paused at the door. "Did you speak to Grandfather about remaining here a few days longer?"

"Aye. He agreed to delay our leaving a day or two, until the *gadjo* either dies or shows signs of improvement."

Lara's voice held a note of anxiety. "You won't let him die, will you, Grandmother?"

" 'Tis in God's hands," Ramona replied, staring intently into the *gadjo*'s face. "Go now. Perhaps you can hurry Rondo along with the cold water."

Ramona continued to stare at the *gadjo* long after Lara left. Why was Lara so taken with the *gadjo*? She sensed his troubled spirit and felt evil surrounding him. She knew not whether the evil emanated from him or from others who wished him harm. Nor did she know how it would affect Lara. She only knew that destiny was at work.

Ramona shifted her gaze to the *gadjo*'s hand. It lay limply upon the blanket, open and vulnerable. Disregarding every tingling nerve ending that warned her not to tempt fate, she cradled his palm in her hands. One sensitive finger traced the lines, pausing as she explored the soft pad of his thumb and deep indentations scoring his palm. Suddenly she let out a cry and dropped the hand as if it had scalded her.

Closing her eyes, she muttered an incantation. Her probing into his destiny had revealed a tormented man courted by danger. Powerful forces were at work. Ramona knew intuitively that the *gadjo*'s enemies were a threat to her beloved granddaughter. And there was little she could do to prevent it.

Somewhere in the murky depths of his brain Julian perceived another presence, but sensed no danger. He was aware of unbearable pain, of heat, then he drifted back to the sublime state where he heard and felt nothing.

"Rondo's here with the water, Grandmother," Lara said, holding the door open for Rondo.

"Set it on the floor, then both of you leave," Ramona ordered.

"Let me help," Lara pleaded.

"No," Rondo argued. "You don't belong in here. I will send one of the married women to help if Ramona needs someone."

"I need no one," Ramona replied. "Go, both of you."

Lara withdrew. Rondo followed. "You are attracted to the *gadjo*," Rondo charged.

"He is sorely in need of my help." With a toss of her curly hair, she walked away to join a group of her friends.

The Rom were sitting around a central campfire eating supper and exchanging gossip when Ramona joined them.

"Does the *gadjo* live?" Pietro asked.

"He lives. He is a stubborn one. He refuses to give up his spirit."

"Eat, Grandmother," Lara urged. "I will sit with him while you rest."

"He is feverish, Lara, and the worst is yet to come. Call me if you need me."

Lara hurried into her wagon and pulled the chair closer to the bed. Despite the golden glow of candlelight, the *gadjo*'s face was pale, and purple shadows dusted the fragile skin beneath his eyes. From time to time he moaned and shivered. Lara pulled the blanket up around his neck and crooned softly to him in the Romany tongue.

She fell asleep with her head resting on the side of the bed, her hand clutching his as if to let him know he wasn't alone.

Lara awoke to the sound of excited voices and daylight shining through the curtained window. She jerked upright just as the door burst inward.

"There's a ship in the cove," Rondo informed her. "They launched a jolly boat and 'tis heading to the beach."

Warning bells went off in Lara's head. "What does Pietro say?"

"He is worried. So is Ramona. We should have left yesterday."

Lara glanced at the wounded *gadjo*, then turned back to Rondo. "I must speak with my grandparents."

The *gadjo* shifted restlessly and groaned.

"Has he awakened?"

"No, he's been doing that all night."

They left the wagon. The entire camp appeared in a state of agitation. A group of Rom had gathered around her grandparents, and she hurried over to join them.

"Does the ship in the cove mean trouble for us, Grandfather?"

"I know not, little one. We must wait and see and be prepared to defend ourselves should they prove unfriendly to the Romany. How fares the *gadjo*?"

"The same. He is barely conscious and feverish. Do you think the men from the ship are the same ones who tried to kill him? What if they're searching for him?"

Ramona's dark eyes turned inward. "We will survive," she said cryptically.

"Please don't give him up," Lara implored.

Ramona never got to answer that question. A dozen armed men burst into the camp.

"We mean ye no harm," a burly sailor growled. "We're looking for a man who may have washed up on shore near here. Have ye seen him?"

Much to Lara's relief, Pietro said, "We have seen no one."

"Are ye sure? 'Tis important. 'Tis important that we know whether he is dead or alive."

"Look elsewhere, *gadjo*," Ramona suggested. "There is no stranger among us."

"Don't believe them, Crockett," a sailor behind him said. He stepped forward, brandishing his pistol in a threatening manner. "Ye can't trust a heathen Gypsy." He waved his pistol in Pietro's face. "I say we beat the old one until we get the truth from him."

"There's another way," Crockett said, glancing at the wagons scattered about the camp. "We'll search every wagon, every nook and cranny. Spread out, men."

Panic seized Lara. These men were the enemy. If she didn't think of something fast, they would find and kill the wounded *gadjo*.

The sailors set off toward the wagons while Crockett held his pistol on the Rom. Lara's heart sank when she spied a sailor heading toward her wagon. Without thinking, she broke away from the group, raced to her wagon, and planted herself before the door.

"Move aside, wench," the sailor warned.

Lara held her ground. "You can't go inside."

The sailor grasped her about the waist and swung her out of the way. "Be good and I'll let ye pleasure me for a silver coin when we're finished here."

"Don't touch me!" Lara blasted.

"Why not? Everyone knows Gypsy wenches are whores."

"What's the problem?" Crockett asked when he noticed the ruckus taking place outside Lara's wagon.

"The bitch won't let me inside," the sailor growled.

Crockett strode over to join them. "Oh, she won't? We'll see about that."

He shoved Lara aside and pushed open the door. Pietro and Ramona rushed to their granddaughter's defense. The Rom followed in their wake.

Crockett glowered at Lara and her grandparents. "Well, well, what do we have here? Who are ye trying to protect?"

Lara uttered the first words that came into her head. " 'Tis Drago, my husband. He's ill." A murmur of surprise rose up from the Rom gathered outside the wagon.

"Ill, ye say. Are ye sure he's yer husband?"

"Aye, the man inside is my husband."

A whisper of warning reached Lara's ears, but it was too late now to back down.

Crockett opened the door and ducked inside the wagon. "Mayhap I'll have a look."

Lara glanced toward the motionless form on the bed and breathed a sigh of relief. The *gadjo*'s face was partially obscured by the blanket. But her relief was short-lived when she realized that Crockett would know the moment he saw the *gadjo*'s white skin that he was no Gypsy. She sent a silent plea to Ramona.

"Ye say the man is yer husband?" Crockett asked again.

"Aye, Drago, my husband," Lara repeated for the third time.

Ramona moved up beside her to lend support and Lara grasped her hand.

"Awaken him," Crockett ordered.

"He's too ill. I don't know if he'll awaken."

Crockett pointed his pistol at the still figure beneath the blanket.

"Don't shoot!" Lara cried, rushing to the bed. "I'll awaken him."

Crockett advanced a step toward the bed. Ramona placed a restraining hand on his arm. "No! Drago has smallpox. Approach him at your own risk."

Color leeched from Crockett's face. "Smallpox? Why should I believe ye?"

"Go look for yourself."

Crockett hesitated, his fear palpable. He stepped back and glared at Lara.

"Awaken him, wench. I wish to question him."

Lara clamped down on her bottom lip to keep it from trembling as she gently shook the *gadjo*. When he failed to respond, she shook harder. He moaned and opened his eyes.

Julian gazed up into a pair of mesmerizing dark eyes. He had no idea where he was, or why he hurt so badly. He only knew that he must be in heaven. The face that went with the eyes was that of an angel. An angel like no other, one with fiery depths and spirit. A wanton angel with curly black hair and snapping black eyes. He liked that.

"Drago, can you hear me?"

Her voice held a smoky quality that pulled him from the depths of his misery.

"Drago. Answer me. 'Tis Lara."

Drago? Who in the hell was Drago? He supposed it wouldn't hurt to play along with the woman. Did she say her name was Lara?

"Aye," he said groggily. Was that his voice? He hardly recognized it.

"Must I continue?" he heard Lara ask someone who must have been standing nearby.

"He's awake. I'll ask the questions now."

"Drago!" Crockett called out. "Can ye hear me?"

"Aye."

"The wench here says yer her husband. Is that true?"

Julian would have laughed aloud had he the strength. Husband, that was rich. Since he never intended to marry, he could be no woman's husband. But Lara was looking at him so intently, he felt compelled to please her.

"Aye, I am Lara's husband."

His words were slurred but understandable, carrying beyond the open door to those standing outside. A collective gasp rose up from the crowd and didn't subside until Ramona's stern look hushed them.

"Do ye have smallpox, Drago?" Crockett probed relentlessly.

Smallpox. It was a possibility. He certainly felt sick enough to have smallpox. He was clinging to consciousness by a slim thread and would agree to almost anything at this point. Besides, for all he knew he *did* have smallpox.

"Aye."

That one word was enough to clear the small wagon of Crockett's threatening presence. He joined his men in their flight to escape the dreaded illness.

"You know what you've done, don't you, Lara?" Ramona asked gently.

"Aye, Grandmother, I know. It couldn't be helped. 'Twas the only way to save him. Thank you for not interfering."

" 'Tis not an easy course you've set for yourself, little one. Fate has taken a hand in your future, and there is little you can do now to stop it. You are married to a stranger you know nothing about. You proclaimed him your husband three times before witnesses and the *gadjo* acknowledged it as the truth. You know the ways of our people. You are now wed to the *gadjo*. May God protect you."

Aye, may God protect me, Lara thought as she gazed at the man she knew only as Drago.

Chapter 3

Julian awakened to pain, and the thrilling realization that he was alive. Though he had no idea where he was, he did know that the bed upon which he lay was not his own. His first thought was that he was back aboard the smuggler's ship, but the clean, sweet-smelling sheets soon disabused him of that notion.

Julian tried to jog his memory but failed. He moved, which proved a huge mistake. A searing flame radiated from his shoulder and traveled down his back, touching every part of his body. The pain was so severe it almost made him wish he *was* dead. He tried to swallow but his mouth was as dry as a desert. He craved water. Had he said the word aloud? He must have, for immediately someone held a cup of cool water to his lips. He drank thirstily. When he'd drunk his fill, he tried to focus his eyes on his angel of mercy.

His sight cleared slowly, revealing an alluring vision that he vaguely remembered from his dreams. He tried to reach up and touch the angel's face, but he lacked the strength to do so, and his hand fell back uselessly to the bed.

"Are you real?" he rasped.

Her husky laugh was mesmerizing. But it was her throaty voice that sent waves of awareness through him. "I'm real. Welcome to the world of the living. For a while we feared you wouldn't join us."

"We? Where am I?"

"In a Romany camp. I am Lara, and this is my wagon."

Julian frowned, trying to recall something of importance that he had forgotten. The woman's name sounded vaguely familiar. "How long have I been here? What is wrong with me?"

"Don't you remember?"

"Not everything. Refresh my memory."

"I found you on the beach and brought you to our camp. You have been with us for several days. Grandmother removed the bullet from your back, and the second wound in your shoulder was badly infected. You lingered between life and death and would have died if not for my grandmother's skill."

Julian's memory was still hazy. "Bullets?"

"Aye. You were shot twice. Once in the shoulder and again in the back. Do you remember who shot you?"

The mist clouding his mind lifted and Julian recalled precisely why he had been shot and who had done it. But he wasn't about to tell this strange Gypsy girl anything, including his name. The last thing he wanted was to bring trouble to the people who had saved his life.

"I can't disclose the answers you are seeking," Julian demurred weakly. " 'Tis best you don't know. I do not wish to bring harm to your people."

Lara mulled over his words. "Can you tell me your name?"

"Call me whatever you wish."

"While you are here with us, we will call you Drago."

Julian's brow puckered. Where had he heard that name before? He dimly recalled . . . No, the memory was gone.

"They came for you, you know."

"Who came for me?"

"The men who want you dead."

Julian tensed. "What happened?"

"Ramona told them you had smallpox. I claimed you were Drago, one of our people."

Julian closed his eyes, pondering everything Lara had told him. He recalled jumping into the firth from the smuggler's ship, and bullets hitting the water all around him. He remembered precious little after a bullet had found a home in his back. He had no idea how he had reached shore alive.

"I'm sorry to cause you so much trouble. I'll leave as soon as I'm able."

"Don't think about leaving until you are well. You'll be safe here with us. Will you tell me nothing about yourself?"

"The less you and your people know about me, the better off you'll be," Julian replied, trying to move and wincing at the effort.

"You're in pain," Lara said. "I'll fetch Grandmother, she'll know what to do."

Julian watched her walk away, not too incapacitated to admire the sway of her curvaceous hips beneath her multicolored skirt, or to note the golden perfection of her shoulders, which were tantalizingly bare above the low cut peasant blouse. He sighed.

The Gypsy wench was quite an eyeful. He wondered what lucky man claimed her favors.

Pain had taken over Julian's body by the time Lara returned with her grandmother, whom she hastily introduced as Ramona. Ramona took one look at his face and produced a bottle from the pocket of her voluminous skirts. She poured a small measure in a glass and held it to his lips. Julian balked.

"Drink, Drago," Ramona urged. " 'Tis naught but laudanum. 'Twill ease the pain and make you sleep. Lara will watch over you."

Ramona's last sentence convinced Julian to drink down the bitter brew. He rather liked the idea of Lara watching over him.

"Lara said you saved my life, Ramona. Thank you."

"We will speak of this later," Ramona said, rising. "I will prepare broth for you and send it over with Rondo. Lara can feed it to you. Try to take as much as you can. Your body needs liquids."

The moment she was gone, Julian slid easily into sleep. When he awakened, Lara was still there. She smiled at him. Then a young Gypsy man arrived with the broth Ramona had prepared.

Rondo handed Lara the bowl and spoon. "This is Rondo."

Julian was quick to note the man's handsome features, and he wondered if Rondo was Lara's husband . . . or lover.

Rondo watched as Lara spooned hot liquid into Julian's mouth.

"Has he told you his name?" Rondo asked.

"His name is Drago," Lara replied.

Rondo's words were ripe with bitterness. "You

mean you don't even know the name of the man you married? Whatever possessed you, Lara? You should have let the *gadje* have him."

Julian listened to the conversation but could make no sense out of it. Who had married Lara? Surely they weren't referring to him, were they? Had he been able, he would have laughed at the notion.

"No more," Julian gasped, pushing the spoon away. His stomach had taken all the broth it could hold.

Sleep was closing in fast when he heard Rondo say, "Does the *gadjo* know he is your husband?"

"He has enough to contend with right now. Besides, you know as well as I that the marriage was a traditional Romany joining. It will mean nothing to him."

"But it means something to us," Rondo persisted. "You have declared yourself before our people. You are a married woman now."

Lara gave her head an angry shake. "I saved a man's life, didn't I? Come Rondo, Drago needs to rest."

Julian felt the lingering effects of laudanum weight his mind, but he had heard every word of the exchange between Lara and Rondo. His ears had to be playing tricks on him. What he'd just heard couldn't be true. Questions still lingered in his mind as he drifted off to sleep, visions of golden skin and swaying hips dancing in his head.

Three days later Julian awoke with his wits intact. With Lara's help he was able to sit up in bed and accept small amounts of solid food. He was far from well, but at least his mind appeared to be functioning again.

Lara had just entered the wagon with his dinner. He gave her a welcoming smile. "Have I properly thanked you and your people for saving my life?"

" 'Tis not necessary. Open your mouth."

"I won't trouble you any longer than I have to," Julian said, opening his mouth to take a spoonful of stew.

"Don't be foolish," Lara scolded. "You're safe here for now, though I suspect those men won't give up on you. They appeared to want you dead . . . badly."

His expression turned grim. "Aye, they do. If your people have no objection, I would like to remain until I've recovered my strength."

Lara's relief was palpable. "Ramona suggested that we darken your skin with walnut oil so you won't stand out among us."

"I'd like to try out my legs," Julian said, "but I seem to have . . . er . . . lost my clothing." A dark eyebrow quirked upward. "Did you undress me?"

A slow flush crept up Lara's neck. "Ramona and Rondo stripped you and burned your clothes. I'll find something for you to wear, something more in keeping with your new identity."

He fingered his beard. It itched. "I'd appreciate a razor, if one is available."

Lara nodded. "I'll see to it."

He touched her cheek. "You're very good to me, Lara. Isn't your husband jealous of the time you spend with me? Is Rondo your husband?"

Mutely, Lara stared at him. Julian understood the reticence behind her hesitation. Obviously Rondo was her lover, not her husband. 'Twas common knowledge that Gypsy wenches shared their favors indiscriminately.

"I'll go fetch something for you to wear," Lara said as she turned and fled out the door.

Julian waited until she was gone, then slid his legs over the side of the bed. A jolt of pain shot through him, but it was bearable. Cautiously he stood, swayed, then steadied himself against the bed. He took a step. And another, until he'd walked the length of the wagon. Satisfied with his progress, he retraced his steps to the bed, sat down, and pulled a blanket over his loins, waiting for Lara to return.

While Lara was gone, Julian studied the inside of the wagon with interest. Built on a long wagon bed, it had wooden sides and a wooden roof just high enough for him to stand. Snug and compact, the space was crammed with colorful cushions, benches, and baskets. An unlit brazier stood in one corner, and the low ceiling was draped with swaths of cloth, giving the interior a cozy, intimate appeal. A single window admitted a small patch of light.

Lara interrupted his visual inspection when she arrived with an interesting assortment of men's garments over her arm. "Some of these belong to Rondo and some are my grandfather's," she explained. "You haven't met Pietro yet, but you will. He's bringing shaving gear for your use."

Julian sorted through the clothing and chose a pair of baggy twill trousers, loose white shirt, and red vest that matched the waist sash.

"Do you need help?" Lara asked.

"I think I can manage on my own."

He stood. The blanket slid away from his loins but

he thought nothing of it. Gypsy women weren't noted for their shyness. 'Twas a well-known fact that they were more knowledgeable in the ways of men and women than English ladies of good birth, and were no strangers to men's bodies.

Lara tried to look away but couldn't. She'd seen Drago's body before, but he'd been ill and unable to do for himself. He looked different now. Trying to keep her eyes above his waist, she concentrated on his face. His hair was thick and black. His eyebrows were steeply arched and oddly elegant. His thickly lashed eyes were the color of a midnight sky. Her gaze settled on his unshaven cheeks and chin, and she wondered how he would look without the beard.

Her gaze strayed downward, over his broad shoulders and wide chest. A mat of dark hair sprouted around his flat nipples and continued in a diminishing line down his corded stomach to his . . . She sucked in a startled breath. She'd seen his manhood when she'd taken care of his needs, but suddenly it had taken on a life of its own. It wasn't exactly aroused, just . . . alive.

Her gaze flew upward, to those incredible dark eyes, grateful that Drago seemed unaware of her flustered scrutiny and flaming cheeks.

"Were my boots salvageable?" Julian asked as he pulled on his trousers. "I know they're not much, but they fit reasonably well."

She fetched his footwear. "I cleaned and dried them. They still look serviceable."

When she turned around, she was relieved to see that Drago had pulled on a shirt and was winding a sash around his slim waist. She set his boots down and helped him don the vest.

"Now you look like a Rom. After we darken your skin, no one will suspect you're not one of us."

A knock sounded on the door and Pietro entered.

"This is Pietro, my grandfather," Lara said. Pride was apparent in her voice and in the way she looked at the older man. "Grandfather, you haven't been formally introduced to Drago."

Pietro stepped forward. His piercing gaze searched Julian's face a long moment. "You are a lucky man, Drago. If Lara hadn't found you, you would have surely perished."

"I am eternally in her debt," Julian vowed.

"You should be. I am not enthusiastic about Lara's choice, but if a *gadjo* pleases her, who am I to judge? Lara said you wish to shave off your beard." He didn't wait for Julian's reply. "Sit down, I will do it for you." He spread out the shaving gear he had brought with him.

Lara placed a cloth around Julian's shoulders. She could tell by Drago's confused expression that he didn't know what to make of Pietro's words.

"Go help Ramona prepare the walnut stain, little one," Pietro said dismissively.

Lara cast an anxious glance at her grandfather, and another at Julian, before taking her leave. She knew Pietro wished to speak privately with Drago and had a good idea what he was going to say, and it worried her. What would Drago do when he learned he had married a Gypsy?

Julian sat stiffly while Pietro shaved off his beard. He knew the old man had something to say and waited with diminishing patience for him to begin. Would Pietro ask him to leave? Julian couldn't blame him if he did. Pietro knew nothing about him. Lara had found him under mysterious circumstances, and Pietro's keen senses surely had warned him that allowing Julian to remain with the Rom could prove dangerous to his people.

Julian's nerves were at a breaking point when Pietro finally said, "I was not happy with my granddaughter's choice, but she made her decision and I will honor it."

Julian had no idea to what Pietro was referring, unless he meant that Lara should have left him lying on the shore to die.

"Ramona said 'tis God's will," Pietro continued. "I am less certain. If Lara was meant to have a *gadjo* husband, why couldn't she choose someone worthy of her? We know nothing about you, except that someone wants you dead. Are you involved in something that will bring dishonor to my granddaughter?"

Julian blinked. He couldn't believe what he was hearing. According to Pietro, and Julian had no reason to doubt him, Lara was his wife. Had a marriage taken place without his knowledge? How? Why? Nothing made sense.

Julian waited until Pietro had scraped the hair away from his throat with the sharp blade before challenging him. "You must be mistaken, Pietro. I recall no wedding. I would never have married Lara, or any other woman. I cried off marriage years ago."

The blade stilled beneath Julian's chin. "Lara claimed you as her husband three times before witnesses, and you acknowledged her claim. 'Tis all that's necessary for a Romany marriage."

Julian blinked. "Why would she do that?"

"To protect you from those who wished you harm. To the Rom, you and Lara are husband and wife. Do not dishonor Lara by denying the marriage."

Julian recognized a warning when he heard one. "I appreciate what Lara did for me and would do nothing to hurt her. But you know I must leave when I am well. My life is in London."

Pietro gave him a cryptic smile. "We are but pawns. We must fulfill what God wills."

Julian squirmed uncomfortably, chilled by Pietro's words. He was vastly relieved when Lara returned with Ramona.

"All done," Pietro said, wiping away the last traces of Julian's beard.

"Oh, my," Lara exclaimed.

Julian glanced at her, wondering why she was staring at him. Did she like him better with the beard? Not that it mattered, he told himself. He and Lara had to speak soon about this husband and wife thing.

"Did you bring the walnut stain?" Pietro asked.

"Aye," Ramona replied. "Lara and I will take over from here."

Pietro left the crowded wagon and Julian submitted meekly as Ramona and Lara darkened his skin with walnut oil. When they finished, Lara handed him a mirror. A man with dark skin and black hair who could easily pass as a Gypsy gazed back at him. He barely recognized himself.

Julian gazed out the window with longing. "I'd like to stroll outside."

"Lara will help you," Ramona said as she gathered up what was left of the walnut stain. "But you must promise to return to the wagon when you start to tire. 'Tis your first day out of bed."

Julian promised, though he had other ideas. How could he regain his strength if he didn't stretch himself to his limits? The moment Ramona was gone, Julian stood and offered his arm to Lara. "Shall we go?"

Julian didn't realize how weak he was until he started down the three steps leading to the ground. Without Lara's support he couldn't have made it.

"Shall we stroll about the camp?" Lara asked.

"That will do for a start." This was going to be more difficult than he'd first anticipated, Julian decided as he concentrated on putting one foot before the other. Though his pain was not inconsiderable, he bore it stoically.

"Lara, 'tis good to see your man up and around," a young woman said in passing.

"May your marriage bring you joy and many children," another woman called out.

Julian grit his teeth and said nothing. He glanced sideways at Lara. She returned his look with one edging on panic.

"Show me where you found me," Julian said.

" 'Tis too far," Lara protested.

"Show me," he insisted. "If I grow tired, I'll stop and rest."

"Very well. This way."

She turned him gently toward the firth.

"Where is this place?" Julian asked. " 'Tis beautiful here."

"We are camped near Dumfries, in Scotland. I was born in Scotland."

"A Scottish Gypsy," Julian mused. "My brother

makes his home in the Highlands. He's married to the Macdonald laird."

"Really?" Lara said, observing him with interest. "Tell me about your family."

Julian's jaw hardened. "I've already said more than I should have. How much further? I can smell the sea."

"We are nearly there. Do you wish to rest?"

Though he leaned heavily on Lara's arm, he wasn't ready to stop yet. "No."

The gorse was thick and lush, slowing their progress, but Julian stumbled on. They were walking uphill now, and Julian paused to catch his breath. The vista was stunning. Mountains rose in the distance, and a wild profusion of heather covered the low hills surrounding them. The air smelled of sunshine and flowers, and the day was so clear he could see forever.

Finally they reached the cliff overlooking the beach. The tide was low. Lara pointed out the strip of sand where she'd found him. The place where his life had nearly ended. He owed Lara more than he could ever repay. But marriage? They needed to talk. He found a flat rock and sat down, inviting her to join him.

"You've exhausted your strength," Lara scolded. "I knew it. Shall I call Rondo to carry you back?"

"A short rest is all I need. Besides, it would be a good time for us to talk."

Lara winced, as if she knew what was coming and dreaded it.

"Pietro said something puzzling," Julian began. "I don't know what to make of it."

Lara smoothed out a wrinkle in her skirt, avoiding his gaze.

"Is it true, Lara? Do your people consider us husband and wife? How did it happen? I don't recall a wedding ceremony."

Lara gazed up at him through lowered lids. "Aye. We are married. 'Twas necessary to save your life. I'm sorry. I would never have said you were my husband if those men weren't going to kill you."

"Saying we are married doesn't make it so."

"It does if you're Rom. I declared myself three times before witnesses, and you accepted. No formal ceremony is necessary as long as two people publicly announce their intentions to become husband and wife."

Julian stared at her. "I'm not Romany. You know I must leave soon. This so-called marriage is a sham."

"Drago, please reconsider. Your life is at stake. What if your enemies return? They will not be looking for a Gypsy man with a wife."

Julian did reconsider. He wasn't a foolish man. Nor did he have a death wish. He had no intention of wedding a Gypsy wench, but he could perpetrate a hoax as well as the next man. Better, actually. He'd had plenty of practice in his line of work.

"Hmmm, perhaps you're right. I will pretend to be your husband for as long as I remain with your people."

"Pretense isn't necessary," Lara replied. "We *are* husband and wife." She rose abruptly. "Are you ready to return?"

Julian felt as if he'd walked into a brick wall. What in the hell had he gotten himself into? English law left no room for doubt. His so-called marriage to Lara wouldn't hold up in an English court of law. Once he returned to London he could safely forget this ever happened and live his life with a clear conscience.

By the time they returned to camp, Julian had exhausted his meager strength. He feared he'd not be able to negotiate the steps into the wagon. Fortunately Pietro recognized his dilemma and took over, supporting him with a firm arm until he reached his bed.

"I hope you don't have a relapse," Lara said, fussing over him. "You were very near death for a long time."

Julian smiled at her wifely show of concern. After Diana and his unborn child had died, he'd let no woman get close to him. He'd had mistresses; he *was* a man after all. He'd treated them with courtesy, but offered them little affection. He wasn't interested in a wife or heirs. His life was consumed with bringing the Jackal to justice.

"Take a nap while I help Ramona fix supper," Lara said, tucking the blanket around him. "I hope you're hungry."

"I can eat," Julian said, surprised that he actually felt hungry for the first time in a long while.

Julian remained thoughtful after Lara left the wagon. He shocked himself by wondering what it would be like to possess Lara's lithe body. She wasn't an innocent. Few Gypsy women were. Lara possessed a natural sensuality that was totally unaffected. Vivacious and spirited, beautiful and tempting, she was a woman no man could resist. Would she turn to flame beneath his mouth and hands? Would she scorch him with her passion?

His body hardened when he imagined how it would feel to be deep inside her. To drive himself into her sweet body. He might lack strength, but he wasn't dead.

* * *

Lara stirred the stew while Ramona busied herself with their meal. She was startled when Ramona said, "Your husband appears well enough now to share a bed with you."

Lara sent Ramona a startled look. "Drago doesn't want a wife, Grandmother. He doesn't consider our marriage valid."

"You should have thought about that before you married the man."

"Do you think it was wrong of me to choose Drago for a husband, Grandmother?"

" 'Tis not for me to say," Ramona hedged. "Sometimes fate works in ways we do not understand. I sense no evil in Drago," she continued, "but he is a troubled man. His palm revealed a history of secrets and contradictions."

Lara wasn't overly surprised that Ramona had read Drago's palm. "What else did you see?"

"Danger," Ramona muttered. "I fear for you, Lara. Your life is now entangled with Drago's, whether he likes it or not. He will leave, aye, but you will meet again and be lured into his intrigues. I tell you this to warn you." She paused. "There is something else."

"What? Tell me."

"There is or was a woman in Drago's life. She is the reason he resists marriage. You may never reach deep enough into his heart to nudge the other woman aside."

Lara had known from the beginning that her Romany marriage meant nothing to Drago. Unfortunately, she couldn't stop the feelings that had taken root in her own heart. Intuition told her that Drago was

someone special. His speech and manners were too re-
fined for a common man. Despite the fact that she
would probably never know who or what he was, her
tender feelings for Drago were impossible to dismiss.

"I will hold Drago to no promises," Lara said with
more conviction than she felt. " 'Tis inevitable that
we should separate. Father is expecting me home
soon, and I cannot disappoint him."

Ramona's dark eyes turned inward and her voice
lowered to a hoarse whisper. "You and Drago will
meet again under different circumstances. He is not
what he seems. He is a man with many inscrutable
facets."

"I've already come to that conclusion, Grandmother. Drago refuses to tell me his real name. If we
meet again, I'm certain he will not acknowledge me. I
will take Drago his supper now."

"Wait, Lara. About your sleeping arrangement . . ."

Lara opened and closed her mouth without uttering a word. What did Ramona expect of her?

"You are a married woman."

"Grandmother! I . . . Drago doesn't accept it."

"You declared yourself before witnesses, little one.
You and Drago are husband and wife. What you do
about it is your business. Intimacy is a private thing.
But Drago is one of us now. We have darkened his
skin and given him a Romany name. Our people will
protect him should his enemies return, but only if
you become Drago's wife in their eyes. They are
clamoring for a feast to celebrate your marriage."

"But, Grandmother, is that wise?"

"It is the way of the Romany."

"Very well, Grandmother, I will bow to your
wishes if it will keep Drago safe."

"Trust me, little one."

"Haven't I always?"

Julian tried to nap but his mind kept returning to his recent conversation with Lara. She couldn't possibly believe she was his wife. He was an earl. Earls did not marry Gypsy wenches. Earls married women of good birth and equal rank. His eyes were finally growing heavy when he heard movement inside the wagon. He sensed Lara's presence before he saw her. His eyes fluttered open.

"You're awake," Lara said. "Are you hungry?"

"Starving," Julian said. He moved slowly to keep the pain at bay as he sat up on the edge of the bed. "Something smells good. Will you join me?"

"I usually eat outside with the others, but I can move a bench beside the bed if you'd like. I brought enough for two."

"I'd like that," Julian said. "I'll join you outside when I'm stronger."

Lara pulled a bench close to the bed and laid out the food. Then she pulled up a chair and joined Julian. They ate in silence, broken only by the occasional comment on the food. When they finished eating, Lara carried the dirty dishes outside and returned with a basin of water.

"I brought water so you can wash." Dark eyes searched his face. "You look exhausted. Did you nap?"

"No, but I'm sure I can sleep now."

"I'll leave so you can ready yourself for bed."

Julian remained thoughtful as he prepared for bed. Dimly he wondered where Lara had been sleeping, grateful that she wasn't taking this bogus marriage seriously. Occupying the same bed wasn't a good idea. Lord knew Lara was an enticing bit of femininity, and he was no saint. He might forget he was a gentleman with Lara's warm body curled next to his.

Julian removed his clothing and washed thoroughly, using the water, towel and washcloth Lara had supplied. Then he climbed into bed and fell instantly asleep.

Sometime later Julian was startled awake by something warm and soft burrowing against him. The sweet scent of her woman's flesh gave him an instant erection.

Lara.

Julian hardly dared to move as she settled into sleep. What did this mean? Did she expect him to make love to her? He was more than willing but wasn't sure he was capable. When he heard the even cadence of her breathing he felt disappointment, and a measure of relief. But the sudden urge to touch her was beyond his meager resistance. He couldn't make love to her but he could bloody well touch her. Carefully he turned on his side, slid his arm around her supple waist, and cupped her breast in his palm.

A little voice inside told him Lara was exactly where he wanted her, and the comforting knowledge lulled him to sleep.

Chapter 4

Lara awakened slowly, dimly aware of warmth, and something else. A sensation that brought her body to tingling awareness. A smile touched her lips, then abruptly disolved when she recalled that she was sharing her bed with a man . . . her husband. One of Drago's hands cupped her breast. Turning her head slightly, she peered into his face and was relieved to see that he was sleeping.

Did he realize he was touching her intimately? Was he so accustomed to having a woman in his bed that he naturally sought out those intimate places? Lying beside Drago felt right to her, but she knew Drago would never honor their Romany marriage, so she carefully removed his hand from her body and scooted out of bed.

Lara dressed quietly, grabbed a towel, soap, and clean clothing, and let herself out the door. The sun was just rising in the eastern sky when she joined a group of women on their way to bathe in a shallow pool fed by backwater from the firth. Instead of listening to their chatter, she let her thoughts turn to London.

Lara wasn't looking forward to the season her father wanted her to have. Her skin wasn't as white as that of the English misses with whom she'd have to compete. Her hair was a wild profusion of ringlets, inky black, not golden blond, and her eyes, tilted up at the corners, were far too exotic to be considered proper.

The years she'd spent at her father's country home outside London had been for the most part happy ones, but a season in London frightened her. She couldn't disguise the fact that she was part Gypsy, nor did she want to. But she didn't have the heart to tell her doting father that her Gypsy blood would prevent her from achieving the success he wished for her. Lara knew she was attractive, but her foreign features would cause much talk and speculation. Regrettably, she couldn't convince her father that she would be happier living in the country.

"Lara, when will we celebrate your marriage?" a girl named Roxy asked. "I saw you walking with your husband yesterday. He looks well, considering his near brush with death."

"Soon," Lara promised. "A few more days perhaps. When he's strong enough to enjoy the celebration."

"We've not had a wedding to celebrate in a very long time," another young woman added somewhat wistfully. "I am looking forward to it."

"Aye," Roxy agreed excitedly. "Just today Pietro told my father that we must leave this place soon if we wish to reach the Lockerbie fair on opening day."

While she bathed, Lara considered the upcoming celebration of her wedding to Drago. After the feasting and toasting, her marriage would become a fact . . . even if Drago and her own father refused to acknowledge it. Lara sighed. Once she returned to her father, her marriage would be real to no one but her people and herself.

Lara returned to camp with the others and helped her grandmother prepare breakfast. She filled a plate with boiled eggs, bread, and tea, and carried them to her wagon. Drago welcomed her with a smile that caused her breath to hitch.

"Where were you?"

"Bathing in the pool with the women. I'll show you where it is later."

"I'd like that."

"I've brought breakfast. How do boiled eggs, bread, and tea suit you?"

"They'll do."

"I'm sorry we don't have bacon, kidneys, and coffee."

He grinned. "You're making my mouth water."

Lara sat the tray on the bench. When she looked up, Drago was smiling at her.

"Is something wrong?"

"Were you in bed with me last night or did I dream it?"

Hot color crept up her neck, staining her cheeks red. "You didn't dream it. Sharing a bed is expected of us. Would you prefer that I sleep elsewhere?"

Julian pictured Lara sleeping in Rondo's arms and felt his stomach lurch. The thought was revolting. "No, though I'm sure Rondo missed you last night." The moment the words left his mouth, he wanted to call them back. Bloody hell, what was wrong with him? He had no business criticizing Lara's morals.

"I'm sorry," he said before she had time to react. "I shouldn't have said that. It wasn't appropriate."

"I'll leave you to your breakfast," Lara bit out as she fled from the wagon.

"Damnation," Julian muttered, frowning at his food. Lara was the last person in the world he wanted to hurt.

Julian bolted down his meal, tasting little of what he ate as he silently cursed himself for causing the stricken look on Lara's face. But picturing Lara with another man, or selling herself at fairs as Gypsy women were known to do, made him angry as hell.

After breakfast Julian decided he felt well enough to venture outside on his own. The quicker he recovered, the sooner he could forget Lara's snapping black eyes and lush lips. Julian did not notice Ramona enter the wagon after he left. Had he been there he would have seen her study the tea leaves in his cup.

Why did Lara climb in bed with him last night? Would she return tonight? 'Twas obvious to him that she was offering herself to him. Was he fit enough to accept her offer if she crawled in bed with him tonight? He doubted it. But it wouldn't be long. After considerable thought, Julian decided it would hurt nothing to avail himself of the fiery Gypsy wench's body if she gave the slightest indication that she was willing.

The moment Julian stepped down from the wagon he was bombarded with greetings.

"Drago, does your wife know you're out and about on your own?" someone called to him.

"When are we going to celebrate your marriage, Drago?" another man asked. "Everyone is looking forward to the feast and dancing. Wait until you see Lara dance. She is magnificent."

Some merely waved, and Julian waved back, accepting their friendship in the manner in which it was offered. These people had accepted him as one of their own, and he vowed to keep them safe from his enemies. The only way he could be sure of their safety was to leave the moment he was well enough to travel. By that time his skin should have returned to its natural color.

Julian's inspection of the campsite led him to a corral where a large number of horses were herded together. Some were of inferior quality, but most were prime horseflesh, the kind that would demand high prices at any fair in the country, or even the auction at Tattersalls. Julian wondered where the Rom had acquired such quality stock. Had they stolen them?

"Do you see anything you like?" Rondo asked as he came up to join Julian.

"You have some of the finest horses I've ever seen. Quite amazing, really. Are they stolen?"

Julian could have kicked himself the moment the words left his mouth. Not all Gypsies were thieves, just most of them. He could tell Rondo was insulted by the belligerent jut of his chin.

"A stallion and three blooded mares were gifts from . . . Never mind, 'tis none of your business. We bred them, and you see the results before you. The herd belongs to Pietro. We care for them and everyone shares in the profits when they are sold at fairs."

Julian didn't know whether to believe him or not. They were fine horses. He knew of few men willing to make gifts of their prime horses.

"Who cares for them?"

"Myself, for one. Others help from time to time."

"Perhaps I can help. I've always been good with horses."

"You? A smuggler?" He sneered. "I wouldn't trust you with my dog."

Julian sent him a startled look. "What makes you think I'm a smuggler?"

" 'Tis obvious. Those men who came looking for you were rough sailors. The only ships that enter this cove are engaged in smuggling. We've seen them before but do not interfere. 'Tis none of our business. Why do they want to kill you?"

"I'm not a smuggler. I cannot tell you more without endangering your people."

"What are you? Who are you?"

"I cannot say. Believe me when I say I will do my best to protect your people."

"What about Lara? You are her husband. What are your plans for her?"

Julian shifted uncomfortably. "I'll always be grateful to Lara for saving my life, but we both know a Romany ritual is not recognized in English courts. Nothing legally binding transpired between me and Lara. Once I leave, you are free to resume your relationship with her. If you will excuse me, I'll continue my exercise."

Julian could feel Rondo's hot gaze on him as he walked away. He didn't blame Rondo. Julian was an interloper among people who did not easily accept strangers. If not for Lara, he felt sure he would have been left on the shore to die.

Julian strolled back to camp. He was tired, and his wounds throbbed like the very devil, but at least he was mobile and gaining strength every day. Soon he would be well enough to return to London and continue his investigation.

Julian saw little of Lara that day. She went along with some of the women to a nearby village to buy supplies for their journey to Lockerbie. Ramona changed his bandages later that afternoon, and he felt so drained he fell asleep soon afterward. He awakened when Lara returned to the wagon to call him to supper.

"You will join us tonight, won't you?" Lara asked. "My family would like it if you ate with them."

"Of course," Julian replied. "I'd like to speak with Pietro about helping with the horses anyway. I can present the idea to him tonight during the meal."

"Are you sure you feel well enough?" Lara asked anxiously. "I wouldn't want you to have a relapse."

"Don't fret, Lara. I'm well aware of my limitations. Can you tell me how to get to the pool? I'd like to bathe before I eat."

Lara gave Julian directions, then left to help Ramona put the finishing touches on the meal.

Ramona and Pietro seemed pleased to have Julian join them when he returned from the pool.

"Do you have family somewhere who might be worrying about you?" Ramona inquired. "Perhaps you'd like to send word to them."

"I have a sister who is probably wondering why I've been away so long, but she's accustomed to my extended absences. My brother lives in the Highlands with his family, and would have no reason for concern."

Ramona and Pietro exchanged speaking glances. "I told you Drago had no wife," Ramona hissed into her husband's ear. "I read his palm after he was brought to us, and I've studied the tea leaves in his cup on two separate occasions."

Paying little heed to the whisperings of the Gypsy couple, Julian stared at Lara instead. She looked exceptionally beautiful tonight. Her tousled ebony curls gleamed with reddish highlights in the moonlight, and the flickering flames from the campfire gilded her skin a creamy gold. Tiny pinpoints of light danced in the dark centers of her exotically slanted eyes, giving mute testimony to her volatile nature. There was little Julian did not admire about the tempting Gypsy, but she was not for him.

"Dance for us, Lara!" someone shouted.

Instruments were brought out and the strains of a vigorous Gypsy melody filled the air. The jingle of tambourines and the energy of fiddles soon had all of them clapping and stomping their feet.

"Dance, Lara!" a chorus of voices urged.

Julian frowned when Rondo bowed before Lara and held out his hand. After a quick glance at Julian, Lara took Rondo's hand. Immediately he swung her into a spirited dance, whirling her round and round, her flashing skirts flying high to reveal shapely legs. Their bodies swayed and twisted together seductively, like passionate lovers swept up in an ancient mating ritual. Julian's gaze was riveted on Lara's lithe body as she leaped into the air and glided like a feather on the wind into Rondo's arms. Never had he seen such gracefulness, such wanton abandon. Never had he been so utterly beguiled.

Never had he felt such overwhelming jealousy.

Hands clenched, teeth grinding together, Julian wanted to jump up and separate the dancers, but of course he didn't. He no longer wondered whether Rondo and Lara were lovers. No one but intimate lovers could dance together in such a manner.

Unable to stand the sight of Lara's flashing thighs and heaving bosom, he quietly rose and returned to the wagon. He lit a candle, tore off his clothes, and threw himself facedown on the bed. The music seemed to go on forever, and he buried his head beneath the pillow to muffle the sound. He had no idea why it bothered him, but he didn't like it one damn bit.

Julian was nothing like his brother Sinjun. In the past he had scolded Sinjun about his wicked ways so often he'd lost count. Julian was the steady, sensible brother, the one who made the rules and followed them. Sinjun had called him stodgy, and Emma thought him too strict. If they could see him now, lusting after a common Gypsy whore, they wouldn't believe it. He hardly believed it himself.

He had cared deeply for Diana, the fiancée his father had chosen for him, and he would have been content to spend the rest of his life with her had she lived. She had given herself to him before their marriage, and Diana had been carrying his child when she died, but he couldn't remember once lusting after her. He was too much of a gentleman for that. He still hadn't recovered from her death, which had occurred two days before their wedding. The accident had been no accident, he'd discovered, but an attempt to end his life. The Jackal did not know that Diana had been riding alone in his coach that fateful day.

The memories still hurt after all this time. He still hadn't found the man responsible for Diana's death, but he was getting closer.

The music stopped and Julian let out a sigh of relief. But his relief was short-lived when Lara opened the door and ducked inside the wagon.

She approached the bed. "Aren't you feeling well? You left early."

"I'm fine," Julian growled. "You and Rondo dance well together."

"We've been doing it since we were children."

Julian heard the rustle of clothing and stiffened. "What are you doing?"

"Getting ready for bed."

"What about Rondo?"

"What about him?"

"Doesn't he want you tonight? The way you were flashing your thighs and throwing yourself at him, I assumed you would go to him tonight. 'Tis obvious he wanted you."

She sent Julian a quelling look. "Rondo and I are childhood friends. As for my dancing, 'tis in my blood. My body moves in rhythm to the music, independent of my mind. I have little control over it." Her eyes narrowed, as if compelled by a sudden thought to speak. "Do *you* want me, Drago?"

"I doubt I'm capable of rising to the occasion tonight," Julian said wryly. "But, aye, I suppose I do want you. Since I am incapable, maybe one of the other men . . ."

Lara's gasp of outrage warned him he'd gone too far.

"Damn you, Drago!" she snarled. "I managed to control my temper while you were so ill, but now that you're better, I won't stand for your insults. I'm a Gypsy, nothing can change that, but you could at least disguise your contempt for me and my people while you're living here. I'm sharing your bed because 'tis expected of me, not because I want anything from a *gadjo*."

God, she's magnificent, Julian thought, eyeing her with appreciation. His gaze was riveted on her heaving breasts, until reluctantly he returned it to her furious black eyes and expressive face. He wanted to pull her down onto the bed and make tempestuous love to her.

He heaved a regretful sigh. "I'm sorry, Lara. I'm behaving badly, but I mean you and your people no disrespect. I'm distraught because you are in my bed and I can do nothing about it."

His words appeared to have little impact on her anger as she turned and flounced out the door.

He believes me a whore, Lara thought as she walked over to the dying fire and plopped down on a bench. Some Gypsy women were promiscuous, but she wasn't one of them. She'd have to love a man before giving herself to him. Lara knew better than to expect Drago to take their marriage seriously, or to care about her. It was inevitable that Drago would leave, and a foregone conclusion that she would join her father in London.

Lara sat beside the fire, hugging her knees to ward off the night chill, until the wood had burned down to ash. Then she rose stiffly and returned to the wagon. The candle had burned down to a stub, but it shed enough light to reveal a sleeping Drago. Lara blew out the candle, undressed down to her shift, and eased into bed. She heard Drago sigh before he gathered her against him. Fearing she would awaken him if she removed his arm, she closed her eyes and settled down to sleep.

She awoke before Drago, arose, dressed, and quietly left the wagon. Pietro was already up and stirring the fire. Ramona had just stepped out of her wagon and was hurrying over to begin breakfast.

"You're up early, little one," Pietro said, greeting her with a smile. "How fares Drago?"

"He grows stronger every day," Lara replied. She said nothing about Drago leaving once he was fully recovered, but she knew Pietro understood that he *would* leave when the time came.

Soon the camp began to stir. Lara went to the pool to bathe. The water was cool, so she washed quickly and returned to camp. She was helping Ramona when she spied Drago walking to the pool with Rondo and some of the other men.

"How soon do you plan to leave?" Rondo asked as he sidled up beside Julian.

Julian stared at him. "Are you anxious to be rid of me?"

"You are dangerous to have around."

"What are you trying to say?"

"You do not appreciate Lara. What do you know about her? Did she tell you anything about herself?"

Julian pushed his fingers through his hair in a distracted manner. "What is there to know? Fear not, I'm no competition to you, Rondo. Once I leave, Lara is free to continue her life as it was before I entered it."

"You're a fool, *gadjo*. Lara is too good for either of us."

Julian had no idea what Rondo was talking about, and obviously Rondo wasn't going to elaborate for he strode away. Julian bathed quickly, taking care to keep his bandages dry, then he returned to camp. Ramona placed a plate and cup in his hands and he sat down to join them.

Julian watched Lara move around the campfire, remembering how she'd looked last night, gyrating to the music. She had moved with unfettered abandon, an earthy blend of feminine allure and sensuality. Was he the only man driven to lust by her flashing thighs and heaving bosom? He doubted it. Watching Lara dance had made his heart pound and the blood flow hot and thick through his veins.

Julian was jarred back to the present when Pietro said, "You're not eating, Drago. Does the food not appeal to you?"

Julian bit into a piece of savory fried bread. "The food is fine, Pietro. I'm sorry if I appear distracted."

Pietro rolled his eyes. "Oh, aye, I know about distractions."

Julian concentrated on his plate. Could Pietro read his mind? He hoped not.

Julian chewed his food thoughtfully. He was finishing his tea when a cry caused him to look up in alarm. A young lad ran toward them, yelling and waving his arms excitedly. "Pietro! Men on horseback are coming."

Voices so recently engaged in conversation fell silent as everyone turned toward Pietro for instruction. Pietro looked at Julian and frowned. "You must be an important man to bring your enemies back."

Julian set down his plate. "You think they come for me?"

"Aye, they come for you," Ramona answered. "We will give them nothing to cause suspicion. Lara, come and sit beside your husband."

Lara set the tea kettle down beside the fire and hurried over to join Julian.

"Perhaps I should hide," Julian suggested.

"Too late," Pietro said. "Fear not. You are one of us now. I have seen to everything."

Pietro's words seemed to reassure the Gypsies, for they returned to their meal and conversation. But Julian remained puzzled by Pietro's last remark. His heart pumped furiously as six armed men rode into the camp. Julian recognized their leader as the smuggler named Crockett.

Pietro stood and waited for the riders to rein in.

"Are ye the leader here?" Crockett asked, dismounting.

"I am Pietro. What do you want?"

"Has the man we were looking for turned up? Have any bodies washed ashore recently?"

"No strangers have appeared in our camp," Pietro assured him. Then Pietro said something that startled Julian. "Strange that you should ask about a body. We did find a dead man on the beach shortly after your first visit to our camp."

Crockett's attention sharpened. "Dead, ye say? Where is the body?"

"We buried it, of course."

Crockett made a slow perusal of the faces peering at him over their plates. His gaze settled on Julian. Julian held his breath, not daring to look up. Would Crockett recognize him without the beard and dressed in Gypsy garb? Obviously not, for Crockett's lustful gaze moved on to Lara. Julian wanted to jump up and shield Lara, but exercised restraint. Drawing attention to himself would doubtlessly bring trouble to the people who sheltered him.

"The dead man. What did he look like?"

Pietro shrugged. " 'Twas hard to tell. He'd been in the water a long time. He was tall, had dark hair, and appeared to be gunshot."

Crockett's beady eyes narrowed. "Show me the grave."

Julian stifled a groan. Things were going from bad to worse, and he didn't even have a weapon with which to defend himself and Lara.

"Follow me," Pietro said.

Julian sent Lara a startled look. He started to rise, but Lara's hand on his shoulder stopped him.

"There is no grave," Julian hissed.

"Trust Pietro," Lara whispered back. "He's thought of everything."

Pietro and Crockett disappeared over a small rise. Julian waited with bated breath, fearing for the old man's life once Crockett learned there was no grave. He allowed himself to breathe again when he saw both men returning. Moments later, Crockett mounted without uttering another word and rode off with his men.

"What happened? There was no grave," Julian said as Pietro returned to his place beside the campfire.

"Rest assured there was a grave," Pietro returned. "Ramona predicted that your enemies would return and had me dig a grave and fill it with rocks. We arranged the clothing you wore when we found you over the rocks. Your enemy didn't bother taking a close look. 'Twas what we had counted on."

Julian felt profound gratitude for the wily Gypsy

couple. They and their people could have betrayed him to his enemies and earned a reward.

"They would never have betrayed you," Lara said, as if reading his mind. "You are my husband, they are loyal to their own."

Perhaps for the first time Julian realized what being Lara's husband, even a temporary one, meant. Dimly he wondered what would happen, how her people would react, when he left to resume his life in London. Would they blame her for being abandoned by her husband? Or would they merely shrug with typical Romany fatalism?

"They won't be back," Ramona said with confidence. " 'Tis time we celebrated your marriage. Tomorrow we will celebrate far into the night. 'Tis just the diversion we need before moving on to Lockerbie. A feast, a day and night of rest, then on to the fair."

Julian could feel their excitement. The Gypsies were eager to celebrate a marriage considered legal by no one but themselves.

After breakfast, Julian asked Pietro if he could help with the horses. He wanted to make himself useful, to give them something back for his life. Pietro gave his permission and Julian hurried off to the corral to begin his day.

At the end of his first full day's work after being seriously wounded, Julian was so exhausted that he bathed and fell into bed without supper. He ached everywhere. He wasn't a stranger to physical exercise, and he normally kept his body in tiptop shape, but outside of fencing, riding, and boxing occasionally at the club, he rarely performed the kind of work

he had done this day. He employed grooms and sta-
blemen for that chore. He fell asleep promptly, unaware when Lara entered the wagon and crawled in
beside him.

Lara lay down beside Drago, glad that he was
sleeping soundly so she could enjoy the solid
warmth of his body without his knowledge. She had
no intention of letting Drago know how much she
enjoyed sleeping in his arms, feeling his hard body
curl around hers as if he truly cherished her. She had
too little time left to be with Drago. Once she returned home everything would change. Intuitively
she knew this would be her last summer with her
Gypsy family.

One day soon her father would introduce her to
the *ton* and she would pretend to be the innocent
maiden society demanded of her. Though she was
still a virgin, living with Gypsies had made her more
conscious of her body, more aware of herself as a
woman. Her English counterparts would be appalled
at her knowledge of the human body. Gypsies believed that what men and women did together was
natural and necessary to well-being. It was her last
thought before sleep claimed her.

The next morning Lara helped prepare breakfast.
Drago arose shortly after she did, ate breakfast, and
went off to the corral. Lara hurried after him.

"You've been working too hard," Lara cautioned
when she caught up with him. "You should rest for
the celebration tonight."

"Consider yourself lucky that I return to my bed
exhausted at night," Julian said in a voice that sent a

jolt of awareness down her spine. "I wouldn't be able to lie beside you each night and not touch you were it not for the physical labor I engage in." He turned away, then spun back around to face her, a smile tugging at one corner of his mouth. "Is this your subtle way of saying you want me to make love to you, Lara?"

Lara blanched and huffed out an angry breath. "Far be it from me to force you to do anything you don't wish to do." Whirling on her heel, she marched away.

She'd wither and die before she'd beg a man to make love to her. She didn't even know Drago's real name. He could be a criminal, or worse.

Maybe he was a spy. He might even be married and the father of several children. Good Lord, what had she done?

Why couldn't he tell her the truth about himself?

Chapter 5

J ulian didn't look forward to the celebration planned for that night. Resisting Lara's tempting body was becoming a problem. He devoutly hoped his virility was still suppressed, but he seriously doubted he could continue to use that as an excuse. His loins stirred restlessly and lust nearly devoured him every time he looked at Lara.

After considerable thought, Julian came to the conclusion that there was no reason he should deny himself as long as both he and Lara were willing. A husband and wife were supposed to consummate their union, even though Lara was the only partner in their marriage who took it seriously. Were Lara an innocent he wouldn't even consider bedding her, but that sensually stimulating dance Lara had performed with Rondo belied her innocence.

The delicious aroma of roasted pig wafted to Julian on the evening breeze. The women had been working all day on the feast, the men fine-tuning their instruments. All the ingredients for the celebration were in place, but he still felt uncomfortable.

That evening Julian bathed and donned the clean

63

clothes Lara had purchased for him on her last trip to the village. He supposed the clothing was elegant for a Gypsy, but it was a far cry from what the *ton* considered respectable for a wealthy nobleman. Still, he was content with Lara's choice of white shirt, colorful brocade vest, green jacket and sash to match, and tight black breeches. She had even purchased a new pair of boots for him, crafted from good leather, that fit him surprisingly well.

Julian had no money with which to pay for his new clothes, but he intended to repay Lara's generosity as soon as he returned home. He planned to send Lara and her people a generous reward for saving his life.

Julian found the camp a beehive of activity when he returned. Everyone had dressed in his or her best. The women pranced about in brightly colored skirts with bells sewn onto the hems. Large gold hoops hung from their ears, and precious gems adorned the rings on their fingers.

The men looked like strutting peacocks in their bright finery. Like the women, they wore gold earrings in their ears and heavy gold chains around their necks. Julian searched the compound for Lara and saw her standing beside their wagon. She must have sensed his gaze upon her for she lifted her eyes to him and smiled.

For all the activity around them, they might as well have been the only two people in the universe. Everything faded for Julian but the sensually stimulating woman who boldly returned his look. A current passed through him, and he shuddered. The air between them was so taut with sexual tension it seemed to vibrate.

His heated gaze slid down her body. Her full

breasts were barely contained within the scooped neckline of her blouse. Tiny sleeves rested on her upper arms, baring both golden shoulders and the upper swells of her breasts. It was obvious to Julian that nothing stood between her skin and blouse, which was tucked into the waistband of a brilliant, multicolored skirt hung with bells at the hem. A thrill shot through Julian when he realized that the ruffled red petticoat, visible beneath the hem of the skirt, was probably the only undergarment she wore.

He went instantly hard. The bulge in his trousers grew and expanded, pulling the material taut against his loins. He adjusted himself and tugged the edges of his coat together. A groan left his throat when Lara started toward him. Her gently swaying hips made the bells on her skirt tinkle merrily. He wanted to grab her and hide her where no one could look at her but him. She was earth. She was light. She was dazzling temptress and artless seductress all rolled into one body that most men would kill to possess.

I want her, Julian thought with dismay. *I want her more than I've ever wanted another woman.*

Unlike Lara, Diana had been a delicate, elegant beauty, all peaches and cream, as lovely as an angel with her blond hair and shy smile. She was everything he'd ever dreamed of in a wife. Good bloodlines, perfect manners, and above all, she was a lady. She hadn't stopped him when he'd wanted to make love to her, but he could tell that she wasn't at ease with his passion. He'd known from the beginning that she had acquiesced to his desire simply because she loved him with a pure heart that transcended passion. Julian had accepted that, and admired her for her purity of spirit, and because she found something worthy in him to love.

He would always remember Diana, always mourn her and their child who had perished with her. He wouldn't rest until he'd found those responsible for their deaths. And he would never care deeply for a woman again, or sire another child. Losing them was too painful.

Julian sucked in a steadying breath, slowly expelling it when Lara reached him. Lust was like a roaring lion inside him.

"Shall we join the celebration? The women are bringing out the food and drink."

Her voice sent chills of awareness racing down his spine. Low and throaty, it put him in mind of sultry nights and hot sex. She was an unsophisticated combination of wantonness and incandescent beauty. Too hot to handle without going up in flames. Just thinking about being inside her brought beads of sweat to his forehead.

He dashed them away and tried to recall what she had just said to him.

Apparently unaware of his discomfort, Lara grasped his hand and led him to the area where tables laden with food had been set up. She picked up a plate and handed it to him.

"We're supposed to start. The others will follow."

Julian regained his wits barely in time to hang on to the plate Lara had thrust into his hands. He paid scant heed to the food he was piling on his plate, and he followed without hesitation when Lara led him to the vacant place of honor around the huge campfire.

Someone handed him a cup of ale, and he drank deeply. The cup was instantly refilled, and he downed it as quickly as he had the first. He dug into his food, tasting little of what he swallowed. He watched Lara's mouth as she chewed, stifling a groan when her tongue darted out to sweep a crumb from her lips. He was bewitched. Honorable, sober, *dull*, Julian Thornton, the Earl of Mansfield, was bewitched by a Gypsy wench.

Exactly what that statement meant didn't bear thinking about. Then the toasting began. Mugs were raised to their health, their marriage, their happiness, their fruitfulness, their good fortune. By the time the toasting ended, Julian's head was spinning.

The musicians took up their instruments. A procession of dancers twirled, whirled, and twisted to the wild tattoo of drums and the wanton refrain of a rousing tune. Julian glanced sidelong at Lara. Her eyes glittered like stars, and her supple body swayed to the beat of the fiddles.

He wanted to kiss her. Was he drunk? Probably, but it wasn't going to stop him. Surprising even himself, Julian grasped her shoulders and pulled her against him. Her lips were parted, their lush contours temptingly moist. He lifted her chin with a fingertip and brushed her lips with his. She tasted of ale and ambrosia. Of sin and wickedness. Of wanton pleasure.

He wanted more.

He seized her lips again, this time with less delicacy, determined to fill his senses with the taste and scent of her. At first her response was tentative, almost innocent. But when he deepened the kiss and thrust his tongue into her mouth, she caught fire, just as he knew she would. She kissed him back, arching and pressing herself against him, digging her hands into the thick folds of his hair. He caught her groan in his mouth and answered it with one of his own. Her response emboldened him. He sucked her tongue into his mouth and drew on it.

He would have continued on to the ultimate end had clapping and hisses of appreciation not alerted him to the fact that they had become the center of attention. He broke off the kiss and grinned sheepishly.

Lara's body was thrumming, her flesh on fire, her head spinning. Drago's kiss made her giddy with delight. She could have gone on kissing him forever. She'd been kissed by Rondo, and one or two other men, but their kisses were mere child's play compared to Drago's kiss.

"Let's go back to the wagon."

The sexual inflection in Drago's voice sorely tempted her, but she shook her head. " 'Tis far too early. The celebration has barely begun."

Ignoring Drago's peevish look, Lara concentrated on the music, swaying and clapping to the beat. The dance was in her blood. Her mother, Serena, had been an accomplished dancer. She had been invited to perform countless times at homes of wealthy noblemen in both Scotland and England. Serena had met Lara's father at one of those performances.

"Dance for us, Lara," Rondo urged. Others lent their encouragement.

Lara leaped to her feet, unaware of Julian's disapproving frown as the music captured her and carried her away. Her lithe body spun and twirled, flickering firelight transforming her into an ethereal figure composed of shadow and light. She danced with abandon, her body weaving before Julian in blatant invitation, her dark eyes gleaming.

She offered him her hand.

Julian stared at it for the space of a heartbeat before placing his hand in hers. Lara pulled him to his feet and drew him into the center of the circle.

"I can't dance," he growled.

Lara didn't care. All he had to do was stand there, she'd do the rest. She pirouetted around him, hips swaying in time to the music, teasing him, leaning toward him, then drawing away before their bodies actually touched.

Never had Julian seen anyone dance like Lara. He knew instinctively that the Gypsy spitfire was dancing for him, and his loins swelled with desire for her. Deliberately she enticed him with her eyes and undulating body, then spun away so fast that his hands clutched empty air when he reached for her. Damnation! She was Mother Earth and Eve. Delilah and Cleopatra. She was every seductress known to mankind, blended together in a tempting body that oozed sexuality.

She was . . . Lara.

When Lara's hips swayed forward, brushing against his loins, Julian gritted his teeth and swore beneath his breath. Did she think he was made of stone? Beads of sweat dripped down into his eyes. Was there no end to the torture Lara was inflicting on him? When she wound a scarf around his neck and gently drew him forward, Julian couldn't help thinking that she was very good at this game, and he wondered how many men she had lured into her web of seduction. His patience shattered just as she pirouetted away from him, but this time he was too fast for her.

His arm snaked out, finding purchase around her waist. His body taut with determination, he pulled her roughly against him. Her face was flushed, her dark eyes glowing, her tinkling laughter an aphrodisiac. It was too much. She had gone too far. His body was brittle, ready to explode. He had to have her.

Ignoring the pain from his healing wounds, Julian swung Lara into his arms and carried her away from the campfire. An opening appeared in the approving crowd, and he charged through, dimly aware of the laughter and rousing cheers following him.

"Drago, we can't leave yet."

"The hell we can't," Julian growled, tightening his hold on her. "A man can take so much. But you knew that, didn't you? You've been begging for this, and I'm going to give you exactly what you want."

"Drago! I didn't mean . . . You don't understand . . . I have no control when I dance. It's like someone else inhabits my body. Sometimes I don't even know what I'm doing."

"I knew what you were doing," Julian rasped harshly as he kicked open the door and carried her inside their wagon. "So did every man watching you tonight. How many men have been lured into your bed by your wanton behavior?"

"Put me down!" Lara raged. "How dare you judge me and find me lacking!"

"I'm not judging you," Julian said, letting her slide down his body until her feet touched the floor. He grinned when she gave him a startled look and backed away. His erection was so hard he knew she had felt it prodding her.

"Feel how hard I am for you, Lara," he said, grasping her wrist and placing her hand on the front of his trousers. "I'm fully capable now of giving you what you've been asking for since the first night you crawled into bed with me."

She tried to pull away but he held her captive in his arms, refusing to release the hand still clasped around his staff.

"This is our wedding night," he reminded her. Just thinking about what he was going to do to her made his mouth dry as dust.

"We're not really married. You said so yourself."

He searched her face. "Do *you* think we're married?"

"Gypsies follow their own laws. My people consider our marriage a valid commitment."

"That's not what I asked," Julian growled. "Do *you* believe we're married?"

Silence.

"Lara, answer my question."

"Aye!" Lara whispered.

"Even though you know I must leave soon? That there can be nothing lasting between us?"

"Aye, dammit! You have your answer, now let me go."

"No. I'm going to love you, my wanton Gypsy spitfire. If your passion for the dance extends to the bed, I have a long rewarding night to look forward to."

Lara stared into Drago's determined features and knew she hadn't the will to stop him. His darkly handsome face gave hint of the dangerous man lurking inside him. She was all too aware of the mystery surrounding him and the pitfalls of loving him. Danger stalked him. He was no ordinary man. Intelligent, enigmatic, and imbued with an unsettling degree of secrecy. She'd have to be crazy to fall in love with a man whose name she didn't know.

"Lara, don't think. Just feel. I know you're thinking that you can't trust me, but I swear I'll make you happy tonight. Don't think about the other men who have made love to you in the past. Pretend that I am your first lover."

Suddenly he went still, giving her a strange look as he searched her face. "I *am* your only husband, am I not?"

Lara shifted nervously. "I have never been married before."

She sensed his relief and wondered about it. He was going to leave anyway, so why should he care if she had another husband? He liked her, maybe even admired her, but that's as far as it would ever go.

Her thoughts were skewered when Drago's arms tightened around her and his mouth came down hard on hers. Her eyes fluttered closed at the startling sensation of his tongue plunging into her mouth. She was lost. Utterly and profoundly lost. She raised up on her toes, wrapped her arms around his neck and kissed him back, with her mouth and with her whole body and soul.

Drago's groan was low and guttural, his lips demanding and possessive as his hands moved determinedly over her curves. She shifted restlessly, wanting more, wanting him closer. Her breasts were crushed against his chest, her hands gripping his shoulders.

"Your clothes, take them off," he growled as his hands swept aside the tumbled mass of her hair to release the ties holding her blouse together.

She shrugged her shoulders and the garment fell to her waist. She wore nothing underneath. She heard him mutter a strangled oath before he lowered his mouth to claim the dusky crown of her nipple.

Lara gasped and arched into his mouth. Her fingers clutched desperately at the dark strands of his hair, and her body swayed with the sweet, drugging sensations washing over her; dark, crushing waves that inundated her with each dragging lap of his tongue. She began to shiver, stunned by the torrid rush of exquisite pleasure plowing deep in her belly and between her thighs. She wanted more; intense need weakened her knees. He must have sensed her desperation, for he swept her into his arms and lowered her to the bed in a froth of skirts.

"These will have to go," Drago grated, grasping a handful of material and tugging.

Skirts and petticoat slid down her hips, her thighs, and he whisked them to the floor. Then he dropped down beside her and bent over her belly, his breath scorching her as his tongue dipped into her belly button. Every nerve ending screamed for something, but she had no idea what. Her breath hitched when Drago parted her legs and eased his fingers into the moist cleft between her thighs. She felt his hot, penetrating gaze upon her and stared up into his eyes, waiting breathlessly, nay, anxiously, for his next move.

The shock of his fingers sliding back and forth over her flesh, then dipping deep inside her, was devastating. She couldn't stifle her startled cry when his mouth replaced his fingers. She shuddered and arched against him, her hands clawing into his hair.

"Drago! No!" Surely such intimacy had to be wicked.

Julian grinned up at her. "Haven't any of your lovers done this to you?" He didn't wait for an answer as he buried his head between her legs and feasted on her tender flesh, his tongue lashing furiously, as if she were an exotic delicacy.

"I . . . ahhh . . . please . . . ohhh . . . stop!"

Julian raised his head. "Stop?"

" 'Tis too much."

He sat back on his heels. "Perhaps you are right. Our passion burns too hot for this kind of foreplay. Perhaps later."

Lara had no idea what he was talking about. She only knew that her body was thrumming with raw, wicked pleasure, but what he had been doing to her couldn't be proper.

Suddenly he reared up from the bed and began tearing off his clothing. Lara watched in fascination as buttons went flying. Moments later he stood before her naked, his bandages starkly white against his magnificent body, now bared for her visual pleasure. Her gaze fell to his engorged staff. It rose full and thick from a nest of dark springy curls.

Lara's mouth flew open. Something that swollen and rigid would never fit inside her. He'd rip her apart. Panic surged through her and she tried to roll away, but she was pressed back against the mattress by the weight of Drago's body as he spread her legs and lowered himself between them. She was momentarily distracted when he kissed her, and of course she had to kiss him back. Then his tongue was grappling with hers and she lost her wits, until she felt his hardness probing between her legs. She stiffened; her eyes flew open.

The heat and heaviness of his own naked need made Julian oblivious to Lara's apparent fear as he pressed inexorably forward and inward, taking his time, wanting to prolong the pleasure. He felt her sheath stretch to accommodate him and flexed his hips, driving himself deeper. He couldn't ever recall being so hard, so rigid, so needy. He was too far steeped in lust to notice that her body was tense, or that fear had replaced the passion-glazed brilliance of her eyes.

She whimpered and he glanced down at her, puzzled.

"Am I hurting you? Am I larger than your other lovers?"

"There have been no other lovers."

Julian laughed. "Don't lie. I doubt there is a Gypsy woman past the age of thirteen still in possession of her virginity. Gypsies are notoriously promiscuous."

"How many Gypsy women do you know?" Lara challenged.

She had him there. He knew damn little about Gypsies. Most of it was hearsay. But he'd learn the truth for himself in another moment. All he had to do was flex his hips and . . .

He broke through the shield of her innocence in one bold thrust. He froze, staring down at her in disbelief.

"Bloody hell! You *are* a virgin." He was more angry than pleased. Seducing virgins wasn't his style.

Her eyes were shiny bright with unshed tears. "Not anymore," she said on a sob.

The pitiful sound tugged at his conscience and put a fine edge to his anger. He held himself rigid inside her. " 'Tis too late for regrets. If you didn't want this you should have told me."

Her chin shot upward. "We're married. 'Tis my understanding that this is what husbands and wives do."

His voice was taut with tension, his control was slowly eroding. "Damnation! *You* may be married but I am not. I would not be making love to you had I known you were a virgin. I am already inside you, however, so I will carry this to a satisfying conclusion for both of us. I promised to give you pleasure and I meant it. Does it still hurt?"

"A little. You're so big."

"Relax." He pressed deeper, then retreated. "Can you feel the friction?" She nodded. "Good." He thrust again. "Concentrate on it and let the sensations build."

He shoved more of himself inside her, moving in and out, once, twice, again. He heard her drag in a shuddering breath and felt her body lose some of its rigidity. Sweat dotted his brow as he gradually increased the movement of his hips. He felt her first tentative response and thanked God, for he was quickly losing what little remained of his control. Then suddenly she caught fire, rising up eagerly to meet his rhythm as he thrust and withdrew forcefully inside her.

Lara felt the pain dissolving, replaced by a far more pleasant sensation as Drago moved inside her.

He was huge. Yet somehow she was able to stretch to fit him, to take more of him. She concentrated on the splendid friction he was creating inside her, on the building tension, on the dazzling sensations spearing through her body. She heard someone moan, and was startled to recognize the voice as her own. She glanced up to see if Drago had heard her, and found him frowning at her.

He paused in mid-stroke. "Are you . . . all right?"

"You are . . . very . . . big," she admitted on a whisper.

Drago closed his eyes and muttered an oath.

"Am I hurting *you*?" Lara asked. "You sound like you're in pain."

"Hurting me? Bloody hell, you're killing me! I don't know how much longer I can hang on."

Her innocent question must have been too much for Julian, for his groans grew louder and deeper as he slid his hands beneath her hips and lifted her, breaching her hard and fast. A tremor passed through her, then another, until her entire body was trembling uncontrollably, but he only held her closer and buried himself deeper until there was nothing between them but hot, damp skin.

She heard him whisper words against her mouth, praising her sweetness, her passion: words of encouragement and reassurance. She felt heat and a rising sense of urgency as their bodies meshed, as he went deeper, thrust faster, harder. Her cries couldn't be stifled now, nor did she try to suppress them. Her body was no longer her own. Drago owned her soul, her will, taking her to places she'd only dreamed about as she shuddered and melted around him.

The contractions came unexpectedly, rushing

along her body in a river of pleasure-drenched heat. Her grip on him tightened, her fingers digging hard into his shoulders as she adjusted to his increasing size and thickness. Pleasure coiled around her. Her body burned. She tilted her hips higher in an effort to ease the grinding, demanding pressure building inside her.

"Drago, please! Do something." She had no idea what she was begging for, but she knew intuitively that Drago could provide it. And if she didn't get it soon, she'd die.

"Aye, my wanton Gypsy spitfire," Julian gasped against her lips. "Come to me now." He thrust deeper. "You've got all of me."

Her head slashing from side to side, her ragged breaths coming hard and fast, Lara was aware of nothing but the wet, sucking slide of his hardness into her softness. He surged forward, she pushed herself feverishly into each rhythmic thrust. Suddenly her eyes widened; a scream vibrated in her throat. Her body exploded, white-hot and brilliant. For a breathless moment her soul left her body as something intensely satisfying, something transcending the greatest pleasure she had ever known, charged through her.

Gritting his teeth against the need to spew forth his seed, Julian couldn't recall when he'd been so carried away by the sexual act. Hot blood sang through his veins and pounded against his temples. Lara was everything he'd expected and more. Her virginal body had caught fire beneath him and responded with matching passion.

Every instinct warned him that taking Lara hadn't

been honorable. Finding an untouched maiden residing in Lara's passionate little body had been the last thing he'd expected. He had thought her just another Gypsy whore. He shouldn't have relaxed his strict morals, he realized. He was doing exactly what he'd preached against to Sinjun. But it was too late now. He was so swollen with lust, so bloody ready to explode, that nothing mattered except finding his own pleasure.

Another stroke or two ... He flexed his hips and drove himself to the hilt. A second stroke wasn't necessary. He responded with a tremendous shudder as his own climax roared through him. He lifted his head and shouted, shattering the silence as he poured his seed into her.

"Are you all right, sweeting?" he asked when he finally found his voice.

"More than all right," Lara answered dreamily. "That was ... I never suspected ..."

He eased back but remained firmly entrenched inside her. "And I didn't expect to find a virgin. I'm sorry. I shouldn't have taken things this far."

Lara went still. "You're sorry?"

"We both know I must leave soon, and that I can't take you with me. You don't belong in my world and I don't belong in yours. I have responsibilities in England and you have your family here. I was engaged to be married once, and she died. I cared a great deal for her. After her death, I swore off marriage for good."

His words hurt. "I expect no commitment from you." She shifted her hips beneath him, easing the weight of him inside her.

Julian sucked in a breath. "Bloody hell, don't

move." He was still hard inside her and growing harder and thicker by the minute.

Lara gave him a startled glance, her eyes wide with disbelief.

"You're still . . . that is . . . how can it be?"

"I still want you." He flexed his hips and went deeper. "Can you take me again?"

Again and as many times as he wanted, Lara thought, moving unashamedly against him. Having Drago inside her, around her, over her, felt right. This time she knew what to expect and eagerly embraced it as she rushed recklessly toward another explosive climax.

Her body was still vibrating with pleasure when Drago reached his own zenith and withdrew from her. She was utterly depleted, awash in the wonderful feeling of well-being and too exhausted to protest when he dampened a cloth and cleansed the blood and semen from between her thighs. When he returned to bed, she sighed happily and turned into his embrace.

Dawn was hovering over the horizon when a pleasant tingling sensation brought Lara abruptly awake. She opened her eyes and stared down on Drago's dark head. She felt a tug on her nipple and realized Drago was suckling her. She moaned and arched her back, pushing herself deeper into the hot cavern of his mouth. He seemed to know when she had awakened for he nipped gently, then soothed the hurt with the rough pad of his tongue.

Her arms went around him, pulling him up and over her body. "Drago! Please."

"I love the way you respond," he whispered raggedly. "You were made for loving. I've always heard Gypsy women were hot-blooded creatures."

Her reply was muffled by his kiss. Then she caught fire. He loved her again, then they slept until the sun was high in the sky.

Drago was gone when Lara awoke. Her body ached in places she never knew existed. She was struggling out of bed when Ramona knocked once and entered. She walked to the bed and stared down at Lara, her eyes dark with concern.

"Are you all right, little one?"

"Oh, Grandmother, what have I done?" Lara wailed. "What will Papa think? He has such high hopes for me. What can I tell him? That I married a man whose name I don't even know? A man so secretive he will tell me nothing about himself? What am I to do?"

"Drago lives a life of intrigue, granddaughter."

"Is that all you can tell me? I know we must each go our own way, but will we meet again?"

"Give me your palm, little one."

Lara extended her hand, palm up, surprised by Ramona's willingness to read her fortune. She had been reluctant to do so in the past. "What do you see?"

Ramona's frown deepened as she stared intently at Lara's palm. "Danger."

"What kind of danger?"

She clutched Lara's palm tightly, her eyes glazing over. "You will become deeply involved with a man you care about."

Lara knew Ramona wasn't simply reading her

palm; she was delving deeply into her psychic powers to foretell Lara's future.

"Is Drago that man? Will we meet in London?"

"You will meet no man named Drago in London."

Chapter 6

You will meet no man named Drago in London. Ramona's words left a deep hole in Lara's heart. How could she continue to exist in a world without Drago? Making love with him had been the most exhilarating, the most exciting thing she'd ever done. There was an element of mystery about Drago. Who was he? Was he loved by another woman? Would he forget her after he left? She had married him while he was too ill to know what he had done, and she was foolish to hope for something more between them.

Lara knew she had no legal hold on Drago. The best thing she could do for him was to cease asking questions about his past and savor whatever time they had left together. Her father would never allow her to marry a man with a violent past and no future, nor would he acknowledge her Rom marriage.

Lara sighed heavily, her heart all but broken. What a silly goose she was. If Drago really cared for her, he would want her with him. But he had admitted quite frankly that their parting would be final.

So be it. When the time came, Lara vowed to let

him go without revealing her heartbreak. Pride was all she had left.

Julian washed quickly at the pool, then returned to camp and helped himself to the porridge simmering in Ramona's cooking pot. Lara hadn't come out of the wagon yet, and neither Ramona nor Pietro was anywhere in sight. After last night's celebration, there were few early risers.

Julian ate, then wandered over to the corral to help Rondo curry the horses. They would leave for the fair tomorrow, and he knew Pietro would want the horses to show well.

Rondo barely acknowledged Julian's presence, and Julian couldn't help but wonder if Rondo was jealous. Julian's thoughts returned to the previous night, recalling how he and Lara had made love endlessly. He freely admitted he had been somewhat foxed, but he knew what he was doing, and remembered how very much he had enjoyed making love to Lara. He had been shocked to find her untouched, and he couldn't stop himself from contemplating who would be her next lover.

That thought produced a fierce scowl. He really shouldn't care, but the thought of Lara lying beneath another man was definitely unpalatable, and even more distasteful when he realized Lara's new lover would most likely be Rondo. Not that Julian had anything against the young Rom, who seemed to genuinely care for Lara.

"Damnation," he muttered beneath his breath. All this speculation was making him crazy. He had a mission; find a killer and break the smuggling ring that was depriving the government of much needed funds. Nowhere in this assignment was there room for a bewitching little Gypsy wench.

Julian intercepted a fierce glare from Rondo and decided to ignore it. He had troubles enough without tangling with a jealous would-be-lover. He owed these people too much to let hostile feelings damage his relationship with them.

Julian didn't return to the camp until suppertime. He joined the others and was handed a plate of food. Moments later Lara sat down beside him.

"Where have you been all day?" she asked.

"Working with the horses."

He studied her face beneath lowered lids, entranced by the sweet curve of her mouth, the exotic slant of her eyes. He shifted, easing his swollen shaft. Just looking at her made him hard. Merely *thinking* about her made him hard. Her full, lush lips, her rounded little body, her passion. Most of all her passion. Last night he had unleashed something wild and wanton inside her.

He leaned forward and whispered, "Are you all right? I was rather hard on you last night."

Her cheeks bloomed a dusty rose beneath the smooth, golden texture of her skin. "I'm fine," she said in a hushed tone. "You're a gentle man, Drago. A woman couldn't ask for a better lover her first time."

Julian suddenly lost his appetite. His mouth went dust dry, and the swelling in his trousers grew more pronounced. Carefully, he set his plate down.

"Shall we retire to our wagon?"

Lara stared at him through luminous eyes. Her slight hesitation gave him pause. Would she refuse him?

"Forgive my eagerness," he drawled lazily. "If I wore you out last night, you have only to say so."

Lara's flush deepened as she set her untouched plate beside his. "I'm tired but not worn out, Drago. Perhaps retiring early would do us both a world of good."

His lips quivered with mirth. The invitation visible in the depths of her exotic eyes was a clear indication that the little Gypsy spitfire knew precisely what he wanted. Furthermore, she wanted it as badly as he did. He rose and held out his hand. She grasped it, and he pulled her to her feet. Hand in hand they walked to their wagon, blissfully unaware of a man's dark gaze following them.

"I missed you," Julian said, surprised to realize he meant it. "You indicated that you had no ill effects from our loving last night. Can you take me again tonight?"

"Aye," she whispered, stepping into his arms.

His arms closed around her. She pulled his shirt out of his trousers and slid her hands inside the opening. He pressed his lips against hers and their mouths became ravenous, their desire unquenchable. He deepened the kiss at the same time he pulled her blouse from her shoulders, freeing her breasts. They filled his hands, and he kneaded them with his fingertips. A groan rumbled deep in his throat. He felt her nipples harden against his palm and wanted to taste the dusky fruits, to suckle them and nip them until she begged for mercy, but Lara had other ideas.

She tore her mouth from his, opened his shirt, and set her lips against his corded throat, then slid her tongue down the muscles of his chest, until they fastened on a hard, male nipple.

Julian had no idea how it happened, but moments later they were both lying naked on the bed, bathed in golden candlelight, their bodies glistening with sweat. Rolling once, he put her atop him, spread her legs, and pushed himself inside her. She melted around him.

"Ride me, sweet wanton," he urged as he flexed his hips and thrust deeply.

Lara took all of him. He felt her stretch as he filled her with his hardness. She eagerly complied when Drago clasped her bottom and lifted her up and down his engorged shaft, showing her what he wanted. Then he pulled out so just the tip of his swollen sex remained inside her, inviting her to take over.

He felt her quivering breath on his cheek as Lara accepted the invitation, riding him like a stallion, until she spent herself upon his great staff. Then his own driving need took over. His roar of ecstasy vibrated the walls of their small wagon.

They slept, then made love again. Few words were exchanged, for they knew what they had found together was doomed. Two unlikely people from different worlds had no right to find happiness together.

The caravan left the next morning for Lockerbie. Julian helped herd the horses behind the wagons. The fair opened the day after tomorrow and Pietro wanted to reach their destination in plenty of time for the opening.

A halt was called at dusk, and they camped that night in a protected valley beside a river. Julian ea-

gerly anticipated the moment he and Lara could disappear and make love again. Within their gaudily
draped wagon, Julian's cares faded into a distant
past. His responsibilities as head of the Thornton
family no longer seemed important. His mission for
the government held no sway when Lara was in his
arms. Not even memories of Diana intruded within
the walls of the cozy refuge he shared with Lara.

The caravan rolled on its way shortly after dawn the
next morning. Julian rode with the horses, his mind
consumed with thoughts of Lara. Her passion had
been inexhaustible last night, almost frantic. Did she
sense that their time together was growing short? The
walnut stain was wearing off his skin. He expected it
to be gone entirely by the time the fair ended.

They reached Lockerbie on the eve of the fair.
Pietro chose a camping site not far from the fairgrounds, and soon the camp was bustling with activity. Lara had explained what would happen on the
day of the fair. The women would wander through
the fair, selling trinkets and telling fortunes. Ramona
would have her own tent, where she would gaze into
a crystal ball and foretell peoples' futures for a silver
coin. Pietro and the men not entertaining with song
and dance would handle the sale of the horses.

Julian decided to keep a low profile in the remote
possibility that some of his friends, or his enemies,
would attend the fair and recognize him. One
couldn't be too careful in his line of work.

The camp quieted down early that night. Pietro
spoke individually to each family before they retired.
He wanted his horses to be in place and his people
ready when the fair opened. The coins earned at the

fair would be hoarded to last through the winter months. After the fair, Pietro intended to return Lara to her father and camp on the grounds of his country estate for the winter. Lara's father had generously allowed Pietro's band of Gypsies to camp on his property whenever they wished because of their ties to his daughter.

Julian made slow, tender love to Lara that night. Twice he brought her to a shuddering climax. Before she drifted off to sleep, he asked her what she intended to do at the fair the next day.

"I usually remain outside Ramona's tent and invite people inside to have their fortunes told," she said sleepily. "Pietro won't allow me to wander about by myself like the other women."

A wave of fierce relief washed over Julian. He knew from experience that Gypsy women often sold their bodies and disappeared into the woods with their marks. Usually the men would return from the tryst missing a valuable piece of jewelry, or their purse. Julian knew Lara wouldn't sell her body, but he feared some coarse man would mistake her for a whore and force her.

"I'm glad," Julian replied, yawning. "That's one less thing I have to worry about. If you intended to wander about with the other women, I would have forbidden it. I won't be nearby to protect you. I intend to remain close to the horses during the fair."

"Pietro always keeps an eye on me. I'll be fine."

Satisfied, Julian pressed her into the curve of his body and let sleep claim him.

Excitement prevailed throughout the camp the following morning. Breakfast was prepared and consumed and preparations were completed for the fair. The sun was not yet visible when Pietro and his followers set out for the fairgrounds. Julian followed behind with the horses.

The stalls were just opening for the day. Lara went off with Ramona and Pietro while Julian helped herd the horses into a crude corral, where prospective buyers could examine the stock and dicker for the best bargain. It wasn't long before fairgoers from towns near and far began streaming to the fairgrounds. Pietro's horses were an instant hit.

Julian had chosen the wrong place in which to maintain a low profile. Men milled around the horses most of the day. Deals were struck and horses were led off by satisfied new owners. At the close of the first day, enough prime horseflesh remained to warrant returning the following day.

Julian was preparing to return to camp when someone tapped him on the shoulder. "I say, my good man, I'm interested in the dappled gray. Can I have a closer look?"

Julian froze. That voice! He knew it as well as his own. Damnation! What was Sinjun doing so far from home? Julian turned slowly, gazing into his brother's handsome face.

To Sinjun's credit, he did nothing to give away Julian's identity. He merely stared, his mouth open, his eyes narrowed in disbelief.

"Bloody hell, Julian, this is the last place I expected to find you. And dressed like a Gypsy, no less. You bloody well better have a good explanation. Emma is frantic with worry. Rory and I were on our way to London to look into your disappearance when we heard about the fair. It wasn't too far out of our way so we made a detour to look over the horses."

"There's no need for you to continue on to London," Julian replied. "I'm returning to town after the fair."

Julian flinched when Sinjun clapped a hand on his injured shoulder. His wound was healed but was still tender.

"Julian, what's wrong?" Silence. "You've been hurt! God's blood, what happened?"

" 'Tis nothing, Sinjun," Julian assured him. "Return home to Christy and the children. I'll make my peace with Emma."

"You're in trouble, Julian, I can sense it. Why are you dressed like a Gypsy? Where have you been? How can I help you?"

Julian's jaw firmed. "I can't tell you. There's nothing you can do for me now. If I need help, you'll be the first to know."

From the corner of his eye, Julian saw Lara approaching and tried to send Sinjun on his way. It was not to be.

"Drago! Are you ready to return to camp?"

"Drago?" Sinjun echoed, one eyebrow raised in question.

"Say nothing," Julian hissed.

"Everyone is leaving," Lara said, sending Julian a beguiling smile. "Are you coming?"

"Run along, Lara, I'll catch up with you," Julian said, praying that Sinjun wouldn't give away his identity. "I was discussing one of the horses with this gentleman."

Lara stared at Sinjun a long moment, then gave Ju-

lian an uncertain smile. "Very well. Don't be long."
She hurried off to join a group of women returning to
camp.

Sinjun whistled softly. "What a little beauty. Do
you want to tell me about her?"

"Some other time," Julian said, staring after Lara.
The gentle sway of her hips sent hot blood surging
through his loins. It took tremendous effort to tear his
gaze away and return his attention to his brother.

"So, 'tis like that, is it?" Sinjun said, chuckling
knowingly. "I never thought you'd fall for a Gypsy
wench. Not Julian, my very proper, very dull
brother."

"Leave off, Sinjun," Julian warned. "Go home. As
you can see, I'm well."

"Are you taking your Gypsy mistress with you?"

"Bloody hell!" Julian swore. "Lara would be out of
place in London. Do you want the dappled gray or
not?"

"How much?"

Julian named a price he knew would please Pietro.
Sinjun looked the horse over and agreed to the price.
Money was exchanged and Julian handed Sinjun the
leading reins.

"Are you sure you're all right?" Sinjun asked.

"Very sure."

"You bloody well better be," Sinjun muttered.
"Rory is around somewhere. I'll collect him and return to Glenmoor. You *will* send word, won't you?"

Julian clapped Sinjun on the shoulder. "Aye, you
have my word."

Sinjun led the horse off and Julian headed back to
camp . . . and Lara. He couldn't wait to make love to
her in the privacy of their wagon again. He thought

suddenly of Sinjun's words. His brother seemed to think he was obsessed with Lara, even hinting that Julian had fallen in love with her. But that wasn't the way of things, Julian reflected. Admittedly Lara was a distraction he hadn't counted on, but he'd never let his obsession for the fiery Gypsy get in the way of duty.

Julian took Lara off to their wagon directly after the meal that night. Though nothing was said, they both knew their time together was drawing to an end. Their loving that night, though no less ardent, was a poignant reminder that nothing was forever.

At the end of the fair, a celebration was held to toast their good fortune during the week-long event. Much feasting, drinking, and merrymaking took place in the camp that night. Most of the horses had been sold and the fairgoers had been most eager to have their fortunes read. Even those selling trinkets were pleased with their success.

Everyone except Julian and Lara were in a celebratory mood. Julian had decided not to continue on with the Gypsies. Before the feasting began, he sought out Pietro for a private word.

" 'Tis time for me to leave, Pietro."

"You must do what is best for you," Pietro answered.

"I will never forget what you and your people have done for me. I owe you my life. Tell me where to find you in the next few weeks and I will arrange for a proper reward."

Pietro shook his head. "We want nothing from you, Drago. Our band of Romany has been fortunate. We prosper and will continue to do so. You may take one of the horses to speed you on your journey."

"Thank you. Who knows? One day our paths may cross again."

"All I ask is that you make peace with my granddaughter. Your leaving will be difficult for her."

Guilt made Julian look away. "Pietro, this marriage . . . how can I explain it? I am English. My marriage to Lara will not hold up in a court of law. Lara is . . ."

". . . a Gypsy," Pietro said with a hint of rebuke. "Far beneath you in rank."

Julian sent him a sharp look. "I do not believe I ever mentioned having a title."

"There was no need. It was obvious from the beginning that you are no common man. Nevertheless, we were pleased to have saved your life. Had not Lara claimed you as her husband, you would be dead now. You used her as a man uses a wife. Let your conscience be your guide where Lara is concerned."

"Conscience has nothing to do with my decision to leave," Julian argued. "Lara was well aware of my intentions from the beginning. I don't want to seem coldhearted, for Lara is a woman worthy of any man, but I will never marry. Certain things occurred in my past, things that made me renounce marriage."

Pietro searched his face. "You are a troubled man, Drago, haunted by events you cannot change. I will not chide you for using my granddaughter, for Ramona insisted that your coming to us was an act of God. If Lara's future does not include you, then so be it. Go in peace, Drago. I believe we will meet again one day."

"Take care of Lara," Julian replied. "In the short time I have known her, she has become dear to me."

He turned and walked away without waiting for Pietro's response.

Pietro stared after him, a thoughtful expression on his face. He placed an arm around Ramona's shoulders when she joined him a few moments later.

"Drago is leaving," Ramona said. There was no question in her voice.

"Aye. Tomorrow."

Ramona's gaze found Lara as she moved about the camp. " 'Tis not the end for them."

"Drago says it is."

"Pah! What does Drago know?" She clutched Pietro's gnarled hand. "I fear for our granddaughter, husband."

Pietro kissed her wrinkled cheek. "We must believe that her father will protect her, Ramona. Should fate bring Drago and Lara together in London, they will find their own way."

Lara saw Drago talking to Pietro and knew intuitively what they discussed. Drago was leaving. She had known the day was coming and had thought herself prepared for it. But being prepared involved more than setting one's mind to something. Her mind knew she and Drago were not meant to be together, but her heart refused to listen.

Drago had made love to her without involving his heart. She couldn't force love where none existed. Drago enjoyed making love to her, she knew that, but she also knew that he was anxious to leave and get on with his life. She wouldn't stop him, although her greatest fear was that his enemies would find him once he left the protection of the Gypsy caravan.

Lara hurried over to Drago the moment she saw him walk away from Pietro. "You're leaving." Her statement seemed to hit a raw note with him.

He looked harried, driven, as if he were being torn in two. "We need to talk, Lara. Come inside our wagon."

Lara wasn't quite ready to listen to Drago's words of farewell. "Can it not wait?"

"No." He held out his hand. "Come."

She placed her hand in his and followed him to their wagon. He shut the door firmly behind them and led her to the bed. "Sit down." Steeling her heart against his hurtful words, she perched on the edge of the bed.

He began to pace; back and forth, back and forth.

"Stop!" Lara shouted. "Just say what's on your mind and get it over with."

Drago stopped abruptly and knelt before her. He grasped her hands. "I haven't told you anything about myself for the simple reason that I wanted to protect you and your people from my enemies. The less you know about me the safer you'll be."

"So you've said," Lara said tartly.

"That hasn't changed. We've already discussed our Rom marriage and you know my position."

Lara's chin firmed. "I asked nothing from you." Once she returned to her father, Drago's name would never leave her lips. Only her heart would know her pain.

"I would never have taken you had I suspected you were innocent," Drago continued. "I lost my head. You seemed so willing to . . ."

"I was willing."

Drago's head jerked up. "I was the experienced

one. I should have known. I will never forget you, Lara. Were things different . . ."

"Things might be different if I weren't a Gypsy," Lara charged. "I can't change what I am."

"No, and I can't change what I am."

"How soon must you leave?"

"Tomorrow. What little walnut stain remains on my skin can easily pass as a summer tan. My responsibilities . . ."

"I don't want to hear about them. Go if you must, I won't stop you. Even Gypsies have pride."

Lara thought she'd never seen anyone so torn.

"Try not to hate me, sweeting. Parting is not easy for me, either. I will always remember this time with you as an idyllic period in my life. Life has never been so simple or enjoyable."

Is that all you can say? Lara's heart cried out.

"I want to make love to you tonight, Lara, but not if you don't want it."

Not want it? She craved it, needed it. "I would like that, Drago. Just tell me one thing. Is there another woman in your life?"

The shadows in his eyes deepened. "Not anymore."

Lara heard all she needed to know. Obviously Drago was one of those men who loved only once, deeply, with their whole hearts. No other woman could ever take the place of the one he lost.

She lifted her face. "Kiss me, Drago. Tonight you are mine. Look at me and tell me you are thinking of another woman when you make love to me."

Drago joined her on the bed. "I think of no one but you, my Gypsy spitfire. Your scent, your taste, you arouse me beyond bearing."

His strong hands cupped her face, bringing their lips together. He kissed her slowly, with such passion, such tenderness, that her eyes grew misty with tears. How would she exist without Drago? He deepened the kiss; his tongue plunged into her mouth, and the ability to think fled.

Excitement roared through Julian, as hot and intense as lightning. No woman had ever made his body sing and his blood thicken like his Gypsy lover. Kissing Lara was pure pleasure. Loving her was pure ecstasy. Leaving her was pure hell. If he wasn't an earl he'd say to hell with propriety, to hell with society, and take her to London with him. People might think the very proper Earl of Mansfield had lost his mind, but he would be the envy of the *ton*.

His thoughts scattered when Lara slipped her fingers between the edges of his shirt. Her hands were warm and soft and infinitely arousing against his chest. He managed to get the front of his trousers undone and his shirt unbuttoned as her hands roamed over the muscular planes of his chest, down his stomach to his . . .

A groan of raw pleasure ripped from his throat when her fingers closed around him. He tore at her blouse, ripping it in his eagerness to render her naked. Clothes flew, mouths clung, hands explored. He skimmed a thumb across a taut nipple. He bent his head and took it between his teeth. Lara gasped; he felt her tremble. Julian knew she was as excited as he when she grasped his head and held it to her breasts. He sucked her nipples, savoring the gasping little moans escaping her throat, sadly aware that he would never hear them again after tonight.

She reached down and circled his staff, and Julian feared he'd spill his seed into her hand. He fought for control. Disgracing himself their last time together was not a pleasant thought. Briefly he considered taking her quickly, as his body demanded, but he swiftly discarded that notion. He turned her on her stomach and lifted her knees.

Lara gave a squeal of surprise. "What are you doing?"

"Have you never seen horses mating?"

"Of course, but what has that got to do with ... oh ..."

He spread her knees and positioned himself behind her, nipping gently at her neck. He stroked her cleft and tested her with his fingers. Wetness flooded his hand. Her heat scorched him. He opened her and buried his sex deep inside her. To prevent their loving from ending too soon, he held himself still inside her a long suspenseful moment.

"Drago, please. End this torture."

Her plea undid him. Grasping her hips to hold her in place, he thrust forward, teeth clenched, head thrown back, a growl rumbling deep in his chest. The explosive end came suddenly, violently. They climaxed together, one in body, one in soul, yet as far apart as two star-crossed lovers could get.

Lara lay quietly in Drago's arms as their breathing returned to normal. She wanted this night to go on forever, but she knew dawn would appear in the eastern sky as surely as day would follow. She wouldn't beg Drago to stay, or beg him to take her with him. It was an impossible situation for both of them. He had those responsibilities he spoke of and she had a father waiting for her. But the thought that Drago could leave her without a backward glance still hurt.

Suddenly, from out of the blue, Lara had a chilling premonition. "We will meet again, Drago," she murmured. "When danger stalks you, I will be at your side."

"I doubt that, sweeting," Drago replied. "I prefer to think of you living safely with your people in some remote part of Scotland. You would hate London and its intrigues."

"Is that where you're going? London? Is London your home?"

He remained silent so long Lara knew she was delving too deeply into his private life. "I'm sorry. You need not answer any of those questions. I know you do not like to talk about yourself. Forgive me."

"We have so little time left, sweeting. There are other things I'd rather do than talk."

"Aye," Lara whispered, winding her arms around his neck. If this was the last night they had together, she wanted to make it special.

They loved again, arms and legs entwined, bodies pressed together, mouths and hands exploring places that might have been missed during their first frantic joining. Then they slept. When Lara awakened the following morning, Drago was gone.

And with him her heart.

Chapter 7

Julian traveled to his country estate for a brief visit before continuing on to London. He didn't want Emma or any of his peers to see him in Gypsy garb. The less anyone knew about his sojourn with the Rom the safer they would remain. Peters, the Thornton Hall butler, opened the door to him.

"Beggars apply at the back door," Peters sniffed, looking down his long nose at Julian. The door started to close in Julian's face.

"Bloody hell, Peters, 'tis me," Julian said as he pushed past the startled butler. "Don't you recognize your own employer?"

The normally unflappable butler was clearly astounded. "I ... that is, my lord, I didn't recognize you. Forgive me. I'm not accustomed to seeing you dressed ... um ... like a disreputable person."

"Stow it, Peters. I want a bath drawn. And quickly. Ask Mrs. Howard to prepare something substantial for me to eat. I'm off to London as soon as I'm presentable."

"Very good, my lord," Peters said. "I will see to it immediately."

An hour later, freshly bathed and shaved, Julian dressed in his usual impeccable attire and sat down to the hearty meal Mrs. Howard had prepared for him. The food was ambrosia compared to the plain Gypsy fare he had become accustomed to, but for some reason it was less enjoyable than the simple meals he had shared with Lara and her family.

Lara. His Gypsy wife who wasn't really his wife.

Thoughts of Lara had plagued him all the way home. Their last night together wouldn't be easy to forget. He wasn't sure he wanted to forget the passion they had shared, though he knew it must remain buried deep within himself while he pursued Diana's killer.

Guilt continued to plague him, however, for the callous way in which he had left Lara. Hurting her hadn't been his intention. If Lara had spoken up about her innocence he never would have taken her. After that first time, there was no way he could stop making love to her. He blamed himself for acting more like his roguish brother Sinjun than himself where Lara was concerned, but her passion was addictive. Wanting her was a hunger he couldn't assuage. Somehow he had to learn how to live without Lara's lush body tempting him beyond redemption, but it wasn't going to be easy. The taste of her didn't satisfy, it only whetted his appetite.

Julian reached London late that night. He didn't have his key and was forced to use the iron knocker to gain admittance.

After a frustrating length of time, Farthingale, Julian's town butler, opened the door, his nightcap askew on his gray head and his spindly ankles sticking out of his nightshirt.

"Lord Mansfield! Welcome h-h-home, my lord."

"Your mouth is open, Farthingale," Julian said, pushing past his stammering butler. "I lost my key. Are Emma and Aunt Amanda out for the evening?"

"Aye, my lord. They're attending Lady Marshall's musicale. Viscount Blakely is escorting them."

"Blakely? Sinjun's rascally friend?"

"Just so, my lord. Lord Blakely has been a frequent visitor during your absence."

Julian frowned. He didn't like the sound of that. Blakely was as much a rogue as Sinjun had been before he'd settled down with Christy. Julian vowed to have a talk with Emma about the company she'd been keeping as soon as possible.

"Shall I summon your valet, my lord?" Farthingale asked, clearly anxious to return to his bed.

"Nay, let Ames sleep. I can undress myself. I'm exhausted. Good night, Farthingale."

"Good night, my lord."

Julian climbed the stairs to his chamber, weary to the bone. He'd been gone from home too long and in the end his investigation had led him back to London. He was convinced that someone high up in the government was the Jackal, the man behind the smuggling ring. The man who wanted Julian dead, the one responsible for Diana's death. One good thing came from Julian's return to London, however. He'd be able to keep an eye on Emma. Obviously Emma was out of control if she was seeing Rudy Blakely regularly.

Julian undressed and collapsed in bed. He was so

tired that he fell asleep before thoughts of Lara could produce the inevitable arousal.

"Julian! Wake up! How dare you stay away so long without letting me know where you were. Julian! Do you hear me? Wake up."

Julian was being shaken violently awake. He opened one bleary eye and saw Emma standing over him like a vengeful angel, hands on hips, one foot tapping impatiently, her violet eyes aglitter with fury.

"Stop it, Emma. What's gotten into you?"

"Where have you been?" Emma demanded.

"It doesn't matter. I'm home now. Kindly wait for me in the breakfast room, I'll be down directly."

"Very well, but don't think you can appease me with your weak excuses this time. I was so worried I sent for Sinjun. I had no idea if you were dead or alive."

"As you can see, I'm very much alive. Ring the bell for Ames on your way out."

Tossing her head, Emma whirled and strode away, giving the bell pull a yank before she stomped out of the room.

Ames showed up shortly bearing a tray with tea and a slice of perfectly toasted bread. He set the tray carefully on the bedside table, poured cream and tea into the cup, and smiled at Julian. " 'Tis good to have you back, my lord. Shall I draw your bath?"

"Aye," Julian said, yawning. "Give me a moment to drink a cup or two of tea and eat my toast. Emma is in a fine froth this morning, and I doubt my breakfast will go down easily with her ranting in my ear."

Two cups of strong tea diluted with rich cream did

the trick. Even the toasted bread tasted good. Julian was in a much better mood when he sank down into the tub of hot water. After his bath, Ames shaved him and helped him into tight black breeches, ruffled white shirt, black jacket, and polished Hessians. Julian observed himself in the mirror. Nothing about his very proper image reminded him of Drago the Gypsy.

Emma was waiting for him in the breakfast room, seated in her normal place. She was attractively attired in a pale violet day gown that emphasized the deep purple of her eyes. The sweetheart neckline showed the barest hint of rounded breasts, reminding Julian that Emma was all grown up. He bent and kissed the top of her head. "Good morning, Emma. Where's Aunt Amanda this morning?"

"Good morning," Emma said without warmth. "Aunt Amanda is still abed, and it's a good thing. I wouldn't want her to hear this conversation. What have you got to say for yourself, Julian? What am I to think when you disappear for weeks at a time without a word in the interim?"

Julian knew he deserved the rebuke, but Emma's words stung nevertheless. He was aware that his absences bothered Emma, but there was little he could do about it unless he removed himself from government service. And he wasn't ready to do that yet.

"Answer me, Julian," Emma demanded. "What will you tell Sinjun? He'll arrive in London soon."

"Sinjun won't be arriving in London," Julian explained. "I saw him but four days past and sent him back to Glenmoor."

"You saw Sinjun? Where?"

"I . . . ran into him at a fair in Lockerbie. He heard about the unusually fine string of horses offered for sale at the fair and made a detour to look them over."

Emma's finely etched brows edged upward. "What were *you* doing at the fair?"

"That, my nosy little sister, is none of your business."

Julian helped himself to food from the sideboard and took his usual place at the head of the table. "How is Aunt Amanda?"

"Well. What a dear she is. I don't know how I would have managed without her after you and Sinjun abandoned me."

Julian sent her a sharp look. "You haven't been abandoned, dear. I expect to remain in London for an indefinite period of time. I'll be on hand to escort you and Aunt Amanda to all the functions you ladies seem to dote upon."

"I wouldn't want you to put yourself out," Emma huffed. "We have a perfectly good escort in Viscount Blakely. Rudy has been wonderfully accommodating during your absence."

Julian's dander rose. "Lord Blakely is hardly the escort I would choose for you, Emma dear. His reputation as a rake and womanizer is well documented. Have you forgotten his escapades with Sinjun? Your brother has reformed, but Blakely has shown no signs of changing his wicked ways."

"Rudy has been nothing but a gentleman," Emma sniffed.

"Nevertheless, I must curtail Blakely's visits now that I am home."

Emma rose abruptly, tossing her napkin into her plate. "I'm not a child, Julian. Why must you be such an ogre? Is your own life so bereft of human kindness and companionship that you wish the same for me?" She stomped her foot. "I won't have it, Julian! I will continue to see Rudy and you can't stop me."

Julian's mouth hung open as Emma charged from the room. What in bloody hell had happened during his absence? How had Blakely gotten so close to Emma? Where was the relationship headed? If Blakely compromised his sister, he'd have his head on a platter.

Julian's fierce expression eased when Aunt Amanda breezed into the breakfast room.

"Julian. How wonderful to have you back. Emma told me you'd returned. Whatever did you say to deserve her ire?"

"I've forbidden her to continue her association with Viscount Blakely. You're looking well," he continued, adroitly changing the subject. "I hope my spirited sister hasn't been too much of a handful for you."

"Never! Emma is a sweet, lovable young lady. She makes me feel young again." She paused, sending Julian a piercing look. "What do you have against Lord Blakely? He has been kind and generous to us. His escort has been much appreciated during your absence. Sinjun asked him to watch over Emma while you were away from London, and the dear, sweet boy has done just that."

"Are we speaking about the same Lord Blakely?" Julian asked, aghast. "Blakely and Sinjun are cut from the same cloth."

"Sinjun reformed, so can Rudy," Amanda argued.

"Nevertheless, we can dispense with Blakely's company now that I'm home."

"Hmmm, whatever you say, Julian," Amanda said, blinking innocently.

Julian finished his breakfast while Amanda chatted about nothing of importance. He listened with half an ear as he made a mental note of all the things he had to discuss with William Randall, the Earl of Chatham, when he reported his findings.

Julian left the breakfast room and went directly to his study, where he pored over the records forwarded to him by his estate manager at Thornton Hall. Everything seemed to be in order there. His other properties were also doing well. He read the exchange report and was pleased to learn that his investments were prospering. All in all, the Thornton family fortune was healthy and growing.

After luncheon, Julian ordered his carriage and drove to Whitehall to report to Randall. He cooled his heels but a short time before being admitted into Randall's office.

"Lord Mansfield," Randall greeted warmly. "I began to fear you had met with foul play. Sit down. I'm most anxious to hear your report. Brandy?"

Julian nodded. Randall filled two snifters and handed one to Julian. Julian rolled the amber liquid around in his snifter, then downed it in one gulp. Thus fortified, he launched into his report.

"The smugglers had access to secret information, my lord. They were expecting an agent to infiltrate their ranks. I was recognized and apprehended while loading contraband with the villagers. They took me aboard their ship. The Jackal was there. I saw him but not clearly enough to identify him. I do know this: He is a person of importance, and privy to our plans."

Randall leaned forward in his seat. "You say you didn't recognize the Jackal?"

"It was dark, and his face was shadowed. I was wounded trying to escape and taken aboard ship unconscious. The Jackal knew I'd be there, and that a reception awaited the smugglers in Cornwall. They bypassed their usual drop-off point and unloaded their contraband on a desolate beach near Dumfries in Scotland."

"I'm glad you survived to tell the story. But how did you escape? And where have you been these past weeks?"

"I dove into the Bay of Solway before the ship landed and took a bullet or two. I don't recall much after that, until I came to in a Gypsy wagon."

"Gypsy wagon," Randall repeated, obviously intrigued.

"Aye. One of their women found me on the beach and had me carried to their camp. There, an old woman treated my wounds. She saved my life. I stayed with them until my wounds were healed."

"Do you suppose the Jackal believes you perished in the sea?"

"I don't know. He sent his cohorts to the Gypsy camp looking for me, but they protected me. Now that I'm back in London, I intend to find the traitor in our ranks. He's raking in profits that rightfully belong to the government."

Julian knew that Randall believed Great Britain's destiny was to become the greatest trading nation in the world, and that he would stop at nothing to see his country reach its goal. Julian hoped that appealing to Randall on that level would convince him to allow Julian to continue his investigation.

"Scorpion has been exposed," Randall mused thoughtfully. "Continuing your investigation could place your life in grave danger. I'll assign another man to the Jackal."

"No!" Julian protested. "You know my history, my lord. The Jackal killed my fiancée. I was the one who was supposed to die in that carriage accident. I am convinced the Jackal is aware of my identity, but that's all the more reason I should continue. I will be more vigilant now. My presence in London will bring the Jackal out of hiding."

"I don't know," Randall said doubtfully. " 'Tis too risky. I've grown fond of you, Julian."

"I have no intention of dying," Julian said tensely, "but catching a traitor is more important than my life. Here is my plan. I will attend every function, every public and private affair. Become a decoy, so to speak. The Jackal won't be able to resist another attempt on my life. This time I will be ready for him. This time there is no fiancée to hurt. There is only my sister, and I can send her to Sinjun in Scotland."

Randall stroked his chin, deep in contemplation. Julian sat on the edge of his chair, waiting for Randall's decision.

"The Jackal must be stopped," he said determinedly. "We are no closer to the smugglers than we were when your initial investigation revealed the plot to cheat the government out of its due."

"Aye, my lord, my sentiments exactly. Do I have your permission to continue my investigation?"

"You have it, though 'tis most unwillingly given. Since you believe there is a traitor within our ranks, 'tis best you do not contact me here. If we need to meet, send a message around to my home."

Julian rose. "Very good, my lord. God willing, the next time we meet I will have run the Jackal to ground."

Julian returned home in a thoughtful mood. He would continue his investigation by escorting Emma to the usual rounds of social events tonight and throughout the season. He strode into the drawing room and was surprised to see Emma and Aunt Amanda taking tea with Viscount Blakely.

"Lord Mansfield," Rudy said, rising to greet Julian. "Emma was just telling me that you've returned home. She said you saw Sinjun. How fares the Laird of Glenmoor?"

"Sinjun appears well." He glanced at Emma. "I'm thinking of sending Lady Emma to Scotland for a lengthy visit."

"Julian! In the middle of the season? I should say not. I'd be most happy to visit Sinjun and Christy in a few months, but not now."

"We'll see," Julian hedged.

He plopped down in an empty chair. Emma poured tea and handed him a cup. "Rudy is to escort us to the Wexinghams' rout tonight. That won't be a problem, will it?"

"Lord Blakely's escort won't be needed," Julian said stiffly. "Since I'm now in residence, I intend to escort you to all your social functions."

Emma shot Julian a disgruntled look, which he promptly disregarded.

"We'll see you there, Rudy, won't we?" Emma asked.

"I wouldn't miss it," Rudy said.

Julian rose abruptly. "A word with you in my study, if you please, Blakely."

Obviously Rudy recognized an order when he heard one. "Of course, Mansfield. Lead the way."

"I hope Julian isn't discourteous to Rudy," Emma whispered to Aunt Amanda as the men disappeared down the hall. "Rudy is really a sweet, kind man. Not at all like the unrelenting rogue Sinjun was before he reformed."

"Is Lord Blakely courting you, Emma, dear?" Amanda asked. "It seems that way to me, but of course Julian must have the last word on allowing his suit."

Emma blushed and looked away. "I . . . care for Rudy, Auntie, and I think he cares for me, though nothing has been discussed concerning our future together or lack of one. You know Julian will say Rudy is too old for me, though barely six years separate us. To his favor, Rudy will inherit his father's title and considerable fortune one day. He can't be all that objectionable."

"That's for Julian to decide, dear," Amanda replied.

Emma's would-be suitor faced Julian over a snifter of brandy. Julian stared at him over the rim of the glass. He could see where Blakely would turn a young girl's head. He was handsome and personable, and his manners were impeccable. But Julian was well aware of Blakely's weakness for women, hard drink, and gambling, not necessarily in that order, and he wanted to protect Emma from falling victim to Blakely's rascally charm.

"What exactly are your intentions toward my sister, Blakely?" Julian asked, going directly to the heart of the matter.

Blakely's brown eyes widened and he nearly

dropped his glass. "Are you accusing me of acting disrespectfully toward Lady Emma, Mansfield?"

"I'm well aware of your reputation, Blakely. Emma is an innocent; 'tis my duty to protect her."

"Lady Emma needs no protection from me, my lord," Blakely assured him. "I hold her in the greatest regard. I would like permission to court her."

"Emphatically no," Julian bit out. "You have wormed your way into her good graces during my absence, but I have no intention of letting it go on. I'm sure there are other ladies who would welcome your attention."

"Be that as it may, my lord, but Emma is the only woman I wish to court."

"I'm withholding permission," Julian barked. "If you'll excuse me, I have business to attend to."

Rudy leveled a flinty glare at Julian and rose stiffly. "I'm as determined as you are, Mansfield. Sinjun changed; what makes you think that I cannot?"

He left before Julian could form a reply.

Julian stared at the closed door a long, thoughtful moment after Blakely left. Emma wouldn't agree, but protecting his sister from her reckless nature was necessary. He knew she considered him harsh and unyielding. She had accused him more than once of having no heart, and in a way she was right.

Would a man with a heart abandon a woman who had been innocent of a man's touch until he had relieved her of her virginity? He doubted it. Lara had been untried and he had taken her with lusty abandon, using her night after night to slake his unrequited hunger for her. Even now he wanted her. He suffered her loss as keenly as he'd felt Diana's death.

Sometimes, during those odd moments of introspection, Julian wondered if he and Diana would have enjoyed a happy marriage. She would have been a perfect countess. Cool, reserved, regal, everything he'd ever desired in a wife. A woman fit for an earl.

It wasn't until he met and bedded a certain Gypsy beauty that he learned the value of a woman's passion. After Diana's death he had taken mistresses, but they had roused little deep passion in him. They had been outlets for his physical needs, but quickly forgotten, whereas Lara's passion had been honestly given and lovingly bestowed.

Lara is a Gypsy, he reminded himself. Not fit to take her place as the wife of an earl, no matter how beautiful or desirable. Society would never have accepted her. Lara would have been miserable as the ostracized wife of an earl. Her wild spirit would have withered and died beneath the strictures demanded by polite society.

Visions of Lara's wanton dancing jarred his memory. With vivid clarity he recalled her lithe, golden body whirling and spinning to a Gypsy refrain. Her blood was hot, her passion stunning, and Julian couldn't bear the thought of another man having her. But his bloody responsibility to family and country made Lara's gift of herself impossible to accept on a permanent basis.

Julian's thoughts were interrupted when Emma burst through the door without knocking. "What did you say to Rudy? He left here in a stew. I swear, Julian, if you've ruined this for me I'll never forgive you."

Julian heaved a weary sigh. Life was so damn complicated. As head of the family his responsibilities were enormous. So many people depended on him that he almost wished he could return to the simple life as Drago the Gypsy.

"You are young, Emma. There are better men than Blakely to choose from among the *ton*. I'll see you at dinner," he said dismissively.

His head was already buried in a ledger when he heard Emma slam out the door.

Dinner that night was an uncomfortable affair. Emma's anger simmered to a fine froth, and Aunt Amanda's quiet disapproval of Julian's overbearing ways grated on his nerves. He excused himself before dessert and paced his room until it was time to dress for that night's social event.

The rout proved boring and a waste of time as far as Julian was concerned. It didn't improve his mood when Emma disappeared into the garden with Rudy while Julian was sniffing out the traitor from among his peers. He learned nothing that night, nor was there an attempt made upon his life. Perhaps he expected things to happen too soon. Frustration gnawed at him. He knew he was handling Emma all wrong but hadn't the slightest idea how to rectify the situation without giving in to Blakely's ridiculous request to court her.

The following weeks were lost in a social whirl. Julian renewed his acquaintance with men he considered prime suspects in his investigation while at the same time keeping an eye on Emma, who, to Julian's consternation, appeared seriously enthralled with Rudy Blakely.

Briefly Julian considered taking another mistress,

but he quickly discarded the idea. He had neither the time nor the energy to devote to a mistress in his present circumstance. Besides, after Lara, the thought of bedding another woman was distasteful. The Gypsy wench had ruined him for another woman. She had bewitched him, and he couldn't shake off her spell.

Julian had been in London a month when Emma informed him at the breakfast table about the ball they were to attend that night to introduce the Earl of Stanhope's daughter to society.

"Do you know Lord Stanhope's daughter well?" Julian asked conversationally as he perused the morning paper.

"I've never met her. Few even knew Lord Stanhope had a daughter until he invited the *ton* to her coming-out ball. I suppose she's been rusticating in the country until now."

"Ummm," Julian said, resigning himself to a boring evening of simpering young women and eagle-eyed mothers looking for eligible husbands for their daughters. He supposed the Stanhope chit was cut from the same cloth.

Julian entered the ballroom of the sumptuous Stanhope mansion situated next to Hyde Park on Park Lane. The line of carriages waiting their turn to discharge their prestigious guests had delayed their arrival, and the ballroom was already crowded to overflowing.

Julian knew Lord Stanhope slightly but didn't see him in the crush of people. He headed over to join a group of peers while Emma and Amanda wandered toward some women acquaintances. The talk was boring and Julian drifted off, looking for other diversion. A crowd of men clustered around a man and woman caught his attention. Curious, he wandered over in their direction. Standing on the edge of the crowd and craning his neck, he felt an odd thrum of excitement pass through him.

Lord Stanhope stood in the center of the eager crowd, beaming down at the woman on his arm. She was turned away from him so that Julian couldn't see her face. She was small, her curvaceous body clad in a stunning silver gown that showed to advantage her dark hair and golden complexion. A chill of recognition raised the hairs on the back of Julian's neck. The young woman raised her head and smiled at one of her admirers. Julian gasped. He felt as if someone had punched him in the gut. Hard.

Lara. As if drawn by the hand of fate, Lara found him over the sea of heads. Their gazes clashed and held. Julian could tell she hadn't expected to see him here, for her skin paled and her eyes grew impossibly wide.

What the bloody hell was Lara doing with Lord Stanhope? Julian wondered. He gave a snort of disgust. Obviously the fiery Gypsy wanton had followed him to London and found herself a protector. Lord Stanhope, a widower, had probably been an easy mark. No one even remembered his wife, and his rich daughter would soon be auctioned to the highest bidder.

Damn! Damn! Damn! How dare she! It didn't take her long to climb from one bed to another. He had taught her passion and she had learned her lesson well. But why had Lara come to London to find another lover? Wasn't Rondo good enough for her?

Lara's knees were shaking. If not for her father's sustaining presence she would have run for the nearest exit. She hated this posturing and pretense. The men vying for her attention did so out of curiosity, not because they thought her wife material. She'd seen the mothers whispering behind their fans, no doubt commenting on her dark skin and unusual eyes. Even the young ladies her age stared at her as if she were dirt beneath their feet.

Lara knew her dowry was sufficient to guarantee her a husband, but the man who asked for her hand would have to be in desperate need of funds to take a half-Gypsy bride. Poor Papa, she silently lamented. He had such high hopes for her. She knew he would be disappointed if she didn't marry one of these posturing fops. But Lara was adamant. If she couldn't have Drago, she didn't want anyone.

Lara summoned a polite smile for Lord Denby, who had just complimented her dress, and wished they would all disappear. Their empty flattery left her cold.

Suddenly Lara felt a finger of apprehension crawl up her spine. Her anxious gaze scanned the crowd of would-be suitors and met the dark, enigmatic gaze of the man she had given up hope of ever seeing again. He was staring at her so intently that her knees began to buckle beneath her and she grasped her father's arm for support.

"Lara, dear, are you ill?" Lord Stanhope asked as he supported Lara's sagging form.

"It's so close in here, Papa," Lara whispered. "Might I go to the ladies' retiring room?"

"Of course, my dear. I will escort you there myself."

He executed a maneuver that led them away from the ballroom and crowd of admirers. "You are a success, Lara," Stanhope gloated. "You have all the young men falling at your feet. I knew you'd be popular. I have such high hopes for you, daughter. You're a welcome addition to society."

I care nothing about society, Lara thought. She hated to disappoint her father, but these adoring young men didn't have marriage on their minds. She was astute enough to know that they were more interested in her as a mistress than a wife. How could Papa be so blind?

When Lara had encountered Drago's gaze over the heads of her admirers, she'd wanted to crawl into the woodwork. He'd looked stunned and angry, though he had no reason to be angry with her. She was the one who had suffered after he'd left her without a hint of remorse or regret.

But he'd looked so wonderful it was all she could do to tear her eyes from him. He was dressed in expensively tailored evening clothes: light blue satin coat, silver waistcoat, gray trousers, white stockings, and leather shoes with buckles liberally sprinkled with stones that looked suspiciously like diamonds. Nothing about him reminded her of Drago, unless it was his brilliant midnight blue eyes.

"I shall wait here and escort you back to the ballroom," Lord Stanhope said when they reached the retiring room.

Lara shook her elegantly coifed head. "No, Papa, return to your guests. I will rest a moment and find you when I feel more confident of myself. This is all so new."

Stanhope kissed her forehead. "I'm proud of you, daughter. You're the picture of your lovely mother. Had I known of your existence I would have married Serena and brought you both to live with me. I pray you forgive me for not making things right with your mother before she died."

"I had a good life with Mama. I lacked for nothing. 'Tis as much Mama's fault as yours that you did not know about me until I was thirteen."

Stanhope smiled. "I promise to make it all up to you. There must be one worthy man among these young puppies making moon eyes at you. Don't stay too long, you will be missed."

Lara slipped inside the retiring room, relieved to find it empty. As far as she was concerned, the only man worthy of her was Drago, and he didn't want her.

Lara hid inside the retiring room as long as she dared before inching the door open and stepping out into the hall.

"It's about time," a familiar voice drawled. "We need to talk."

"Drago."

"Aye, my wanton little Gypsy." He grasped her arm and pulled her toward the open French door leading from the hallway directly into the garden. Once outside, he dragged her through the sweet-smelling flowers and into a maze of hedgerows. He didn't stop until they reached a moon-drenched gazebo at the center of the maze.

Roughly he swung her around to face him. "What

the bloody hell are you doing in London? Did you follow me here?"

Lara couldn't believe her ears. Drago's accusation made her furious. He was the one who had abandoned her, so why was he so angry? If looks could kill, Drago would have already met his maker.

Chapter 8

"**H**ow dare you manhandle me!" Lara blasted.

"I'd like to do more than that," Julian growled. "Why did you follow me to London, you little fool? It didn't take you long to find a new protector."

Lara's mouth fell open. Drago's cruel, unjust accusation nudged her anger into full bloom. She shook herself free of his grasp and started to walk away. But it was not to be. Drago renewed his hold and dragged her up against him.

"Stanhope is an old man. Does his soft shaft please you?"

"Arrogant bastard," Lara hissed. Finding Drago at her ball was shock enough, but to have him speak to her as if she were a common whore was insulting. Who was he? And what was he doing at her party? How did he come by an invitation? He was dressed like a fine lord and acting like an idiot.

Enough was enough. Before she had time to change her mind, she hauled back and slapped Drago across the face.

"Go away, Drago," she spat. "You know nothing

about me. Why should you care what I do? You left me without a backward glance. Did you ever think of me once during the weeks since we parted? I don't know who you are, or how you came by an invitation to Lord Stanhope's party, but I suggest you take yourself off and leave me alone before I call a footman to evict you."

A nerve twitched in Julian's jaw, but other than that, he gave no sign that she had hurt him. Judging by the way her hand stung, the blow should have been painful.

"Don't ever do that again," he hissed through clenched teeth. "What happened, Lara? You weren't a whore when I left you. Did you discover you couldn't do without a man in your bed? I'm surprised you didn't turn to Rondo." His eyes narrowed. "Or did you? Perhaps you decided to seek your fortune in higher places. I understand Stanhope is a wealthy widower. He won't marry you, spitfire. Earls seek wives from their own ranks."

"You disgust me, Drago. I believe you owe me an apology."

Julian stared at her as if she'd lost her mind. "For what must I apologize?"

"There are so many things I can't begin to name them. For one, you called me a whore. For another, you accused me of following you to London when it never occurred to me to chase after someone who cared so little for me."

"Then explain what you're doing in London."

"This conversation is beginning to bore me. There should be a law preventing pompous, overbearing asses from circulating in polite society. Excuse me, I must be getting back. Lord Stanhope will come looking for me if I don't return to the ballroom soon."

"Let him look," Julian growled as his arms tightened around her. "Shall I remind you how it was between us? Would you like a small demonstration of how it feels to be kissed by a real man?"

Panic shuddered through Lara. If Drago kissed her she'd never find the will to stop with just one kiss, and knowing Drago, he wouldn't, either. Lara didn't know this elegantly dressed gentleman. He looked like Drago yet he wasn't Drago in any of the ways that counted. His demeanor was more commanding, more tyrannical. Less admirable.

"Kiss me, Lara."

"No! I don't know you."

He gave her a feral smile. "You know me, Lara, and you know my kisses. You tempt me beyond reason."

His mouth slammed down on hers. His kiss was hard, almost brutal, as if he were punishing her for showing up in London and complicating his life. The kiss went on forever, until her mouth softened beneath his and his lips became coaxing and gentle, just like the Drago she remembered from the Gypsy camp. His hand found her breast. He squeezed gently, then tormented the nipple with the pad of his thumb. A moan slipped past Lara's lips. Abruptly he dragged his mouth away and removed his hand, holding her at arm's length and staring at her so intently she wanted to melt.

"Go back to your own kind, Lara," he commanded. "I have no time for you."

"I did not follow you to London, Drago, so ease your mind of that notion. You made it perfectly clear that you didn't want a Gypsy wife. By the way, what name are you using in London? I assume 'tis not the one I gave you. Drago is a Gypsy name and you look like no Gypsy I've ever seen. What kind of skullduggery are you involved in? Have your enemies found you yet?"

"I can tell you nothing, Lara, except to repeat my request that you leave London."

"I will do as I please," Lara retorted.

"Does that mean you will continue to serve as Lord Stanhope's mistress?"

"Go to blazes, Drago!"

Dark eyes burning with fury, Lara whirled on her heel and left Julian standing in the shadows. Why did he have to be so damn hurtful? When she first spied him tonight her heart had pounded with excitement. Never would she have expected this kind of reaction from the man she loved.

Julian felt as if he'd just been trampled by a horse. Seeing Lara dressed like a lady and consorting with society had thoroughly shocked him. He was confused and disoriented. He shook his head to clear it of the vision in silver that still danced before his eyes. The elegantly coifed and robed lady wasn't the Lara he knew, and he wasn't sure he liked this new image of her.

He preferred to remember her as the tawny, long-limbed spitfire who danced like a wood sprite and made love like a wanton. The Lara he recalled was all fire and seduction. Innocent and temptress neatly packaged in a body that would entice a saint. He wanted to tear her away from Lord Stanhope, to claim her as his own, but his mission was too vital for him to become involved with a woman. He knew

Gypsies had low moral standards, but he had assumed Lara was different. Tonight he'd learned that she was like every other Gypsy woman. The kind who did just about anything, legal or illegal, for money.

Julian strode back to the house. He'd had enough surprises for one night. As soon as he collected Emma and Aunt Amanda, he intended to leave. His plans went awry the moment he appeared in the ballroom. Lord Stanhope hailed him from across the room.

"Ah, Mansfield, how good of you to come tonight. You haven't met my daughter yet. She was just here a moment ago." He grasped Julian's arm. "Come along, I'm sure we'll find her somewhere in this crush of people."

Julian muttered an oath beneath his breath while trying to maintain a pleasant façade. He didn't want to offend Stanhope, but neither did he wish to meet the man's marriageable daughter. He'd seen enough of pale young women with empty heads to last a lifetime. Since he never intended to marry, they held no interest for him. But rudeness was not Julian's style and he let himself be dragged forward to meet the chit.

"Ah, there she is." Stanhope beamed, pointing vaguely toward a group of young people.

Julian groaned when he spotted Lara standing near the group. He had no wish to encounter her again, least of all in Stanhope's company. The knowledge that Stanhope was bedding Lara produced unaccountable fits of violent jealousy, an emotion Julian had no business feeling. The passion he and Lara had shared during his sojourn with her people had been of short duration. Theirs was never meant to be a permanent association, and he had ended it out of necessity.

Julian's gaze locked on Lara when they halted before her.

"Lara, my dear, may I present Julian Thornton, the Earl of Mansfield. Mansfield, this is Lady Lara, my lovely daughter."

Stanhope's words exploded inside Julian's head. His Gypsy lover was an earl's daughter? Bloody hell! He had compromised an earl's daughter! Lara was staring at him as if he had two heads, and he supposed he looked as shocked as she. Why had an earl's daughter been living with Gypsies? Nothing made sense. Finally his impeccable manners prevailed and he bowed over Lara's delicate hand, murmuring appropriate words of greeting.

Julian's vision narrowed. Everyone became invisible but for Lara, the woman he had taken to his bed and left without a backward glance. An earl's daughter deserved better than what he had given her. Resentment welled inside him. Why hadn't she told him the truth about herself? Berating himself for a fool, he knew he shouldn't blame her when he'd been as secretive as she, but he couldn't help himself.

The strict moral code under which Julian had conducted his life reared its ugly head, reminding him where his duty lay. One didn't compromise an earl's daughter without consequence. He knew what he had to do and was prepared to make the sacrifice.

Abruptly Lara was whisked away to the buffet table by an admirer, leaving Julian feeling as if his world had just collapsed.

"She's something, isn't she?" Stanhope bragged. "I

wasn't aware that I had a daughter until Lara's grandparents brought her to me a few years ago. Her mother was a Gypsy. The loveliest woman to walk the earth. She disappeared from my life after a short acquaintance and I never saw her again." He sighed. "Eventually I married, but my wife and I produced no children. Lara came to me after my wife died, and my life suddenly took on new meaning."

"How very fortunate for you," Julian said dryly.

"Aye, very fortunate. Now I must see that she marries well." He sent Julian an assessing glance. "I understand your betrothed died tragically some years ago. How sad. You have mourned long enough. Have you thought of settling down and getting yourself an heir?"

Stanhope's broad hint was not lost on Julian. The earl wouldn't be the first parent to throw his daughter Julian's way. This time the circumstances were different. This time he knew the daughter far too well to ignore Stanhope's invitation.

"With your permission, I'd like to call on Lady Lara tomorrow afternoon. Perhaps she'd consent to a drive through the park with me. Shall we say two o'clock?"

"Splendid, Mansfield, splendid," Stanhope said, his face alight with pleasure. "I'll tell Lara to expect you."

Julian wandered off, his mind awhirl. Finding Lara in London and learning she was the daughter of an earl was spectacularly bizarre. A coming-out ball was the last place in the world he would have expected to see his Gypsy lover.

"I say, Mansfield, good to see you in town again. Have you put your wanderings behind you?"

Julian gave Viscount Hurley, a passing acquaintance, a tepid smile. "Good to see you, too, Hurley. I plan to stick around awhile."

"I saw you talking to Stanhope's Gypsy bastard. Quite a beauty, isn't she? I hear he legitimized her years ago."

"Indeed," Julian said, keeping his expression purposefully blank.

"Harry Lister and I were just discussing her," Hurley said, motioning for his friend to join them. "Her dowry is generous, but I strongly suspect it will take a man with empty pockets to offer for her."

"Hello, Mansfield," Harry Lister, the Marquis of Avondale greeted. "What a crush of people. What do you hear from Sinjun? 'Tis hard to picture him rusticating in Scotland."

"Sinjun is a different man since he and his family settled in the Highlands."

"We were discussing Lady Lara," Hurley confided to Avondale.

A leering smile twisted the corner of Avondale's mouth. "Ah, the luscious Gypsy wench. Half the men attending the ball tonight want her for their mistress, while the other half are put off by her tawny skin, exotic eyes, and all that black curly hair. She's too bloody different to fit in."

"I wouldn't mind having her in my bed," Hurley acknowledged. He lowered his voice. "You know what they say about Gypsy women and their passionate natures."

"You go too far, Hurley," Julian warned.

"Defending the chit, Mansfield? Do I sense a liaison in the making? Seems to me you haven't had a mistress for some time. If you fancy her, we'll stand aside. She's probably too hot for either Avondale or myself to handle anyway. Tell me, how does one approach an earl when one wants his daughter for a mistress?"

Avondale and Hurley shared a private laugh while Julian simmered inside. How dare they insult Lara! Aye, she was different, but not a woman present tonight outshone her in beauty or spirit. There was nothing pallid or wan about the dark-eyed goddess who had once called him husband.

"Stow it, Hurley," Julian said, clipping his words for emphasis. "Lord Stanhope will have your head if he hears you insult his daughter. I suggest you keep your improper thoughts to yourself. Excuse me, gentlemen."

Julian strode away, so angry he could barely contain himself. Lara didn't deserve their disparaging remarks. They had no right to judge her and find her lacking.

Julian looked around for Emma and failed to see her. He found Aunt Amanda chatting with a group of elderly ladies and headed in her direction. From the corner of his eye he saw a brilliant slash of blue and immediately associated it with the color dress Emma had chosen for tonight's outing. He turned just in time to see Emma disappearing through the open French door with someone looking suspiciously like Viscount Blakely.

Spitting out a curse, he hurried after them, and nearly ran over Lara on his way out. Dimly he wondered if one of her admirers had lured her into the garden to seduce her. She was naive in the ways of the world, and he feared she might mistake men's flirtations for genuine interest. After speaking with Hurley and Avondale and overhearing snippets of conversation here and there, he feared she might be seduced with fancy words into doing something she'd later regret.

"Were you going out for some air, my lady?" Julian inquired politely.

She met his stare with icy dignity. "If I was, my lord, 'tis no concern of yours."

"If you're thinking of trysting with one of the randy fops here tonight, then I'm making it my business. You know nothing about the games men play with women."

"Don't I, my lord? Since meeting you, I've learned much about those games."

Julian grasped her arm and pushed her out the door before they caused a spectacle. "It seems we were both playing games, Lara," he grated as he guided her down the path and behind a row of tangled vines. "We have both withheld vital pieces of information from each other. I did it to protect your family. What excuse do you have?"

"It wouldn't have been wise to reveal information about myself to a man I knew nothing about. You could have been a smuggler, a spy, a secret agent, a . . ." Her eyes narrowed, then widened with sudden comprehension. "That's it, isn't it? You're a secret agent!"

"Quiet, little fool! You don't know what you're saying. I asked your father's permission to call on you tomorrow. I'll come for you at two o'clock in my carriage."

"I think not, my lord. I'm not going anywhere with you. Papa wants me to choose a husband from among the *ton* and I'm seriously thinking of doing so. You, my lord, are not in the running."

His voice turned hard, implacable. "I've ruined you, spitfire. You should bloody well consider me."

"Julian, is that you?"

Julian groaned. Emma and Viscount Blakely had spotted him in the shadows and were fast approaching. He grasped Lara's arm to keep her from fleeing and turned to greet his sister.

"I've been looking for you, Emma. 'Tis time to go."

"Oh Julian, must we?" Emma groused. "I have yet to meet the earl's daughter."

Lara's voice held a brittle edge. "Be so good as to introduce me to your . . . friend, my lord."

Julian saw no help for it. "May I present my sister, Lady Emma? Emma, this is Lady Lara, the Earl of Stanhope's daughter. And this," Julian continued, gesturing carelessly at Blakely, "is Viscount Rudolph Blakely."

Polite words were exchanged, then Julian said, "Would you kindly take Emma inside and inform Lady Amanda that I am ready to leave, Blakely? I will be with you in a moment."

Emma looked as if she wanted to say something, but Julian's stern visage must have persuaded her otherwise. She nodded politely at Lara and followed Blakely inside.

"They make an exceptional couple," Lara said wistfully. "They look perfect for one another."

"They are *not* a couple," Julian insisted. "Lord Blakely is my brother's friend, nothing more. Emma is too good for him."

"Just like you're too good for me?" Lara charged. "Do you think I don't know what the *ton* is saying about me? I'm neither blind nor deaf, I know people are whispering among themselves about the color of my skin, my unusual eyes, my strange looks. I'm just the thing for a mistress but not good enough for a wife. I can't make my father understand that bringing me to London for a season was a mistake. I'd be much happier in the country, or with my grandparents."

Julian wanted to wring the neck of the men who thought themselves too good for Lara, until he remembered that he'd thought the same thing.

"I must go, Lara. Blakely is sniffing around Emma and I have to put an end to it. We'll talk further tomorrow."

"Your sister looks old enough to make up her own mind," Lara defended. "Perhaps she sees something in Lord Blakely you do not."

"Ah, there you are, my dear. I saw you go out the door for a breath of air and wondered why you did not return."

"Papa," Lara said, sending him a fond smile. "I was just about to come back inside when I ran into Lord Mansfield. You will excuse me, won't you, my lord?"

"Of course, my lady. Until tomorrow," Julian answered.

He watched Lara disappear through the door on her father's arm and felt heat rising inside him. He'd wanted to kiss her again, and he would have if Emma and Blakely hadn't interrupted. To look at Lara was to want her. He knew intuitively that every man present had the same thought. And it made him mad as hell.

Julian collected Emma and Aunt Amanda and hurried them out the door to their waiting carriage. Blakely joined them.

"Do you have your own transportation, Blakely?" Julian asked bluntly.

"Not tonight," Rudy said, grinning at Emma. "Would you be so kind as to drop me off?"

"At home or at one of those gambling hells you're so fond of?"

"Julian, don't be rude," Emma chided. "Of course we'll take you home, Rudy." She moved over to make room for him. He slid in beside her before Julian could intervene.

Grumbling to himself, Julian gave his driver Rudy's direction and settled down beside Aunt Amanda.

"You do recall the little talk we had in my study, don't you, Blakely?" Julian asked curtly.

"Indeed," Blakely said without taking his eyes off of Emma.

"Julian," Emma began when Julian's displeasure became palpable. "Have you met Lady Lara before? You two appeared to be on *very* friendly terms. What a little beauty she is. It's hard to believe that Lord Stanhope kept her hidden in the country all these years."

Julian remained stubbornly silent as he stared out the window.

"The gossips raked her over the coals," Rudy offered. "Her looks are too exotic to be considered proper. Men were put off by her background and women were jealous of her beauty. She's part Gypsy, you know."

"How dreadful to be the subject of vicious gossip," Emma commiserated. "I hope someone has the good sense to offer for her."

"What about you, Emma?" Julian challenged. "How many men have you turned down this season?"

"Now, Julian, don't fuss at Emma," Amanda chided. "The child will make her choice when she's found the right man."

Julian felt sick when Emma sent Blakely a shy smile. His relief was palpable when they discharged Blakely at his townhouse.

"I'll see you tomorrow, Lady Emma," Rudy said, ignoring Julian's cold glare. "I'll bring my new rig around and take you for a drive in the park."

"I daresay Emma will be busy tomorrow," Julian ventured.

"Not at all," Emma said, ignoring Julian's scowl.

"Emma, I wish you wouldn't flout my wishes in this matter," Julian chided.

"You're such a bluenose, Julian," Emma chided. "Don't you ever do anything on the spur of the moment? Must you always be so proper, so disapproving of everything I do? Sometimes one does things because it makes one happy. But I don't suppose you know anything about that, do you?"

Julian went still. Was that really how Emma saw him? A strict guardian with no joy in his soul? He'd been happy once, before Diana and his unborn child met their untimely deaths. But he knew even then that he'd been a strict taskmaster. As head of the Thornton family, he had taken his responsibilities seriously. Sinjun had been no help, and his family's welfare had sat heavily on his shoulders.

Lord Randall had recruited Julian as an undercover agent ten years ago. At the time the excitement of undercover work appealed to him. But look what it had gotten him. The deaths of two innocent people. After those senseless deaths, Julian had made a solemn vow to himself. Once he ran Diana's killer to ground, he would never again place the lives of those he loved in danger.

Julian dressed carefully for his visit to Stanhope Hall the following day. He looked every bit the elegant lord in buff breeches and coat, snowy white linen shirt, and polished Hessians. The carriage was waiting for him outside the door when he left the house precisely at one forty-five. He drove the matched grays himself, threading the ribbons between his fingers with practiced ease. At exactly two o'clock he turned up the circular driveway of Stanhope Hall. Another carriage was parked before the door, and Julian scowled. He hoped it wasn't one of those young puppies who had made disparaging remarks about Lara's heritage.

Julian rapped on the door with his walking stick and was promptly shown into the drawing room by the imperturbable butler. Lara was sitting on a sofa, perusing a book. She looked up when he entered, barely concealing her displeasure. He studied her through lowered lids. She looked tired, he thought. Mauve shadows marred the fragile skin beneath her eyes, and there was a tightness about her mouth that hadn't been there before.

Julian glanced about the room, pleased that he was the only caller. The other carriage must belong to someone visiting Lord Stanhope, he decided.

"I brought my carriage, Lady Lara," Julian said. "You look tired. A drive in the park is just what you need. Will you join me?"

A fringe of long, dark lashes made it difficult to read her mood. Truth to tell, she appeared none too pleased to see him.

"I have no intention of going anywhere with you, Lord Mansfield," Lara said coolly.

"Lara, did I just hear you dismiss Mansfield?" Lord Stanhope asked. Apparently he had entered the room in time to hear Lara's reply to Julian's invitation. "You're being exceptionally rude, my dear. Are you ill?"

"I'm fine, Papa, really," Lara said. "I'm just not inclined toward a ride in the park today."

"Nonsense, Lara. I gave Mansfield permission to call on you. The least you can do is take that ride he offered. 'Tis a beautiful day. The air will do you good. Get your wrap while I have a word with Mansfield."

Lara sent Julian a resentful glare and left the room. Lord Stanhope stared after her, a puzzled expression darkening his pleasant features.

"I don't know what's got into the gel, Mansfield. She seems to have taken a dislike to you."

"So it would seem," Julian drawled.

"I'm worried about Lara," Stanhope confided. "I love her dearly, Mansfield, but I'm not blind. I saw how the *ton* treated her last night. She's too different, not English enough to gain their approval. Men, bah, they don't recognize a jewel when they see one. They can't see past her golden skin and exotic eyes."

"Someone is sure to see her worth," Julian ventured.

"I was pleased when you asked permission to call on her. You're the only one, you know. The others coveted her, but had nothing respectable in mind."

"I'm sure you're imagining things, Stanhope," Julian bluffed. If any man showed disrespect to Lara in his presence, or made untoward advances, he'd skin him alive.

"Time will tell." Stanhope sighed. "I must get back to my guest now. I left him when Simms informed me you had arrived. Government business, you know."

Julian's interest sharpened, but he was disappointed when Stanhope said nothing more. Stanhope wasn't particularly close to Randall so Julian had no reason to be suspicious, though Stanhope was a powerful man in Parliament.

"Of course," Julian said smoothly. "I'll wait here for Lady Lara. I won't keep her out long."

Stanhope quit the room. Julian moved closer to the door and surreptitiously watched him enter a room halfway down the corridor. Lara still hadn't come downstairs, and no servants were nearby. Throwing caution to the wind, Julian crept down the passage and halted before the door Stanhope had just gone through.

Voices drifted to him through the panel. They were muffled, but loud enough for Julian to make out. Stanhope was speaking.

"The Scorpion, you say? He cannot be allowed to . . ." The last words were lost to Julian as Stanhope's voice lowered. He picked up the conversation when Stanhope's voice grew louder. "I'll keep my eyes and ears open. We can't let a dangerous man like that roam the streets."

Another voice answered, too low and strident for Julian to recognize, and he dare not linger. Was Stanhope involved with the smugglers? It certainly seemed that way. But he mustn't jump to conclusions. He'd have to wait and watch how this played out. He hurried back to the drawing room, arriving seconds before Lara returned with her wrap.

Julian took the cape from her and placed it around her shoulders.

"Where's Papa?" Lara asked.

"He returned to his study. He has a visitor. Did you happen to see who it was?" Julian asked casually.

"No, I was upstairs when he arrived." She sent Julian a sharp look. "Why? What are you up to, my lord? More secret business? Leave Papa out of it."

"You misjudge me, Lara," Julian replied in an effort to allay her suspicious nature. "Shall we go?"

"I really don't want to go anywhere with you, my lord, but if you insist, I suppose I can survive a drive in the park in your company."

Julian handed her into the carriage and climbed into the driver's seat beside her. A slap of the reins and they were off.

"There is no reason for this coldness between us," Julian said as Lara stared stonily ahead.

Lara's dark gaze knifed into him. "Is there not? You left me, my lord. You insulted me horribly. You thought yourself too good for a Gypsy wench."

Julian had the grace to flush. "You could have told me the truth. What else was I to think?"

"You could have believed me. You could have told me you were an earl. I deserve an apology."

Julian gritted his teeth. She did indeed deserve an apology. "I'm sorry, Lara. Forgive my bad manners. I jumped to conclusions."

"It's *not* that easy, my lord," Lara replied curtly. "Perhaps in time. Tell me, why all the secrecy? Who is trying to kill you?"

Maybe your father. "There are things I cannot tell anyone, not even my family."

Lara gave a brittle laugh. "I gave you my love, my

innocence, my heart. You took them and gave nothing of yourself in return, save for empty passion."

"Not empty passion, Lara. Never that. You're the only woman who . . ." His words fell off. Now was not the time to make declarations, not when his own feelings were confused. He did know his duty, though.

"No lies, Drago. You abandoned me. What if I'm carrying your child? Did you ever think of that?"

Julian started violently. "God's blood! I never considered that." He searched her face. "Are you expecting my child?"

"No, thank God. Would it have made a difference? No, don't answer. I know it would not. Earls marry from their own ranks."

"Things have changed," Julian began. "I'm an honorable man, whether you believe me or not. I've compromised an earl's daughter and now I must make amends."

Lara's eyes widened. "I hope you're not suggesting what I think you are. You didn't want a wife then, why do you want one now?"

"I told you. I thought you were—"

"—a Gypsy, I know. The color of my skin hasn't changed, nor has the shape of my eyes."

"Let me be the judge of what's best for you," Julian advised.

"You presume too much, Drago. My destiny is mine to fulfill. You still love your dead fiancée. I won't take second place in your heart."

Julian's expression hardened as he turned the carriage into the park. "Will you just listen to me?"

"No. Unless you wish to tell me how and why you ended up in Pietro's camp with two bullets in you."

" 'Tis a long story."

"I have time."

"Anything I tell you will put your life at risk. I have many guises. I'm the Earl of Mansfield, of course, but I also work for the government. I was on an important mission. A traitor I have yet to identify recognized me. Attempts have been made on my life before, and one of them ended in Diana's death." He paused, looking off into the distance. "Diana was carrying my child when she died. I won't rest until I find the man responsible."

The sharp intake of her breath told Julian his revelation had shocked her. "So I was right. You *are* a government agent."

"Aye, and a damn good one, until someone discovered my identity."

"I'm sorry about Diana and . . . and your child, but getting yourself killed won't bring them back. What has the traitor done?"

"I can't say. 'Tis best you forget I ever mentioned it. I will never speak of it again during our courtship."

A weighted pause. "Our what?"

"I intend to court you in a timely manner and marry you in a ceremony grand enough to satisfy the *ton.*"

"I thought we already *were* married."

"That marriage wasn't legal," Julian countered. What did she want from him? He had offered for her, done what society demanded of him. He had ruined her and was willing to right the wrong he had done her.

"Good," Lara blasted, "because I don't want to be married to you. You have too many secrets, too much pain, too much anger inside you to give me the love I deserve. You have room in your heart for nothing but revenge. I'm sorry, my lord. I can't live without love."

Julian grimaced. "Why is love so important? You'll have respect, my name, everything within my power to grant you. We'll always have passion, no one can take that away from us. Let it go, Lara."

"I can't let it go. Until you tell me you love me, don't mention marriage again."

Chapter 9

The drive in the park hadn't turned out exactly as Julian had hoped. Lara remained stubbornly resistant to his courtship. Her position on love had made it impossible for him to convince her that marrying him was necessary, whether she liked it or not. He had even reminded her that his proposal was likely to be the only one she would get, but that had only made her more adamantly opposed to the match.

Julian drove purposely slow through the park so anyone out and about could see them and draw their own conclusions. People on horseback and in carriages stopped and ogled them, a few drawing abreast for a word with Julian. One of the men who stopped to chat was Clay Merritt, Earl of Tolliver, one of Randall's confidants. When Julian had questioned Tolliver's loyalty, Randall had assured Julian that Tolliver had no knowledge of Scorpion's identity. That was a secret only Randall and Julian shared.

"Lord Mansfield," Tolliver greeted affably. "You've been missed in London. Business abroad?"

"You could say that," Julian replied. "Have you met Lady Lara?"

"Lord Stanhope's daughter, is it not?" Tolliver purred, smiling at Lara. "Indeed, we chatted at the ball last evening, though I doubt you remember me with the crush of people vying for your attention. But we actually met briefly before that at your home, when I had occasion to visit your father."

"Of course I remember, my lord," Lara said. "How nice to see you again."

Julian scowled. For some unexplained reason Tolliver rubbed him the wrong way. He was personable enough, but the man's narrow face, sharp chin, and intense brown eyes reminded Julian of a ferret. He was of medium build and always dressed in the height of fashion. Julian and Tolliver were acquainted socially, but not professionally.

A sudden suspicion made Julian view Tolliver in a new light. Tolliver was close to Randall and could be the elusive Jackal. Tolliver, however, gave no indication that he was aware of Julian's secret investigation.

"Enjoy your ride," Tolliver said as he took his leave.

Julian stared after him, his mind working furiously. "Is Tolliver a frequent visitor at your home?" he asked as he set the horses into motion.

Lara's brow furrowed. "I've seen him a time or two when he called on Papa. He and Papa are sponsoring a bill together in Parliament, I believe, and confer together often. But so is Viscount Dunbar a frequent visitor."

Viscount Dunbar was another of Randall's confidants, Julian reflected. Of the three men, Dunbar, Tolliver and Stanhope, was one of them a traitor? Were all three traitors? One way or another, Julian intended to find out. What worried him was Lara's proximity to men who might pose a danger to her.

He didn't like to think what might happen to her if she was recognized as the Gypsy girl from Pietro's camp. Lara's life could be in danger simply because she had helped him.

"What are you thinking, my lord?" Lara asked when the silence became oppressive. "You're becoming secretive again."

"My name is Julian, Lara. I think we know one another well enough to use first names. After all, you're going to be my wife soon." He had to get her out of the intolerable situation in which she existed so he could protect her. At this point, even her father was suspect.

Lara gave Julian a wistful smile. "I knew Drago, but the Earl of Mansfield is a stranger to me."

Lara suddenly became aware that Julian had turned down a deserted path. The clatter of carriage wheels other than their own could no longer be heard. Trees grew thick and dense on either side of the path, creating a canopy that nearly blotted out the sun.

"Where are we?" Lara asked.

"Still in the park but on a little used path," Julian replied as he guided the carriage off the path and behind a stand of dense bushes that concealed them from passersby.

Her heart thudded against her ribcage. "Why are we stopping?"

"So I can do this," Julian said, roughly pulling her against him. "And this," he continued, clamping his mouth over hers and stealing her breath as surely as he was depriving her of her will.

He kissed her deeply, thrusting his tongue into her mouth. She breathed in his essence. His scent stirred her senses and sent them reeling. Then it happened. She returned his kiss with a sense of euphoric desperation, igniting something hot and deliciously wicked deep inside her. She clutched his shoulders, arching against him. She felt her will evaporating, until memories too painful to visit, dreams too shattered to be resurrected, brought her back to reality.

Julian hadn't wanted her when he thought she was a Gypsy and he didn't deserve her now. He didn't love her. Strong feelings for his dead fiancée still haunted him. Lust wasn't enough for her. She wanted it all, and Julian wasn't prepared to give her what she needed.

Wresting herself from his arms, she held him at bay. "Stop, Julian. Why are you doing this?"

"Is it not obvious? There is something explosive between us that defies reason."

"Lust," Lara said in a voice ripe with disgust.

"Aye, there is that."

" 'Tis not enough, my lord. Take me home."

He brought her back into his arms. "I've declared myself, Lara. I wish to marry you. Why are you resisting?"

"I do not wish to marry you . . . again," she added meaningfully.

"I dishonored you. You're an earl's daughter and I intend to make amends. I want to protect you."

There was a sarcastic edge to her words. "How good of you. Forget it, my lord. I don't need protection."

"Tell me you don't need this," Julian growled as he held her chin between his palms and lifted her mouth to his.

Don't let him do this to you! her mind screamed. But

then she felt herself melting against him, taking the heady taste of him deep into her mouth, writhing beneath his hands as they roamed freely over her body. What made her love this particular man? she wondered despondently. Why did every other man seem weak and insubstantial compared to Julian?

She felt his hands on her back; his warm palms trailed a line of fire down her spine. She groaned a desperate sigh, the beloved familiarity of his touch shattering her willpower. Then she felt a rush of air against her chest and realized that he had unfastened her bodice, baring her breasts. His mouth went unerringly to her nipple as his hands lifted them from the confines of her corset. She tried to push him away but her resistance fled as he licked and sucked the taut buds, moving easily from one to the other.

Lara scarcely had time to catch her breath when she became aware of a new sensation. Excitement raced through her. Julian had lifted the hem of her skirt and was skimming his hand along the insides of her legs. Deliberately she pressed her thighs together, but he merely chuckled and continued past the meager barrier. Then his hand was there, where she ached for his touch, his fingers dancing upon her heated center.

"My lord!"

"Julian."

"Julian, please."

"You're wet and hot for me, Lara. You were always hot for me, weren't you, sweeting? Even when you were innocent of a man's touch you wanted me, just as I wanted you."

"Julian, I . . . can't . . ."

"You can. For me, love. Come." He pushed a finger inside her, working it in and out.

He groaned and grasped her hand, placing it on his erection. "Feel what you do to me? Oh God, I have to have you. I've never been like this with a woman before. I've always prided myself for my restraint, but you put my control to shame."

Julian's words barely registered as tremors shook Lara's body. All her sensory organs were centered on his hand and the torment his talented fingers were putting her through. The tremors began deep inside her, traveling outward, making her skin tingle and the flesh beneath burn with incandescent fire. Needing something substantial to hang on to, she dug her fingers into his shoulders. Then the world shattered around her.

She regained her wits slowly. Julian hovered over her, his face taut with purpose as he eased her down upon the seat. Then he was inside her, moving forcefully, his breath exploding from his lungs in tortured gasps. Something inside her reawakened. Feelings intensified and sensations returned with renewed brilliance. Flames seared along her nerve endings. A shimmering light exploded inside her, until her body became one with it.

She felt Julian stiffen, felt his hot seed flood her body, heard him shout, then her mind went blank. She burst into a million pieces and died a little. Long moments later, she sighed and opened her eyes, dimly aware that someone was calling her name.

"Lara, wake up, sweeting. Someone is coming along the path."

"Oh, God, what have we done?"

"We made love. Let me help you."

Gathering her scattered wits, Lara sat up with Julian's help and began fastening her clothing. Julian had already put his clothing to rights, for he looked as impeccably dressed as he had before they'd set out for the park.

"You had no right! I'll never forgive you. Look at me, I'm a mess."

"You look adorable," he replied. "When we are husband and wife we can make love whenever the mood strikes us."

Lara smoothed her hair and shoved it beneath her hat. "I was your wife, I *am* your wife, but you never saw it that way. I'll not give you another opportunity to thrust me aside, my lord."

"Fear not, sweeting, I will do what's right this time."

Julian pulled the rig back onto the path. Moments later another rig rolled past. The two male occupants nodded in polite greeting. Julian paid them little heed but before Lara turned away, something in her brain seemed to click. She recognized the man! He wasn't dressed in rough sailor garb, but she'd vowed never to forget his face that day he and his companions barged into their camp looking for Julian.

"Is something wrong?" Julian asked. "Did you recognize those men?"

Lara shook her head. She could be mistaken. If she told Julian about her suspicions, he would insist upon investigating. Obviously Julian hadn't noticed anything out of the ordinary.

"I'm just . . . upset, Julian. I never expected to encounter you in London, and after what just happened between us, I'm not sure we should see each other again."

"A month should be sufficient time for the *ton* to get used to our engagement," Julian said without any indication that he had heard her. "We'll marry one month from Saturday at my country estate. There hasn't been a wedding in the chapel since my grandparents were married there in the sixteen hundreds. We'll make it a grand affair."

"I hope you find the perfect bride," Lara snapped. "You've said nothing to convince me that I should marry you."

Lara bristled with suppressed indignation. Why couldn't Julian accept the fact that they were already married? Why couldn't he let the past go and love her? His fiancée was dead, life went on, the future beckoned. But there might not be a future if his enemies found him.

"Your father won't object," Julian continued. "We'll announce our intentions in a few days."

Lara gave a forlorn little sigh as Julian joined the line of carriages leaving the park. She wouldn't be opposed to Julian's plans had he indicated that he cared for her. Lust was a powerful emotion, but not substantial enough to bind two people together for a lifetime.

Julian pulled the carriage into the driveway and halted before the imposing entrance of the Stanhope mansion. He leaped to the ground and walked around to hand Lara down, but she hadn't waited for him.

"Good-bye, my lord," she said stiffly.

"I will call for you at nine tonight to escort you to the Ailsworth musicale."

"I'm sure I'll have a headache," Lara defied.

"Lara," Julian reminded her, "after this afternoon, you could be carrying my child."

Lara sent him a frosty look. "I doubt that. Find yourself a woman more worthy than I of your exalted title. Excuse me, I feel that headache coming on already."

"Nine o'clock, Lara, be ready," Julian said in a tone that brooked no argument. "I'll speak with your father tomorrow about our engagement."

Lara tossed her head. A wealth of dark curls tumbled down from the top of her head as she stormed into the house. Julian stared after her. This stiff-backed, elegantly clad young lady looked nothing like the scantily garbed Gypsy temptress who had captured his fancy, but all the elegant clothing in the world couldn't mask her fiery nature. He recalled with aching clarity how her lithe body, flashing legs, and unfettered breasts had tempted him beyond redemption. He wanted desperately to peel away the exterior layers of refinement and bare her wanton Gypsy soul.

Julian climbed into the carriage, picked up the reins, and tooled down the driveway. He hadn't meant to take advantage of Lara this afternoon. He didn't know what had gotten into him. For a man admired for his control, his lack thereof this afternoon had been a breach of his strict moral principles.

Two men watched avidly from their closed coach as Julian drove away from the Stanhope mansion.

"Are you quite certain Stanhope's daughter is the same woman you saw in the Gypsy camp?" a tall, well-dressed man in top hat asked.

The second man, looking uncomfortable in formal

servant's garb, nodded enthusiastically. "Aye, my lord, the very same. She's wearing fancy dresses now, but 'tis the same wench who insisted that the sick man named Drago was her husband."

"Bah," the nobleman scoffed. "They duped you. It had to be Mansfield, and I'd bet my best racer that he was wounded, not ill. The Gypsies were protecting him. Mansfield has the devil's own luck. I want him dead, Crockett, is that clear? He infiltrated our ranks and is becoming a painful thorn in my side. It took persistent sleuthing to identify Scorpion, the agent bedeviling my operation, and now that I know Mansfield is Scorpion, he must be gotten rid of. He's too close to unmasking me for comfort."

"Aye, my lord. Leave him to me."

"He won't be easy to run to ground. He's too canny." The nobleman tapped a finger against his chin, his pale blue eyes narrowed in thought. "Perhaps the Gypsy wench holds the key. He's already lost one woman he cared for. Should another be threatened, he may decide to give up his investigation. Our enterprise is too lucrative to let one man destroy it."

"What about the girl's father?" Crockett questioned. "Won't he be a problem?"

"Leave Stanhope to me," the nobleman said. "Here's what you're to do."

The nobleman tapped on the roof with his cane and the coach lumbered forward. Inside, the nobleman whispered his plan to his henchman.

A message was waiting for Julian when he arrived home. Farthingale told him it had been delivered by a street urchin who swore he didn't know the man who had paid him to deliver it. Julian stared at the missive, then took it into his study to read.

The note was a strongly worded warning. A threat, really. Whoever had sent it knew too much about Julian. The note, written in sprawling script, suggested that if the Earl of Mansfield valued his life and the life of a certain female close to him, he'd be well advised to drop his investigation.

Julian let out a string of curses. The implication of the message was clear. The Jackal knew he was Scorpion, knew he was close to unmasking him, and also knew that Lara was the Gypsy woman who had protected him. A nerve clenched in his jaw. His first thought was that he had to protect Lara whatever the cost. His second was to wonder if Stanhope was capable of harming his own daughter.

Julian sat at his desk and dashed out a note to Lord Randall, requesting a secret meeting, either during the musicale, if he was attending, or later that night. He sent it off with Farthingale, whom he trusted implicitly. An hour later Farthingale returned with Randall's answer. Randall was going to attend the same musicale and agreed to meet with Julian sometime during the evening.

Lara's first inclination was to plead a headache when Julian arrived that night to escort her to the musicale. But she feared he wouldn't accept no for an answer. With her father pushing her toward an alliance with Julian, she had little hope of getting her own way in this. No one could force her to marry Julian, however. Not as long as a dead woman still held his love. He could beg and plead all he wanted, insist that she needed protection, but nothing short of a declaration of love would change her mind.

Another thing that bothered Lara was the fact that Julian considered their Romany marriage invalid. Well, two could play that game. If he refused to acknowledge it, neither would she, but she wouldn't marry him for the reasons he had given her. It was obvious to Lara that once Julian had discovered she was an earl's daughter, he'd felt obligated to marry her.

Furthermore, Julian's line of work worried Lara. She had inherited a bit of her grandmother's canny ability to "see" things, and she saw danger surrounding Julian. No matter what she did or did not feel for Julian, she was compelled to admit that she feared for his life. Therefore, she decided, it was up to her to see that nothing happened to him. With that thought in mind, she bathed and dressed for the musicale that night.

Julian arrived promptly at nine o'clock, looking splendid in blue satin coat, gray breeches, silver vest, and white stockings. Lara saw admiration in his eyes as she came down the stairs to join him and her father. Her own costume was an elegant confection of green and gold tulle with short puffed sleeves, fitted waist, and neckline that dipped provocatively low over the rounded tops of her breasts.

"You look stunning," Stanhope beamed, moving forward to grasp Lara's hand. "Mansfield will be the envy of the *ton* tonight."

A footman handed Lara's cape to Julian and he placed it over her shoulders. Lara felt the warmth of his palms as they rested a moment longer than necessary on her arm.

They were on their way out the door when another carriage pulled up behind Julian's.

"Who in the world could that be?" Stanhope asked.

Lara felt Julian stiffen beside her and wondered if he was expecting trouble.

The carriage door opened and Lord Tolliver stepped out. "Ah, I'm just in time. I have something of importance to discuss with you, Stanhope. 'Tis about the bill we're sponsoring in Parliament."

Stanhope looked annoyed. "Can't it wait? I'm accompanying my daughter and Mansfield to the Ailsworth musicale tonight."

Tolliver nodded at Julian, then returned his attention to Stanhope. "I'm going there myself after we've spoken. You can ride with me."

Stanhope appeared torn.

"Go on, Papa, have your talk," Lara urged. "You can join Lord Mansfield and me later. Don't keep him too long, Lord Tolliver."

"Indeed I won't, my lady," Tolliver said smoothly.

Lara shivered. The more she saw of the man the less she liked him. There was something oily about him. He was too smooth, too sure of himself. And she didn't like the way he looked at her, as if he could see through her clothing.

Lara sensed Julian's tension and wondered if he felt the same about Tolliver as she did. She glanced at him beneath a fringe of spiky lashes, but his expression gave away nothing of his thoughts. She did know, however, that something about Lord Tolliver bothered Julian.

"Shall we go?" Julian said, offering Lara his arm.

"Go on, my dear," Stanhope urged. "I'll be along directly."

Lara cast a surreptitious glance over her shoulder at her father, then moved off with Julian. The night was damp, and Julian had arrived in a closed coach with a driver and his tiger hanging on to the back. Julian handed her inside and climbed in after her. He seemed preoccupied as he stared out the window.

"Is something bothering you, my lord?"

Julian turned his midnight blue gaze on her and smiled. " 'Tis nothing to be concerned about."

"Are you concerned in some way about Lord Tolliver?"

A long pause. "Perhaps."

"When are you going to stop being so secretive? Are you in danger? Is Lord Tolliver involved?"

"Don't pry, Lara. And don't worry. I'll protect you."

"From whom do I need protection, my lord?"

"Your father, perhaps?"

"Don't be ridiculous. I wish you wouldn't interfere in my life."

" 'Tis too late. Our lives became entangled when you brought me into your camp. One woman lost her life because of me and I won't let it happen to another."

Julian's pain was palpable and Lara's heart went out to him. He must have loved Diana dearly. Losing her so tragically had altered the fabric of his existence. His life now revolved around finding her killer and bringing him to justice. He was opposed to opening his heart to another love, and she was a fool to think she could change him.

They arrived at the Ailsworth mansion and Julian handed Lara down from the coach. The butler opened the door and they ascended the stairs to the music room, where chairs had been set up for the guests. The featured entertainer for tonight's performance, a busty Italian diva, was standing beside the pianoforte, preparing to deliver her first aria.

"I'll fetch you something to drink," Julian whispered as he settled Lara into a chair beside a young lady in pink organza.

The diva began her recital and Julian drifted away. He hated opera. At the refreshment table he helped himself to whiskey and poured a cup of punch for Lara. He started to walk away when Lord Randall joined him.

"I see we both have the same idea," Randall said jovially. "My wife enjoys opera, but I find it tedious."

"As do I," Julian remarked.

Randall leaned close. "Meet me in the garden in ten minutes. Look for the statue of Venus."

Julian nodded and Randall disappeared into the crowd.

Julian returned to the music room and pressed the cup into Lara's hand. She smiled her thanks and returned her attention to the diva, who had hit a high note that almost perforated Julian's eardrums. Glancing furtively about to make certain no one was watching, he sidled toward the door.

Moments later he exited through the pantry on the lower floor and worked his way around to the garden. He spied the statue of Venus keeping watch over a fountain and hastened toward it. Lord Randall was already there, sitting on a bench beneath the shadow of a boxwood.

"Make it fast, Mansfield," Randall said. "It wouldn't do for someone to notice we went missing at the same time. Have you learned something?"

"What do you know about Clay Merritt, Earl of Tolliver?"

"Tolliver? He's not exactly a confidant, but he has important connections and we meet occasionally. He knows nothing about Scorpion. He's aware of the smuggling situation and is using his connections to gather information. He agrees that the loss of government revenue is a threat to the crown."

"Who else knows about our investigation?" Julian asked.

"Lord Dunbar, the Duke of Crawford's second son. He's been in my service nearly as long as you have."

"What about Stanhope? Is he one of your confidants?"

"No. Stanhope is active in Parliament but he knows nothing about our investigation."

"Could any of the men just mentioned be the brains behind the smugglers?"

Randall remained thoughtful. "I suppose anything is possible, but I'd hate to think one of those men is a traitor. Be very careful, Mansfield. We don't want to accuse unjustly."

Julian removed the note he'd received earlier and handed it to Randall. "It's too dark here to read, so I'll tell you what it says. It's a warning against continuing the investigation. I can handle the threat to my own life, but the threat was also directed at Lady Lara, Lord Stanhope's daughter. The Jackal must know that she is the woman from the Gypsy camp who aided me."

"Good Lord!" Randall said, aghast. "We can't involve another innocent victim in our investigation.

You told me the lady saved your life by claiming you were her husband. Just how involved are you with her?"

Julian's jaw stiffened. "I'm going to marry her. I had no idea Lara was an earl's daughter when I . . . when we . . . Needless to say, I owe her my name."

"You're relieved of duty immediately, Mansfield. Keeping you on the case now can endanger your life and hinder our investigation. Your future usefulness is questionable. I don't want your death on my conscience, Julian."

"I can't quit now, my lord," Julian argued. "I'm on the threshold of unmasking the Jackal. I'm convinced I can protect myself and those I care about. I just wanted you to be aware of a traitor within your ranks. Keep an eye on both Tolliver and Dunbar. I'll take care of Stanhope. Don't give them any useful information."

"I'd feel better if you got out of this now."

"I'll contact you again in a few days," Julian replied, deliberately ignoring Randall's suggestion. "I'm getting closer every day."

Lara dragged her gaze away from the diva, searching the room for Julian. A prickling sensation tickled the back of her neck. Something dangerous was afoot. Where was Julian? What mischief had he gotten himself into now? Without a thought to her own welfare, she rose and slipped from the room. Julian was not in the hallway. She descended the stairs. A few couples lingered in the open doorway leading to the garden, fanning themselves.

Something in the waiting darkness drew Lara's attention. She could see nothing, hear nothing but silence, but her nerve endings sent a silent warning to her brain.

Julian was out there.

Lara slipped past a couple obviously engrossed in one another and strode purposely down a path toward a statue of Venus standing guard over a bubbling fountain. Footsteps crunched in the gravel behind her. She whipped around. There was no one. Her imagination was working overtime. She continued down the path, then stopped abruptly when she sensed someone behind her, close enough to feel his breath touch the back of her neck. A hand on her shoulder.

She opened her mouth and screamed.

Julian and Randall were just parting company when a muffled scream pierced through the darkness.

"What's that?" Randall asked sharply.

Somehow Julian knew. He felt it in the deepest marrow of his bones. Something had happened to Lara. His face contorted with terror as he raced along the path toward the house. He came upon her abruptly, sprawled on the ground in a puddle of moonlight. Her face was as pale as death and a trickle of blood oozed down her forehead.

He dropped to his knees and cradled her head in his lap, his fingers dashing the blood from her eyes.

"Lara, can you hear me? Oh God, Lara, speak to me."

"What happened to her?" Randall asked when he reached them a moment later.

Just then Lara moaned and opened her eyes. "She's been injured," Julian snarled, touching the lump rising on her forehead. "I'll kill the bastard who did this."

"What happened?" Lara asked groggily.

"Did you see who attacked you?"

"No. I heard someone behind me, but didn't see him. Help me up. I'm fine, my lord, really."

Julian helped her to sit up, then to stand. She swayed, but quickly gained her equilibrium.

Julian swept her into his arms. "I'm taking you home."

"Julian, wait, I just remembered something," Lara said. "Moments before I blacked out, my attacker spoke to me. He said to let this be a warning for Scorpion. What did he mean?"

Julian and Randall exchanged meaningful looks over Lara's head.

"It means you're not leaving your house without me or an escort," Julian growled.

Chapter 10

Julian spirited Lara away from the musicale without causing a scene. He circled around to the front of the house where his coach awaited and set Lara on her feet. But as luck would have it, they ran into Stanhope and Tolliver, who were just arriving.

"Mansfield, Lara," Stanhope greeted. "Leaving already?"

"Uh, Lara has a headache," Julian said, stepping before Lara to shield her from view.

Concern furrowed Stanhope's brow. "I'll come with you."

"No need," Julian said. "I'll see Lara home."

"Nonsense," Stanhope blustered. "I wouldn't enjoy the musicale knowing Lara is unwell." He turned to Tolliver. "Please excuse me, my lord. I must see to my daughter's welfare."

"Of course," Tolliver said smoothly. He peered at Lara through darkness eased only by moonlight. "Have you injured yourself, my dear? Is that not blood on your forehead?"

Julian cursed beneath his breath as Stanhope maneuvered his daughter so he could get a better look at her. "My God, what happened?" Stanhope exclaimed.

" 'Tis nothing, Papa," Lara said weakly. "I . . . I fell."

Julian glanced at Tolliver, but could read nothing in his shuttered expression. Then his attention was diverted when Lara slumped against him. Fear lanced through him. She could be badly injured. He had to get her home and summon a doctor.

Scooping her into his arms, he placed her inside the coach while his tiger held the door open, and clambered in beside her.

"Wait for me," Stanhope said, hurrying after them. The door had barely closed behind him when Julian thumped on the roof and the coach lurched forward. Lara groaned and opened her eyes.

"How did it happen?" Stanhope asked. Julian sensed Stanhope's anger and couldn't blame him. He felt the same way. This shouldn't have happened.

"I fell," Lara said before Julian could answer. "Julian had gone to fetch refreshments and I felt in need of air. I stepped outside to catch a breeze and tripped on a tree root when I started down the path toward the fountain. I . . . I must have hit my head on a rock."

Stanhope sent her a skeptical look. " 'Tis not like you to be clumsy, Lara. Are you telling me everything?"

"Aye . . ."

"No," Julian contradicted. It was time to test Stanhope's devotion to his daughter. "Lara was attacked in the garden."

"Attacked!" Stanhope gasped. "Someone attacked

my daughter? How dare they? Who was it, Lara? I'll have his hide. I'll bring charges."

Lara sent Julian a disgruntled look. "Really, Julian, there's no need to frighten Papa."

"There's every reason in the world," Julian maintained. "He's your father. He has a right to know."

Stanhope glared at Julian. "What should I know?" Suddenly his brow cleared and he smiled. "I say, Mansfield, have you declared yourself to my daughter?"

"I was going to speak to you tomorrow, my lord. I want your blessing to court your daughter. I intend to marry her."

Stanhope stared at him. "What does Lara have to say about it? I'll not force her to marry someone she dislikes."

"I don't dislike Lord Mansfield, Papa," Lara explained. "I'm not ready to marry yet."

"We'll marry in one month, in the chapel at Thornton Hall," Julian said over her objection. "Meanwhile, Lara is to go nowhere alone. I intend to hire a guard to watch over her when I'm not available."

Stanhope looked thoroughly confused. "I don't understand. Why was Lara attacked? Why would anyone want to harm her?" His eyes narrowed with sudden comprehension. "What are you involved in, Mansfield? Is Lara's life in danger because of you?"

"What are *you* involved in, Stanhope?" Julian returned.

"Me? I'm involved in nothing that could hurt my daughter. Can you say the same? I'm not sure I approve of your suit."

Unfortunately, like it or not, without his offer,

Lara's future prospects were grim. "I'm an honorable man, Stanhope. I'd offer my name to any lady I've compromised."

"Julian!" Lara cried, stunned by Julian's words. "How dare you!"

"I dare because I care what happens to you."

"Now hold on just a bloody minute," Stanhope blustered. "You owe me an explanation. When did you compromise my daughter?"

Julian realized he had blundered, but there was no help for it. Since he couldn't mention the Gypsy camp, he quickly improvised. Besides, it was the truth.

"The day we rode out in my carriage. We were seen in a ... uh ... compromising position. Don't blame Lara, my lord. I thoroughly compromised her without her consent, and I'm more than willing to marry her."

Stanhope looked thunderstruck. "Well, ahem," he could barely look at Lara, "I can hardly refuse you after what you've just told me. I must say I'm disappointed in both of you, but I'm pleased Lara is making a suitable match."

The coach rattled to a halt before the Stanhope mansion. The tiger opened the door and pulled down the steps. Stanhope stepped down first, then Julian. When Lara would have followed, Julian lifted her out and carried her past her father.

"Put me down, my lord, I'm perfectly capable of walking."

Stanhope hurried to open the door, and Julian carried Lara inside. "Which room is Lara's?" Julian asked.

"I can take her from here," Stanhope insisted.

"Show me the way," Julian said curtly as he started up the stairs.

"My lord, Julian, I'm not badly injured. Put me down."

Stanhope opened a door off the hallway and Julian pushed through to Lara's bedchamber. Her maid, who waiting for her mistress to return home, jumped to her feet.

"Oh, my lady, what happened?"

Julian placed Lara in the center of the bed, then issued crisp orders to the maid as if he had every right to do so.

"Cold water and cloths," he barked as he moved the lamp closer to the bed.

"What are you doing?" Stanhope asked.

"Trying to determine if a doctor is needed."

Stanhope watched closely as Julian ran his fingers over the purple lump on Lara's forehead.

"Really, Julian, must you act the tyrant?" Lara complained. " 'Tis only a small bump."

"I don't believe it will need stitching," Julian remarked, "but I'll know more as soon as that infernal maid returns with the water and cloths."

The maid returned a moment later and set the basin of water and cloths on the nightstand. Julian wet a cloth and gently probed the wound. Lara winced but uttered no sound.

"The skin is broken but the wound is shallow. It appears that she was struck with a rock, or a hard object of some sort. The bleeding has slowed to a trickle."

"I told you I was fine," Lara maintained. "Just go away and leave me alone."

"Come along, Mansfield," Stanhope ordered briskly. "Let's leave Lara to her maid. I think a stiff brandy is in order."

"I'll be back tomorrow, Lara," Julian promised. "You're to remain inside until I can arrange for an around-the-clock guard."

"Despot," Lara hissed as Julian strode out the door behind Stanhope.

Once in Stanhope's study, Julian accepted the snifter of brandy and dropped down into a chair.

Stanhope chose a chair opposite him. An uneasy silence ensued as Stanhope frowned into his drink. He lifted his head. "You owe me an explanation, Mansfield. You and my daughter appear to know one another quite well, despite having met a few days ago. *Have* you and Lara met prior to your introduction?"

"You're going to have to trust me on this, Stanhope," Julian said. "I have your daughter's best interests at heart. No one is going to hurt her. I'm announcing our engagement in the papers tomorrow."

"Lara appears reluctant to marry you."

"She has no choice." He emptied his snifter and rose. "I must go. There is much to do tomorrow before the announcement appears in the paper. Good night, Stanhope."

"Are you in danger, Mansfield?" Stanhope asked abruptly as Julian reached for the doorknob. "What secrets are you keeping from me?"

"I can't divulge that information. Suffice it to say, Lara will come to no harm. But," he added on an ominous note, "if I find you're involved in . . . something that could hurt Lara, you'll have me to answer to."

Lord Stanhope's brow furrowed in consternation as Julian took his leave.

* * *

It was very late when Julian reached his town-house. He let himself in and went directly to his room. Ames was seated before the fire, awaiting him.

"Go to bed, Ames, I won't need you tonight," Julian said. "See that I'm awakened at seven. I have a full day ahead of me."

"Very good, my lord," Ames said. "I shall have your bath drawn at precisely seven. Good night, my lord."

"Good night, Ames."

Julian lay awake a long time, pondering the irony of his situation. For a man who had sworn never to marry, he was damn anxious to make Lara his wife. Perhaps it was because he'd never compromised a lady of quality before and was beset by guilt. He and Diana hadn't made love until after they had set the date for their wedding. After Diana's death he had taken mistresses, and occasionally he'd bedded bored wives of his peers who themselves kept mistresses. But he'd never taken an innocent, or debauched a woman of his own class. Until Lara, the lively beauty who had married him in a heathen ceremony and lied to him about her identity.

The memory of Lara's sweet body clinging to his was still with him when sleep finally claimed him.

Lara was in the breakfast room when the newspaper arrived the next morning. Her head ached and her hands shook as she picked up the paper to look for the announcement of their engagement. She found it posted prominently on the second page and groaned aloud. He could announce their engagement in every broadsheet in the country but she'd still refuse to marry a man who didn't love her.

Julian arrived promptly at ten o'clock. Lord Stanhope had already left for the Exchange and Lara was preparing to go out for a ride in the park, despite her father's admonition that she wasn't to go out alone. Julian took one look at her riding habit and nearly hit the ceiling.

"Where do you think you're going?"

She raised her chin. "Riding."

"You aren't supposed to leave the house alone. Does your father care nothing for you?"

"Leave Papa out of this. He told me not to go out alone but I saw no danger in riding in the park with a groom to accompany me."

"You're not in a Gypsy camp," Julian asserted. He grasped her shoulders and gave her an ungentle shake, then he pulled her against him. "Little fool. This is London. You were assaulted once. What will it take to convince you to heed my warning?"

"I saw no danger," she repeated.

" 'Tis all around you."

"No, 'tis all around *you*. I'm but a pawn in your secret affairs. The best thing you can do to ensure my safety is stay away from me. Once you lose interest in me, the danger will die of natural causes."

Julian wasn't convinced the solution was that simple. Or maybe he didn't want to see it as clearly as she.

"If you're so eager to ride, I'll join you. I rode my horse over today. Come along."

With marked reluctance, Lara picked up her crop and preceded him out the door. Once they were both mounted, they walked their horses onto the thoroughfare.

The moment they entered the park, Julian knew he

had made a mistake. There were too many people and Lara was too obvious a target should someone wish to hurt her. A frisson of apprehension rolled down his spine. Though he recognized no one who might hurt Lara, he had a gut feeling that they were being watched.

Lara headed down the bridle path and Julian followed, alert for trouble. The pistol he always carried was tucked snugly into the waistband of his trousers, and the short dagger he'd placed in his boot at the last minute was a comforting weight against his leg.

"It feels wonderful to be out riding," Lara said as Julian rode up beside her. "My loss of freedom in London makes me long for the country. I rode every day at our country estate in Kent. And my life is simple when I'm with Ramona and Pietro."

"London has its charm, but one must be on guard when out and about. That's why I'm so strict with Emma. I know the dangers that exist for unsuspecting innocents."

The bridle path made a jog through a wooded area. Traffic had thinned out to an occasional rider or two and Julian grew tense, watchful.

"I'll race you to the other side of the woods," Lara threw over her shoulder as she spurred her horse into a full gallop.

A relentless fear pierced him. "No! Stop!" An errant breeze could have picked up his words and flung them away for all Lara heeded them.

Lara raced away. Her hat flew off, hairpins scattered, loosing a silken curtain of curly black hair. Her laughter floated back to him as he touched his crop to his horse's flank and gave chase. Had Lara gone mad? Or had the wild Gypsy blood in her taken charge, obliterating any sign of Lady Lara?

He caught up to her on the other side of the woods. She had already dismounted and stood waiting for him.

He leaped to the ground and hauled her roughly against him. "Don't ever do that again. You were out of my sight far too long."

"You can't watch me twenty-four hours a day," Lara defied.

"Why do you think I want to marry you?"

"I was hoping for more," Lara said on a sigh.

Julian didn't catch what she'd said, but her lips looked so damn inviting he couldn't find the breath to ask her to repeat it. Resisting the lure of sweet, red lips was suddenly beyond his control as he lowered his mouth and tasted her. That one taste wasn't enough. He deepened the kiss, pulling her closer, his tongue delving deep to savor her sweet essence. His kiss grew frenzied; he guided his hands over her back, her hips, cupping her bottom and bringing her into the vee of his legs, making her aware of his almost painful erection.

Lara broke off the kiss and looked up at him, her eyes huge and luminous. "Julian . . . I . . ."

"No, don't say anything." He lowered her to the ground, his arms cushioning her descent.

Suddenly the world around them exploded. Something hot singed his ear. It took but a brief moment for Julian to realize they were being shot at, and instinctively he covered Lara's body with his own. Another bullet whizzed past his head. Grasping Lara firmly in his arms, he rolled with her behind a tree and lifted her to her feet, flattening her against the thick trunk.

"What is it? What happened?" Lara asked breathlessly. "Was that a shot?"

"Damn bloody right it was," Julian growled. "Now do you understand why I don't want you going out alone?"

"That bullet doubtlessly was meant for you," Lara ventured.

"Maybe," Julian allowed. "And maybe not. Needless to say, London is becoming too dangerous."

Lara shuddered. Since meeting Julian, her life had become remarkably complicated. Ramona had predicted danger, but Lara never imagined she'd become a target. Julian led a secretive life, and because of him, danger stalked her.

The shots had stopped. She glanced at Julian to ask him if he thought the shooter had departed and was stunned to see blood streaming down the side of his neck.

"Julian, you're hurt!"

"A bullet nicked my ear. The bleeding has already stopped. Don't fuss, Lara, 'tis nothing."

Lara peered over his shoulder, toward the open space where they had been kissing a few moments ago. "Do you think the shooter is gone?"

"Stay here, I intend to find out." He pulled his pistol from his belt and stepped out from behind the tree.

"Julian, no! Don't expose yourself."

Lara's admonition was ignored as Julian stepped out into the open.

"Be careful!" Lara hissed.

Nothing stirred in the ominous silence.

"It's all right," Julian called back as he returned his pistol to his belt. "He's gone. You can come out now." After a tentative look around, Lara joined him.

"Let's get out of here," Julian said. "Our horses bolted at the first shot but I doubt they went far."

Julian whistled and his horse obediently trotted out from the woods. Lara's mount followed close behind. Julian helped her to mount and swung himself into his saddle.

"I'll lead the way back through the woods," Julian said. "Stay close. The shots came from the woods, so whoever was shooting at us is likely to be ahead of us."

"We'll ride side by side," Lara argued.

Julian's face hardened. "Do as I say, Lara."

Lara sighed and did as she was bidden, though she spent more time looking over her shoulder than watching where she was going. The thought that someone wanted Julian dead made her physically ill. They retraced their route along the bridle path. More people were about now and Lara allowed herself to breathe easier. Numbers meant safely. They left the park and retraced their route back to the Stanhope mansion.

A groom ran up to help Lara dismount and to take charge of the horses. "Leave my horse," Julian ordered as he grasped Lara's arm and ushered her up the stairs. "I'm leaving immediately."

"Julian," Lara protested. "We're safe now. There's no reason to rush away."

"I don't trust anyone," Julian bit out. "It's no longer safe for you in London."

Lara stared at him. "You're exaggerating. I'm perfectly safe here with Papa."

"Not any longer. I'm taking you where I'm sure you'll be safe."

"Where is that?" Lara challenged.

"Pack your belongings for an indefinite stay. I'm going home to pack and have my coach readied."

The door opened and Julian swept Lara past the butler.

"That will be all, Jeevers," Lara said as she pulled off her gloves. She rounded on Julian the moment the butler disappeared. "Come into the kitchen. Your ear needs tending."

"I'm fine, Lara," Julian said dismissively. "We're leaving London within the hour."

Lara assumed a belligerent stance. "I'm not going anywhere with you, my lord."

Julian's jaw firmed. "I beg to differ with you, my lady."

"What will I tell Papa?"

"Leave a note. Tell him you're going away with me. Don't tell him where to find us."

"How can I? I don't know where you're taking me. What will Papa think? I can't just disappear without an explanation."

"I don't care what he thinks. We'll explain everything when we return."

Never had Lara seen Julian so serious, so adamant. "Do you really think I'm in danger?"

"Don't argue, Lara. Go upstairs and pack. If you're not ready in an hour, I'll carry you away with or without your belongings."

He grasped her shoulders and gave her a hard kiss. Then he pushed her away. "Go."

Lara walked up the stairs, pausing once to peer over her shoulder at Julian. He was speaking earnestly to Jeevers, who had appeared as if on cue to open the door for Julian.

"I understand, my lord," Jeevers said with only a slight arching of one eyebrow. "I'm to admit no one into the house until you return. And I'm to tell Lord Stanhope that you and Lady Lara are leaving for an extended period of time."

"That's correct," Julian said.

"Anything else, my lord? May I give Lord Stanhope your direction?"

"No you may not, Jeevers. Just give Lord Stanhope my message. I believe Lady Lara is penning a note to her father."

Julian reached home without incident. Farthingale opened the door and Julian hurried inside. "Have Ames pack a bag, Farthingale," Julian said. "None of my fancy duds, just plain trousers and jackets. I want my coach and driver out front within the hour. And ask Mrs. Roark to prepare something substantial to take along with me. Enough for two."

"May I ask how long you'll be gone, my lord?"

"I have no idea, Farthingale. Is Lady Emma home?"

"No, my lord. But Lady Amanda is in the small parlor."

Julian frowned. What was Emma doing out alone? He found Amanda bent over an embroidery loom.

"Good afternoon, Aunt Amanda."

Amanda looked up and smiled. "Good afternoon, Julian. Lovely day, isn't it?"

"That depends on how you look at it. Where is Emma?"

"Riding in the park with that nice Viscount Blakely."

"Bloody hell! Does no one follow orders? I told her

to stay away from Blakely. I believe you are abetting the couple. I thought you would understand my objections to Blakely and direct Emma's attention away from him. Blakely isn't the man for Emma."

Amanda's hand fluttered to her chest. "My goodness, Julian, you know how determined Emma is."

"Hardheaded, you mean," Julian muttered. "I can't wait for her, Aunt Amanda. I'm leaving within the hour. I'm trusting you to—"

His words were interrupted by a commotion in the hallway. Julian walked to the door and peered down the long corridor. His heart jumped into his mouth when he saw a pale, disheveled Emma leaning heavily against Blakely.

Julian burst into the foyer, scowling fiercely at Blakely. "Bloody hell! What did you do to Emma?"

"Rudy didn't do a thing," Emma defended. "He saved my life."

Julian went still. "What do you mean?"

"Someone took a shot at Emma," Blakely explained. "I saw sunlight glitter on something shiny. I spotted a gun barrel poking out from behind a tree and pushed Emma from her horse. The bullet missed her by scant inches. What in the hell is going on, Mansfield? I have a sneaking suspicion that this senseless attack has something to do with you."

Julian looked stunned. Had his whole family become targets for a madman? He couldn't let this go on. Something had to be done immediately.

"Are you all right, Emma dear?" This from Amanda, who had followed Julian into the hallway.

"I'm fine, Aunt," Emma said shakily. "A trifle bruised, maybe, but otherwise unhurt." She looked adoringly up at Blakely. "Thanks to Rudy."

"Go up to your room and have your maid pack a bag for you. And one for herself. You're leaving for Scotland immediately. Will you accompany her, Aunt Amanda?"

"Oh, dear me, no," Amanda said, appalled. "I couldn't possibly embark on so long a journey at my age." She shuddered. "The Highlands are not to my liking. Too wild for my tastes, and those savage Scotsmen frighten me. I don't know how Sinjun endures."

Julian nodded briskly. "Very well. Emma's maid will have to serve as chaperone."

"I'm not going anywhere, Julian," Emma protested. "What is this all about? Why is someone trying to harm me?"

"Aye, Mansfield," Blakely said. "I think you owe Emma an explanation."

Julian saw no help for it. He'd kept his identity as a government agent concealed from his family, but now that the Jackal had identified him, it was imperative that his loved ones be made aware of the danger that existed for them. And he supposed it wouldn't hurt to inform Blakely since he had saved Emma's life.

"Emma, your life is in danger because someone wants to hurt me," Julian confided. "You see, someone tried to kill me and Lady Lara today."

"Lady Lara!" Emma said, aghast. "Why Lady Lara?"

"Because I plan to marry Lara within the month. Our engagement should have appeared in the morning paper."

"I didn't read the paper today," Emma said. "Why was I not informed of your plans? Why am I the last to know?"

"You're right, of course," Julian conceded. "I was

going to discuss it with you at dinner this evening, but plans have changed. I'm taking Lara away and you're going to Scotland. Tell Sinjun I'll contact him if I need him."

"Am I finally to know what you're involved in, Julian?"

"I'm a government agent, Emma. My current assignment is to unmask the man behind a band of a smugglers. I believe he is the same man who killed Diana."

Aunt Amanda plopped down on a bench and reached for her smelling salts. "Oh, my."

Emma turned pale. "Julian! I thought Diana died in a carriage accident."

"It was no accident, Emma dear. I was supposed to be inside the carriage that day, not Diana. Diana died in my stead." He didn't mention the child. That was too personal.

"Oh, Julian, how dreadful," Emma commiserated. "But why would anyone want to hurt me?"

"To force me to drop my investigation," Julian revealed. "I received a threat, warning me that my loved ones would be hurt if I continued my investigation. London is no longer safe for you and Lara. Don't argue, Emma, you're going to Glenmoor and that's final."

"I'd be happy to escort Lady Emma to Glenmoor," Blakely offered. " 'Tis past time I paid Sinjun a visit."

"I'm perfectly capable of providing an escort for my sister," Julian argued.

"But no one will be as careful of her safety as I," Blakely persisted. "Think about it, Mansfield. I will protect Emma with my life."

Julian was torn. He knew of Blakely's reputation

with women, but the rogue *did* seem inordinately fond of Emma, and he'd heard no gossip about Blakely since his return to London. He had to get Lara out of town, and he couldn't be in two places at once.

"Come on, Mansfield, you know I'm your best choice. I'll see that Emma gets to Glenmoor safely."

"Aye, Julian, listen to Rudy. If I must leave, let him accompany me if you cannot."

"Very well, but I want you both gone within the hour. I'll arrange for a coach and six outriders. I'm trusting you with my sister, Blakely. If I learn there is anything . . . untoward going on, I swear you'll feel the fine edge of my steel."

"You won't be sorry, my lord," Blakely swore. He took Emma's hands. "I'll pack a bag and return within the hour." Then he was gone.

"Thank you, Julian," Emma said. "I'll feel safe with Rudy."

"I hope I'm not making a mistake," Julian muttered.

Emma started up the stairs, then paused. "Julian, do you love Lady Lara? Is that why you're marrying her?"

Julian frowned. Love? He cared for Lara. He wanted her with a desperation that stunned him. He couldn't keep his hands off her. She kissed like an angel, and her passion . . .

"Julian, answer me. Do you love Lara?"

"What nonsense, Emma. A man doesn't have to love a woman to want to protect her. I cared deeply for Diana. I don't think I'm capable of caring like that again."

Emma sent Julian a knowing smile. "Methinks you protest too much, brother dear." Then she proceeded up the stairs, leaving Julian with a stunned look on his face.

Amanda rose somewhat unsteadily from the bench. "You will be careful, won't you, Julian? I do so worry about you." She gave a delicate shudder. "To think you've been pursuing danger all these years."

"Don't worry, Aunt," Julian said. "Perhaps it would be best if you visited Thornton Hall while we're gone. I'd be devastated should anything happen to you."

"If you say so," Amanda said. "I'll make arrangements immediately."

The townhouse bustled with activity as preparations for their various departures got underway. By the time Blakely returned, packed and dressed for travel, Emma was ready to leave. Julian had arranged for six burly footmen to serve as escorts and saw her off with a final admonition to Blakely.

Aunt Amanda left in the carriage shortly afterward with her maid and suitable escort for the short journey. Julian was last to leave. Before he left the house, he dashed off a brief note of explanation to Lord Randall that Farthingale was to deliver after he left.

The moment Julian left her, Lara dashed off a note to her father, asking him to return home immediately. When a footman arrived at Parliament, he was denied access to Lord Stanhope until Parliament adjourned for the day. While Lara packed, the footman cooled his heels in an anteroom. Julian arrived long before Lord Stanhope, and with a regretful sigh, Lara climbed into the coach without her father knowing what had happened or where to find her.

Chapter 11

The coach clattered over the bridge, leaving London far behind. Lara shrank back against the squabs, looking anywhere but at the determined man sitting beside her. It wasn't until the stench of the Thames could no longer be detected that she finally deigned to speak to him.

"Where are you taking me?"

"Ah, so you do have a tongue," Julian teased.

"I've a notion to give you the sharp edge of it if you don't answer my question," she returned tartly. "Really, Julian, do you think this reckless flight out of town is necessary? I'm worried about Papa."

"You left him a note, didn't you?"

"Aye, but it won't satisfy him. I hope you know what you're doing."

"London is not a healthy place for us at the moment. I'm taking you where you'll be safe."

"Where exactly is that?"

"We'll leave the coach at the next coaching inn and send it and the driver back to London," he continued. "A plain carriage will carry us to our destination."

"You're being very mysterious."

"Do you know where to find Ramona and Pietro?"

She gave him a startled look. "Of course. They are always at the same place this time of year. Somewhere on Papa's property in Kent. They have a standing invitation to camp there during the winter months. Papa makes sure they have enough food and warm clothing to see them through the cold season." She gave him a speculative look. "Why?"

"I figure you'll be safe with Ramona and Pietro. My enemies won't think to look for you there."

"What about you? Where will you be safe?"

"I'll be there too . . . for a while. I want the Jackal to assume I've given up my investigation now that they are aware of my identity."

"Have you really given up?" Lara asked, stunned by Julian's disclosure. He didn't seem the type to give up on anything, much less let the man who killed the woman he loved go unpunished.

Julian's expression hardened. "Not while there's a breath left in my body. The man responsible for Diana's death will hang for his crime."

Lara's heart sank. The proof that Julian could never love her as he had Diana was in his fierce expression, his heated words. She remained silent. What could she say in response to Julian's staunch devotion to his dead fiancée?

The coach rattled to a stop. Julian pulled back the curtain and peered out the window. "We've arrived."

He opened the door. The coachman pulled down the steps. Julian climbed out first and handed Lara down. Lara waited while Julian retrieved their bags and spoke briefly to the coachman. He returned shortly and ushered her inside the inn.

"Wait here while I find out if the carriage I ordered is available," Julian said.

"You really are worried, aren't you?"

"I know the Jackal, Lara, and what he is capable of. I've been on his trail for over two years. I *will* catch him," Julian vowed. "I won't let him harm another innocent victim."

Lara warmed herself beside the hearth while Julian spoke to the innkeeper. Money changed hands.

"Everything's in order," he said when he returned for her. "The carriage is being brought around as we speak. We should reach the Three Feathers Inn by nightfall."

Julian ushered her through the door, helped her into the waiting carriage, and climbed into the driver's seat. A flick of the reins sent the horses stepping out smartly.

A damp fog arrived with the darkness, making Lara long for a cozy room with a fire. Then she saw the lights from the Three Feathers Inn twinkling in the distance and her spirits lifted. She supposed Julian was armed, but fear of being stopped by highwaymen terrified her. Country roads weren't safe at night.

"You'll be in a warm room soon," Julian promised. "I've always found food at the Three Feathers to be good." He searched her face when she remained uncommunicative. "Are you all right? You haven't said much since we left the coaching inn."

"I'm still trying to come to grips with the fact that someone wants to hurt me. I don't like the idea of fleeing London like thieves in the night."

"I know what I'm doing, Lara."

"I suppose," she said doubtfully. "It's just that my life was so simple before . . ."

"Before I entered it?" he asked grimly.

"I suppose."

Julian guided the horses into the yard and reined in. A stableman hurried over to take charge. Julian climbed down and removed their bags from the boot. Then he dug in his pocket for a coin.

"Rub the horses down and give them a measure of oats with their feed," Julian instructed, tossing the man the coin. "Have them harnessed and waiting out front by seven tomorrow morning."

"Aye, my lord," the man replied.

A lad burst from the door and fetched their bags as Julian ushered Lara inside. The common room was noisy and filled to capacity with travelers and locals, enjoying the food and drink. Lara pulled the hood of her cloak up but soon learned it wasn't necessary, for no one paid more than token attention to the new-comers. She stood aside while Julian arranged for their rooms, baths, and a meal.

They climbed the stairs together, followed by the lad with their bags.

Julian stopped before the door to their room and fit the key in the lock. He opened the door and ushered Lara inside. The lad placed their bags inside the room and held out his hand. Julian found another coin, and the lad departed with a smile on his face.

"Is this your room or mine?" Lara asked.

" 'Tis *our* room," Julian answered. "You saw how full the inn was. 'Tis the last and only room available."

Lara went still. She didn't dare share a room with Julian. 'Twas asking too much of her. She would never stop thinking of him as her husband, or stop remembering how his loving made her blood sing through her veins and her body soar.

Her voice was quiet but emphatic. "No. You'll have to sleep elsewhere."

An amused smile kicked up the corner of his mouth. "We're betrothed, Lara. As good as married."

"Are we?" Lara challenged.

"I'm not leaving, sweeting," Julian vowed.

Lara opened her mouth to protest but a knock on the door forestalled her. Julian opened the door, admitting two strapping lads wielding a large wooden tub. The lads set the tub down before the hearth and built up the fire. Moments later a procession of chambermaids carrying buckets of hot and cold water marched through the door.

"Wait two hours before serving our meal," Julian instructed the last maid as she was about to leave.

"Aye, my lord," the perky gal said, casting a flirtatious glance at Julian over her shoulder as she closed the door behind her.

"You first," Julian said, indicating the steaming tub.

Lara turned her back on him. "I think I'll forgo a bath until we reach our destination."

"What are you afraid of, Lara?"

Lara bristled. "Certainly not you."

Julian grinned and started to undress. "I don't know about you, but that water looks too inviting to waste. Are you certain you don't want to go first?"

Lara eyed the steaming tub with longing. After the damp fog she'd had to endure, a bath would be heavenly.

"I . . . oh, all right, but I want you to leave the room while I bathe."

"Not bloody likely," Julian muttered. "Shall I help you undress?"

He stepped behind her and removed her cloak. She felt the heat of his hands linger on her back and her protest died in her throat. His touch sent a frisson of excitement down her spine. Her cheeks flushed and her skin suddenly felt too tight for her body. She started to step away from him before she was drawn into his web of seduction, but abruptly he turned her around and drew her into his arms.

"I've missed you," he said in a voice husky with wanting.

Lara flattened her hands against his chest, holding him at bay. "I'm just a substitute for Diana, Julian. Nothing more than a warm body. I won't let you do this to me."

He pressed her struggling body closer. The entire length of him felt hard and hot; his manhood stirred against her loins.

"Don't bring her into this."

"Why not? She's very much alive in your heart. So much so that you'd risk your life to avenge her death. I don't want to be a substitute for another woman. Did you pretend I was Diana when we made love? Was I ever anything more to you than a Gypsy lover unworthy of your name?"

Lara's words gave Julian pause for thought. Lara *did* mean something to him. He just couldn't figure out what. If he'd known who she was from the beginning, perhaps he would have . . . What? Would he have done anything differently? He'd wanted Lara from the first moment he'd become aware of her.

"You should have told me you were Lord Stanhope's daughter," he said resentfully. "I believed you were a Gypsy wench who had saved my life by claiming me as her husband. I'm willing to marry you, Lara, does that count for nothing?"

" 'Tis your honor speaking. Honor is good and well, but I need more from a husband."

"What about this?" Julian asked as he tunneled his fingers through her hair and tilted her head up. "What about passion? That's something we have in abundance."

He kissed her, breathing in her sweet essence, exulting in the satiny feel of her lush lips, the softness of her curvaceous body pressed intimately against his. He deepened the kiss. Too damn many clothes between them, he decided as he frantically worked the buttons free at the back of her bodice. His hand slid over smooth, bare flesh, but it still wasn't enough.

"Let's get you out of these clothes," he whispered against her lips.

"No! Stop! Passion isn't enough."

"You want me, Lara. You can't deny what I know to be the truth."

His mouth clamped down on hers. He swallowed her protest as his hand moved unerringly to the swollen crests of her breasts. He felt them hardened against his palm and groaned. He thrust his tongue into her mouth as he pressed his hips into the vee between her legs. When he finally freed her mouth, she stepped back and glared at him. Sparks of anger glittered in her dark eyes, but it did not make him want her any less. If anything, her anger fueled his passion.

Lara curled her hand into a fist and aimed for the crest of his cheek. He blocked the blow easily and yanked her hand behind her back. Then he kissed her again, tasting her anger, and something else, something profoundly arousing.

Lara whimpered. His lips were hard and bruising, his tongue thrusting with a determination that robbed her of the will to resist. Then suddenly his mouth softened, the pressure eased. Perhaps it was her whimper, or it could have been the result of her body pushed fiercely against his, but whatever the cause, her passion suddenly kindled and caught fire. When his mouth settled more firmly over hers, she sucked his tongue into her mouth and held it hostage. Abruptly he released her wrist, using both his hands to free her breasts from her bodice and chemise. She wore no corset. She couldn't bring herself to wear one after enjoying the freedom of Gypsy clothing.

He held her against him, cradling her head and turning it so he could reach every part of her mouth. His hands molded around her breasts and rode the curve of her hips. When she was too weak with longing to resist, he rid her of her skirts. Her chemise followed, leaving her naked but for her shoes and silken stockings tied with dainty ribbons around her thighs.

Lara clutched his arms. A desperate need compelled her to reach up and claw her hands into his hair, to hold him fast against her. Hunger for this exasperating man fueled her passion. Lara savored it, responding to it with a need that was as raw and ungovernable as his. Then his hands delved between them and she felt him fumbling with the buttons on his breeches. She sucked in a shuddering breath when he lifted her against him and slid his hand between her thighs.

His hand came back glistening with moisture.

"You're ready for me, sweeting," he moaned softly. Then his engorged sex replaced his hand, gliding along her wet, silky cleft. One upward thrust sheathed him snugly within her heat. She inhaled sharply and sucked him inside her. She took him deep, deeper, willingly obeying his terse command to wrap her legs around his waist and ride his powerful strokes.

His thrusts became urgent, almost violent as he drove into her with increasing vigor. His legs, his arms, his entire body shook with the force of his need.

"The bed," he gasped, staggering forward.

Lara glanced over her shoulder, saw that they had reached the bed, and felt herself being tumbled backward. Julian followed, the downward plunge causing him to surge into her with a ferocity that made them both gasp and cry out. His breath rasped harshly in her ear as his strokes became harder, stronger, faster. Lara thought she'd already experienced the ultimate in pleasure the last time Julian had made love to her, but her memory of it paled compared with the incredible, shimmering orgasms ripping through her now, shattering her body into a million white-hot fragments, each one brighter than the one before.

Dimly she felt him grasp her hips, lifting her into his driving thrusts. Felt his mouth pull on her nipple, suckling her forcefully. Then she heard the roar of his voice in her ear and felt a surge of incredible heat splashing against her womb. When he slumped against her, she accepted the weight of his body and held him close.

Lara regained her wits slowly. She opened her eyes

and found Julian gazing down at her. His eyes were darkly probing, uncomfortably intense. As if he were trying to make sense out of what had just happened between them. Her own thoughts were perfectly clear. It was appalling to feel this powerful need for a man who would never love her.

"Forgive me for losing control," Julian said, lifting himself off her. "I meant to do this slowly, savoring you as I would a fine wine. Just let me catch my breath and we'll do it right this time."

Lara watched him through slumberous eyes as he shed his coat and vest and unbuttoned his shirt. She seriously doubted she could survive another of his passionate assaults.

"The tub will grow cold," she protested weakly.

"Let it."

He tossed his shirt aside and slid his breeches down his legs. She stared at him, astounded that his sleek body could harbor so many muscles. Not an ounce of spare flesh resided anywhere on his body. His shoulders were broad, his chest a mass of rippling tendons, and his entire frame, clear down to his elegant feet, bespoke his noble birth.

His boots hit the floor, one by one. He stepped out of his breeches, rolling his stockings down with them. The sight of him standing over her was so daunting she couldn't look away. She loved this man, she realized with a start. Loved him too much to marry him. Loving Julian with little hope of being loved in return would utterly destroy her.

Julian moved to the tub, wet a cloth, and returned to the bed. She offered a tepid protest when he spread her legs and washed away the remnants of his seed. Then he cleansed himself and sank down on the bed, his hot gaze flowing over her body like warm honey.

He touched her breasts, then lowered his head to suckle her. A groan formed in her throat and left her mouth in a whoosh of air when his lips traveled downward, over her belly, to the tops of her stockings. He released one ribbon with his mouth and kissed a path down her leg, slowly rolling the stocking down and away. He repeated the movement on the other leg. Her body caught fire. She arched against him as his mouth climbed upward, to the triangle of curls nestled between her legs.

"Julian . . ."

"Aye, sweeting."

"We shouldn't . . . you don't . . ."

He buried his face between her legs and touched her with his tongue. She grasped a handful of bedclothes and arched against him.

He raised his head and favored her with a devastating grin. "What shouldn't we do, sweeting?"

His mouth returned to the tender flesh between her legs. Lara's mind drew a blank. She could think of nothing save for Julian's hungry mouth on her. His tongue grew bold, slipping into the moist sheath of her womanhood in a long, thrilling slide, and her wits flew out the window.

"What was your question? I can't think with you . . . you . . . oh, God, you're killing me."

"Don't think. I want to feel you shudder beneath my mouth, I want to taste your passion."

His erotic words spurred her ardor as she writhed beneath the punishing ecstasy of his mouth and tongue. Her breath rasped loudly in the waiting silence as he drove her higher and higher, her body tense, swollen, moving closer, ever closer to the release he demanded of her. Then she was there, screaming his name, clutching his hair in her fists, fearing he'd stop, loving everything he did to her.

She was still shuddering in the aftermath of her climax when Julian raised up and buried himself deep inside her throbbing sheath. He held himself still for a breathless moment, establishing control, but the need to drive himself to completion overpowered him. He groaned and thrust forcefully. It didn't take long. Within minutes he was lost in the throes of a violent climax. His seed spewed forth and he shouted her name.

Julian regained his wits first. Lara was lying beside him, her body limp, a sweet smile on her face.

"How about that bath now?"

"Not now," she murmured sleepily.

"Now," Julian insisted.

He scooped her up and carried her to the tub. Lara squealed a protest as he lowered her into the water. "It's cold."

"Move over," Julian said, stepping over the rim of the tub.

"There isn't room."

"We'll make room."

She scooted forward; he sat down behind her. It was a tight fit but Julian didn't complain. He picked up the washcloth, lathered it with soap, and ran it over her back in a long, sensual slide. By the time they had washed each other in the cramped space, more water resided on the floor than in the tub. A knock on the door announcing the arrival of their food sent them scrambling from the tub and into enough clothing to satisfy the chambermaid's sensibilities.

They ate in silence. Julian was starved, and from the way Lara was devouring her dinner, he knew she was as hungry as he. After their meal, Julian sat back in his chair and stared at her.

"How long do you think it will take to find the Romany camp?"

"Papa's estate is vast, but there are several sites Pietro prefers above others. We'll look at those first. How long will we remain with the Rom? Not that I'm complaining, mind you. The best times of my life are those I've spent with Ramona and Pietro."

"I don't know," Julian mused. "In a few weeks I'll return to London and speak with my superior. I narrowed the suspects to a few men with high connections. He's someone with access to secret information.

"You have someone in mind, don't you?" Lara questioned.

"Aye."

"Tell me."

"No. Knowledge is dangerous. I'm close, I know I am. The Jackal is showing signs of fear. He's striking back at me by threatening you and my family."

"I don't like this, Julian."

"I'm sorry you became involved. I'll explain everything to your father once I'm certain he's not involved."

Lara leaped to her feet. "You believe that Papa is dealing with smugglers? Are you mad?"

Julian knew he'd made a mistake. He shouldn't

have named Lord Stanhope as a suspect. There wasn't enough proof to prove or disprove his suspicion.

"I am suspicious of anyone who has contact with the man who might be the Jackal."

"You wanted to get me away from Papa, that's why you all but abducted me," Lara charged.

"Partly," Julian admitted. "Those attacks on you are what really convinced me to take you away."

"Papa would never hurt me."

"I hope not," Julian said uncertainly.

"You're the most exasperating man!" Lara contended. "I insist that you take me home. Papa wouldn't lie to me. I'll ask him outright if he's involved in smuggling."

"That's out of the question," Julian argued. "Whether or not Lord Stanhope is involved is irrelevant. There are unscrupulous men on the loose in London. Until I learn the truth, you'll remain with your grandparents."

"I'm going to bed," Lara huffed.

"You're angry at me."

She rounded on him. "Of course I am! What did you expect? First you try to force a marriage you're really not keen about, then you spirit me out of London and accuse my father of conspiracy."

"Make no mistake, Lara, we *are* going to marry."

"No. You are mistaken, my lord. I'm still a Gypsy, or have you forgotten?"

"Half Gypsy," Julian corrected. "And an earl's daughter. What if you're carrying my child?"

" 'Tis no sin among my people to bear a child within a marriage."

"If you're referring to our Gypsy marriage, rest assured society will not accept it. 'Tis my understanding that this was to be your last summer with Ramona and Pietro, that your father wished you to find a husband of equal rank or higher. Your father could never hold his head up in public again were you to bear a bastard. English laws must prevail over heathenish rituals."

Lara's bristled indignantly. "Are you calling me a heathen?"

Julian heaved an exasperated sigh. "I don't wish to argue with you, sweeting. Let's go to bed. I want to get an early start tomorrow."

"Find your own bed, my lord. I do not wish to share mine with a man who considers me a heathen."

Julian watched in amusement as Lara found her nightgown in her bag, donned it over her clothing, and undressed beneath it. Then she crawled into bed, pulled the blanket up to her neck, and turned away from him.

"Sorry, sweeting, this is the only bed available and I have every intention of sharing it with you."

He undressed quickly and climbed in beside her. When he tried to take her into his arms, she stiffened and moved to the edge of the bed.

"Very well, Lara, have it your way. I only wanted to hold you."

Lara didn't want Julian to hold her. She was too vulnerable to his loving, too raw inside. How could Julian suspect her father of being involved with smugglers? Her father was an honorable man. She was living proof of his loving spirit and generosity. He didn't have to take her in when she showed up at his door thirteen years after his brief encounter with her mother, but he did.

Lord Stanhope could have denied ever knowing her mother and no one would have faulted him. But he had accepted her without question, and loved her without reservation. Somehow she would prove that her father was innocent, that Julian's suspicions were unfounded.

Sleep finally claimed her, but when she awoke in the morning she found herself nestled in Julian's arms, legs entwined, her body pressed snugly against his. Her gaze flew to his face. His eyes were open and he was grinning at her. If he said one word about their closeness in bed she'd smash the smug smile off his face with her fist.

"You're awake," Julian drawled lazily. "It's time to get up. I'll perform my ablutions first. While you're at your toilette, I'll order breakfast and make sure our carriage will be ready when we need it."

Lara nodded and carefully removed herself from his arms. Then she turned her back and stared at the wall while Julian washed, shaved, and dressed. Not until Julian left did she rise to perform her own toilette. Julian was seated at a table in the common room when she arrived downstairs.

"I ordered a substantial breakfast," Julian said.

Lara nodded, still too angry to engage in conversation with Julian.

Lara ate her breakfast in silence, her anger building with each morsel of food she consumed. How could Julian be so complacent when she was seething inside? She couldn't wait to join Ramona and Pietro. Her grandparents always seemed to know what was best for her. Perhaps they could help solve her dilemma where Julian was concerned. The way she saw it, Julian would never love her, so why should she marry him in a *gadjo* ceremony?

It bothered her that Julian believed her father capable of harming her. That hurt almost as much as the knowledge that Julian didn't love her. Lara's mental musings ceased when Julian finished his meal and ushered her out the door. He handed her into their waiting carriage and vaulted up beside her. They started forward in a clatter of wheels and jangling harnesses.

The sun had reached its highest point when Stanhope Manor came into view. "We're on Papa's land," Lara pointed out.

"I'm going to bypass the house," Julian said. "Being seen by servants would defeat our purpose in coming here. No one is to know where you are."

"Turn off the main road," Lara advised. "Head for the trees to the right. You'll find a narrow wagon path that should lead us to one of Pietro's favorite camping sites."

Julian followed Lara's directions and soon arrived at a clearing beside a bubbling brook.

Disappointment colored her words. "They're not here. Follow the brook downstream. There's another camping site not far from here."

The carriage rolled along a grassy delta. Lara began to fear her grandparents had decided to winter elsewhere. Then she heard voices in the distance.

"It's them!" she cried, clapping her hands excitedly. "They're up ahead."

A dozen or more colorful Gypsy wagons soon came into view. They were scattered about a sun-dappled clearing beside the meandering brook. A

Rom child saw them and alerted the others. Since this was Stanhope land, they knew they had nothing to fear from the visitors, for few dared to trespass upon another's holdings unless invited.

Lara recognized Pietro immediately and waved. She smiled as Pietro's face lit with pleasure. He waved back and started forward to greet them. Ramona was close on his heels. Julian drew in the reins and leaped to the ground to hand Lara down. But Pietro was there before him, swinging Lara down from the carriage and into his brawny arms. He gave her a bear hug before handing her over to Ramona.

Ramona gave Lara a swift hug, then held her at arm's length, her knowing gaze moving over her. Then her dark face split into a huge grin.

"Did I not predict that you and Drago would find one another in London?" Suddenly her grin faded and her expression turned grim. "Danger. You are both in grave danger, that is why you are here."

Chapter 12

Julian had suspected that Ramona possessed amazing powers, but her quick understanding of the situation stunned him.

"I will explain later," Julian said tersely when he realized that he and Lara had become the center of attention. He had every intention of telling Lara's family the truth about himself, but this wasn't the time.

Watching through shuttered eyes as Rondo swaggered forward, Julian scowled at the way the handsome Rom's gaze devoured Lara. Jealousy was a new emotion for Julian, and he found it difficult to swallow.

"Welcome back, Lara," Rondo said, purposely ignoring Julian. "Did your father learn of your unfortunate marriage and send you away?"

Julian stepped forward, his face carefully composed. He wanted to do nothing to rile the people who had saved his life, nor did he wish to tell them anything that could bring harm to Lara.

"I brought Lara back for a visit because she missed her grandparents," Julian explained. "If it is agreeable to Pietro, we'd like to stay awhile."

He felt Ramona's dark eyes upon him and boldly

returned her gaze. He knew she was weighing his lies and giving him the benefit of the doubt, even though she was ignorant of his true identity and the danger in which he had involved Lara.

" 'Tis always a pleasure to have our granddaughter with us," Pietro assured him. "You are Lara's husband and welcome, Drago. Is that not right, Ramona?"

After a long pause, Ramona said, "Aye." Julian could tell she was withholding judgment. Ramona turned and smiled warmly at Lara. "Old Gregor drove your wagon here, little one. It is ready for you and Drago. I've been expecting you."

"You knew I was coming?" Lara asked with surprise.

"I know many things," Ramona confided. "Come to my wagon, where we can speak freely."

People began drifting back to what had occupied them before Julian and Lara arrived, but Rondo hung back.

"Why are you and Drago together, Lara? He abandoned you," he asked snidely. "What manner of man is he? I would not be so heartless were you my mate."

Lara was rendered speechless by Rondo's words. Julian leaped to Lara's defense. "We need not explain ourselves to you. But if you must know, circumstances beyond my control made leaving Lara necessary."

Rondo's eyes narrowed. "There is more to your appearance here than you have told us. I can smell your lies. Lara's father must have been enraged to learn she had married a man with little to commend him, a man with dangerous enemies."

"Pah, Rondo! You smell your own jealousy," Ramona charged. "You fool no one. You've always wanted Lara, but her father had plans for her future that didn't include a Gypsy husband. Cast your eyes elsewhere; Lara was never meant for the likes of you."

Rondo's eyes darkened with malice. "Nay, you cannot believe that Drago, a man with a mysterious past, is better than I. The *gadjo* left Lara behind. I would not."

His gaze settled disconcertingly on Lara. " 'Tis easy enough to divorce the *gadjo*. You know our customs. I'm surprised you did not see to it immediately, before you returned to your father."

Julian looked askance at Lara. Rondo's words gave him pause for thought. Why hadn't Lara divorced him if Gypsy customs made it easy to do? Lara's answer left him more confused than ever.

"I did not wish to divorce Drago, Rondo. Why I did not do so is none of your concern."

"Come with me," Ramona said. "You must be tired. As for you, Rondo, heed my granddaughter's words. None of this concerns you."

Properly rebuked, Rondo strode away, but not before slanting Julian a menacing look. Intuitively Julian knew that the jealous young man would bear watching.

Ramona prepared tea for them inside her wagon on a small brazier. She poured each of them a cup of the strong brew. After a bracing sip, Ramona's penetrating gaze settled on Julian.

"Tell me about the trouble you have visited upon my granddaughter."

" 'Tis a long story," Julian ventured.

"We have time," Pietro encouraged.

"Very well," Julian said, dragging in a sustaining breath. "First, my name is Julian Thornton, Earl of

Mansfield. But I prefer to be called Drago while I am here. Revealing my identity to others could prove dangerous to your people."

Pietro tensed. "Danger from whom?"

"My enemies. What I tell you now must be held in the strictest confidence. And if you wish me to leave after you've heard me out, I will do so at once."

"We will not judge until we've heard your explanation," Ramona assured him.

"I am a government agent," Julian began in a hushed voice. "My current assignment involves smugglers. I was very close to discovering the name of their leader when something went awry. A man, quite possibly the leader, is privy to government secrets. He learned the identity of the agent known as Scorpion."

Lara's eyes widened as comprehension dawned. "You're Scorpion!"

"Aye. Things took a deadly turn when the smuggler, a man called the Jackal, tried to end my life. I was supposed to be inside the carriage that carried my betrothed. She died in my place. I vowed on her casket that her death would be avenged."

"How did you end up floating in the sea, shot full of holes?" Pietro asked.

"The Jackal got wind of the trap that been set for the smugglers. I had joined a group of peasants who were loading contraband into a jolly boat. The contraband was to be rowed out to a ship anchored off the French coast. I was there to keep an eye on the operation, but the Jackal must have known about me for I was singled out and marked for death. I was shot trying to escape. I woke up aboard the smugglers' ship and was wounded a second time when I jumped overboard in another bid to escape. I have no idea how I ended up on the beach where you were camped." He glanced at Lara and smiled. "Divine intervention, perhaps?"

"The men who came looking for you wanted you dead," Ramona mused thoughtfully.

"Aye, Lara saved my life when she claimed me as her husband."

"Why did you not take Lara with you to London?" Pietro demanded.

"I can answer that, Grandfather," Lara cut in. "Julian is an earl. He didn't wish to damage his high standing in society by claiming a Gypsy wife. He maintains that a heathen marriage such as ours is illegal and will not hold up in English courts."

Julian bit back a groan. The way Lara explained it made him out to be a hard-hearted bastard. The look in Pietro's dark eyes did not bode well for him.

"I'm more than willing to marry Lara again in a ceremony recognized by English law," he offered.

Lara sent him a dismissive look. "Julian and I met at a ball Father gave in my honor. Needless to say, we were stunned to see one another in such a setting. Once Julian learned Papa was an earl, he decided to do the honorable thing and offer for me. A Gypsy wench was good enough to bed, but not to wed. My being an earl's daughter made all the difference in the world to Julian."

"Is that true, my lord?" Ramona asked.

Julian could not lie. He owed these people too much. "More or less, but in my own defense I might add that my leaving had more to do with removing danger from your ranks than abandoning Lara. Unfortunately my enemies decided to act against Lara when they discovered my interest in her. Our engagement has already been announced in the papers."

"I have no intention of marrying Julian," Lara said defiantly.

"Pay Lara no heed. We *will* be married," Julian insisted.

"Tell me what your enemies did to harm Lara," Ramona said.

"Nothing, really," Lara said, forestalling Julian's reply. "Someone hit me on the head at a musicale and . . . and someone shot at me in the park the other day. But that could have been an accident. I still think the bullet was meant for Julian."

"It matters not," Julian said dismissively. "I refuse to play loose with Lara's life. She is safer here with you than in London with her father."

Lara made a sound of disgust deep in her throat. "Julian suspects Papa of being involved with smugglers. 'Tis ridiculous. Papa would never hurt me."

Pietro nodded solemnly. "I agree, little one. Your father is an honorable man. Your suspicions are unfounded, my lord."

"I agree with Pietro," Ramona concurred.

"Time will tell," Julian muttered, wishing he was as sure of Stanhope as Lara and her grandparents.

"You were wise to bring Lara to us, my lord," Pietro said.

"Drago. Call me Drago," Julian returned. "My only concern is for Lara's safety. 'Tis my fault she's in danger."

Ramona searched Lara's face, as if looking for something no one else could see. "I wish to speak alone with my granddaughter."

"I'll wait outside for your decision," Julian said, rising.

"I will leave, also," Pietro echoed. "Whatever Ramona decides is fine with me."

* * *

Lara lowered her gaze to her lap and waited for Ramona to speak. Her grandmother was wise beyond this world and Lara knew better than to try to fool her. All Ramona had to do was look into her eyes and her thoughts would be laid bare.

"I know why you did not divorce Drago after he left you, little one," Ramona began.

"How can you know that when I do not even know myself?"

"I looked into your heart. You returned to your father but you never intended to wed another, despite the fact that your Romany marriage would not be recognized by *gadje.*"

"Perhaps," Lara admitted.

"You loved Drago even then," Ramona continued. "Your heart told me what you refused to acknowledge. I read your palm and studied Drago's tea leaves. I knew fate would bring you and Drago together in London, and that danger would find you."

"You are wise, Grandmother."

"But not wise enough to know why you will not marry Drago in a *gadjo* ceremony when you love him."

Lara's head shot up. "Drago will never love me like I love him. He is grateful to me and cares what happens to me, but I want more from a husband. I cannot marry a man who will never return my love."

"How do you know this, little one?"

"Julian loved his betrothed dearly. She was killed by his enemies, though 'twas made to look like an accident. His heart resists another love. He remains faithful to a dead woman while I yearn for his love. How can I stay with Julian knowing I am not the one for whom he is pining?"

"Shall I send Drago away?" Ramona asked.

Lara's hand flew to her throat. "No! Do not send him away. It could mean his death, and I couldn't exist in a world without Julian."

"Do you intend to live as his mate during your visit?"

Lara averted her gaze. "I . . . don't know."

"What if Drago plants his child in you?"

A tiny smile curved her lips as she touched her stomach and pictured a miniature Julian growing there. "If God wills it," she whispered, "I will love it as much as I . . ." Her words fell away.

"As much as you love his father," Ramona said, nodding sagely.

"Oh, Ramona, what shall I do?" Lara wailed on a note of despair. "When Julian learned he had taken the virginity of an earl's daughter, his honor demanded that he marry me, but I cannot live without love."

"Give me your palm, little one," Ramona said, holding out her hand.

Trustingly Lara placed her small hand in Ramona's, then waited with bated breath while the old woman traced the lines with a gnarled finger. Ramona seemed to go into a trance. She closed her eyes. An eternity later she spoke.

"You will have love, little one," she said in a singsong voice. "The kind of love you desire."

"With Julian?" Lara asked hopefully.

"I know not, but I see happiness at the end of a long tunnel through which you will travel. You must beware, little one. Danger lurks in places least expected."

"What else can you tell me? What advice can you give me about Julian?"

Ramona's eyes jerked open as if awakening from a

dream. "You must follow your own heart. Do you still want Drago to stay with us? Before you answer, think carefully. Everyone here considers you and Drago husband and wife."

Lara searched her heart, seeking answers that could prove painful. In the end, her problem had but one solution. Julian needed a safe refuge, and a Romany camp perfectly suited his needs. She loved him too much to send him back to his enemies.

"Julian must stay," she whispered shakily. "Do not send him away, Grandmother."

Ramona touched Lara's cheek and smiled. "I knew your answer before you gave it, little one. Finish your tea. Then you can go and tell Drago that he may remain with us for as long as he desires."

Julian sat on the steps while Lara and Ramona were inside the wagon. If he was allowed to remain, it wouldn't be beyond a week or two. That should be long enough to make sure he and Lara hadn't been followed, and that the Jackal was no longer a threat to Lara.

Julian was so engrossed in his thoughts that he failed to notice Rondo heading his way. He was more than a little surprised to find the handsome young Gypsy standing beside him.

"Why have you come back?" Rondo asked curtly. "We do not need your kind here."

Julian slanted him a condescending smile. "What kind is that, Rondo?"

"You dishonored Lara. You never intended to honor your marriage to her."

"She should have told me she was the daughter of an earl."

"Do not lie to me. Admit that Lord Stanhope sent her away when he found out she was ruined, that no *gadjo* would have her now. That would not matter to me. I've always wanted Lara. But it was you, a man with a violent past, who stole her affections. Go away and leave Lara to me. She was never comfortable with *gadje*. You will only hurt her."

"I fear you have misjudged my commitment to Lara," Julian drawled. "I've asked her to marry me. We will wed in a ceremony sanctioned by English law."

The color drained from Rondo's face. "What can you give her besides danger and heartache?"

Julian had a good notion to tell Rondo that he was an earl and that Lara would be his countess, but wisely remained silent. He couldn't trust Rondo to keep the information private.

"Sheath your claws, Rondo, nothing will happen to Lara as long as she's under my protection."

"Can you guarantee that?" Rondo challenged.

Julian frowned. He'd like to guarantee Lara's safety, but the truth was, he wasn't sure. That's why he'd brought her here.

"Can you?" Julian shot back.

"I would if Lara were mine."

"Ah, but she isn't. That's the crux of the matter, isn't it?"

"Aye. I expected Lara to grow tired of London and return to us. Then I would press my suit. Lara is happiest here, with those who love her."

Julian's reply was forestalled when the door opened and Lara stepped out, followed by Ramona. He rose and waited for them to join him.

"Allowing Drago to remain here is a mistake," Rondo charged.

"Let me be the judge of that," Ramona said with asperity.

Without another word, Rondo whirled on his heel and stalked off.

"He's jealous," Julian said.

A stunned expression marched across Lara's face. "Jealous? Why is he jealous? We were never more than good friends. He always knew my father would choose a husband for me when the time came to marry."

"But you chose your own husband, did you not, little one?" Ramona said with a chuckle. "Take Drago to your wagon. Pietro will see to your carriage and horses."

"I'll get our bags," Julian said, striding away. He needed a moment alone to think. Rondo's animosity was not a good thing. He didn't want to cause strife for the people who had saved his life. 'Twas best that he limit his stay to a few days, just long enough to see Lara settled before returning to London to continue his investigation.

Julian helped Pietro unhitch the horses, then carried their bags to the wagon he was to share with Lara. Lara had arrived before him and had already changed into the comfortable clothing she preferred. He set the bags down and studied her profile as she loosed her hair from its prim bun and ran a brush through the curly raven tresses. Each downward stroke brought new life to those lustrous strands that refused to be tamed no matter how industrious her efforts to conform to society's dictates.

He stared with appreciation at an elegant bare shoulder exposed by the low neckline of the peasant blouse she had changed into, admiring the way her colorful skirts swung temptingly around her slim ankles. Julian felt a tightening in his groin and had to clench his fists to keep from tossing her on the bed, pushing her skirts up, and thrusting himself inside her. He looked away lest his expression give away his thoughts.

Lara hadn't felt so free since she'd left the Romany camp weeks ago. The restrictions society placed on her and all women was unbearable. She glanced at Julian, wondering if he'd ever felt like abandoning his title and duties and just enjoying his life. Somehow she doubted it.

Her gaze settled on his face, catching him momentarily unaware. She inhaled sharply, for she'd never seen him quite so focused, so intense. His midnight blue eyes held a certain gleam she'd seen only during their most intimate moments. He caught her watching him and she smiled guiltily.

"What are you thinking?" Lara asked. "You seem so absorbed. Are you worried about Rondo? Don't be. Pietro will keep him in line."

"Rondo doesn't worry me."

Lara resumed brushing through her tangle of curls. "What is it, then?"

She could hear his breathing, the harsh intake and exhalation, as if he were consciously regulating it. He stepped closer. Her gaze returned to his face and she backed a shaky step away from whatever emotion he strove so hard to control.

"What's wrong, Julian?"

"I . . . bloody hell, I don't understand any of this." He shook his head and turned away. "I don't know why I cannot control this raw hunger for you that constantly gnaws at my soul. Have you bewitched me, little Gypsy? If so, release me. I do not like this state of upheaval in which you hold me. Not even Diana . . ."

He groaned out an oath and stormed out the door without looking back. Had he glanced over his shoulder, he would have seen Lara's face crumple and tears gather in her eyes.

Why couldn't Julian see what was before him? Lara wondered dismally. Was his love for his dead fiancée still so alive and vital that he refused to let another woman supplant her in his affections? Why did he have to be so heedless of her feelings? Could he not trust his emotions to tell him what was in his heart?

Lara dried her eyes and turned her mind in another, less painful, direction. She had been surprised at Rondo's jealousy. He had been, and still was, her friend. How could he think otherwise? He'd always known she must eventually wed an Englishman. Julian and Rondo had been engaged in conversation while she and Ramona were inside the wagon, and from the looks on their faces, it had been a serious discussion. What had Rondo said to Julian?

That night they ate with Pietro and Ramona. After the meal, people drifted by to welcome them back. Later, Lara noticed that Julian appeared restless and asked if he'd like to take a walk.

"Aye," Julian said. "I'm too unsettled to sleep. There is something I wish to discuss with you and now is as good a time as any."

"And I have something to ask of you," Lara answered.

Arm in arm they strolled off toward the brook. Nights were cooler now, and Lara shivered in the damp air.

"You forgot your cloak," Julian commented as he removed his coat and placed it around her shoulders.

They followed the brook around a bend, moving farther away from the camp. When they reached a grassy knoll Julian's steps slowed.

"Shall we sit down?"

Lara sank down to the ground. She drew her knees up, folded her arms around them, and waited for Julian to begin. She couldn't imagine what he wanted to say to her.

"You go first," Julian invited. "What did you want to ask me?"

" 'Tis about Rondo. I saw you speaking together earlier. He appeared angry."

A long pause. "He was. He's jealous of me."

Lara shook her head in dismay. "Rondo and I are friends. Nothing more, nothing less."

"Tell that to Rondo. Our Romany marriage disturbs him. He was happy when I returned to London. He thought you would divorce me and remain with the caravan."

"That's ridiculous. I joined my father in London shortly after you left."

"Rondo expected you to tire of London and the restrictions imposed upon you and return to your grandparents. He thought I'd abandoned you and hoped to gain your affections. He wanted to be more than a friend to you. I suppose he expected you to divorce me however Roms do it, and turn to him."

"Rondo thought wrong. I would have done as my father wished no matter how much I disliked English ways."

"Would you have married the man your father chose for you?" Julian asked.

"I . . . don't know. 'Twould have been easy enough to divorce you and forsake our Romany marriage, but I probably wouldn't have. Divorce you, that is. As you pointed out countless times, our marriage isn't recognized by English courts, so there was no need for a Romany divorce."

"I think Stanhope was pleased when I offered for you."

"I believe he finally realized it wouldn't be easy to marry off his Gypsy daughter. The Earl of Mansfield was more than he had hoped for in a son-in-law."

"Have you finally accepted that we will marry?"

"No."

"I want our children to be legitimate," Julian explained. "A legally executed marriage will solve that problem."

"Why do you want to marry me, Julian?"

"I'm an honorable man, Lara. My family thinks I'm too strict and too damn honorable, but 'tis the way I am. I dishonored you, though 'twas as much your fault as mine. Nevertheless, the moral code by which I conduct my life demands that I marry you."

"So you've told me," Lara returned dryly. "Honor is not enough to base a marriage upon. Deep in your heart you really don't want to marry me. I understand that and accept it. I am still your Romany mate but I will not become your English countess. Now, what is it you wanted to tell me?"

Julian's fingers plowed through his hair. "You're the most exasperating woman I've ever met. Very well, we'll drop the subject for the time being, though in the end I'll have my way."

Lara heaved an exasperated sigh. "Time will tell. What is it you wanted to say to me?"

" 'Tis about our sleeping arrangements," Julian began. "There's no way I can keep my hands off you if we share the same bed. I'll be returning to London soon, and I don't know what the future holds for me. Until the Jackal is dealt with, my life is in danger. The Jackal has a number of thugs in his employ. He knows I'm close to exposing him and he's desperate. He wants me dead, Lara, and he might succeed."

"Does no one know the Jackal's identity?"

"Only those close to him. I suspect Crockett knows."

"You'll be safe as long as you remain here," Lara maintained.

"I intend to remain no longer than it takes to see you settled with your grandparents. I must return to London to continue my investigation and avenge Diana's death."

Lara's heart sank. Diana, always Diana. "What's Diana got to do with our sleeping arrangements?"

"Nothing, really. Except that I have no desire to leave you with a bastard in your belly."

"Of course not," Lara mocked. Oh, the pain. "That would be a tragedy."

"A tragedy, aye. My first child was—"

"You have a child? Why didn't you tell me?"

Julian went still. "I'm sorry. No one knows that . . . that Diana carried my child when she died."

"Oh, Julian, I'm the one who's sorry. How devastating for you."

"Devastating, aye. Sometimes I wonder what our child would have been like had he lived."

A sob slipped past Lara's lips. Then another. There was no hope for her, none at all. Julian was still obsessed with Diana and the child they had made together. He didn't want a child of hers. A thought occurred to her and she spoke aloud her fears.

"What if we had married in London? Would you have wanted a child of ours then?"

Lara couldn't see Julian's expression in the darkness but she sensed his anger.

A small sound of surprise was wrung from her when he grasped her shoulders and dragged her roughly against him. "Little fool. What makes you think I wouldn't welcome a child we made together? The timing is wrong, that's all I'm saying. We aren't married yet."

He grew thoughtful. " 'Tis odd how things turned out. I was fully prepared to accept that I would never have an heir, since I never intended to marry. Sinjun's son was to be my heir. But when you and I marry there *will* be children," he said fiercely.

But they will not be Diana's children, Lara thought despondently.

"If I should die, I want my child to have legal proof of its legitimacy."

"You won't die, Julian," Lara said passionately.

"I sincerely hope you're right."

"I may already be carrying your child."

She heard him suck in a breath. "Do you think . . . bloody hell, why wasn't I more careful?"

Her hand fluttered against his chest and settled there. She felt his heart thumping wildly against her palm. "I said 'tis possible, not that I know it to be a fact."

A charged silence hung between them. Lara felt the unaccountable need to soothe his fears. "I can ask Ramona for a potion," she offered.

"A . . . potion?"

"Aye, you know, to keep me from conceiving."

"She can do that?"

"She's done it for others."

His voice held a note of dismay. "Don't ask it of her. We will be married long before you conceive my child."

"We *are* married, Drago," she whispered, deliberately using his Gypsy name. " 'Tis you who refuses to accept it."

"Bloody hell, Lara, why are we at an impasse when we both want the same thing?"

"Perhaps we want the same thing in different ways, Julian. You want me in your bed and I . . . I want your . . . love." There, she'd said it.

"Love!" Julian sputtered, as if the word were foreign to him. "I want you. I've never denied that. Mutual passion is a good basis for a marriage."

"Did you love Diana?"

The quiet shattered around them as he spit out a curse. "Bloody hell! What is this, an inquisition? I can't recall Diana ever being so needy. Diana and I were betrothed as children. She would have made me a perfect wife. Everything about her was perfect. We were alike in many ways. Background, religion, all the ways that counted."

"What about passion?" Lara challenged.

He hesitated. "We shared a sweet passion."

The moon suddenly appeared from behind a cloud, revealing the stark planes of Julian's face. He was frowning, as if he were remembering something he didn't want to recall.

"Sweet." Her voice held a note of mockery. "The wild, abandoned passion we share is anything but sweet."

He gave her a rough shake. "What are you trying

to do? I cared deeply for Diana. Her death devastated me. So much so that I swore never to marry and sully her memory."

"Yet you're determined to marry me," Lara reminded him.

"Honor . . ."

"The hell with honor!" Lara swore. She leaped to her feet. "I'm going back. You can sleep beneath the wagon tonight."

"I care for you, Lara," Julian admitted. "Does that count for nothing?"

"Less than nothing," Lara flung over her shoulder. "Good night." She stalked away.

Julian leaped to his feet and stumbled after her. "Do you refuse to share my bed?"

"I have no desire to sleep with you, Drago." She glanced up at the lowering sky, noting that the moon had slipped behind a cloud. "It looks like rain. I hope you enjoy your damp bed beneath the wagon."

Julian couldn't stop the foolish smile that came unbidden. His wild Gypsy wench had returned with a vengeance. In all her splendid, defiant glory. Ferocious as the storm threatening to break, untamed as the Scottish moor upon which she had been born.

He wouldn't change her for the world.

Chapter 13

❧

Rain came down in buckets. Julian huddled beneath the wagon, teeth chattering, wondering why Lara had to be so bloody stubborn. If not for her temper and her need for an emotion that was a myth, they'd be snug in bed right now, with rain pounding on the roof instead of plaguing him. He was lying in a river of mud beneath the wagon and it was damn miserable.

The storm raged on unabated. The wetter Julian became, the angrier he grew. When a bolt of lightning struck a nearby tree, Julian jumped so high he bumped his head on the underside of the wagon.

"Enough is enough!" he shouted. His words were lost to the roar of the wind, but his decision had been made. He crawled out into the fury of the storm and made a dash for the door. The knob turned beneath his hand and he burst inside, dripping mud and water onto the floor.

"Julian! What are you doing?" Lara cried, reaching over to light a lamp.

"Not sleeping beneath the wagon," he growled.

"In case you haven't noticed, 'tis pouring rain out there. I refuse to sleep in a sea of mud."

"You're dripping all over the floor."

Julian sent her an aggrieved look and began tearing off his clothes. When he had rendered himself completely naked, he calmly gathered up his wet clothes and tossed them out the door. Then he reached for a towel that lay on the bench and dried himself.

"Move over," he commanded as the mattress dented beneath his weight.

"I'm not sleeping with you, Julian," Lara insisted.

"Then *you* go outside in that storm. I'm sleeping in this bed with or without you."

A bolt of lightning followed by a crack of thunder sent Lara scooting over to make room for Julian. Shivering uncontrollably, Julian ducked beneath the covers and pulled them up to his chin.

"Your teeth are chattering," Lara said, sounding slightly remorseful. "I really didn't think it was going to storm like this."

"Show me how sorry you are," Julian said, reaching for her. "Warm me. I need your body heat."

He pulled her against him, grinning when he heard her gasp. "You're icy cold!"

"Tell me something I don't know, sweeting. I'll forgive you for trying to freeze and drown me if you put your arms around me and share your body heat."

"I don't need your forgiveness," Lara argued. "I never meant for you to freeze to death." Nevertheless, she flung her arms around him, shivering as his cold flesh clung to her warmth. "But I still won't forgive you for . . . for . . ."

"For what, sweeting?"

"Never mind, you wouldn't understand."

"Are you still angry over that little argument we had earlier? I shouldn't have mentioned Diana again."

"I'm glad you did. Now I know exactly where I stand in your affections."

"Forget about emotions and concentrate on what we *do* have together. What about this?"

His lips touched her neck, nibbling at her flesh, trailing kisses up the line of her jaw, across her cheek, until he found her mouth. "Or this." He kissed her, hard, filling his senses with her taste, her scent, the very essence of her.

Why did Lara want to complicate matters with all this talk about love? he wondered dimly. *Why couldn't she just enjoy what they had together?*

Despite the coolness of his flesh, heat coursed through Lara as Julian showered kisses upon her. She gazed up into his midnight blue eyes and surrendered to the hot, sweet melding of lips and tongues. She knew she shouldn't yield so easily but this was the man she loved, the only man she'd ever love.

Sighing with pleasure, Lara ran her hands down his back, reveling in the play of corded muscles beneath the taut satin of his skin. She didn't even whimper a protest when Julian raised himself above her and lowered his body over hers.

"Isn't this better?" he whispered against her lips. "You sure know how to warm a man, sweeting."

He rubbed his chest against her breasts. Heat surged through her; her nipples budded against the hard wall of his chest. She heard him groan and felt his sex prod the crevice between her legs.

"This is what I didn't want to happen tonight, Julian," Lara said raggedly. "You're difficult to resist."

"Don't try," Julian answered as he eased back on his haunches and stared at her.

"What are you looking at?"

"You. You're so bloody beautiful."

He filled his hands with her breasts, moving them in a slow, expert design of arousal, palming their fullness, teasing her nipples to diamond-hard points. She arched against him just as he leaned forward, pressing his belly against hers as he licked her breasts and sucked a turgid nipple into his mouth, tonguing it into painful arousal.

Heat consumed her. Torturous tremors of need racked her. Her fingers twined in his hair, holding him against her as he suckled her.

"Julian! I . . ."

As if he knew what she needed, he moved between her thighs and shoved them wide with his knees. Then his fingers parted her, massaged the center of her desire, slipped inside her. She cried out, wanting him, needing him.

"Julian! Please!"

He reared up, his body looming over her, his nostrils flaring as he exhaled her name on a strident whisper. "Aye, love, now."

He slipped his hands beneath her buttocks, lifting her against his hot, engorged tip. "Here I am, Lara, take me inside you. Take all of me."

Lost in a haze of passion, she raised her hips and

felt him ease inside her. He was big and solid and hot, filling her with his strength, his hardness. She took him, all of him, her heat closing around. She felt him shudder, then he began to move.

"You're mine, Lara," he groaned into her ear. "What we have together is better than love."

In the dim recesses of her conscience, Lara heard him and felt a crushing blow of rejection. But she was too close to the edge to stop her body's response to Julian's loving. She hovered on the brink, then tumbled into a maelstrom of seething sensation. Indescribable pleasure overwhelmed her as she rode the crest to sweet oblivion. Moments later, Julian followed her.

"That was incredible," Julian said, panting. He snuggled her against him. "Spending the rest of our lives together won't be nearly as bad as you seem to think."

Lara said nothing. No matter what he said, she wouldn't marry him. Without love, sexual attraction wouldn't . . . couldn't last. She'd be his wife for the short time they remained with the Romany, she decided, but if she couldn't make him love her before they left, she saw little hope for a future together.

Julian tried to remain as inconspicuous as possible during his stay with the Rom, tending the horses and enjoying the company. It was an easy life. Cold weather had arrived and the Gypsies were content to remain in one spot until spring, when they would hitch up their wagons and resume their nomadic wandering.

Julian spent many pleasant evenings around a roaring campfire, listening to music and watching dancers twirl and dip to the beat of drums and twang of fiddles. Whenever Lara joined the dancers, her fly-ing skirts, flashing legs, and bouncing breasts never failed to arouse him. And he burned with jealousy whenever Rondo joined her.

Julian refused to accept that the anger plaguing him where Lara and Rondo was concerned was jeal-ousy. He never considered himself a jealous man. But seeing Rondo and Lara together made him want to do physical harm, and he was surprised that it both-ered him as much as it did. He didn't love Lara, yet the thought of her with another man drove him to fury. His reason for wanting to properly marry Lara was simple, he told himself. He had taken her virgin-ity; he owed her his name. She had saved his life; he owed her his protection.

Despite his confusion he still made love to Lara each night in the privacy of their wagon, even though he knew it might result in Lara's pregnancy. *What in bloody hell was wrong with him?* He didn't even take the usual precautions.

One week after Julian joined the Romany, unin-vited visitors rode into camp. Julian was consulting with Pietro about the horses when they arrived.

A curse rasped past Julian's lips. " 'Tis Crockett and his cohorts. They're looking for me. How in the hell did they know where to find me? Unless . . . do you suppose Lord Stanhope sent them here?" Julian's lips compressed into a thin line. "I was hoping he wasn't involved, but now"—he shrugged—"the evi-dence against him is growing."

"No," Pietro maintained. "Lord Stanhope would never place his daughter in danger. I will send them on their way. Try to remain inconspicuous while I speak with them."

Julian hung back as the Rom gathered in a knot around Pietro.

"This is private land," Pietro said. "You are trespassing."

Crockett gave a dismissive gesture. "We're looking for a man. Ye lied to us before. The man we sought was in yer camp but ye were protecting him. I will ask one more time. Who among yer people is not Romany?"

"We are all Romany," Pietro said. "We have Lord Stanhope's permission to camp on his land during the winter months. I can personally vouch for each and every man, woman, and child in my caravan."

Crockett appeared unconvinced. "Very well, if that's the way ye want it. My mates will search the wagons."

The six men accompanying Crockett dismounted and fanned out toward the wagons. Frantic, Julian searched for Lara and failed to find her. He recalled seeing her walking down to the stream for water and prayed she wouldn't return until the danger was over. While Crockett spoke with Pietro, Julian drifted out of sight behind a wagon. He was still close enough to watch and listen without being seen. Before he'd let one Rom suffer, he'd give himself up.

"Look what I found!"

The shout came from behind Crockett. Julian stifled a groan when he saw a thug coming up the path from the stream, pulling Lara along behind him.

Crockett smiled. " 'Tis Stanhope's daughter. If she's here, Scorpion can't be far away."

"Release my granddaughter!" Pietro demanded.

"Be quiet, old man," Crockett hissed. "I just want to ask the wench a few questions."

Julian went rigid with fear when Lara was dragged before Crockett.

"Where is Scorpion?" Crockett asked harshly.

Lara's chin rose defiantly and Julian had never been more proud of her. She had more grit than some Englishmen he knew. More than was wise.

"I don't know who or what you're talking about," Lara claimed. "A scorpion is a bug, isn't it? We don't have them in England."

Crockett raised his hand as if to slap her and outrage burst inside Julian. A growl rumbled in his chest as he prepared to charge from behind the wagon and launch himself at Crockett. Fortunately intervention wasn't necessary. Pietro stayed Crockett's hand with a few well-chosen words.

"There are more of us than you. I'd think twice before hurting my granddaughter."

Crockett gave Lara a murderous look and shoved her into Pietro's arms. "Aye, we don't need the wench. We'll find Scorpion without her. Search the wagons, men. He's got to be here someplace."

Pietro handed Lara over to Ramona, who quickly whisked her out of harm's way.

"They want Julian, Grandmother," Lara whispered. "Do you know where he is?"

"No, little one. But let's hope he had the good sense to hide where those men can't find him."

Julian sat on the horns of dilemma. Showing himself could prove fatal. But standing by and letting Crockett and his cohorts manhandle his Romany friends didn't set well with him. Had they hurt Lara, he wouldn't have hesitated to retaliate, even if it meant losing his life in the bargain.

He glanced back at Lara and was surprised to find

that she was no longer standing where he had last seen her. Ramona was there, but not Lara. Where had she disappeared to?

There was no help for it. He took one step from his concealment when someone grabbed his sleeve and pulled him back.

"No! Stay."

Julian spun around. "Lara? How did you know?"

"I saw you, and so will those men if you don't find a better hiding place. The grass is tall here. Get down on your belly and crawl to the wooded area behind the wagons."

Julian wagged his head. "I want to be where I can watch. I'll give myself up before I'll let them hurt your family."

"Pietro and the others can take care of themselves, they're used to it. Have you ever seen a Romany use a knife?"

Julian let that sink in. "I'm not going anywhere without you."

"They won't hurt me. Pietro and the others will protect me. Go!"

Julian didn't like it, not one damn bit. "No. I'll only go if you come with me."

Rough voices sounded from inside the wagon behind which Julian crouched, warning him that it was only a matter of time before he was flushed out. Lara must have come to the same conclusion for she clutched his arm and whispered urgently, "Very well. Lead the way."

Julian dropped down on his belly and slithered through the high grass into the wooded area behind the wagon. He looked back over his shoulder once, could not see Lara crouching behind the wagon, and assumed she was following behind him. It wasn't until he reached the forest and hid behind a sturdy tree trunk that he realized Lara hadn't followed.

"Bloody hell!"

Then he saw her. Even from a distance he recognized the proud tilt of her shoulders, the defiant angle of her chin. She was standing with Ramona, watching the smugglers make a shambles of their wagons.

Lara glanced over her shoulder toward the wooded area and prayed that Julian would remain hidden. She'd hated to deceive him but felt it would be too conspicuous for both of them to disappear at once. The men had given up the search, she noted, and were reporting back to Crockett.

"I must go to Pietro," Ramona said when Crockett turned his angry gaze on Pietro. "Stay here, little one."

"Where is Drago?" Rondo asked as he sidled up to join Lara.

"Hiding in the woods. I'm hoping he'll remain there until the danger is over."

"Who is Scorpion? In what manner of dangerous business is your man involved? I do not like this, Lara."

"I cannot say," Lara said. "Hush, listen."

Crockett made a motion for quiet. "A purse of gold to anyone with information about the man known as Scorpion. I know he has been here. He is a dangerous man. The right information could line yer pockets with gold. Think about it. We will camp nearby tonight should anyone wish to unburden himself."

"My people know nothing," Pietro insisted. "Leave. You are not wanted here."

"We shall see, old man. Perhaps there is one among you who knows something and is willing to talk. Look for my camp to the south."

Lara watched with trepidation as Crockett wheeled his mount and trotted off. She didn't like the way Rondo stared after the men, or the way his eyes had bulged when he'd heard about the purse of gold. But she felt reasonably certain Rondo would not betray Julian for fear of earning Pietro's wrath.

"I'd best go see to the horses," Rondo said, striding off toward the corral.

Lara felt a prickling of disquiet crawl up her spine, then promptly dismissed it. She was becoming paranoid. She trusted Rondo. He'd do nothing to hurt her. She glanced toward the forest where Julian was concealed and sidled off in that direction. She found Julian leaning against a thick elm.

"What happened?" Julian asked, clutching her in his arms and bringing her against him.

"Crockett offered a purse of gold for information about you. He's camped nearby, waiting for someone to accept his offer. But don't worry, no Rom will betray you."

"I'm not so sure," Julian muttered beneath his breath.

"Stay here. Wait till dark to return to the wagon."

"You know what this means, don't you, Lara?"

Lara did indeed know. "Aye, but where will you go?"

"Back to London. I won't rest until I run the Jackal to ground."

"Aren't there are others who can do that as well as you?"

"No. It has to be me. I've narrowed the field of suspects down to three. Another week or two of intensive investigation should yield the results I need. I have to do this, Lara. I've explained all this before."

Lara pushed herself away from him. "Of course. I understand perfectly. I must return to camp before I'm missed. Remember, don't return until after dark. We'll discuss this more fully then."

Julian reached for her but she slithered away, losing herself in the deepening shadows.

The evening hour approached. Cooking fires popped up all over the camp. Lara helped Ramona prepare their meal, remaining alert for trouble. A cool breeze wafted through the trees. She shivered. It was too cold to eat outside so she took her plate into her wagon and lit the brazier for warmth. She glanced out the window, wishing Julian was here with her.

She was staring absently out the window when she saw Rondo slip away from camp and disappear into the shadows. Alarm bells went off in Lara's head. Where was he going? He usually took his supper with his sister and her family. Curiosity got the best of her. Grabbing a wrap from a hook, she left her wagon and hurried after Rondo.

Lara was relieved to see that Rondo didn't appear to be looking for Julian, though he did seem to know precisely where he was going. She followed behind at a discreet distance, grateful for the darkening skies.

The walk wasn't a short one. Her legs began to ache and she was panting when Rondo suddenly stopped, looked around him, then ducked through a hedgerow. Lara crept forward until she reached the place in the hedgerow through which Rondo had disappeared. Crouching low, she peered through the narrow opening, stunned at what she saw. Hurt and betrayal would better describe her feeling.

Rondo had led her directly to Crockett's camp!

Crockett saw Rondo and rose from his seat beside the campfire to greet him. She strained forward to listen to their conversation. What she heard made her heart pound violently in her chest.

"I suppose you're here for the gold," Crockett said with a sneer.

"Aye," Rondo answered. "I have information about the Englishman you seek."

"Speak, Gypsy. You'll have yer gold if yer information pleases me."

"The man you call Scorpion is in our camp."

"My men searched every wagon."

"I know, but Drago wouldn't go anywhere without Lara, and she's still here."

"Drago?"

"Aye, 'tis what we call him. No one knows his real name, except perhaps for Lara and her grandparents."

"I've been told Scorpion wears many guises," Crockett mused thoughtfully.

"Who told you he'd be here?" Rondo asked curiously.

"The Jackal has his ways. Why are ye so anxious to betray Scorpion?"

"What does the Jackal want with him?" Rondo shot back.

"He knows too much about our operation. The Jackal wants him dead."

"The Jackal?"

"Aye, and 'tis all you're getting from me. Tell me what you know."

"I don't know anything about Scorpion, but Drago is hiding in the woods. You'll find him in Lara's wagon. 'Tis the blue and green one with the red door. You're not to hurt Lara, is that clear?"

"We'll not touch the wench. Unless you're lying. If we fail to find Scorpion, we've instructions to take the wench. The Jackal believes the girl can be used to flush Scorpion from hiding."

"I guarantee you'll find Scorpion in Lara's wagon, sleeping in her arms," Rondo said bitterly. "Leave Lara out of this."

Lara was shocked by Rondo's betrayal. Why was he doing this? The answer was given a few moments later.

"Yer jealous!" Crockett crowed. "Ye want the wench for yerself." He gave a bark of laughter. "I understand now why yer betraying Scorpion. I hope the wench is worth it."

Crockett reached beneath his coat and removed a purse. He counted out half the glittering coins and placed them in Rondo's palm. "Ye'll get the rest when we have Scorpion. Come, share a bottle with us to seal our bargain."

Lara had heard enough. With the agility of a young doe, she took to her heels. There was much to be done before Crockett returned for Julian. Her side ached and her breath was nearly gone when she tripped past the burning embers of their campfire and rapped on Pietro's door. A few minutes later, Pietro answered her summons. He saw Lara and hurried her inside.

"What is it, little one? Is it Drago? Have the *gadje* found him?"

"No. Oh, Grandfather, I cannot believe it."

Ramona appeared beside Pietro, her voluminous nightgown billowing around her ample figure. "Tell us what happened."

"There is little time. I saw Rondo leave his wagon and followed him to the *gadje* camp. He spoke with their leader. He betrayed Julian and accepted their gold. We cannot stay here. I must find Julian and leave before the *gadje* come for him."

"Once you are safely away, Rondo will be punished," Pietro promised. He wagged his head. "Why would he do such a thing?"

Ramona gave him an exasperated look. "Think old man. Rondo wants Lara and he's smart enough to realize that Drago stands in his way."

"Rondo has always known that Lara would marry a *gadjo* one day," Pietro said. " 'Twas her father's wish."

"Sometimes hot-blooded young men think with the organ hanging between their legs," Ramona said disparagingly.

"How did the *gadje* know to come here for Drago?" Pietro asked, stroking his mustache thoughtfully.

"A man called the Jackal told them where to look," Lara explained. "I fear that Julian is right . . . I fear Papa might be involved in all this. I didn't want to believe it," she wailed in despair.

"Things are not always what they seem," Ramona intoned cryptically. "But you are right about one thing. You and Drago are no longer safe here. Go pack your things. Pietro will saddle horses for you. The carriage you arrived in will only be a hindrance where you're going. I will pack food for your journey."

"Where we're going? I . . . I don't know where we are going. But apparently you do," Lara whispered.

"Drago knows. He has always known. Trust him. Go now," Ramona urged. "Before Rondo returns."

Lara hurried to her wagon. She found the small valises she and Julian had brought with them and stuffed their clothing inside. Then she removed their warmest cloaks from a trunk and took a last look around for anything she might have missed.

Ramona entered the wagon a moment later, carrying a cloth sack. "This should stave off hunger a day or two. Do you have sufficient coin?"

"Aye," Lara assured her. "Julian had the foresight to bring a cache of gold and silver coins with him. I found them at the bottom of his valise."

"Go to Drago," Ramona urged. "Leave your valises. Pietro and I will take care of everything and meet you at the edge of the forest."

"I'll bring horses," Pietro added.

Lara dashed out into the night. The forest was a dark and frightening place after sunset. Shadows mingled with shafts of pale moonlight filtering through the trees, creating distorted images. Lara shivered and pulled her cloak tighter about her as she plunged deeper into the woods.

Her voice held a hint of urgency. "Julian. Where are you?"

A shadow passed in front of her, then someone reached out and snagged her about the waist. She started to scream but a hard hand covered her mouth.

"Hush, sweeting, 'tis me." He released her mouth. "What happened? I was going to return to the wagon soon. Why are you thrashing through the woods? Have Crockett and his men come back?"

"Rondo betrayed you. We must leave before Crockett returns with his men. Pietro is bringing horses for us. He and Ramona await us at the edge of the forest. Hurry."

Julian spit out a curse. "I knew that young hothead was trouble from the beginning. He'd betray his own people if it meant he could have you."

"Perhaps we should return to London," Lara suggested. "Papa can protect me and—"

"No! 'Tis too dangerous for you there. The Jackal will try to hurt you to get to me. I can't let that happen."

"What are we going to do?"

"I've thought about this a long time," Julian began. "There's only one place you'll be safe. I should have brought you there straightaway. I'm taking you to the Highlands, to my brother Sinjun and his wife, Christy. When I return to London, I want to know you are with someone I trust implicitly."

"You're not staying with me?"

"I'll remain long enough for our wedding to take place," Julian said. "Even if you don't wish to marry me you have no choice now that I can see. When this is all over, the scandal resulting from our being together without benefit of marriage will be brutal. Your father will demand it of me."

"We'll see," Lara muttered. Loving Julian was easy, having him love her back was more complicated. There were times she pined for the man she'd once known as Drago, that mysterious man who had entered her life unexpectedly and stolen her heart. Sometimes she felt she didn't really know the dangerous earl still bound to his dead love by invisible ties.

* * *

Julian's thoughts ran along similar lines. He couldn't understand his need to bind Lara to him legally when he'd sworn off marriage. He told himself his reason for proposing to Lara was pure and unselfish. Lara was not the immoral Gypsy wench he'd thought her. But he was beginning to doubt his own motives. He wanted to protect her, which was certainly true. But even that line of reasoning was suspect.

"Let's get out of here," Julian said, grasping her small hand and guiding her through the forest. The lines along which he was thinking were discomfiting and better left for another day.

Pietro and Ramona were waiting in the clearing with two of Pietro's best horses.

"Rondo hasn't returned yet," Pietro said in a hushed voice as he handed the reins to Julian and Lara. "You must hurry. Where will you go?"

" 'Tis best you don't know," Julian said. "Trust me to take care of your granddaughter. What will you do to Rondo?"

Pietro's lips thinned. "He will be punished in the Romany tradition."

Lara threw her arms around Pietro first and then Ramona for one last hug, then Julian lifted her onto the back of her mount. "I will trust you both to do what is best where Rondo is concerned."

"Your valises, food, and warm blankets are attached to your saddles," Ramona said. "Lara said you had sufficient funds for your journey."

"Aye," Julian said. "We'll be fine. I'll try to send word when we've arrived at our destination."

"God go with you," Pietro intoned.

"Wait!" Ramona interjected.

The spirited horse danced beneath his thighs, eager to be off, but Julian held him in check.

"I would have a private word with my granddaughter," Ramona said.

Julian nodded and turned to speak to Pietro.

"What is it, Grandmother?" Lara asked anxiously.

"You must beware, little one," she warned. "I read the tarot cards. There is no safety until the enemy is vanquished."

"I will take care," Lara promised.

"Are you ready?" Julian asked.

"Aye, we must not linger. Good-bye Grandmother, Grandfather, I love you both very much."

Lara's parting words rang in Julian's ears as they rode away from the Romany camp. *Love*, he thought. If that tepid sentiment he'd felt with Diana was love, then what name would he give to the powerful emotion he experienced with Lara?

Chapter 14

They reached the Highlands ten days later. Garbed primly in traveling clothing an English lady would wear, Lara raised little curiosity during their stays at coaching inns, or at the homes of noblemen acquainted with Julian. The first time Lara was introduced as Julian's wife, she darted him a look that did not bode well for him. One that Julian promptly ignored.

"Why did you tell Lord and Lady Compton that we were married?" Lara challenged.

Julian slanted her an exasperated glance. "Would you have me tell them you were my lover? Your name would be dragged through the mud long before we returned to London. Think of the embarrassment to your father. Besides," he said with a careless shrug, "our marriage is a foregone conclusion."

After that, Lara learned to grit her teeth and be as pleasant as she could be to the people who thought her Julian's countess. Let Julian believe what he wanted, she decided. Until she heard the word "love" from him, she wasn't about to marry him in an Anglo ceremony.

Lara adored the Highlands. She'd spent many a pleasant summer on the Scottish moors, gathering heather beneath towering mountains in the clean, fresh air. She had been born in the Highlands, not far from Inverness, and had always considered herself more Scottish than English, though above all, she proudly proclaimed herself half Gypsy.

Each year until she'd turned thirteen and joined her father, she had traveled with the caravan between their summer quarters in the Scottish Highlands and their winter home in the lowlands. At the first hint of spring they returned to their roots in the Highlands. Not even the raw wind blowing across the moors could dim Lara's enthusiasm when Julian informed her that they were on Sinjun's holdings.

" 'Tis like coming home again," Lara said. "My family traveled throughout Scotland, but the Highlands were always special to me. It wasn't until they brought me to Papa that they began spending winters in England, on Papa's land. Now 'tis your turn. Tell me about your brother."

"Sinjun defies description. A few years ago he'd been headed for perdition. He was married at fourteen by order of the king to a seven-year-old Scottish lass, heir to Glenmoor and the future laird of the Macdonald clan.

"The marriage was not to Sinjun's liking and he never claimed his bride. Instead, he set out to become the most notorious rake in all of England. He succeeded beyond his wildest dreams, until Christy Macdonald showed up in London pretending to be Lady Flora Randall. Sinjun didn't recognize her as his abandoned wife, but from the moment he saw her he was bewitched."

"My goodness," Lara said. "Why didn't Christy tell Sinjun she was his wife?"

"Christy was no more eager to have an English husband than Sinjun was to have a Scottish wife. But she needed an heir for Glenmoor. Sinjun had all but ignored Christy and Glenmoor during his years of carousing and womanizing, so that heir seemed unlikely unless Christy took matters into her own hands. Needless to say, when Christy returned to Glenmoor some months later she was carrying Sinjun's child, and my dim-witted brother had no idea he'd taken his own wife as his mistress."

"My goodness," Lara repeated.

"All turned out well," Julian said. "They have a son, Niall, and a small daughter, Althea. Sinjun is now respected by Christy's clan, and has become a fine laird.

"See the sheep grazing on the hillside," Julian pointed out. "They belong to Glenmoor."

Lara let her gaze roam freely over heather-covered moors and verdant hills, impressed by the vast number of fat sheep grazing upon lush grasses.

"There's Glenmoor!" Julian exclaimed as the towers and turrets of the fortress came into view. " 'Tis a fine place. Sinjun has made improvements both inside and out, though he's never gotten around to making a decent road through his property," he groused.

Lara gazed at the gray castle rising out of the mist and thought it magnificent. She'd never been in a real castle before. Her father's country estate was of recent vintage and could in no way be described as a fortress. Lara couldn't wait to explore the ancient stone towers.

They rode over a bridge and through the curtain

wall. Since enemies were few in this remote corner of Scotland, no guard was posted at the gate, although they could see men patrolling the ramparts. They rode through unchallenged and drew rein before a set of stone steps leading to a scarred wooden door four times larger than Lara.

They were preparing to dismount when a man came striding from an outbuilding. He hailed them with a shout and hurried over to greet them.

" 'Tis Sinjun," Julian said.

Lara stared at Sinjun, her breath catching in her throat. Julian had failed to mention how handsome his brother was. He was tall and muscular, and his smile alone could charm the leaves off the trees. She was more than a little surprised to see Sinjun wearing kilts, a garment banned after Culloden.

"Julian! Welcome. I was going to send a message to you in London and here you are. I was worried. You're much too secretive." Suddenly, his eyes narrowed and he caught his breath. "Something is wrong, I can sense it! What is it?" Before Julian could answer, his gaze settle on Lara. "Is this the lady I saw you with at the fair?"

Suddenly Lara recalled seeing Sinjun with Julian at the fair. Julian had told her that Sinjun was merely someone interested in buying one of Pietro's horses.

"Your memory is intact," Julian drawled. "Sinjun, this is Lady Lara, Lord Stanhope's daughter. Lara, this is my brother Sinjun. I'll explain everything once we're inside, 'tis bloody cold out here."

Sinjun's eyes were the same color as Julian's, Lara reflected as she mentally compared the two men. Sinjun was younger, but no less handsome than his brother. They both had dark hair, dark eyes, and devastating smiles, but to Lara, Julian was far more attractive. The mystery and danger surrounding Julian gave him a distinct edge over his brother.

Sinjun bowed over Lara's hand. "Welcome to Glenmoor, my lady. Come inside where it's warm." He sprinted up the stairs and threw open the door. "Christy will be pleased to see you, Julian. I don't believe you've met our daughter yet."

Lara's eyes widened as she entered the great hall. The room was huge; its whitewashed walls were hung with colorful tapestries, and there was real glass in the windows. Servants moved about the room, involved in various chores and chatting back and forth. Sinjun led them to chairs set before a huge hearth that dominated one side of the room.

A handsome woman wearing the Macdonald plaid hurried over with cups of warmed ale.

"Margot, where is Christy?" Sinjun asked.

"In the solar, Sinjun. Shall I fetch her for ye?"

"Aye. Tell her we have guests."

"Your servants call you Sinjun?" Julian asked, taken aback by the informality at Glenmoor.

"Margot is Christy's kinswoman. You'll find that we're all family here, and that English titles mean little to Highlanders."

Lara slumped back in her chair, warmed by the fire and ale. Her eyes felt heavy and she had started to drift off when a high-pitched squeal and the patter of small feet on the fresh-smelling rushes jerked her awake. She glanced up just as a small lad toddled forward and threw himself into Sinjun's arms. Sinjun laughed and tossed the boy high in the air, much to the lad's delight.

"This is Niall," Sinjun said with a hint of pride. "The little imp would rather run than walk."

An old stooped woman wearing a white apron over her plaid came bustling behind Niall. "There ye be, ye little scamp. Dinna bother yer papa and his guests."

" 'Tis all right, Mary, let him stay. This is his uncle Julian and Julian's . . . friend, Lady Lara."

"Will they be staying, Sinjun?"

"Aye, Mary, prepare rooms for them, will you? Ask Rory to bring in their luggage and see to their horses."

"Aye," Mary said, scooting off.

"Julian! How nice to see you. What brings you to the Highlands? Dare I hope 'tis your desire to see your nephew and new niece?"

Lara's attention was captured by the vision who had just entered the room. Lara thought the Macdonald laird the most beautiful woman she'd ever seen. Hair the color of copper tumbled over her shoulders, and her slim figure belied the two children she'd borne. She wore the Macdonald plaid with inherent pride.

"Christy!" Julian leaped to his feet and embraced his sister-in-law. "You're more beautiful than I remember. Marriage and motherhood must agree with you. I hope my sister hasn't run you ragged with her usual shenanigans. Where *is* Emma, by the way?"

"Emma?" Christy said, exchanging a puzzled look with Sinjun. "Is Emma supposed to be here?"

Julian paled. "I sent her north some time ago. She should have arrived long before now."

Sinjun's expression turned grim. "I'll instruct Rory and his clansmen to initiate a search immediately. If Emma reached the Highlands, we'll know in a day or two. To my knowledge, no danger to travelers exists at this time. Did you send her alone?"

"I assigned six guards to her, and Rudy Blakely offered to accompany her, though I was against it. Did you know Blakely asked permission to court Emma? I refused, of course, but it seemed to do little good. You know Emma."

Sinjun rolled his eyes. "Indeed I do. But Blakely? Surely you jest. His reputation is nearly as bad as mine was before I settled down to marriage."

"He's not *that* bad," Christy defended. "All he needs is the right woman to reform him." Her brilliant gaze settled on Lara. "Isn't someone going to introduce me to Julian's lady?"

"Forgive me," Julian said. "This is Lady Lara Stanhope, my—*oomph*." Julian rubbed his leg where Lara had kicked him.

"Julian and I are acquaintances," Lara said before Julian could finish his sentence. She didn't want Julian's family to think of her as Julian's wife when Julian himself refused to recognize their Romany marriage.

Sinjun stared at Lara, clearly confused. "I could have sworn I'd seen Lady Lara dressed in Gypsy garb the day I ran into you at the fair."

"Lara's mother was a Gypsy," Julian explained. "She visited her grandparents each summer after she went to live with her father at age thirteen. She was spending her last summer with them before settling down for good in London when I met her."

"I see," Christy said, eyeing Lara with speculation. "Are you two traveling alone? Where is Lady Lara's chaperone?"

"I suppose I can't keep anything from you two," Julian said on a sigh. "Very well, here's the way it is. Lara dragged me from the sea and saved my life. Her grandmother treated my wounds and the Romany protected me from my enemies when they came searching for me."

"You were wounded? Someone tried to kill you?" Christy gasped.

"Aye, there are people who want me dead."

"You're in danger now," Sinjun inferred.

"Aye, so is Lara. Attempts have been made on both our lives."

Sinjun sucked in a harsh breath. " 'Tis time for you to give up your dangerous life and go back to being just plain Julian Thornton, Earl of Mansfield."

"I suspect you're right. My identity as a secret agent has been compromised. But I refuse to retire until Diana's death is avenged."

"Where does Lady Lara fit into all this?" Christy ventured.

"I had no idea Lara was an earl's daughter until I returned to London weeks later and met her at a ball given in her honor by her father. Due to the . . . unusual circumstances of our . . . association, I felt honor bound to offer for her. My enemies took note of my interest in Lara and decided to use her to get to me."

"So you had to flee London before your wedding day," Christy surmised.

Lara decided it was time to put an end to all the speculation. "Not exactly. I refused to marry Julian for reasons of my own."

Julian's jaw hardened. "We *will* be married, make no mistake. I've placed your reputation in serious jeopardy."

Christy cleared her throat. "You both look exhausted. I'll show Lara to her room. We have dinner early in the Highlands but there's plenty of time to freshen up and take a nap."

"Take Niall with you," Sinjun said. "The lad is falling asleep in my arms."

Lara rose while Christy gathered up her son, grateful for Christy's timely interference. She followed the Scotswoman up a winding stone staircase to the solar.

"I'll take Niall to the nursery first," Christy said. " 'Tis time for his nap."

Lara stood aside while Christy entered a room at the top of the stairs. A young woman came forward to take Niall from his mother's arms.

"This is Effie," Christy said. "She cares for the children. Effie, this is Lady Lara. She'll be staying with us for an indefinite period of time."

Effie gave Lara a shy smile. "Pleased to meet ye, my lady."

Lara smiled a greeting, then her gaze fell on a cradle holding a tiny babe. "That must be your daughter?"

"Aye," Christy said proudly. "Would you like to see her?"

"Oh, yes, I'd love to see her."

While Effie tucked Niall in bed, Christy plucked her tiny daughter from her cradle and offered her to Lara to hold. Raised in a Gypsy camp where babies and children abounded, Lara naturally nestled the babe in the crook of her arm.

"She's beautiful," Lara breathed, mesmerized by the infant's sea green eyes and mop of reddish fuzz atop her small head. "How old is she?"

"Althea is in her third month," Christy said, "and already she has her father wound around her little finger."

" 'Tis no wonder," Lara said wistfully. "I wish . . ." Her sentence fell away as she handed the babe back to Christy.

"I'll take her, Christy," Effie offered.

"Aye," Christy said. "I'll return to feed her later, after I've shown Lady Lara to her chamber."

Lara's chamber was just a short distance down the narrow hallway. From the long windows Lara caught a glimpse of towering mountains, blue skies, and heather-laden hills. A woven rug covered the floor and the high bed sported heavy velvet curtains that could be closed to keep out the chill. Tapestries covered the stone walls and the windows were hung with velvet drapes, keeping winter's chill at bay.

"I chose this room for you for its magnificent view," Christy said. "Your clothing has already been unpacked and placed in the chest at the foot of the bed. You didn't bring much with you so feel free to ask for anything you lack."

She eyed Lara critically. "I'm taller than you but Margot is a wizard with a needle. Most of my London clothing is going to waste here in the Highlands where I favor plaids and simple shirtwaists."

Christy lingered so long that Lara suspected she had something on her mind. She did, indeed, as Lara soon found out, and the beautiful Highland laird wasn't one to mince words.

"I can't imagine any woman refusing Julian's proposal. I take it you don't care for him."

Lara flushed. If Christy only knew how much she *did* care . . . "Julian is . . . a special man," Lara said, choosing her words carefully. "What woman wouldn't care for him?"

"I thought as much," Christy said smugly. "Is there a specific reason for your refusal?"

Lara hesitated. "Aye."

"I'm sorry," Christy apologized. "I don't mean to

pry, but Julian seemed quite eager to marry you. I thought it strange, for Julian told Sinjun he'd never marry or father a child after Diana's death." She clapped a hand over her mouth. "Oh, forgive me. Sometimes I talk too much."

"It's all right," Lara assured her. "I know all about Diana and Julian's vendetta against those responsible for her death. She's the reason I *won't* marry Julian. I want the man I marry to love me as much as I love him."

"But Diana's dead," Christy protested.

"Her ghost stands between us," Lara maintained. "I won't marry Julian until he buries her for good."

Christy touched her hand. "I hope that happens soon. I'll leave you to your rest while I tend to my daughter. Would you like a bath? Dinner isn't until six-thirty, Lara. May I call you Lara?"

"Of course, and I'll call you Christy. A bath sounds wonderful, Christy."

Julian and Sinjun sat before the fire, discussing the situation at hand.

"I fear something has happened to Emma," Julian announced worriedly. "If Blakely lets harm come to her I'll call him out."

"If Rory fails to learn anything about our impulsive sister, I'll head a search party myself. Do you think you were followed here?"

Julian mulled over his answer. "Not to my knowledge, but I can't be sure. But make no mistake, my enemies won't leave a stone unturned until they find me."

"Why do they want you dead?"

"I'm very close to discovering the identity of the

man behind the lucrative smuggling operation that's depriving our government of revenue. I've narrowed the field to three men. One of them is Lara's father, but I pray I'm wrong."

"Bloody hell! What a coil. Would Stanhope hurt his own daughter?"

"I can't believe it of him, but I'm not ruling him out. 'Tis why I brought Lara here. I'm depending on you and Christy's clansmen to protect her."

"You can count on us, Julian," Sinjun vowed. "I'll alert the chieftains to be on the lookout for strangers."

"I can take care of myself, Sinjun, 'tis Lara I'm worried about. She doesn't deserve all this. Saving my life and claiming me . . . well, needless to say, I owe her more than I can ever repay."

Sinjun frowned. "Is that why you want to marry her? From what I've observed, it appears that, well, that you and Lara are . . . well, more than friends."

Julian flushed and looked away. "We *are* more than friends. You'll probably find out anyway so I may as well tell you. Lara and I are lovers. I didn't know she was an earl's daughter when I . . . took her virginity. 'Tis only right that I offer her my name."

"Lara seems reluctant to accept your proposal. Why is that?"

"It has to do with Diana," Julian admitted. "Lara thinks I'm in love with a dead woman."

Sinjun's eyebrows inched upward. "Are you?"

"Bloody hell, Sinjun, you too? Diana's been dead for many years. Her death cost me a great deal and I'll not rest until she is avenged. But Lara is flesh and blood. I feel many things for Lara, among them the kind of lust I never felt for Diana. I can't help feeling that I'm betraying Diana for experiencing deep emotions with Lara, but I'm not ready yet to face that. I have to deal with Diana's killer first."

"Far be it from me to give you advice," Sinjun said, "but it seems to me that refusing to acknowledge your strong feelings for Lara is an error. Learn from my mistakes, brother. Being too stubborn to say the words Christy wanted to hear nearly cost me my wife and children."

"I have to follow my conscience," Julian explained. "But I *will* marry Lara before we return to London whether she agrees or not. She could be carrying my child."

Sinjun chuckled. "And you called *me* a rake."

"You don't understand," Julian said earnestly. "Lara and I have a Romany marriage. She married me to save my life when the Jackal's men came looking for me. Of course I never considered it legal or binding, but I can't deny I wanted to bed Lara once I recovered from my wounds. Lara never mentioned that she was an earl's daughter."

"And I thought Christy and I had problems," Sinjun said, wagging his head. "I suppose you and Lara will have to work this out on your own. But you can rely on me to provide all the protection you require."

"Thank you," Julian said solemnly. "I knew I could depend on you."

"Are you two catching up on news?" Christy asked as she strode into the hall. "Have you discussed Emma and what might have happened to her?"

"I'm on my way to speak with Rory and Gavin," Sinjun said, rising. "Would you show Julian to his chamber? He'd probably like to clean up before dinner."

Sinjun strode from the hall, and Julian followed Christy up to the solar.

"Can I peek in on my new niece?" Julian asked.

"Both Niall and Althea are sleeping, but it won't hurt to look in on them," Christy answered.

She opened the door to the nursery and Julian tiptoed inside, startling Effie, who sat sewing beside the cradle.

"It's all right, Effie, this is Julian, Sinjun's brother. He wants a peek at Althea."

Julian approached the cradle and stared down at the tiny scrap sleeping peacefully in her snug bed. He couldn't resist the urge to caress her cheek with the back of his hand, amazed at the softness. One day he and Lara might have a child like this, he reflected. That thought startled him, but it had definite appeal. Deep in thought, he turned away and followed Christy from the chamber.

"That's Lara's chamber," Christy said, gesturing at a closed door farther down the corridor. "She's probably bathing now. Your chamber is across the hall."

Julian wanted to protest separate rooms but thought better of it. This wasn't his home; he had to follow the rules set by its lady. But surprising Lara at her bath did sound tempting.

"Dinner will be served at six-thirty. You can escort Lara downstairs," Christy said as she opened the door to a large chamber furnished with an array of solid, masculine furniture. "Your clothing has been put away. If you need to supplement your wardrobe, I'm sure Sinjun can find something to fit you. He wears mostly kilts these days and has plenty of clothing to spare."

"Thank you, I'll keep that in mind," Julian said, eyeing the bed with longing. The narrow bed they'd occupied at the inn the night before left much to be desired.

Julian prowled the chamber like a restless animal once he was alone. Lord knew he could use a nap, but curiosity about Lara's sleeping accommodations wouldn't allow it. Plus, he wanted to know what she thought of Sinjun and Christy, and how she liked Glenmoor, and if she was comfortable, and . . . There was no help for it. He wouldn't rest easy until he spoke with Lara.

No one was about when Julian stepped out into the hallway. He quickly crossed the narrow corridor and rapped lightly on Lara's door. When no one answered he turned the knob and let himself inside. She was still at her bath, her head resting on the rim of a tub that had been set up before the hearth.

The glow of leaping flames softened her golden skin. A riot of midnight black curls cascaded over the rim of the tub. Her eyes closed, she appeared to be sleeping. Julian crept closer, his body taut with wanting. Would desire for his wild Gypsy lover ever wane?

As if she sensed his presence, Lara's eyes flew open.

"Julian! What are you doing here? This is my chamber."

"I wanted to see if you were comfortable. When you failed to answer my knock, I let myself in."

"I suggest you let yourself out," Lara said curtly.

Julian stared at her. "What's the matter, sweeting? You offered no objection when I watched you bathe in our room at the inn last night."

"This is your brother's home, Julian. Everything has changed."

Julian bristled. "Nothing has changed. Our wedding will take place as soon as I find Emma. You'll be my wife before I leave the Highlands. There's a kirk in the village, and a minister who I'm sure will be happy to perform the ceremony."

"We'll see," Lara demurred.

"Meanwhile," Julian said, giving her a rakish smile, "there's no reason for us to deny ourselves."

Lara gave a startled cry when he reached into the cooling water and lifted her out of the tub. He snatched a linen towel from a bench near the hearth and wrapped it around her as he carried her to the bed.

"Julian, put me down. We're in your brother's home and—"

"And what?"

"We should be circumspect."

"Circumspect be damned! It occurs to me that I've been far too prudent and sensible most of my life. Sinjun once called me an insufferable prig, and I have to agree. That's what responsibility and duty does for one. But you changed all that, my wild Gypsy wench. I can think of nothing but spreading your legs and filling you with myself."

His words set off a clamoring in Lara's blood, a clamoring she tried desperately to ignore. But her love for this impossible man was so strong she could deny him little.

The mattress dented beneath Julian's weight. He grinned down at her. "We've plenty of time before dinner."

"We're not married, Julian, you said so yourself. I'd feel guilty taking advantage of Christy's hospitality."

He whisked the towel from her body. "Christy doesn't have to know. Besides, Christy is no fool.

She's probably guessed we're lovers." He bent his dark head and lingered a long moment over the corner of her mouth, pressing gentle kisses against it.

"Each time we're together increases my risk of conceiving your child," Lara argued.

He found her mouth. Lara sighed softly as she offered her lips. He kissed her breathless, then he lifted his head and said, "Don't you think I know that?"

Lara reared up on her elbows. "You *want* to get me with child! I don't understand."

"I told you we were going to marry. It won't matter in the least if you are increasing when our wedding vows are exchanged. At least you'll have no excuse to beg off."

Lara stared into his brilliant, determined gaze and gave him a tremulous smile. "Do you love me, Julian?"

"Does it matter?" Julian whispered against her lips.

"It does to me. Will you give up your vendetta against those responsible for Diana's death?"

"Give it up?" Julian gasped, clearly astounded. "Not until the bastards are in prison."

Lara's heart sank. How could she be so wrong? Julian didn't love her. For a brief moment she'd thought—no, hoped—he'd finally searched those dark reaches of his heart and discovered love.

"I'll arrange everything, Lara," Julian continued. "I've had a special license since before we left London, though I doubt one is necessary in the Highlands."

He sat up and began stripping off his clothing. "Don't worry about Christy or Sinjun. They know how it is between lovers. Besides, Sinjun already knows about our Romany marriage."

"You told him?" Lara gasped.

"I had to explain about us." He threw off the last of his clothing and covered her with his body. "Are you going to shut up and let me love you?"

"I think not," Lara said, squirming out from under him. She picked up her robe and shoved her arms inside. "I'll marry you *and* let you make love to me when you can say that you love me and mean it."

"I care for you deeply," Julian said, reaching for her. She scooted away.

"What do you have against loving again? Diana is dead. Why is finding love with another woman abhorrent to you?"

Julian charged to his feet. "Bloody hell, Lara, what do you want from me? My soul? Loving is dangerous. Loving means dying a little when someone you care about is taken from you. There, are you satisfied?"

Lara's mouth gaped open. She would never have guessed that Julian was afraid to love again. Afraid to lose again. Afraid that the one he loved would be taken from him.

"So you prefer to keep your feelings buried deep inside you rather than love again," she said dully. "I feel sorry for you, Julian. When you realize how wrong you've been, I might decide you're not worth the waiting."

"Dammit, Lara, there'll be no need to wait. We're going to be married in a few days and I won't take no for an answer."

He closed the distance between them and pulled her into his arms. "Go ahead and be stubborn, deny me your bed, but once we're married we'll sleep in the same bed every bloody night."

He kissed her hard, the strength of his determination overwhelming her. Julian *did* love her. He *did*. He just didn't know it yet. Or if he did, he was too stubborn to admit it.

A low growl rumbled in Julian's chest as he swept her into his arms and carried her back to bed. She stared up at him; his heated gaze raised goose bumps on her flesh.

Her own gaze swept the length of him, held in thrall by the ripple of muscles over his magnificent body. The scars from his wounds did nothing to detract from his seductive allure. If anything, they made him more attractive. Her gaze shifted downward, to his rampant sex, and her breath hitched.

"Keep looking at me like that, sweeting," Julian whispered thickly, "and I swear you'll never leave this bed."

His eyes glittered as he lowered himself to the bed. Just as he reached for her, someone rapped on the door. Seconds later, the door opened and Christy entered.

"I hope I didn't awaken you, Lara," Christy said. "I brought a plaid for you to wear over your shoulders. The castle can be drafty this time of the year and—oh . . ."

Julian groaned and dove for his breeches.

"I'm sorry," Christy said. Her eyes sparkled with mirth. "I didn't realize you had company. I'll just leave the plaid on the bench."

Lara went pink with embarrassment, but Julian appeared unflustered as he calmly stepped into his breeches.

"No need for you to leave, Christy," Julian said once he was decently covered. "I should leave." He glanced over at Lara. "We'll continue this . . . conversation later."

He gathered up his remaining clothing and let himself out of the chamber.

"I didn't mean to interrupt," Christy apologized after Julian had left.

"I'm glad you did," Lara replied. "As you observed, I have little willpower where Julian is concerned."

"You should marry him," Christy advised.

"Would you marry a man who didn't love you? Lust is all good and well, but I want more."

"I married a man I didn't love," Christy admitted. "In fact, I hated Sinjun the first time I set eyes on him. Of course I was but seven years old and my whole family except for my grandfather had been killed by Englishmen. I never counted on falling in love with Sinjun when I traveled to London to seduce him. Give Julian time to realize how much you mean to him. He's determined to marry you, you know."

"Humph," Lara snorted.

"Think about it, Lara. Julian wouldn't be so determined to marry you unless he loved you."

"His honor—"

"Honor be damned," Christy said. "Julian loves you. Marry him and put him out of his misery."

Chapter 15

L ara locked her door against Julian that night and the next two nights, and was grateful that he hadn't raised a ruckus. She wasn't lying when she'd told Christy she had no willpower where Julian was concerned. Unfortunately, Lara knew that Julian *would* have his way, whether she liked it or not.

More worrisome was the lack of news about Emma and Lord Blakely. No one seemed to know a thing about them. They hadn't been seen or heard from since they left London. Sinjun and Julian had mustered fifty clansmen and had spent two days searching for them.

Julian hadn't mentioned marriage to her again after that first night when Christy had walked in on them, and that made Lara nervous. Knowing Julian, she suspected he had something up his sleeve. Something he'd probably spring on her when she least expected it.

The two-day search for Emma turned up no clue to her whereabouts. Everyone was understandably tense. That night Lara donned one of Christy's dresses Mary had altered for her, tossed the plaid around her shoulders, and hurried downstairs to join the family for dinner. Everyone was gathered before the hearth in the hall.

"Oh, that dress is perfect on you," Christy exclaimed. "Blue is definitely your color. And the plaid sets everything off beautifully."

"I agree," Julian said. His arm circled her waist, bringing her against him. "Has our guest arrived yet, Sinjun?"

"Not yet, but I'm sure he'll be here soon."

"We're having guests?" Lara said.

"Just one," Julian answered.

Lara didn't like the wicked gleam in Julian's eyes. He was up to something, and it didn't bode well for her.

Her thoughts scattered when Rory rushed into the hall. "Sinjun, they're here!"

"You mean the guest we were expecting?" Sinjun asked. "Show him in."

"Nay, 'tis Lady Emma and Lord Blakely."

"Emma is here?" Julian exclaimed on a rising note of euphoria. "Good God, man, show them in."

"Here we are, Julian," Emma said, hurrying forward. Rudy Blakely was two steps behind her. "Forgive me for worrying you."

"Where in bloody hell have you been?" Sinjun all but shouted. He glared at Blakely. "What detained you, Rudy, and this had better be good."

Rudy smiled tenderly down at Emma, his eyes glowing with love. He took her hand and brought it to his lips. Then, stiffening his jaw, he met the steely gazes of Emma's brothers without flinching.

"Emma and I were on our honeymoon. We were married before we left London."

"What!" Sinjun and Julian's combined voices resounded like thunder in the immense hall.

"You bloody bastard!" Julian said, lunging at Rudy.

"Betrayer!" Sinjun snarled, pushing Julian aside to get to Rudy.

Emma stepped in front of her husband, shielding him from her brothers' wrath. "Don't you dare hurt Rudy!"

"Step aside, Emma," Sinjun ordered.

"He's my husband now," Emma declared.

"I can defend myself, love," Rudy said, setting her gently aside.

"They don't understand," Emma cried. "I love you and you love me, that's all that matters. We're married, there's nothing they can do about it."

"She's right," Christy said, joining Emma. "Emma is a grown woman. Give her credit for knowing her own mind."

Sinjun glowered at his wife. "You forget, Christy, I know Rudy better than anyone. I know everything there is to know about him, and he isn't good enough for my sister."

"A renowned womanizer like you has no room for criticism," Christy reminded him. "You've reformed, why can't Rudy?"

"Thank you, Christy," Emma said softly. "Don't blame Rudy. It's all my fault. I knew my brothers would never allow us to marry so I convinced Rudy to marry me in secret. The ceremony was performed by an ordained minister incarcerated in debtors' prison. 'Tis done all the time by couples desiring to marry without parental consent."

"I love Emma, Sinjun. I'd never do anything to

hurt her. If you can be a faithful husband, give me credit for being able to do the same. Since I've come into my inheritance, I'm wealthy enough to support her. Emma will want for nothing. I . . . I'm sorry we had to do this in secret."

"Dammit, Blakely, this isn't well done of you," Julian spouted. "Emma should have had a grand wedding, with her family and friends present."

"I don't care about any of that," Emma insisted. She gazed adoringly at Rudy. "I have all I want right here."

"What happened to the six guards I sent along with you?" Julian asked.

"I sent them back," Emma defended. "I told them they weren't needed. Rudy and I went directly to Fleet prison and were married. We spent our honeymoon at Rudy's country estate in Northumberland. Please don't be angry at us. You left us no choice but to do it this way."

Lara could remain silent no longer. She had watched Emma and Rudy together and knew intuitively that Rudy was sincere. The tender way in which he smiled at Emma, the way he touched her, with so much love. Perhaps Julian didn't recognize true love, but she did.

"Julian, can we speak in private a moment?"

Julian glared at her. "Can't it wait?"

"No. It won't take but a moment."

"Very well." He moved away from the others and waited for Lara to follow. "What is it, Lara?"

"Just because you refuse to believe in love doesn't mean it doesn't exist. Can't you see how happy Emma is? Not everyone has the luxury of marrying for love."

"You're too sentimental to see the situation clearly," Julian scoffed.

"And you're too hard-hearted to admit love exists!" Lara all but shouted. "Sinjun reformed, what makes you think it can't happen to Rudy? Emma is too sensible to love an unreformed rake. Give your sister credit for recognizing love, Julian. I applaud her courage for doing what she thinks is right for her and the man she loves."

Julian's eyes narrowed. "What do you think I should do? Let my sister make the biggest mistake of her life?"

Lara's chin firmed. "Let her be with the man she loves. Trust Rudy." Her voice lowered. "And believe in love. It does exist, you know."

Julian said nothing, merely stared at her. Then he turned and joined the rest of the family.

His voice tense with repressed anger, he said, "Emma, dear, I cannot condone what you've done or the way it was accomplished, but I'm willing to give Rudy a chance to prove himself."

" 'Tis too late to change things," Sinjun allowed. "What's done is done. But that doesn't mean we won't be watching Rudy like a hawk," he added, sending Rudy his sternest look.

"I swear you'll have no reason to doubt my love for Emma," Rudy declared.

Julian silently acknowledged the wisdom of Sinjun's words. Emma had chosen Rudy and they appeared to love each other deeply. Who was he to tear them apart when his own relationship with Lara was far from perfect?

"Very well," he said grudgingly, and though it cost him a great deal, he offered his hand to Rudy.

"You won't be sorry, Julian," Rudy said, grasping Julian's hand and beaming.

"You've always been my best friend," Sinjun admitted, "now you're my brother-in-law. I promise not to kill you for stealing my sister as long as you toe the line."

He held out his hand and Rudy grasped it. A frown still lingered on Julian's brow when the door opened and Gavin entered, accompanied by another man.

"He's arrived, Julian," Gavin said breathlessly. "Reverend Gordon is here to perform the ceremony."

A tall Scotsman wearing the black robe of a clergyman followed in Gavin's wake.

Lara sent Julian a suspicious look. "Ceremony?" she repeated. "What is he talking about, Julian?"

Julian cleared his throat. "It's most fortuitous that Emma and Rudy arrived when they did. Now the whole family can be present for our wedding."

"You and Lara are getting married!" Emma exclaimed, clapping her hands gleefully. "How wonderful! I was beginning to worry about you, Julian. I hoped you'd find a woman to love one day."

Lara bristled. "Julian doesn't love me and we're not getting married. I'm sorry, Reverend, you made the trip to Glenmoor for nothing."

Julian muttered a curse beneath his breath. Never had he met a more stubborn woman. "My bride-to-be is nervous, Reverend. Please commence with the ceremony."

Lara glared at him. "I'm warning you, Julian . . ."

"May I have a word with Lara in private?" Christy said, pulling Lara aside.

"You won't change my mind," Lara hissed as

Christy all but dragged her away from the knot of people gathered before the hearth.

"Do you love Julian, Lara?"

"Aye," Lara admitted grudgingly.

"Do you trust him?"

Her answer was more hesitant this time. "I shouldn't. He left me because he thought I was a Gypsy and unworthy of him. But, aye, I suppose I do."

"Then take my advice and marry him. Sinjun told me all about Julian and Diana. From what I gather, Julian cared deeply for her but it wasn't a grand passion. They were compatible, and they had been promised to one another as children. It would have been dishonorable of him not to love his betrothed."

"He loved Diana enough to get her with child," Lara charged. "Diana was carrying Julian's child when she died. The children I bear him would come second behind the child he lost."

"Julian is an honorable man. Far more honorable than Sinjun," Christy allowed. "Like Sinjun, he's a passionate man. Unlike Sinjun, Julian would not cheat on his betrothed. Diana and Julian were all but married. A legal betrothal had taken place. They probably saw no reason to wait until after the nuptials to consummate their relationship.

"Diana is dead. What you and Julian have together is rare. I saw the way he looks at you, the way he follows you with his eyes. If that's not love I don't know what is."

"My heart tells me that Julian loves me, but he's too stubborn to admit it."

"Then take a chance on him, Lara. Marry him. I

guarantee those words you covet won't be long in coming."

"What do you suppose they're talking about?" Julian asked Sinjun as they watched the two women speak earnestly to one another.

Reverend Gordon had moved close to the hearth, sipping mulled wine Margot had brought him, and Emma and Rudy were engrossed in each other, looking deeply into each other's eyes and exchanging sweet words.

"Christy is probably trying to talk some sense into Lara," Sinjun speculated.

"I hope Lara listens to her."

"You must love Lara a great deal," Sinjun mused. "I can't ever recall hearing you express particularly strong emotions for Diana. Oh, I know, you said you loved Diana, and I believe you, but there are different degrees of love."

"Humph. What makes you such an expert?"

Sinjun sent him a wicked grin. "You forget, you're talking to Lord Sin, the notorious rake. I know everything there is to know about love."

"You know everything there is to know about sex," Julian scoffed. "You're the last person I'd come to for advice on love."

"No matter, I'm giving it. I'm not stupid. A simpleton can see that you love Lara. If you can't see it, then you're a bigger fool than I suspected. You've lectured me many times in the past, now it's my turn."

"I know you mean well, Sinjun, but there is something you don't know. Before I can offer my heart to Lara, I have to lose the guilt I feel over loving Diana less than I should have. She died because of me, for godsake! I got her with child. I didn't know Lara then and had no idea stronger feelings existed."

"Guilt is not an easy thing to live with. Perhaps you should—Beware," Sinjun hissed. "Christy and Lara have finished their conversation. Here they come."

Julian held his breath as Christy and Lara joined them. He tried to read her expression but it was carefully masked behind a bland smile. Would she reject him again? No matter, he decided, stiffening his resolve. Willing or not, she would marry him this very night.

The minister saw the women approaching and left his place by the hearth. He smiled benignly at them. "Is everything settled? Shall I begin the ceremony?"

"What do you say, Lara?" Julian asked, giving her the choice before forcing her to it.

When Lara looked up at him, Julian nearly lost the ability to speak. Her dark eyes were filled with so much love he felt unworthy. He wondered if he was capable of returning that same devotion. He had fallen short with Diana, could he trust himself to give Lara the kind of love she deserved?

His introspection ended abruptly when Lara said, "I'll marry you, Julian, though this Anglo ceremony will be no less binding than our Rom one. I'm marrying you because I believe in you, and because I believe in love."

Her acceptance brought Julian a measure of comfort. He was doing the *right thing*. Lara would never be disparaged by the *ton*. She would be his countess.

Julian reached for Lara's hand and brought it to his lips. "You may begin the ceremony, Reverend."

The family gathered round as Reverend Gordon

opened his book and began reading the marriage rites. Both Sinjun and Christy were misty-eyed, and Emma sobbed openly. Macdonalds seemed to creep out of the woodwork, filling the huge room.

Julian forgot to breathe when it came time for Lara to repeat her vows, but he needn't have worried. She pledged her troth loud and clear. The only time she appeared surprised was when Julian fished an emerald-encrusted band from his pocket and slid it on her finger. It fit perfectly, just as he had known it would.

"It belonged to my mother," he whispered. "I've carried it with me since our engagement appeared in the newspapers."

Then he drew her into his arms and kissed her amid a burst of applause and laughter. He was married! Finally. Bloody hell! Why did he have to feel so good about it?

Lara stared at the ring Julian had just placed on her finger and happiness burst inside her. She'd held out for a long time, but now that the deed was done she felt as if a great burden had been lifted from her. She believed that Julian loved her, and she prayed she wouldn't have to wait a lifetime to hear those words from him.

An enormous celebration followed the ceremony. So many Macdonald clansmen crowded into the hall to partake of the feast that Lara realized Julian had planned this day carefully, and that everyone had known but her. So much food, she thought as dish after dish was placed on the groaning tables.

There were sea trout, oysters, turtle, racks of lamb, roasted venison, a variety of vegetables, the last of summer's bounty, and a half-dozen different tarts and puddings. Lara sampled only a few of the tasty dishes before giving up. Her stomach could hold only so much.

After the meal, musicians came from the village, accompanied by a troop of Gypsy dancers, acrobats, and jugglers. Wine, ale and fine Scottish whiskey flowed like water. Scotsmen were a rowdy lot, and when Julian asked if she was ready to retire, she was only too happy to comply.

Hoots, jeers and ribald suggestions followed them up the stairs to the solar.

"I had my things moved to your room while we were eating," Julian said as he opened the door to her room and ushered her inside. "It has the better view, not that we'll need it tonight."

Lara stood in the center of the room and looked around. Her heart skipped a beat. The bedcovers had been turned down and the draperies pulled across the window. The sweet smell of violets drifted to her from the bed, and Lara realized that someone had sprinkled scent on the sheets. Christy's handiwork, she supposed.

She looked at Julian, her gaze wandering over him in appreciation. He must have borrowed something from Sinjun for he was fashionably garbed in midnight blue satin breeches, light blue coat, and silver vest. A froth of ruffles adorned his white linen shirt at both neck and wrists, and his shoes sported silver buckles.

"You haven't said much tonight," Julian said as he peeled off his coat. "Do you regret marrying me?"

"Not yet, Julian."

"You don't sound convinced. What can I do to change that?"

His gaze held hers with almost hypnotic intensity. After a weighted silence she whispered, "You know, Julian, you've always known."

"I know I want you, sweeting. These last few days without you in my arms, in my bed, have been hell. Another day or two and I would have battered your door down."

Lara smiled at that. She didn't doubt it a bit.

"Come here, love." He opened his arms and she walked into them. They closed around her and Lara felt as if she had come home. She had held out as long as she could, but a determined Julian was like no other force on earth. He had worn down her resistance, and Christy's advice had pushed her toward the ultimate decision.

"I want you naked," Julian whispered against her ear. "I'm going to make love to you all night and beyond."

"Aye, Julian, love me," she crooned softly. She'd have his body if not his heart.

Julian's dark blue eyes glittered with desire as he kissed her. What began as a gentle melding of lips became hotter, hungrier, more needy and demanding. She twined her fingers in his thick hair, pulling him closer as she opened her mouth beneath his. His tongue darted inside, deep and hot. Their bodies strained against each other, their breath coming in ragged gasps, their hands touching, arousing, possessing. But that wasn't enough.

He tore his mouth away from hers. Candlelight revealed a face stark with hunger and intense yearning. His hands tightened around her waist to set her away from him. Then he began to undress her, ripping a sleeve in his haste to render her naked. Grasping her dress in his hands, he lifted it up and away. With shaking fingers he released the tape on her petticoat. It pooled around her feet and he lifted her up, pushing it away with his foot.

She stood before him in her chemise, expecting him to remove that too, but the gleam in his eyes warned her that he had other ideas.

"Can you manage the rest yourself?" he asked. His voice was low and mellow, his eyes smoky dark.

She nodded mutely. He sat on the edge of the bed and removed his shoes and stockings. She could sense his desire for her, saw it in his set features and the tense expectancy of his body. Her breasts felt swollen and she felt moisture gathering between her legs.

With provocative slowness she untied her garters one at a time, rolling her stocking down one leg, then the other, removing them along with her shoes. She heard him hiss in a quick breath.

"Your chemise," he said on a ragged sigh. "Take it off."

Smiling seductively, she pulled it over her head with tantalizing slowness. He stood to remove his breeches, then sat down again. His heated gaze slid over her like warm honey; delicious shivers coursed down her spine. The room was so quiet she heard nothing but the sound of candles sputtering in their holders over his strident, aroused breathing.

He drew her forward, until she stood between the vee of his spread thighs, her hands resting on his shoulders. She moaned softly and closed her eyes when she felt his fingers digging intimately into the cheeks of her buttocks. A heavy, dewy moisture collected between her legs, intensifying her rampant desire for this man.

"You're so beautiful," he whispered. "When the Gypsies were dancing tonight, it was you I pictured spinning before me. I've never seen anyone dance like you, my wild Gypsy beauty. Music unleashes something wanton and abandoned inside that incredible body of yours."

"Julian, you don't have to say those things," Lara said, surprised by his sincerity. "We're married now." Did he truly mean them?

"Why do you doubt me? I meant every word."

He began moving his hands, palming the fullness of her breasts, taunting her nipples with his tongue. She whimpered and arched against him as he sucked a nipple into the wet heat of his mouth. He released her nipple and pulled her into his lap.

"This is our wedding night," he whispered against her lips.

"We had our wedding night weeks ago," she reminded him.

He turned suddenly, bringing her beneath him, his hard body pressing her into the mattress.

"Julian!" She was trembling, consumed by heat, racked by torturous waves of desire. Her fingers twined in his hair, guiding his lips to hers. His kiss was everything she wanted, needed, but it wasn't enough.

She seemed to know precisely what she needed. His hand slid down her belly, his weight shifting as he brought his knees between hers, shoving them wide. Her breath hitched when she felt his fingers part her. Then his mouth came down to taste her. She bucked her hips, wild now for what only Julian could give her, but he took his time, tasting her thoroughly, his tongue a wicked sword as it stabbed repeatedly into her dewy center, then laved her tender bud.

She cried out, arching her neck, her shoulders lifting off the bed as she flew into the turbulent eye of a storm, hurtling toward a wild, shattering release.

When she regained her wits she found him crouched over her, his face stark with his need and driving hunger. Her fingers wrapped around his wrists, pulling him against her. "Inside me, Julian, please."

He reared up, his big, dark body looming over her, his nostrils flared. "Lara," he said in a strident whisper. "You're mine. All mine."

"I've always been yours, Julian."

He gave no hint of having heard her as he slipped his hands beneath her buttocks and positioned her against his hot, smooth tip.

"Put me inside you," he groaned. "Guide me to heaven."

Her hand fastened around his staff, bringing him to her entrance. She heard his breath rasp against her ear as he eased into her moist sheath, stretching her, filling her with his heat and strength, until he was buried so deep she felt as if he'd pierced her soul.

"I can't remember when I've been this hard," Julian gasped. Gazing deeply into her eyes, he raised himself up on his arms and thrust. In and out, increasing his tempo until they were both gasping and breathless.

She clutched at his back and wrapped her legs around his wildly undulating hips. She sucked in a breath and drew him deeper. He pumped harder, faster, each thrust taking her higher and higher, until she was nearly incoherent with exquisite pleasure.

He dipped his head, his mouth catching her abandoned cries of delight she hadn't even realized she was making. Sensations were mounting, piling one on top of the other as she strained toward a peak that dangled temptingly within reach. Then those sensations burst through her, over her, inside her, in a shattering crescendo of whirling colors and rapturous ecstasy.

"I love you, Julian!"

If Julian heard, he gave no indication, for he was hurtling toward his own climax. She felt him stiffen, heard the harsh rasp of his breath, and felt the wet heat of his seed explode inside her.

Afterward they slept. She woke sometime during the night and felt Julian's hands slide across her stomach and dip down between her legs. Without hesitation she turned into his arms, letting him love her again.

Julian awoke first the follow morning. He stretched and smiled. He couldn't recall when he'd been so hungry, or felt so well. His mouth watered at the thought of eggs, a rasher of bacon, kidneys, and hot coffee. He bathed, shaved, and dressed without waking Lara and quietly left the chamber. The family was gathered in the hall, eating breakfast when he arrived.

"Where's Lara?" Christy asked with a hint of amusement.

"Still sleeping," Julian replied with appalling male arrogance. "She didn't sleep well last night."

Sinjun gave a loud guffaw. "And whose fault was that, I wonder?"

"I really like Lara, Julian," Emma said shyly. "Please don't hurt her."

Julian frowned. "What's that supposed to mean?"

"I . . . you're gone so much, and, well . . ."

"Out with it, Emma."

"Quit badgering my wife, Julian," Rudy said, placing a protective arm around Emma.

"What's the argument about?"

Everyone swiveled around as Lara walked into the hall and seated herself beside Julian.

"I thought you were sleeping," Julian said.

"I was, but I woke up when you left the chamber."

Julian slid a warning glance at Emma. "There is no argument, sweeting."

Just then Mary shuffled into the hall and set a steaming bowl before Julian. "What's this?" Julian asked, frowning at the glutinous mass quivering before him. Certainly not breakfast.

"Oats, me fine lord," Mary said gleefully. "If yer brother can eat them, so can ye."

Sinjun covered his laughter with a cough as Julian cocked an eyebrow at him. "I don't like oats," Julian said.

Mary grinned, apparently enjoying Julian's discomfort. "Neither did yer brother but he learned to like them."

"Try them," Lara urged. "I find them fortifying. I'll have a bowl, Mary."

Beaming, Mary returned to the kitchen for Lara's oats. Julian glared at her departing back as he dipped his spoon in the bowl and brought it to his mouth. He did his best not to gag as the oats slid down his throat but lost the battle.

"I'm accustomed to something more substantial," Julian complained.

"Come now, Julian, they're not that bad," Sinjun chided. "They grow on one when they're served every day. I've even grown to like bannocks."

"Thank God I'll soon be returning to London and a civilized breakfast of eggs, kidneys, toasted bread and bacon."

He swallowed another mouthful with difficulty and grimaced. Julian had nearly finished the entire bowl of oats when Mary returned. She set down a plate of eggs and bacon in front of Julian and whisked away the empty bowl.

"Ye'll do, Yer Lordship," Mary said with smug satisfaction. "Yer brother dinna do nearly as good the first time as ye did. Enjoy yer eggs." Still grinning, she shuffled back to the kitchen.

Sinjun and Christy burst into laughter. "You passed the test, Julian," Sinjun said, wiping tears from his eyes. "It took me a bit longer."

Mary appeared a moment later with a bowl of oats for Lara. "Would ye like some eggs, Lara?"

Lara looked at Julian's eggs and felt her stomach turn over. She had to look away quickly else she'd be forced to leave the table. She took a deep breath to steady her queasy stomach and shook her head.

"The oats is all I'll require this morning, Mary, thanks anyway." Lara managed to swallow two spoonfuls before she pushed the bowl aside.

Christy must have taken note of her sudden loss of appetite. "Perhaps tea and toasted bread would suit you this morning, Lara."

Lara's sent Christy a grateful look. "I believe it would." Margot started to rise. "Finish your breakfast, Margot, I'll get it myself."

Julian leaned over and asked, "Are you all right? Was I too rough on you last night?"

Lara sent him a reassuring smile. "I'm fine, Julian. I never eat much breakfast." She slid her chair back. "I'll be right back. I'm sure Mary won't mind if I invade her kitchen."

Christy rose. "I'll come with you. Mary may not be in the kitchen and you don't know where things are kept."

After they left the hall, Christy placed a hand on Lara's arm. "What is it, Lara? You look a little peckish this morning. Did Julian hurt you last night?"

"Oh, no, nothing like that," Lara assured her. "Julian would never hurt me. My stomach is somewhat queasy this morning, but I doubt it has anything to do with my wedding night."

Christy gave her a knowing look. "I recall that feeling. You're increasing, aren't you?"

"It's possible," Lara admitted. "I hope you don't think ill of me. You see, Julian and I have been married for many weeks now. We were wed according to Rom tradition and lived as man and wife even though Julian refused to acknowledge our marriage. It really hurt when he left me, as if I meant nothing to him. I was a Gypsy wench, not worthy of his exalted name."

"Sinjun already told me a little of your history together, but I didn't know Julian left you at the Gypsy camp."

Lara sighed, indulging in a generous dose of self-pity. "Julian never intended for us to meet again. We met by accident in London."

"When are you going to tell Julian about the baby?"

"When I'm sure," Lara hedged.

"Very well, I'll keep your secret," Christy vowed. "I wasn't honest with Sinjun, either, and it nearly cost me my marriage. Keep that in mind."

They entered the kitchen. "Ah, Mary is in the kitchen after all," Christy said. "We'll talk later."

Everyone but Sinjun and Julian drifted away from the hall after Lara and Christy left the table.

"Lara looks pale this morning, brother," Sinjun chided. "Did she get any rest at all last night?"

Julian had the grace to flush. "I may have been a little rough on her, but she didn't complain."

Sinjun rolled his eyes. "I doubt there's a woman in the world who would complain about being made love to by a Thornton."

"Speak for yourself, Sinjun," Julian said curtly. "I'm not the notorious rake and womanizer you are."

Sinjun laughed. "Those days are gone forever. Would you like to ride out with me today? I need to make sure the villagers are prepared for winter. New thatch was put on the roofs and the cottages repaired last year, but I want to check on their needs before the first snow arrives."

"You're a good landlord, Sinjun," Julian said. "I'm proud of you. I'll be ready to join you as soon as I tell Lara I'm leaving."

High on a hill above Glenmoor, a dozen men crouched behind boulders, spying on the castle.

"Are ye sure Scorpion is here, Crockett?"

"The Jackal assured me that we'd find him and his woman at Glenmoor, Dorks," Crockett said. "That stupid Lord Stanhope is so worried about his daughter that he doesn't have an inkling he's been feeding information to the Jackal. He knew we'd find them with the gypsies, and we did. Unfortunately Scorpion escaped before we got to him. The Highlands is the one place Scorpion believes himself safe." He snorted. "Little does he know."

"We ain't seen hide nor hair of him," Dorks complained. "He ain't left that damn fortress."

"Patience, Dorks. He can't leave without us seeing him."

"Then what?"

Crockett grinned. "Then we kill him."

Chapter 16

"Those fat sheep grazing on your land are a tribute to you, Sinjun," Julian said as he scanned the hillsides with an eye toward profit. "I'm also impressed with the horses you raise here. My mount is a particularly fine animal. You've done well, brother."

"That's a compliment coming from you, Julian," Sinjun replied. "One day my children will inherit all this. And Christy's clansmen will never fear hunger again. I was a selfish, hedonistic fool for neglecting my duty all those years when I prowled London as Lord Sin. Thank God Christy turned me around before I became a lost cause."

"We should both be grateful to Christy," Julian agreed. "She convinced Lara to marry me. How far to the village?"

"Not far."

"Can I have a closer look at the sheep first? Wool is bringing a high price in London."

"Of course. You won't find finer sheep anywhere in Scotland," Sinjun bragged.

*   *   *

"What the hell are they doing?" Dorks asked as he watched Julian and Sinjun veer off in another direction. "We've waited days for Scorpion to show himself, and now he's riding away from us."

"Don't worry, we'll get him," Crockett snarled. "Pass the word to the men. They're to arm themselves and be ready to ride at a moment's notice."

"What about the other one? The brother?"

"Kill him," Crockett ordered. "The Jackal don't want no witnesses."

After inspecting the sheep, Julian and Sinjun continued on to the village. "Your wool is of prime quality, Sinjun," Julian said. "Glenmoor appears to be in good shape financially now that you're no longer gambling or supporting an expensive mistress. My lectures must have gotten through to you."

Suddenly Sinjun's shoulders stiffened. "We have visitors."

Julian glanced up and saw a dozen riders heading toward them. They were close, too close, and coming fast. "They don't look especially friendly."

"They're not clansmen," Sinjun bit out. "Are you expecting company, Julian?"

Julian's lips flattened. "They must be the Jackal's henchmen. We can't fight them all, Sinjun. I suggest we run while we can."

Turning their mounts, they galloped full tilt back to Glenmoor. But they had waited too long. "They're nearly upon us," Julian yelled over the din of pounding hooves.

A loud report disturbed the silence. Moments later

a bullet whizzed past Julian's ear. "Bloody hell, they have flintlocks, and all we have between us are a pistol and a pair of short swords. Head back to the castle."

The castle was ahead of them, and Julian feared they would be cut down before they could reach their safe haven. The last thing he had wanted was to bring trouble to his brother and the Macdonalds. But it appeared that's exactly what he'd done. Both he and Sinjun were bent low over their horses' withers, trying to make as small a target as possible as they made a hasty retreat.

"We aren't done for yet, Julian," Sinjun yelled as another bullet flew dangerously close. "Look!"

Julian raised his head a fraction and saw a dozen or more Macdonald clansmen spilling out of the castle gate, wielding sufficient weapons to discourage the devil.

" 'Tis Rory and Gavin, leading some of their kinsmen," Sinjun said gleefully. "The guards patrolling the ramparts have seen us and sent out help."

The clansmen galloped past them to meet the enemy. Rory shot them a grin in passing. Both Julian and Sinjun wheeled their mounts to join in the fray.

When Crockett saw the fearsome band of savage Highlanders riding toward them, screaming a battle cry, he motioned for a full retreat. Turning tail, he and his men rode back into the hills, losing themselves in the thick trees, gorse and rocks.

"We'll never find them up there," Sinjun said, bringing the Highlanders to a halt.

Rory rode up to join them. "We routed them this time but ye ken 'twill happen again if ye go out without an escort. The bastards seem determined." He gave Julian a hard look. "Do ye expect them to give up and leave?"

Julian gave a snort of disgust. "Not bloody likely. But you're right about one thing. The bastards are determined to kill me. I left the Gypsies to avoid placing them in danger and I can do no less for my family. They'll keep plaguing Glenmoor and the clan until they have what they came after. Me."

"You're not going anywhere, Julian," Sinjun argued. "There are enough Macdonalds, Camerons, and Mackenzies to protect you and Lara."

"At what cost?" Julian charged.

Sinjun smiled. "Look around you, brother. Who in their right mind would want to do battle with a tribe of savage Highlanders? They're a warrior clan, and itching for a good fight."

Julian had to agree. The huge Scotsmen were indeed a ferocious lot. The assortment of battleaxes, claymores, swords, and flintlock rifles they wielded made them appear even more bloodthirsty than they probably were.

"You're right, Sinjun. With this lot behind us we have nothing to fear."

They encountered no more interference as they continued on to the village. Julian was impressed with Sinjun's easy way with the villagers and their friendliness toward him. His roguish brother had come a long way from his sinful past.

Lara and Christy were anxiously awaiting them when they returned to the castle some hours later. They were aware of the attack and had watched from the castle walls as the enemy was routed.

"Are you hurt?" Lara asked, throwing her arms around Julian. "Did you recognize them?"

"I didn't get a good look but I'd be willing to bet that Crockett was one of the men. He's the Jackal's toady, does all his dirty work."

"Do you think we've seen the last of them?"

Julian shot Sinjun a warning look. He saw no reason to worry the women. "I think Christy's clansmen scared them off for good. Nevertheless, I don't want either you or Christy to venture outside the curtain wall alone."

"I usually visit the sick in the village every Friday," Christy said, looking askance at Sinjun. "Shall I take a guard with me?"

"Several," Sinjun said. "At least until we're sure the ruffians have left the area. Rory is alerting the clansmen to danger now. Any strangers in the area will be reported to Rory."

"I'm starving," Julian said, changing the subject. "How soon before supper?"

"You have sufficient time to clean up," Christy said. "Dinner is in an hour. Mary said to tell you she's making something special for you tonight."

Julian rolled his eyes and groaned. "I'm almost afraid to ask. How many ways can she prepare oats?"

"Don't complain, Julian," Lara said, laughter coloring her words. "You're lucky Mary doesn't serve oats at every meal."

Everyone except Julian was amused. He wouldn't put it past Mary to do just that.

"I had a bath prepared for you," Lara said as they climbed the staircase to their chamber.

A wicked gleam darkened Julian's eyes. "Christy said we had an hour. What I have in mind won't take that long."

Lara opened the door to their chamber. "Don't you ever think of anything else?"

She squealed in surprise when Julian swept her from her feet and carried her into the chamber, slamming the door with his foot. "How *can* I think of anything else when a wild Gypsy tempts me beyond endurance?"

"Julian Thornton! I do no such thing."

"You don't have to do anything, sweeting," Julian rasped. "I find your scent, the way you walk, the way you look at me highly arousing." He spied the tub sitting before the fire and let Lara slide down his body. "You can scrub my back."

He began tearing off his clothing. From the corner of his eye he saw Lara watching him. He heard her sigh, a soft, sweet sound of longing, and he smiled. Soon he'd change that sigh into a scream of ecstasy. Driven by an urgent need of his own, Julian stepped into the tub and scrunched down into the water.

"Would you care to join me?" he asked hopefully. "I can make room for you."

"I've already bathed," Lara informed him. "Besides, I want to hear about the attack and what it means."

"Later," Julian hedged. He leaned forward, bringing his knees up to his chin. "Can you reach my back?"

Lara stared at his broad back a moment, then dropped to her knees behind him. She soaped a cloth and began scrubbing with more vigor than was warranted.

"Take it easy, love, I've grown rather fond of my hide."

"Sorry," Lara muttered, easing the pressure. A moment later she tossed the cloth into the bathwater and stood up. "Done. You can wash the rest yourself."

"Pity," Julian said, looking for all the world like a child who'd just been denied dessert.

Lara turned away while Julian completed his bath. She didn't dare watch him. She'd become aroused just scrubbing his back. Last night and again this morning she'd been so thoroughly sated she wouldn't have believed she could still feel desire scant hours later. The power Julian wielded over her senses was frightening. It wasn't right that she should love him so much while his feelings for her were tepid at best.

"Hand me the drying cloth," Julian said, rousing Lara from her silent ruminations.

Lara picked up the cloth she'd placed on the hearthstone to warm and offered it to him.

"Hold it out for me," Julian said, splashing water on the floor as he rose from the tub.

Lara stretched out the cloth, peering over the top at him. Her breath stalled in her lungs when he lunged from the tub and shook himself like an animal, a magnificent animal. He was even more impressive nude than he was dressed. Even at rest his manhood was imposing. But it didn't remain at rest for long. Her cheeks pinkened when it began to stir and stretch. Scant seconds later it was fully aroused. Thick and hard, it rose proud and defiant from a dark forest. Lara literally tossed the drying cloth at him and turned away. Letting him see how much she wanted him would only fuel his arrogance.

She felt his hand on her shoulder and stiffened. "Look at me, sweeting. There's no shame to feel desire for your husband."

Lara whirled around. " 'Tis not shame I feel, Julian. 'Tis regret. I wish . . ."

He dropped the drying cloth and drew her into his arms. "What do you wish, love?" She hesitated. "The truth, Lara. I'll give you whatever you desire, if it's within my power to do so," he added.

"I love you, Julian. I won't be happy until I make you love me."

He kissed her with such insistent fervor that her world spun with heady delight. She knew he loved her. Why couldn't he just say it?

"Perhaps my problem is that I care about you more than I should, more than I have a right to care about another woman," Julian whispered against her lips.

Stunned, Lara leaned back and stared at him. "What is that supposed to mean?"

"It's something I have to work out on my own, love."

She whirled away from him. "Diana and your dead child will always be closer to your heart than me and the children we have together."

"You're wrong, Lara."

"Prove it, Julian," Lara challenged. "Why can't you just say the words?"

"I've never made love to anyone like I make love to you. I've never felt the things I feel with you."

Lara frowned. "That's a good start. Was it so difficult?"

"Aye, for reasons you can't even guess."

"Tell me."

"I don't know how to explain this, love. It's difficult. Diana would be alive today if not for my involvement with the government. She was an innocent victim and now she's gone. The guilt I feel over her death is a tremendous burden."

"Why can't you move past Diana's death?"

"Because her death isn't the only guilt I carry. I didn't love her enough, Lara. I realize that now. I've known it for a very long time but didn't want to acknowledge it. My feelings for you are stronger than those tepid emotions I felt for Diana, and the knowledge eats at my soul. I caused an innocent woman's death, a woman I didn't love as much as she loved me. I can't put that behind me, not yet. Do you understand now what I'm trying to say?"

"Not really, Julian, tell me more."

He glanced over at the clock sitting on the mantle. "Not now. 'Tis late. We've barely time . . ." He bore her backward, toward the bed. Her knees hit the edge and he lifted her onto the mattress. "I've thought of nothing but this all day."

His expression was taut, his emotions concealed in the shadows created by the thick fringe of his lashes. A lock of hair fell over his forehead. Sweat gleamed on his bunched shoulder muscles and straining biceps as he leaned over her.

He undressed her slowly, arousing her with great passion and admirable restraint, making her body sing and her blood thicken. She was sobbing incoherently when he finally parted her thighs and rocked into her. She clung to him, riding the increasing tempo of his thrusts, gyrating her hips against the torrent of sensation buffeting her.

She tried to make it last, tried to will away the exquisite, wrenching pleasure that beat through her, in her, over her. But it was no use. She sobbed his name and let go, splintering, careening, spinning as pulse after pulse of intense sensations battered her.

She was floating in a sea of raw pleasure as Julian

drove into her one last time, then stiffened. His head snapped back and his hips ground against hers. A deep, body-wrenching convulsion set him free. He climaxed violently, then collapsed.

He was heavy, but Lara relished his heat and hardness. Her arms came around him, holding him tightly. After a few minutes, he raised up and pushed himself away.

"I always get a little wild when I make love to you," he rasped. "I didn't mean for it to go so fast."

"It's a good thing it did," Lara said, smiling. "We're already late for supper."

Julian gave an exhausted moan. "If I weren't so hungry I'd be tempted to skip the evening meal."

"You might be willing to go hungry but I'm not," Lara said, pushing herself out of bed. "Get up, lazybones."

They washed and dressed quickly and hurried downstairs. The buzz of conversation came to a halt and everyone stared at them when they entered the hall. Moments later the hall erupted in a cacophony of laughter and clapping. Blushing, Lara slipped into her chair and pulled Julian down beside her.

"Julian," she hissed into his ear. "Do you think they know why we're late?"

Julian spared her an indulgent grin. "They know exactly what kept us, love. Don't fret, it's expected of newlyweds."

Sinjun confirmed Julian's words.

"We started our meal without you and Lara," he said with a twinkle. "Actually, I'm surprised to see you made it at all."

"What? And miss Mary's surprise?" Julian scoffed.

"Ah, there ye be, me fine lord," Mary said, bustling

into the hall bearing something on a plate that didn't look edible. "I made this specially for yer pleasure." She set the plate before Julian with a flourish. "Enjoy, Yer Lordship."

Julian glanced down at the grayish blob quivering on the plate and wrinkled his nose. It looked and smelled like a bloated piece of offal. "What in bloody hell is *that*? Is this a joke, Sinjun?"

Sinjun nearly choked on his laughter. " 'Tis no joke, brother. Have you never heard of haggis? 'Tis a delicacy in these parts."

Julian glanced at Lara. She was trying not to laugh and losing the battle. "What in bloody hell is haggis? Is it edible?"

Mary glared at him. "I wouldna be serving it to ye if it wasna edible," she huffed. "I thought to honor ye by making ye a dish relished by all Highlanders."

"Do you know what's in this?" Julian asked in an aside to Lara. "Am I expected to eat it?"

" 'Tis a mixture of liver, oats, and spices cooked in a sheep's stomach," she replied. " 'Tisn't so bad once you get used to it."

"Cut into it, Julian," Sinjun urged. "Mary is a wonderful cook."

Julian didn't want to offend Mary, and rather than suffer her disappointment, he cut into the haggis. The revolting filling oozed from the stomach, assaulting Julian's senses with its odious scent. His gut clenched and he swallowed convulsively.

"Dig in, Yer Lordship," Mary said gleefully. "I've made enough for everyone."

As if on cue, the kitchen help brought out steaming platters of haggis, which they passed around the various tables. Julian's face paled as he watched the

Highlanders cut into their haggis and stuff it into their mouths with obvious relish.

"Go on," Sinjun urged. "It won't kill you, Julian."

"I'm not so sure about that," Julian muttered. Still and all, how bad could it be when everyone seemed to be enjoying it. Even Sinjun, who had eaten food prepared by the finest chefs in England, seemed to have acquired a taste for haggis.

Julian knew everyone, including Mary, was watching him. Girding himself for the worst, he placed a small portion in his mouth and chewed. Taste burst in his mouth, and it wasn't pleasant. He started to gag, thought better of it, and chewed slowly, aware that this was the greatest trial he had ever faced. If he spat out the haggis, everyone would laugh at him. If he swallowed, he wasn't sure he could keep it down.

"How is it?" Sinjun asked in a teasing tone. "Does it suit your palate?"

Unable to swallow, Julian spoke around the haggis that seemed to grow in his throat. " 'Tis . . . tolerable."

"Ye have to swallow it to enjoy it," Mary encouraged.

Julian forced the haggis down his throat, felt the mess hit his stomach, and turned visibly green. After a few deep breaths and a long swallow of ale, he was able to speak normally. " 'Tis not something I'd care to eat every day."

"Nor once a year. Nor again in your lifetime," Sinjun guffawed.

"Pass it down the table, someone will gladly eat your share," Christy said. Julian eagerly obliged. Mary appeared satisfied that Julian had at least tried it and retreated into the kitchen with a pleased smile curving her lips. He was relieved when the main course arrived moments later.

"That woman is diabolical," Julian muttered in Mary's wake. That only brought on more good-natured laughter.

As the meal progressed, Julian couldn't help thinking about the men who had been sent to kill him. Protecting Lara and his family came before any consideration for himself. He knew what he had to do.

After the prolonged meal, Julian saw Lara stifle a yawn. He promptly excused them and took her off to bed. The moment the door closed behind him, Lara turned on him, all signs of exhaustion vanished.

"You're not getting off that easily, Julian. You never did tell me what you intended to do about the attack. They won't go away, you know. They're just waiting for you to leave the castle again. I can't bear to see you killed."

Julian plowed his fingers through his hair in a distracted manner. "Remaining at Glenmoor could endanger you and my family. Those men would have killed Sinjun today and thought nothing of it. I refuse to become a virtual prisoner within the walls of Glenmoor. I have to leave. Sinjun offered his Highlanders as escort should I decide to return to London."

"When would we leave?"

"You mean when would *I* leave," Julian corrected. "You're not going anywhere until the Jackal and his cohorts are in prison. They're not above using you to get to me."

"You're not going anywhere without me," Lara said, giving her head a stubborn shake.

"Don't make this any harder than it is, love. Your life is precious to me. You'll stay here with Sinjun and Christy until I say 'tis safe to leave."

"We'll see," Lara muttered as she began to undress. A few minutes later she slid naked beneath the sheets.

Julian undressed and joined her. His arms went around her and he pulled her close. "Sleep, love. You look exhausted. We'll decide what's to be done later."

A week passed with no further attempts on Julian's life. Whenever he left the protection of Glenmoor, enough Highlanders accompanied him to discourage even the bravest of men. At the end of the week the consensus was that danger no longer existed, that the Jackal's men, fearing the Highlanders, had left. Neither hide nor hair had been seen of them since that initial attack.

Christy decided it was safe to travel to Inverness for winter supplies and consulted with Sinjun. Sinjun agreed and recruited several burly clansmen to accompany them.

Lara was looking forward to visiting Inverness. It was a fairly large city with many shops, and she was in need of warm clothing.

They started out early in the morning. Julian, Sinjun and the women rode beside the Highlanders. A wagon to carry supplies back to Glenmoor followed.

They reached the bustling city shortly before the noon hour. Lara's stomach was grumbling so loudly that when she saw a pie seller hawking his wares, she asked Julian to buy her a meat pie. Julian complied, buying pies for everyone. He laughed as she gobbled down the savory pastry and licked her fingers afterward.

"Hungry were you?" he teased.

"Famished." She and Christy exchanged meaningful looks, then joined in the laughter. Soon she'd have to tell Julian about the baby, but not yet. She wanted to give him every opportunity to declare his love first.

"Oh look," Lara said, pointing to the shop bearing the sign of a mantua maker. "What a lovely fur-lined cloak in the window. Can we stop there?"

"It's right next to the weaver's shop where I buy woolen material," Christy said. She looked at Julian. "Is it all right if Lara and I shop while you and Sinjun go about your business?"

"Only if guards accompany you," Julian replied, looking to Sinjun for confirmation.

"Aye," Sinjun agreed. "Normally the women would be safe in Inverness, but no sense taking chances. We've seen no sign of the Jackal's men, but that doesn't mean they're not still around. Gavin and three other men will accompany them while they shop."

The party split up then, four men tagging along with the women and the rest forming a protective ring around Julian.

"I knew if we bided our time we'd find the opportunity we've been waiting for," Crockett said gleefully.

Crockett and Dorks were disguised in plaids and bonnets, making them difficult to differentiate from the townspeople going about their business on this fine market day. "They didn't even know they were being followed," Crockett continued. "Had we been stupid and brought all our men to town, we would have been conspicuous, but just the two of us raised no suspicion."

"What now?" Dorks asked. "What can two men accomplish with those savage Highlanders protecting Scorpion?"

" 'Twould be foolhardy to attack Scorpion with the odds against us, but we might fare better with his woman. Once we have her, Scorpion will follow."

"Look!" Crockett crowed, "the group is splitting up. Come on, keep the wench in your sights."

They turned the corner and dogged the women's trail. With their bonnets pulled low over their foreheads, they followed on foot, garnering scant attention.

"The Gypsy wench is entering the mantua maker shop, and the Macdonald laird is going into the weaver's shop," Dorks hissed.

Crockett grinned delightedly. "Everything is working in our favor. Hie yerself to the livery and rent a closed coach. Bring it around to the alley behind the shops. Leave the rest to me."

Dorks didn't question his superior as he sprinted off down the street to do Crockett's bidding.

The cloak in the shop window was exactly what Lara wanted. "Are you coming in with me?" she asked Christy.

"Why don't you buy your cloak and browse around a bit while I duck into the weaver's shop and purchase the woolen material I need. I'll join you when I'm finished."

She turned to Gavin. "Is that all right, Gavin?"

Gavin thought a moment, then nodded. "The shops are side by side, two men can wait for ye outside the weaver's shop and the other two can wait for Lara outside the mantua maker's."

"I won't be long, Lara," Christy promised. "Take all the time you need. Our husbands will spend hours examining the weapons Sinjun intends to purchase as replacements for the old and obsolete ones in our armory."

Lara entered the shop and looked around, delighted with the array of ready-made clothing. A small, birdlike woman came from behind a curtain and flitted around her.

"How may I help ye, my lady?"

"That cloak in the window. I'd like to purchase it."

" 'Tis of the finest quality, and feel the fur. 'Twill be warm and soft against yer tender skin."

"How much?"

They haggled over the price a few moments before reaching a mutually satisfying conclusion.

"I'll wear it," Lara said, taking off her old cloak and replacing it with the new one. "Wrap up the old one, I'll take it with me. Show me what you have in ready-made gowns."

"This way, my lady," the shopkeeper said, leading Lara to a corner of the shop where several gowns were displayed.

Lara heard the shop door open and close but paid it little heed as she inspected the gowns.

"Excuse me a moment, my lady," the shopkeeper said, "while I take care of the gentleman's needs. Take yer time. Browse to yer heart's content."

Lara found two gowns that would suit her and started sorting through a pile of petticoats. A strange sound behind her caught her attention and she turned slowly, gripped by a sudden chill. Her gaze scanned the small shop for the shopkeeper but failed to find her. She saw the man who had entered while she was browsing and a frisson of fear slid down her spine. Clutching her cloak about her, she sidled toward the door.

Suddenly the man was upon her, his large hand covering her mouth. "Be quiet, wench!" he hissed.

Lara struggled as he dragged her toward the curtain in the back, but it did little good. He was so much stronger than she. Then she spied the shopkeeper lying on the floor behind the counter and fear escalated to raw panic. Had he killed the woman? She prayed not. What did he want with her?

The ruffian pulled her through the curtain toward a rear door, and suddenly it dawned on Lara what was happening and why.

Protesting violently, Lara was shoved through the back door and hustled into a coach waiting in the alley. The ruffian relaxed his hold on her mouth long enough for Lara to gather a scream in her throat. Unfortunately it never left her mouth. Her attacker realized what she intended and let his fist fly against her jaw. Then she knew no more.

Christy hummed to herself as she left the weaver's shop. She had purchased all the fine woolens she needed as well as flannel to make swaddling clothes for the baby, and she was eager to tell Lara about her purchases. The cloak Lara coveted was gone from the window, she noted as she opened the door and stepped inside.

The shop was empty. Alarm shot through her. She called Lara's name. No answer was forthcoming. The Highlanders must have sensed her panic, for they rushed inside behind Christy.

"What is it?" Gavin asked. "Where's Lara?"

"I don't know," Christy answered.

"She dinna leave the shop by the front door," one of the Highlanders offered.

"Search the shop," Gavin ordered.

The men spread out. Gavin found the unconscious shopkeeper lying behind the counter.

"Is she dead?" Christy asked, falling to her knees beside the woman.

"She's alive," Gavin said on a note of relief. "She's beginning to come around."

The woman opened her eyes and tried to focus on Christy's face. "Who are ye?" she whispered.

"The Macdonald laird from Glenmoor. What happened to the woman who bought the cloak from you?"

"Och, I dinna know. A man came into the shop while she was browsing. I went over to speak with him and he struck me."

"Can ye identify him?" Gavin asked.

"Och, nay, I dinna see his face."

Consumed by misery, Christy sat back on her heels. Four strong Highlanders hadn't been able to protect one small woman. And now Lara was gone.

How was she ever going to tell Julian?

Chapter 17

"**S**he's what!" Julian roared when told of Lara's abduction. "Where was everyone when my wife was abducted? How could it happen beneath your very noses?"

"We were right outside the door," Gavin defended. "Only one other customer went inside. I peeked through the door and saw the customer speaking with the shopkeeper and Lara browsing through a stack of female frippery. Nothing looked amiss to me so we remained at our stations outside the door."

Julian grit his teeth in frustration. "I checked behind the curtain and found the rear exit. 'Tis obvious he took Lara out that way. Where's the shopkeeper?"

"Over here, Julian," Christy called. "The poor woman is just coming around. She received a nasty clout on the head."

Julian knelt beside the woman. Christy helped her into a sitting position. The woman's eyes were still dilated and she moaned softly as Christy supported her in her arms.

"Can you tell me what happened to my wife?" Julian asked in a gentle voice. He wanted to yell and

scream but was astute enough to realize his bluster-
ing would only frighten the injured woman.

"Och, I dinna know," the woman wailed. "One
minute I was speaking to a customer who had entered behind yer wife and the next I felt a crushing
pain in me head. I knew nothing more until I awoke
and found the Macdonald laird leaning over me."

"What did the man look like? Can you describe
him?"

"Och, nay, my lord, I dinna get a good look at him.
He was wearing a plaid and bonnet and looked like a
Highlander. I'm sorry, my lord," she wailed, hiding
her face in her hands. "Why would anyone want to
abduct yer wife?"

Julian's face hardened. " 'Tis a long story." He
fished in his pocket and dug out a gold sovereign,
pressing it into the shopkeeper's hand. "For your
trouble and pain, my good woman."

"I hope ye find yer wife, my lord. Such a pretty little thing."

"Aye," Julian muttered, his voice harsh with determination.

Sinjun entered the shop and pushed his way
through the Highlanders crowded around Julian.
"I've checked the area, Julian, and no one seems to
know anything. But one piece of information stuck
out in my mind."

"Out with it, man!" Julian exploded.

"A woman said she saw a closed coach speed from
the alley about the time Lara was abducted. She said
it nearly ran her down. When I questioned others
about it, they too remembered seeing a black coach
barreling down the street."

"Bloody hell! The bastards who attacked us didn't

go away like we thought. They've been holed up somewhere spying on Glenmoor, biding their time for the right opportunity to strike. When they couldn't get to me, they took Lara. They were that certain I'd follow."

"What are you going to do?" Sinjun asked worriedly.

Julian's jaw firmed. One had but to look into his eyes to see the dark promise of retribution burning within their glowing depths. "I'm going to get my wife. And God help those responsible for her abduction."

"Amen," Sinjun said. "Do you think they took her to London?"

"I have to believe that's where they took her. It makes sense. The Jackal wants to lure me to London where I'll be accessible to his hired thugs. He knows that as long as he has Lara I won't continue my investigation."

"I'll go with you," Sinjun offered.

"No. I've already placed your family in danger by coming here. I was naive to think the Jackal would give up on me. Stay here with your wife and children, Sinjun. I appreciate your offer but I'd rest easier knowing my life is the only one at risk."

"Will you ask Lord Randall for help?"

"I'm not sure that would be a wise thing to do. I'll do nothing to anger the Jackal and place Lara's life in more danger than it is now."

Julian strode out of the shop as if the devil were on his tail. One of the Highlanders handed him his reins. "I'm for Glenmoor," he told Sinjun as he leaped into the saddle. "Then I'm off to London to confront Lara's father. If that bastard knows anything about

Lara's abduction, his life is forfeit. I'll find Lara if it's the last thing I do."

Lara regained her wits slowly. Her jaw hurt like the very devil and her head spun dizzily. The only thing she knew for sure was that she was inside a coach that was rattling down the road at breakneck speed, bouncing her about. She tried to steady herself against the seat and collided with a solid form.

Her abductor!

She raised her head and looked into the hard, colorless eyes of a man she recognized.

Crockett.

"Why?" she asked tremulously.

"Yer awake," he growled.

"Where are you taking me?"

"Yer a nosy wench. Don't fret none, I ain't gonna hurt you. What will happen to ye once ye've outlived yer usefulness is another matter. 'Tis for the Jackal to decide."

A shiver slithered down Lara's spine. "You're taking me to London, aren't you? Am I finally to meet the Jackal?"

"Mayhap."

"What does he want from me?"

"Nothing. 'Tis Scorpion he wants. Yer the bait to lure him."

"I don't know any Scorpion. You've made a mistake."

"The Jackal doesn't make mistakes, wench," he snarled. "Julian Thornton, the Earl of Mansfield, is Scorpion, right enough."

"If Julian is Scorpion, you're making a big mistake

thinking he'll come after me. He doesn't care for me all that much."

Crockett gave a bark of laughter. "Yer crazy if ye think that, wench. Now shut up, ye talk too much."

Lara's mouth snapped shut. Not because she was ordered to do so but because she needed time to think. Julian *would* come after her, she knew it as well as she knew her own name. She loved him so much, yet it appeared that she was to be the instrument of his death. She wished, no, prayed, that he would remain at Glenmoor and escape the trap set for him.

Perhaps she could devise her own escape. Traveling all the way to London with only Crockett and the driver of the coach to guard her presented many interesting possibilities. Surely she could outsmart two men who had more brawn than brains. She spent the next hours planning her escape, only to have her hopes dashed when a dozen men joined them at the coaching inn where they stopped to change horses and purchase food.

"Who are those men?" Lara asked. They all seemed to be under Crockett's authority.

"They're my men," Crockett bragged. "They'll be handsomely rewarded for this day's work once we reach London."

"So you *are* taking me to London."

Crockett cursed beneath his breath. "I don't suppose it matters that ye know where we're taking ye." He handed her a pastry. "Eat up, I don't know when another meal will be forthcoming."

Hunger pangs convinced Lara to eat the greasy tart. She was eating for two now and had to nourish her babe.

"Won't we be stopping for the night?" she asked, licking the crumbs from her fingers.

"Too dangerous."

"But I have to . . ." She bit her lip and blushed.

"The jakes are behind the inn," Crockett said. "I'll escort ye."

He opened the door and stepped down. Lara followed. Outside the coach at last, she thought gleefully as she scanned the area for a source of help. The stable boy came into view. Perhaps she could catch his eye, or call out to him to let him know she was being abducted. Unfortunately the stable boy was so busy with the horses, he didn't even look in her direction. Nevertheless, it wouldn't hurt to scream.

"I wouldn't if I were ye, wench," Crockett growled. "Not if ye value the lad's life."

"You wouldn't! He's an innocent boy."

"Aye, a boy who means nothing to me."

Lara gasped, realizing that she was dealing with a heartless madman. She finished her business quickly, stopped briefly to wash her hands and face in a barrel of rainwater, and reluctantly returned to the coach. When she hesitated at the door, she was unceremoniously tumbled inside by an impatient Crockett.

Lara scooted into the far corner, rested her head against the squabs, and pulled her cloak tightly about her. She was exhausted. But far worse than exhaustion, the greasy tart had upset her fragile stomach, and nausea plagued her. As the coach rolled off into the night, Lara's stomach roiled dangerously, until she could no longer control the appalling urge to vomit. She sat up and clapped a hand over her mouth.

"What ails ye now, wench? Can't ye see I'm trying to sleep?"

"I'm sick," Lara moaned. "If we don't stop now, I'll foul the coach."

"Bloody hell!" Crockett blasted. "Is this a trick?"

The gagging sound she made must have convinced him, for he rapped on the roof and the coach rolled to a stop. One of the outriders yanked open the door. "What's amiss?"

"The wench is sick," Crockett said, moving aside as Lara stumbled out of the coach. "Watch her. I don't know what she has up her sleeve but 'tis not going to work."

Lara was beyond caring what Crockett said or did as she headed for the side of the road. Crossing her arms over her belly, she bent over and lost the contents of her stomach. When she finished, she ripped a ruffle from her petticoat and wiped her mouth. One of Crockett's men must have felt sorry for her, for he offered his water pouch. Lara accepted gratefully. She poured water on the scrap of cloth and cleaned her hands and face, then she rinsed out her mouth and drank deeply.

"What's keeping ye?" Crockett hollered from the coach.

"Are ye ready?" the guard asked.

"Thank you," Lara said. "You seem like a reasonable man. Would you help me escape?"

The man cast a nervous glance over her shoulder and saw Crockett watching him. "I'm loyal to Crockett." Grasping her arm, he turned her around and shoved her toward the coach. "Get ye inside, wench."

So much for kindness, Lara thought as she climbed inside the coach and settled in the far corner.

"I've changed my mind," Crockett said. "There's

another inn down the road. My men could use the rest, and so could I. Besides, I don't fancy spending the night with a sick woman in the coach."

Lara said nothing lest Crockett change his mind. She felt terrible and wanted to do nothing to harm her unborn child. Lara didn't speak again until they reached the inn and Crockett dragged her inside.

"I'd like a bath," she said in her haughtiest tone after Crockett paid for two rooms. "Please have someone bring a tub and hot water to my room."

"That'll be extra," the innkeeper said.

Crockett shot her a venomous look and placed another coin on the counter. "Prepare a bath for the lady." Then he grasped Lara's arm and pulled her up the stairs.

"I'm setting a guard outside yer door," he said as he opened the door and shoved her inside. "I'll be in the room next to yers, and this is the second floor so don't even think about leaving through the window." He made for the door. "Enjoy yer bath, wench." He paused at the door and stared at her. "Yer a fetching little piece. If I wasn't afraid of the Jackal I'd sample yer wares myself."

"Get out!" Lara hissed. "Julian will kill you if you touch me."

Crockett's laughter followed him out of the room. Lara slammed the door and leaned against it. She was still there when servants arrived with the tub and hot water.

Four days later they reached the English border. After that first night, Crockett decided that stopping at inns was less dangerous than traveling on snow-covered roads at night.

Once they crossed the English border the snow turned to chilling rain. Not for the first time since her ordeal began, Lara was grateful for the fur-lined cloak she'd purchased in Inverness. That thought brought forth another. She hoped the shopkeeper hadn't suffered any permanent injury from the blow Crockett's henchman had dealt her.

They were well into England now, and Crockett sought rooms at an inn on the outskirts of Coventry. Soon they would reach London and Lara was desperate to escape before meeting the Jackal.

Lara had learned that the men who had accompanied Crockett to the Highlands were smugglers from his ship. Once they reached England, the men, except for Dorks, who was driving the coach, parted company with them. Crockett told her they were returning to their ship, which awaited them in a hidden cove on the Cornish coast. Crockett and Dorks were to join them once Lara was delivered into the Jackal's hands.

Lara dragged her feet into the inn. She was exhausted, ill, and barely able to function. Apparently she was too slow for Crockett's liking. Grasping her arm, he all but dragged her through the door. She almost collapsed when he released her and used a chair to steady herself. She had eaten little of the unappetizing food Crockett provided for her and had lost weight. Her face was noticeably thinner, and purple shadows smudged the delicate skin beneath her eyes.

Once Crockett had secured their rooms he shoved

Lara toward the stairs with unnecessary roughness. Dorks followed behind them. Neither Lara, Crockett, nor Dorks noticed the young Rom sitting in the corner near the fire, nursing a flagon of ale. But he saw them and recognized both men as well as Lara. He waited until they disappeared up the staircase, then followed. Lurking in the shadows, he saw Crockett escort Lara inside a room and slam the door behind her.

He hugged the wall, not liking what he saw. A rough looking man settled down before Lara's door and placed his loaded pistol in his lap. The young Rom slunk back down the stairs, returning to his seat before the fire. He had no weapon, and he wasn't as foolish as he had once been. He had done something incredibly stupid, and because of it was no longer welcomed by his people.

Rondo remained in the common room the entire night. He was awake and watchful the following morning when Crockett descended the stairs and ordered breakfast for his party. Moments later Rondo sidled out the door, saddled his horse, and waited. He'd done Lara a terrible wrong and had accepted his punishment. Now fate was giving him a chance to right that wrong. Obviously Lara was in deep trouble and he was to blame.

He'd never meant Lara harm. True, he had been jealous of Drago and had betrayed him, and he sincerely regretted it. Now it was up to him to help Lara.

Lara lay on the bed fully clothed. She hadn't bothered to undress any of the nights since she'd been abducted, for Crockett had a habit of barging into her room each morning and dragging her out of bed so they could be on their way. This morning was no different. The door burst open. Crockett entered.

"Time to leave," he growled. "I sent a messenger to the Jackal. He's expecting us in London tonight."

Lara raised up on her elbows. Her head started to spin. "I don't feel well."

Crockett grabbed her arm and pulled her to her feet. "Ye haven't been hurt yet but yer trying my patience."

"Who is the Jackal and what does he want with me?"

"Ye'll find out soon enough. I had the cook wrap up something for ye to eat in the coach. Come along, now, no dawdling."

Lara was hustled downstairs and into the coach. Crockett climbed in after her and thrust a greasy cloth sack into her hands. "Eat, it may be all ye'll get for a while."

The smell made Lara nauseous. She set the sack aside. "I'm not hungry."

Crockett shrugged. "Suit yerself."

The day dragged by endlessly. Lara knew they were getting close to London for she recognized familiar landmarks. She was hungry, but she still couldn't stomach the food Crockett had offered.

Lara hugged the secret of Julian's child to herself, aware of the pressure on her to save the innocent babe she carried. She wanted this child fiercely, and hoped Julian would want it once she told him. Perhaps having a baby with her would be exactly what Julian needed to finally relegate Diana to his past, where she belonged.

An ominous darkness shrouded the streets of London as the coach lumbered toward the waterfront.

Lara knew instinctively that the section of town through which they traveled was one of the worst London had to offer. Prostitutes openly plied their trade on street corners and footpads prowled for likely victims. Warehouses interspersed with disreputable saloons lined the litter-strewn streets, and the smell of rotting garbage mixed with tangy salt air assaulted Lara's senses.

"Where are you taking me?" Lara asked.

"Where ye'll be safe while we wait for Scorpion to show up."

"What makes you think he'll show up? Maybe you've got the wrong man."

Crockett sent her a knowing grin. "He'll show up."

The coach pulled into the yawning maw of a dark alley and rattled to a stop. Lara looked out the window at a blank wooden wall.

"What is this place?"

Crockett opened the door and stepped down. Then he grasped Lara's arm and pulled her out of the coach. A rat scurried past; Lara shrieked in surprise. Bile rose in her throat; the stench was nearly unbearable.

"Come along with ye," Crockett said, all but dragging her down the alley.

Lara feared they were going to murder her and leave her body for the rats. Then she saw Crockett push open a door she hadn't noticed before and she breathed a little easier.

He pulled her forward and sent her through the opening. "In ye go, wench."

Dorks, having found a lantern somewhere, pushed past them to light their way. The glow revealed an abandoned warehouse. The room was cavernous. The play of shadow and light against the filthy walls made it appear sinister and foreboding. Empty boxes and crates lay haphazardly about. The musty smell of mold and rotting wood nearly gagged her.

"Keep moving," Crockett said.

He prodded her across the room to a closed door. Flinging it open, he shoved her inside. Lara stumbled and fell, catching herself with her hands to cushion the fall. She scrambled to her knees.

"Ye'll be safe enough here," Crockett growled.

"You're going to leave me here?"

"For the time being. I don't know what the Jackal has planned for ye once he gets rid of Scorpion. I doubt he'll let ye live. Ye know too much about his operation."

"Julian won't walk into the Jackal's trap. He's too smart."

He laughed. "Tell that to the Jackal. I'm going back to sea soon. Smuggling is what I do best." Still laughing, he headed out the door.

"Wait! Don't leave me in the dark."

Crockett considered her request, then spoke to Dorks. Dorks disappeared, returning moments later with another lantern. He set it down on an upturned crate.

Lara's voice rose on a note of panic. "When can I expect the Jackal?" She didn't want to stay in this place. She didn't want to lure Julian to his death. She had to escape.

"He'll arrive when he's good and ready." Dorks handed Crockett the sack of food Lara had rejected that morning and he set it next to the lantern. "Here's something in case ye get hungry. Mayhap 'twill be more to yer liking when hunger gnaws at yer innards."

Lara swallowed hard against the panic rising in her chest as Crockett and Dorks exited and slammed the door behind them. The scrape of a wooden bar being lowered into place sent a bolt of fear through her. What if the Jackal didn't come? Would this warehouse become her tomb? Her hands flew to her stomach. No! She wouldn't accept death meekly. She'd live to give Julian his child.

Lara was so exhausted she couldn't think straight. The trip to London had been grueling. Gathering her reserves, she picked up the lantern and conducted a thorough search of the room. It appeared to have once been an office, for a rickety desk and broken chair still remained. Two wooden crates sat beneath a window that had been boarded up. More crates were scattered about the room.

Lara sat down on one of the crates to think. The window was too high up for her to reach, even if she could knock out the boards nailed across it. She eyed the crates beneath it with speculation. She could reach the window if she stood on the crate, she reflected, but that still didn't solve her problem. There seemed to be nothing available to use as a battering ram against the window.

Tired, so very tired. Perhaps if she rested for a bit she'd be able to come up with an idea. Pushing the two crates together, she lay down and closed her eyes. Sleep came almost immediately.

Lara awoke to daylight poking through the cracks of the boarded-up window and the terrible feeling that she was doomed to die here. She sat up, suddenly aware that she was hungry. Her gaze fell on the sack of food Crockett had left for her. With a grimace of distaste, she opened the sack and rummaged about for something that might agree with her stomach. She found two pieces of dark bread among the greasy fare and nibbled on one of them.

The lantern had burned low, but enough light seeped through the cracks of the boarded window for Lara to see just what she was up against, and it didn't look hopeful. There had to be something she could do, but what?

Julian reached London a day behind Lara. He'd ridden like the very devil, stopping a few hours during the darkest part of night to sleep on the hard ground. Exhausted and haggard, Julian stopped first at the Stanhope residence.

Jeevers opened the door to Julian's insistent rapping and Julian barged inside, his expression grim.

"Where's Stanhope?"

"Lord Mansfield, is something amiss? Lord Stanhope will be pleased to see you. Is Lady Lara with you?"

"A great deal is amiss. I'm hoping Stanhope can clear up the matter. Is he home? I need to see him immediately."

A door opened off the foyer and Stanhope stepped out. "I'll handle this, Jeevers, thank you. Come inside my study, Mansfield, I'm quite anxious to speak with you."

"And I with you," Julian said harshly. "Where's Lara?"

Shock, then fear marched across Stanhope's face.

"Are you telling me my daughter isn't with you? You're the one who dragged her away from London without so much as a by-your-leave. I'll see you in hell if Lara has come to harm because of you."

Julian's probing gaze searched Stanhope's face. "I was just going to say the same about you."

"Why would you say that? Lara is my daughter, I love her."

"Lara is my wife, and I love her."

The moment the words were spoken Julian realized he meant them. He loved Lara. Loved her as he'd never loved Diana, although he cared for Diana, although he had fully committed himself to being an excellent husband to her. But his passion for Lara was a powerfully compelling force within him. The kind that ate a man alive. He should know, he'd experienced it often enough. Lara was the air he breathed and the water he drank. She was imbued with life and spirit and a wildness that made his heart sing. He cursed himself for not recognizing love when he was first smitten.

"What happened to Lara? Why isn't she with you? You say she is your wife? 'Tis a good thing, else I would have demanded that you marry my daughter after you ruined her."

"Lara and I were married in Scotland, at my brother's estate. She was kidnapped ten days ago."

Stanhope turned pale as death. "Kidnapped? Why? Who would do such a thing?"

"Have you no idea?" Julian queried.

"Me? What in God's name are you talking about? Why would I know anything about my daughter's kidnapping? Only a monster would do such a thing."

Julian found it difficult to believe Stanhope had anything to do with Lara's kidnapping. But there was only one way to learn the truth.

"How deeply involved are you with the smugglers operating off the English coast?" he asked bluntly.

"What! Are you mad? I know nothing about smugglers. I would never consort with men of that ilk. I have all the money I need, why would I resort to smuggling?"

Julian was inclined to believe him, but not entirely. "What about Lord Tolliver? You and Tolliver seem especially close lately. He's been a frequent visitor in your home."

Stanhope appeared perplexed. "What does Tolliver have to do with any of this? We're pushing a bill through Parliament."

"Have you ever heard of Scorpion?"

"Are you referring to Scorpion the traitor? Tolliver suspects that Scorpion is the brains behind a smuggling ring. He asked me to keep my ears and eyes open." He paused, as if comprehension finally dawned. "Are you insinuating that Tolliver is Scorpion?"

"No, of course not. I know for a fact that Tolliver is *not* Scorpion."

Stanhope's eyes narrowed. "How can you be sure?"

"Because I'm Scorpion. I've been an agent for the crown for some time, working under Lord Randall. My current assignment is to bring the Jackal to justice. Regrettably, Lara got caught in the middle."

"You'd better explain yourself, Mansfield," Stanhope demanded harshly.

Julian quickly explained how he and Lara had met.

"So my daughter saved your life and married you in a Gypsy ritual," Stanhope mused after Julian finished speaking. "But you didn't consider it legal. I'll have something to say about your appalling conduct once this is over, but right now my daughter's life is in danger and that's my primary concern. Tell me why Lara was kidnapped and by whom."

"The reason I fled London with Lara was that the Jackal noted my interest in your daughter and intended to use her to get to me. You see, the bastard had figured out my identity and set out to kill me before I had enough evidence to put a noose around his neck. Lara and I hid for a time with Pietro and Ramona, then fled to Scotland when one of their people betrayed us."

"Are you telling me that Lara's life is in danger because someone wants you dead?"

"Exactly. That someone is the Jackal."

"And you suspect Tolliver of being the Jackal?"

"What do you know of Tolliver's finances?"

"A few years ago Tolliver's pockets were empty. Somehow he recouped his losses and of late seems well heeled."

Julian digested that piece of information, then asked, "What about Dunbar, Lord Crawford's second son?"

"Don't know anything about Dunbar. Seems a likable chap. Is he a suspect?"

"Both he and Tolliver have access to privileged information."

"I'll do anything to help. My daughter means more to me than all my wealth. I'll meet any ransom the Jackal demands."

" 'Tis not a matter of ransom," Julian said. "They want me, not money."

"What are you going to do?"

"I'm going home to wait for a message from the Jackal. I'll do whatever it takes to free Lara."

"Even at the risk of your own life?"

Julian smiled grimly. "Even at the risk of my own life, but I hope it won't come to that."

"Are you going to inform Randall of the latest development? What can I do to help?"

"Randall would insist upon dispatching dragoons to aid me. I fear they would anger the Jackal and further endanger Lara's life. Remain here, where I can reach you. I'll send word around when I hear from the Jackal. I suspect he'll demand that I meet him in some disreputable section of town, unarmed and alone."

"I want to come with you."

"No. I need you here. I'll let you know where I'm to meet the Jackal and you can take the information to Randall." His face hardened. "The Jackal wants me and he shall have me."

"Keep my daughter safe, Mansfield," Stanhope pleaded. "I never knew my daughter the first thirteen years of her life. She's been a blessing to me these last years. I can't lose her now."

"Neither can I," Julian muttered through clenched teeth.

Chapter 18

J ulian prowled his study, waiting for the message
that would direct him to Lara. He'd already
alerted his staff, and Farthingale was stationed at
the door, waiting for further developments. The Jackal
had probably known the very minute he'd returned to
London, and that he'd called on Lord Stanhope.

Finding the man responsible for Diana's death was
no longer a priority in Julian's life. He still wanted
the bastard punished, but not at the expense of a
loved one. At long last he was able to put Diana's
death behind him, and it felt damn good. He was free
now to give his heart to Lara without reservations.
But was he too late?

Farthingale called to him from the other side of the
door and Julian grew instantly alert. He reached the
door in two long strides and flung it open.

"The message you've been waiting for has arrived,
Lord Mansfield," Farthingale said, handing a folded
sheet of paper to Julian.

"Did you detain the messenger?"

"Aye, my lord. One of the footmen has him under
restraint. But I fear he's not what you're expecting."

"Bring him in," Julian bit out.

Farthingale stood aside as a brawny footman dragged forth a scrawny street lad no more than a dozen years old. He was small, wiry, belligerent, and incredibly filthy.

"I ain't done nothin'!" the lad whined as he tried to shake himself free of his captor. "Some bloke give me a shilling to deliver a note to Lord Mansfield. That ain't no crime."

"I'm Lord Mansfield," Julian said. "I'm not going to hurt you, lad. Can you describe the person who gave you the note?"

"I never seen his face. I swear. He stayed inside his fancy coach the whole time. 'Twas his driver what give me the note and shilling. That's a lot of blunt. I ain't gonna give it up."

"I'm not asking for your blunt, lad. Is that all you can tell me? What about the coach? Did it bear a coat of arms?"

"If ye mean fancy markings on the side, no, it were plain black. Can I go now?"

"Let him go, Jenkins," Julian told the footman. "The lad knows nothing of value. See that he's fed before you turn him loose."

"Thank ye, milord, thank ye," the lad said, bobbing his head respectfully.

Jenkins hauled the boy away. "Is there anything I can do, my lord?" Farthingale asked.

"Pray, Farthingale. Please wait outside the door. As soon as I read the note, I'll need to send a message around to Lord Stanhope. You're to give it to a footman to deliver with all due haste."

"I understand, my lord," Farthingale said as he let himself out of the room and closed the door behind him.

Julian stared at the note, almost fearing to read it. Though he knew he was being fanciful, he imagined he could feel evil vibes emanating from the sheet of paper. His hands shook as he unfolded the note. The words leaped out at him. It was no more or no less than he expected.

Short and to the point, the message stated that if he wanted his Gypsy wench to remain alive and healthy, he should come to the abandoned textile warehouse on the waterfront at ten that night. There was no signature but none was needed. It was from the Jackal.

Julian spit out a curse. There was nothing in the note to indicate that Lara hadn't been harmed. Shaking with anger, he crumbled the paper in his fist and tossed it into the hearth.

Julian knew exactly where to find the abandoned textile warehouse. It was in the seediest part of town, a place so dangerous that few ventured there at night except for hardened thugs and cutthroats. The thought of Lara in such a place sent tremors of panic racing down his spine. Sweet, innocent Lara. She knew nothing about the dregs of London society, and the experience could traumatize her.

He looked at his watch. Nine o'clock. He had one hour to prepare for the encounter that might very well result in his death. Before he left, he dashed out a note to Stanhope and gave it to Farthingale to send on its way. If all went well, Randall would arrive with dragoons in time to help, but not too soon to ruin his rescue attempt.

Lara had no conception of time. She knew it had begun to rain for she heard it splattering against the side of the building. When hunger struck again, she nibbled on the remaining hunk of stale bread from the sack and tossed the rest into a corner for the rats. If they had something to gnaw on they might ignore her.

She had examined the boarded up window countless times throughout the day. She'd even stood on an upended crate to study it more closely. Disappointment was a bitter pill to swallow. What she needed was a crowbar of sorts, but she had nothing.

She resumed her pacing, ignoring her growling stomach and the nausea plaguing her. Suddenly her gaze fell on the desk. Long spindly legs held it upright, but it was tilted at a precarious angle, as if a good wind would knock it over. Or a good push. Mustering her strength, Lara shoved the desk, hard. It fell over and shattered.

Crowing in delight, Lara pulled one of the legs free. Regrettably, it didn't look sturdy enough to do the job for which she intended it, but Lara wasn't about to give up that easily.

Holding the leg like a bat, she swung with all her might at the boards barring the window. They didn't even budge. She tried again. And yet again. Her arms ached clear up to her shoulders, but what happened next sent her spirits plummeting. The desk leg shattered.

"Oh, no! Please, God, no."

She sank to her knees and sobbed into her hands. Julian was going to die and she couldn't do a thing about it.

Lara didn't know how long she remained like that. Daylight waned and the lantern sputtered out. The room grew dark. She heard the scurry of tiny feet and panic rose hard in her throat. She climbed onto a crate and gathered her skirts about her. There was nothing left for her now but to wait.

A scraping noise at the window caught Lara's attention. More rats? A whisper of sound sent her off the crate and to the window.

"Who is it?"

"Lara? Is that you? Thank God I found you."

The voice wasn't Julian's, she was sure of it. But it was as familiar as her own.

" 'Tis Rondo. I've been hours searching for you. This building is enormous; every opening is locked or boarded up. I saw you through the slits in the window but waited to make sure you were alone."

"Rondo! What are you doing in London? How did you find me?"

" 'Tis a long story, I'll tell you later."

"What are you going to do?"

"Get you out of here. But first I have to find something to pry these boards off with."

"Hurry," Lara urged. "The Jackal intends to kill Julian. He'll be here soon."

"The Jackal?"

"Aye, the man who wants Julian dead. You betrayed Julian to the Jackal's men. Oh, do hurry, Rondo," she added on a note of desperation.

"I'm sorry, Lara. I swear I'll make it up to you. I'll be back."

Lara listened to the silence outside the window and felt a glimmer of hope. Who would have thought Rondo would show up in London? So many unanswered questions, but none of them mattered right now. What mattered was getting out of this dangerous situation and saving Julian's life.

Rondo returned a short time later. Lara heard him at the window. "Rondo, is that you?"

"Aye. I found a metal pipe in the alley. It should do the job. Stand back."

Excitement pounded through her as Rondo used the metal bar to pry off the boards. When one of the nails gave way, Lara nearly cheered. Another nail popped loose and one board fell away, but the space was too narrow for her to climb through. She waited with bated breath as Rondo pried furiously at another board.

Suddenly Lara froze. Voices. Coming from beyond the locked door. "Quiet," she hissed. "Someone's coming."

She could see sweat dripping off Rondo's forehead, but despite his frantic efforts she sensed defeat. It was a bitter pill to swallow.

"You have to leave, Rondo. Quickly, before you're discovered."

"I won't leave you, Lara."

"You have to. Pass the pipe to me through the window. It may be of some use to me."

"I can't leave you," Rondo repeated.

"Go Rondo. Now. You have no weapon, you'll be killed. Go to my father. You know where he lives. Tell him where to find me and ask him to bring help."

She must have gotten through to him for he thrust the pipe at her through the window and disappeared. It wasn't a moment too soon. Seconds later the door opened. A man she didn't recognize pushed through. He looked like a thug. Could he be the Jackal? Then someone entered behind him and a chill skittered down her spine. Instinctively she concealed the pipe in the folds of her skirt as she gazed into the face of the Jackal, a man she knew at once.

"You!"

"Good evening, my dear. I trust you approve of my hospitality."

"You're the Jackal? The man who wants Julian dead?"

"Surprised?" the Jackal asked smoothly. "Where is your Gypsy intuition? I thought you'd have figured that out by now. I'm sure your lover has."

"If you're referring to Julian, he's my husband. We were married in Scotland."

"Mansfield married you? That does surprise me. I thought he merely wanted you for bed sport. I can't imagine Mansfield tainting his noble bloodline with Gypsy blood, not that it matters. Your husband will die today, and you with him."

"My lord, look there!" the Jackal's hired thug exclaimed, calling his attention to the window. "The wench was tryin' to escape."

The Jackal stared at the window, his face a mask of rage. "Blast that Crockett! He said this room was escape-proof. What did you use to pry off the board?"

Lara tightened her hold on the pipe hidden in the folds of her skirt. Her words dripped with sarcasm. "My hands."

Tolliver whirled around to face her. "A smart mouth won't save you, my lady." He turned to his hired thug and snapped out orders. "Wait outside for Scorpion, Barnes. Position the others in various places around the warehouse. There may be trouble. Bring Scorpion to me as soon as he arrives. Leave the light, there's another outside the door."

"What if Scorpion ain't alone?" Barnes asked.

"He'll be alone," the Jackal said with confidence. "He fancies his Gypsy wench too much to disobey my instructions. If for some reason he isn't alone, take care of him yourself and let the others handle his companions. Remember, however, I prefer to kill Scorpion myself. I want him alive so I can watch his face when I kill his wife. I want him to know she's the second woman to die for him."

Barnes set the lantern down on a crate and left the room. The Jackal took a menacing step toward Lara. "You're a fetching little witch. There's just enough time before your husband arrives to sample your charms. I've never had a Gypsy, and I've heard they're hot and eager for it."

"Don't touch me," Lara said with deadly calm despite her racing heart.

She retreated, until she felt the wall at her back. The Jackal pressed forward. His body pushed ruthlessly against hers. She felt his erection rising thick and threatening between his legs and sucked in a breath of courage. He grasped her breasts with both hands, his fingers hurtful on her tender flesh, and rage emboldened her. When he leaned down to seize her lips with his, she placed her hands on his chest and shoved hard. He stumbled backward.

It was now or never, she thought as she whipped out the pipe from the folds of her skirt, put all her strength behind it, and swung it toward the Jackal's head. Caught off guard, he raised his arm to ward off the blow. The pipe landed midway between his elbow and wrist with a sickening crack. He howled and cradled his arm against him.

"Bitch! Bloody, Gypsy bitch! You broke my arm!"

"I wish it were your head!" Lara cried, eyeing the door with renewed hope.

She took one step, then another, but the Jackal reacted swiftly despite his injury. Raising his good arm, he backhanded her. She crumpled to the floor, clinging to consciousness by a slim thread.

"That will teach you." He pulled a pistol from his belt. "You'll be the first to die. Your lover will watch you draw your last breath before I kill him."

Julian hired a hackney to take him to the docks. He instructed the driver to let him out at the far end of the street and cautiously made his way on foot to the abandoned warehouse. He felt eyes following him and knew he was being watched. Ignoring the prickling sensation at the nape of his neck, he paused before the warehouse door and tried the latch. The door opened beneath his hand, but before he could enter, he felt the business end of a pistol pressing into his back.

" 'Tis good ye came alone," Barnes snarled. "Inside with ye, Scorpion."

Julian froze. "Where's my wife?"

"Ye'll see her soon enough. Move."

The steady pressure of the gun in his back persuaded Julian to do as Jackal's hired thug directed. He entered the cavernous room and paused, his gaze darting about to get his bearings. Barnes picked up the lantern sitting on a crate near the door and prodded Julian forward.

"Are you taking me to Lara?" Julian asked. "Is the Jackal with her?"

"Ye ask too many questions," Barnes growled. "See that door yonder?" Julian nodded. "Walk toward it."

Julian approached the door, his body tense, his senses alert. He knew the odds were stacked against him and he'd gladly give up his own life to spare

Lara's. The only bright ray in the otherwise dismal future was the hope that the message he'd sent to Lord Stanhope had reached its destination, and that Stanhope had gotten through to Lord Randall. But would help arrive in time?

Barnes nudged Julian in the back with the pistol. "Stop at the door."

Julian halted before the closed door. His body tensed when he heard a thud on the other side of the door, and another strange sound that sent chills down his spine. Nothing, not even the threat of death, could prevent Julian from flinging the door open and rushing inside. He skidded to an abrupt stop, rendered motionless by the scene unfolding before him.

Lara lay motionless on the floor. Was she hurt? Dead? Rage exploded inside him. He raced to her side and dropped to his knees. With gentle care he lifted her head. She groaned and opened her eyes. Julian breathed a sigh of relief.

"Julian. Why did you come? The Jackal is going to kill you."

"He can try, my love." When she tried to rise, he helped her to a sitting position. "Don't move," he warned. Then he rose to his feet and spun around to confront the Jackal, his teeth bared in a snarl.

"So it *is* you. My suspicions were correct."

The Jackal's left arm hung limply at his side. Julian eyed him narrowly, speculating on his injury and wondering whether his feisty Gypsy wife had caused it.

"Scorpion. How good of you to come," the Jackal said through clenched teeth.

"What happened to your arm?"

The Jackal's eyes glowed with dark malice. "Ask

your lover. I've decided she'll be the first to die. Before I kill you, I want you to tell me how it feels to have two innocent women die for you."

"Bastard!" Julian snarled. "Why? Why would a man with your background turn to smuggling and murder?" The longer he kept the Jackal talking the better the chances of help arriving.

"You've never had empty pockets," the Jackal spat. "You've never worried about going to debtors' prison. Not the high and mighty Earl of Manchester. You don't know what it's like to face a bleak future."

"So you turned to smuggling," Julian contended.

"At least I have funds to maintain the lifestyle I enjoy. Smuggling is quite lucrative, actually, that's why you must be eradicated. Randall will never know I'm the Jackal after you and Lara are dead."

Keep him talking, Julian told himself. "Why were you courting Stanhope's friendship?"

"At first, 'twas merely business. Later, after I figured out that Scorpion had been aided by Gypsies, I wanted to keep tabs on Stanhope in the event his Gypsy daughter was involved. My suspicions proved correct, for it wasn't long before you were sniffing around Lara's skirts. Your identity as Scorpion has been known to me for some time."

"Let Lara go," Julian demanded. "Killing her will solve nothing. 'Tis me you want."

"I can't let her live. She knows too much."

"Julian . . ."

Until now Lara had kept blessedly silent. He turned toward her, his expression dark with warning. "Let me handle this, love."

She started to rise and he helped her up. He felt her trembling beneath his hand and pulled her close.

"Step away from him, my dear," the Jackal said smoothly. "I promised you'd be the first to die and I meant it. I want to get this over with quickly, so I can have my injury treated."

"She's not moving," Julian confronted, shoving Lara behind him.

Silently Julian contemplated his chances should he decide to rush the Jackal. It might work if the Jackal's hired thug wasn't in the room. He stood just inside the door, his beady eyes and steady gun trained on Julian.

"Don't even consider it," the Jackal warned. "My men are placed strategically around the building. You wouldn't get far, even if by some miracle you got past Barnes and out the door."

He raised the pistol with his good hand and pointed it at Julian. "I wanted the wench to die first, but I suppose it doesn't matter which of you goes first. You're both going to die."

"Drop to the floor, I'm going to rush him," Julian hissed in a voice meant for Lara's ears alone.

Three things happened at once. Julian launched himself at the Jackal, Lara hit the floor, and the gun went off. The bullet went wild as the Jackal fell beneath Julian's weight, and the pistol went skittering across the floor. The Jackal fell on his broken arm and screamed.

Barnes aimed his pistol at Julian, but Julian used the Jackal as a shield, spoiling Barnes's shot.

"Don't shoot, you fool!" the Jackal screamed. "You might hit me."

Barnes looked confused, then he turned and aimed at Lara. Lara scrambled for the gun the Jackal had lost. Barnes had Lara in his sights when the remaining boards covering the window shattered and a man's lean, lithe body hurtled through the opening. The man lunged for Barnes. Barnes fired. The bullet found a home in soft flesh. The man grunted and fell. Light from the lantern illuminated his face, and Lara screamed his name.

"Rondo!"

Julian was stunned by Rondo's sudden appearance through the window. What in bloody hell was he doing here?

The Jackal, obviously in great pain, was easily subdued, but Julian didn't dare release him to see to Lara and Rondo. A quick glance told him that Barnes was reloading, and that frightened the hell out of him, for he knew instinctively that Lara would be Barnes' next target. Rondo was trying to rise but appeared too hurt to be of much help. Then Julian spied the Jackal's pistol, which had flown out of his hand when Julian rushed him.

"The gun, Lara, the gun!"

Everything was happening so fast Lara found it difficult to take it all in. Rondo was hurt and Julian was fighting for his own life. She had to do something. She realized the Jackal's pistol was within reach even before Julian alerted her. She stretched out her arm, curled her fingers around the weapon, and brought it toward her. Her hands were shaking as she raised the pistol and aimed at Barnes, who by that time had reloaded and had his gun trained on Lara.

Without allowing herself time to think, Lara

squeezed the trigger. Barnes screamed and dropped his pistol. It discharged harmlessly into the wall. Lara stared at the weapon in her hand and dropped it as if it had bitten her. Never in her wildest dreams did she imagine she could shoot another human. But the threat to her own life, the life of the child growing inside her, and Julian's life was more than enough justification.

Unfortunately Barnes had more stamina than Lara had counted on. She watched in horror as Barnes retrieved his pistol and started to reload, albeit awkwardly. The blood soaking his sleeve seemed not to bother him as he calmly raised the weapon and took aim at Lara. She heard Julian scream her name and braced herself for the pain that would rip through her body with the bullet. All she could do now was close her eyes and pray.

Lara heard a burst of gunfire but felt no pain as her eyes flew open. Barnes was lying on the floor, and beyond him, a man wearing a uniform stood in the open door, calmly reloading his pistol. Unable to comprehend what had just happened, she watched in trepidation as a tall, powerfully built man pushed past the dragoon. He wore authority like a perfectly tailored coat.

The man who entered behind him was as dear to her as Julian. "Papa!" Lord Stanhope opened his arms, and Lara flew into them.

"Lara! Thank God. I feared we'd get here too late."

"You couldn't have arrived at a better time," Julian said. "Lord Randall, may I present the Jackal to you?"

Lord Randall eyed the Jackal with contempt. "Lord Tolliver. I should have known. You'll hang for this.

You have betrayed my confidence and your own country for personal gain."

"I would have succeeded but for Scorpion," Tolliver snarled. "He'll pay with his life."

From Lara's vantage point she saw something no one else seemed to notice. Though Tolliver's left arm still hung limply at his side, his right arm and hand were free. As Julian shoved Tolliver toward Randall, Tolliver reached inside his coat pocket and retrieved a small pistol. It must have been loaded and ready to fire for he whirled abruptly and shoved the pistol in Julian's gut.

Lara screamed a warning but it was too late. The gun exploded. Fortunately Julian had reacted the moment he felt the gun pressing into his gut. At the last possible moment he managed to shove Tolliver's arm upward, deflecting the shot and taking the bullet in a less vulnerable part of his body.

Almost immediately men swarmed around Tolliver, taking him in tow. He was dragged from the room, screaming for a doctor to treat his broken arm. Lara tore herself from her father's arms and raced to Julian's side, sobbing in relief when she saw the steady rise and fall of his chest.

Randall knelt beside her, concern wrinkling his brow. "Is he alive?"

"Aye, but he's losing a dangerous amount of blood."

" 'Tis best not to move him until a doctor arrives. I'll send for one immediately. Press on the wound, it may help to stem the flow of blood."

Lara tore a piece of her petticoat and wadded it into a pad. Then she opened Julian's shirt, placed the cloth over the wound, and pressed on it. The pad turned red and she increased the pressure, relieved when the flow slowed.

"I just checked on Rondo," Lord Stanhope said as he came up to join them. "He's alive. I don't know how he got here or why, but he needs medical attention."

"Rondo saved my life," Lara said.

Randall rose to summon help.

"How is Mansfield?" Stanhope asked.

"I've felt better," Julian groaned. "You arrived with Lord Randall and the dragoons in the nick of time."

"Julian!" Lara cried, overjoyed to see him alert. "Thank God! Lord Randall sent for a physician."

Julian started to rise but Lara wouldn't allow it. "No, don't move. You've lost a great deal of blood. Wait until the physician arrives."

"How is Rondo?"

"Alive," Stanhope said. "You'll both be taken care of. That was some scene I walked into."

Julian's gaze settled on Lara. "Are you . . . all right? Tolliver didn't . . . hurt you, did he?"

"I'm fine. I wouldn't allow Tolliver to hurt me. Don't talk, Julian, conserve your strength."

"Lara's right, Mansfield," Stanhope concurred. "Everything is under control."

Julian felt himself start to fade. Pain kept him from blacking out completely, but he knew it was only a matter of time before consciousness left him, and there was so much he wanted to say to Lara. If only he could think straight.

"I . . . we . . . need to talk," he said weakly. "Something . . . you should know."

"Can't it wait?" Lara asked.

"No, I want . . . to say it . . . now. Our marriage . . ."

Her breath caught in her throat. "What about our marriage?"

He wanted to tell her he was sorry for refusing to accept the love she had so freely offered. For being such a fool about their Gypsy marriage. For believing a Gypsy not good enough for an earl. He needed to tell her that Diana was his past and she was his future.

"I'm sorry . . . about our . . . marriage. I was a . . . fool to think our marriage . . . Diana is . . . was . . . What I feel for you isn't . . ." His words fell off, then stopped altogether.

Had Lara understood what he'd been trying to tell her? he wondered in his last moment of clarity. Diana was dead. What he and Lara had together transcended those feelings he'd felt for Diana. Words of explanation were trapped in his throat as his eyes fluttered shut.

Lara sat back on her heels, stunned by Julian's words. Had be been about to say that he didn't love her and never would? Is that what he meant?

"The physician will be here soon," Stanhope said, placing a hand on Lara's shoulder. "I'm sure your husband will be fine."

"Did you hear, Papa?" she whispered. "Julian doesn't love me. He still has feelings for his dead fiancée."

"I'm sure you're wrong," Stanhope consoled. "Why, Mansfield told me himself that he loved you."

Lara dropped her head, despair blinding her to all but her own heartache. "I heard him, Papa."

"What you heard were the ravings of a wounded

man. He came to your rescue, didn't he? He was ready to sacrifice his life for yours."

"That's because Julian is an honorable man. He married me because it was the right thing to do. He would have honored his vows for that reason. I won't accept those terms. He went to extraordinary lengths to bring the man responsible for his fiancée's death to justice. That's how much he loved her."

"We'll speak of this later, my dear. Things are often different from what they seem."

The physician arrived soon afterward. He poked and prodded at Julian a few minutes, then went to examine Rondo. In an impervious voice he announced that he couldn't possibly operate in such filthy surroundings.

"Is it safe to move them?" Randall asked.

"Better to move them than risk infection from God knows what," the doctor said shortly. "Digging out bullets is risky business."

"There's room in my coach for both men," Stanhope said.

"You can follow in your carriage, doctor."

"Be careful," Lara cautioned as dragoons carried Julian and Rondo out of the room.

Stanhope patted her shoulder. "Don't worry, Lara, they'll be very careful."

As Lara followed the dragoons out the door, her mind was in a turmoil. She had a great deal to think about. Her entire future was at stake. Of one thing she was certain. If Julian had been trying to tell her he'd never love her, she wouldn't force herself on him.

Chapter 19

Lara paced outside the bedroom door while the doctor worked on Julian. He'd already assured her that both Julian and Rondo were in no danger of dying, and that all they had to fear now was fever, but Lara was still edgy. Julian hadn't regained consciousness in the coach and was still out when he was carried into a guest bedroom in her father's house. Randall had sent word around to Julian's staff so they wouldn't worry, then he'd left to see to Tolliver's interrogation.

"Rondo is conscious and would like to speak with you," Lord Stanhope said as he stepped into the hall from Rondo's room.

"Did he tell you why he was in London?"

"Aye, he told me everything. He's sorry for what he did and wants to beg your forgiveness."

Lara gazed longingly at Julian's closed door and sighed resignedly. "Very well. I'll go to Rondo now, but I won't stay long. Call me when the doctor finishes with Julian."

Lara hurried into Rondo's room. A brace of candles burned on the bedside table. She made her way to the bed. Rondo's eyes were closed and she debated whether to leave, but he took the decision from her when he opened his eyes.

"I'm glad you've come," he said weakly. "I need your forgiveness."

"You don't have to talk now, Rondo. Wait until you're feeling better."

He clutched her hand. "Please, Lara, hear me out."

"Very well," Lara said, "I'll listen."

"I was mad with jealousy and reacted without thinking of the consequences. I never wanted anyone's death. I didn't know those men wanted to hurt you, nor did I realize the grave consequences of my jealousy would turn me into an outcast. I'm a man without a home. My own people revile me."

His face contorted in pain and he sucked in his breath. Lara felt a surge of compassion. He had tried to make amends by coming to her aid and had nearly lost his life.

"How did you know where to find me?"

"I was in the inn in Coventry when you arrived with Crockett and his henchman. Don't ask me how I ended up there. I had nowhere to go and was simply roaming the countryside without direction. I knew you were being held against your will so I waited, then followed when you were taken away the next day. Helping you was the only way to make amends for what I had done."

"You did make amends, Rondo," Lara assured him. "The Jackal's thug was about to kill me when you intervened. You probably saved both my life and Julian's."

"Your father wasn't home when I arrived to seek his aid. I didn't know it then, but he was already on his way to the warehouse with help. When I found him gone, I returned to the waterfront to rescue you myself."

"Thank you, Rondo. I'm sure you'll be welcomed back into the fold once Pietro learns about your brave act."

"I've always known you weren't meant for me," Rondo continued, "but I've always loved you."

"You were always my friend, Rondo, and today you proved it. I loved you as a brother and protector throughout my childhood. But the moment Julian walked into my life, I wanted no other."

The doctor rapped and entered the room, his black bag clutched in one hand. "His Lordship is resting, Lady Lara. You may see him now, but only for a moment. I dosed him with laudanum so he probably won't respond to you."

"How is he?" Lara asked anxiously.

"As well as can be expected, considering the gravity of the wound. Luck was with him. The bullet lodged in his chest but missed his lung by a hairsbreadth. He's weak from loss of blood, but he's young and healthy and should heal without complication, if he follows my directions," he admonished.

"Thank you, Doctor," Lara said with a note of relief. She hurried off.

Lara met her father in the hallway. "The doctor said Julian is going to be all right."

Stanhope sent her a reassuring smile. "Didn't I tell you as much? Your husband is a vigorous man. He wouldn't let a little bullet do him in."

"Of course not," she said with a smile. "I must go to him."

She opened the door and crossed the room to his

bedside. His complexion was waxen, and Lara stretched out her hand to touch his cheek. He was cool to the touch and seemed to be breathing easily. He was also sleeping deeply, and probably would for several hours. She kissed his forehead, pulled a chair beside the bed, and sat down to watch over him.

Her father arrived a few minutes later. "Go to bed, Lara, you must be exhausted. Most women would have been hysterical after the harrowing ordeal you've been through. I always knew you were strong and resilient, but I didn't realize to what extent until today."

"I'd like to sit with Julian a little longer, Father, then I'll go to bed."

"Let me sit with Julian."

"No, Papa, I'll be fine, really."

Stanhope gave Lara a skeptical glance. "You don't look fine. You've grown quite thin, and I don't like those circles under your eyes."

"Please, Papa, let me stay."

"Very well. An hour, no longer."

Lara curled up in the chair after her father left and stared at Julian. *He's so handsome*, she thought, gazing lovingly at the strong slant of his jaw, his full lips and aristocratic nose. *Why can't he love me as much as he loved Diana?* she silently lamented. She had his lust but not his love.

A thought whirled out of nowhere. Perhaps there was a way to learn once and for all how deeply Julian cared for her. She'd be taking a risk, but wasn't life a risk? There was so much at stake in this marriage. She had a child to nurture, and that child needed a father who would love him or her.

Lara fell asleep in the chair. She never heard her father come into the room, or felt him lift her and carry her to bed. She slept soundly, deeply, dreamlessly.

Julian's condition continued to improve. Thus far no signs of infection appeared, and the doctor assured Lara that her husband was out of danger. Since Julian had begun to think clearly, they had spoken little of personal matters. Many times Lara wanted to ask what he had meant when he'd spoken about their marriage the day he'd been wounded. But pride kept her from broaching the subject. She wondered if he even recalled those hurtful words.

Julian appeared pleased to have her with him in his sickroom. One day she entered his room and found him sitting up in bed, freshly shaven.

"Julian, should you be sitting up?"

"The doctor said it was all right to sit up for short periods of time. I can't just lie here all day like a slug-a-bed. I was hoping to talk with you today about our future. It's the first day I've felt well enough to concentrate."

Lara's heart plummeted to her feet. "Can't it wait? You're weak and—"

"No, we need to settle this between us. Or rather, there is something I wish to tell you. Something that should have been said weeks ago. This is difficult for me, Lara, so bear with me."

Oh, God, he's going to tell me he doesn't want me, Lara thought. "Not now, Julian, it will have to wait. There's . . . something I must do first."

"Lara, I don't want to put this off. The sooner 'tis said, the sooner we can get on with our lives. I want you to know exactly how I feel about you. In the past I've been reticent about—"

Lara clapped her hands over her ears. "Julian, please. I don't want to hear this now." Turning abruptly, she raced from the room.

Julian stared after her, wondering what in the devil he'd said to upset her. All he'd wanted to do was to apologize for being such an ass about their relationship. He knew he had hurt her in the past and wanted to set their marriage on the right path. He was finally ready to bare his heart to her. He wanted their future together to be a long and happy one, with children to brighten their lives. He'd tried to tell her while he lay wounded in the warehouse, but he wasn't sure it had come out as he'd intended.

He sighed. The next time he saw Lara he was going to insist that she listen to him.

Lara found her father in his study. The door was open, so she walked inside unannounced. "Are you busy, Papa?"

Stanhope set his ledger aside and smiled at her. "Come in, my dear, come in. I'm never too busy to talk to my daughter." He searched her face. "Are you all right? You look pale. You've worn yourself out nursing your husband. You must rest more. In fact, I insist upon it."

"I'm fine, Papa," Lara assured him. "I wish to ask a favor of you."

Stanhope beamed. "Anything, daughter, within my power to grant, of course."

Lara took a deep breath. "I'd like an escort to Kent. I want to spend some time with Ramona and Pietro."

Stanhope looked thunderstruck. "Now? What does your husband say about this? He's hardly up to traveling."

"I . . . didn't tell Julian, and I don't intend to. I'm going alone."

Stanhope frowned. "You're still not worried about those words Mansfield spoke in the warehouse, are you? They were the ravings of a sick man. Has he brought them up again? Did he tell you what he meant?"

"He tried a little while ago but I wouldn't listen."

"You're being foolish, Lara."

"Perhaps," Lara admitted. "But there's one way for Julian to prove his love and I'm not settling for less."

"You think running away will solve your problem?"

"Not exactly."

"What am I to tell Mansfield?"

"Tell him I need time to evaluate our marriage. Don't tell him where to find me. And . . . and tell him he's free to divorce me if he wishes."

"Lara, you're talking nonsense. This isn't like you."

"I'm sorry, Papa, but this is something I have to do. You see, Julian spent the better part of our relationship denying his feelings for me. I have to be sure."

"I can't condone your behavior. Mansfield is your husband. He came to your rescue, didn't he?"

Lara sighed. "We've been over this before. Julian is an honorable man. He'd rescue a dog in trouble. And it was important to him to capture the Jackal."

"To avenge his fiancée, or so you've told me."

"Exactly. She was his one true love."

Stanhope sat back and stared at Lara. "You're serious, aren't you? 'Tis winter. A Gypsy wagon can't be all that comfortable this time of year."

"You're wrong, Papa. I spent most of my childhood inside a Gypsy wagon. 'Tis most comfortable, and very cozy during the winter months. I'll be fine. I can always take refuge at your country estate should I change my mind. The staff at Stanhope Manor is perfectly capable of seeing to my needs."

Stanhope sighed resignedly. "Very well, if you're sure this is what you want."

"Very sure. Besides the reason I've already given, I want to clear the way for Rondo to return to the fold, and this will give me a chance to extol his bravery."

"How soon do you want to leave?"

"Today. As soon as possible. I can pack and be ready in an hour."

"Lara . . ."

"Please, Papa."

"When have I ever been able to deny you anything? Let's say two hours. It will take that long to prepare the coach and select the outriders. Does that suit you?"

"Perfectly. Now if you'll excuse me, I have preparations to make."

Two hours later Lara was on her way to Stanhope Manor in Kent.

Julian chafed restlessly. Lara hadn't returned to his room all day. He couldn't imagine what was keeping her away. When he'd hinted that he wished to talk about their future, she'd seemed frightened. What in bloody hell was wrong? Did she decide all of a sudden that she no longer loved him?

When a maid brought his dinner, Julian asked about Lara. The maid seemed suddenly tongue-tied and left without answering his question. When Jeevers came to prepare him for bed, he'd asked the same question of the stoic butler.

"I'll tell Lord Stanhope you were asking for Lady Lara," Jeevers said obliquely.

"What's going on, Jeevers? Has something happened to my wife?"

"To my knowledge, Lady Lara is well. Do you require a dose of laudanum tonight?"

"No, dammit! I don't want to be drugged. Please tell Lara I want to see her."

"As you wish, my lord."

Julian waited. And waited. And waited some more. When Lara failed to arrive in a reasonable length of time, Julian slid to the edge of the bed and attempted to stand. If Lara wouldn't come to him, by God he'd go to her.

Unfortunately his will was stronger than his legs. They crumpled beneath him the moment he put weight on them. He made a grab for the nightstand and succeeded only in bringing it down with him, as well as the candle resting atop it, which set the carpet on fire. Stanhope came rushing into the room, his nightshirt flapping around his legs. Jeevers was close on his heels. Together they stomped out the fire, until nothing remained but a charred section of carpet.

Stanhope righted the nightstand while Jeevers rescued the candle and relit it.

"What happened?" Stanhope asked. "Are you all right, Mansfield? Damn, man, you nearly set the house on fire."

"No, I'm not all right," Julian bit out. "Where's my wife?"

"Help me get His Lordship back into bed, Jeevers," Stanhope said, evading Julian's question.

It took both men to maneuver Julian back into bed. "You shouldn't have tried to rise by yourself," Stanhope admonished. "You've lost a great deal of blood and are still weak."

"You're ducking my question, Stanhope," Julian growled once he was settled back in bed. "Has everyone gone mad around here? What's happened to Lara?"

"You may return to bed, Jeevers," Stanhope said. "Lord Mansfield isn't going anywhere tonight."

Julian waited until Jeevers shuffled off down the hall before turning his angry gaze on Stanhope. "Are you ready to tell me what the bloody hell is going on? I want Lara, where is she?"

"I was hoping to wait until tomorrow but I can see you're not going to give up."

"What's happened to Lara?" Julian roared, struggling to control his fear.

"Calm down, Mansfield. Nothing has happened to Lara. She was fine when she left."

Julian's attention sharpened. "Are you telling me my wife has gone somewhere?"

"Damn," Stanhope said, shoving his fingers through his hair. "I told Lara to speak to you first. I knew you weren't going to like it. But you know how stubborn Lara can be."

"Indeed," Julian said dryly, remembering how long she'd kept him waiting before consenting to marry him. "What exactly am I not going to like?"

"Lara left early today."

Confusion marched across Julian's face. "Left? Lara left without consulting me? Where has she gone?"

"I'm not at liberty to say."

"I beg your pardon?" Julian bit out. "I believe I'm Lara's husband. I have a right to know where she's harried off to in the middle of winter."

"I'm sorry, Mansfield, but I promised Lara I wouldn't disclose her destination."

A muscle flexed in Julian's jaw. "Never mind, I already have a good idea where to find her. Did she leave a message for me?"

Stanhope shifted uncomfortably. "Aye, as a matter of fact, she did. She said you should seek a divorce if that is your wish."

"She knows bloody well that's not what I want! Apparently she's not thinking straight. Being kidnapped, dragged cross country, then incarcerated in an abandoned warehouse must have unsettled her more than any of us knew. Obviously she's not herself."

"I tried to stop her but she wouldn't listen," Stanhope lamented. "I believe she is testing you."

"Exactly," Julian agreed. "Stubborn wench. I'm ashamed to admit, Stanhope, that I put Lara through hell, but I felt we had finally come to terms with our feelings for one another."

"What, precisely, are your feelings for my daughter?"

"I thought I'd already made that clear. Nevertheless, I'll say it again, and keep saying it until both you and Lara believe me. I love your daughter, Stanhope."

"Lara believes you will never love her like you loved your dead fiancée."

"At one time I might have given her reason to believe that was so, but loving Lara has changed my way of thinking about Diana. Believe me when I say I've never loved another woman like I love Lara."

"You don't have to convince me, Mansfield. 'Tis Lara you need to persuade."

"I will, as soon as I can get out of this bed."

* * *

Lara reached the Gypsy camp without mishap. She was enthusiastically welcomed and immediately whisked into her grandparents' wagon. She sipped hot tea and basked in the glow of their love despite her uncertainty over her rash decision to leave London.

Was Julian angry at her? Angry enough to get the divorce she'd recommended? She sighed wearily. Time would tell. Meanwhile, she would sit back, enjoy her pregnancy, and try not to think about Julian and his response to her leaving.

"Why are you here alone?" Ramona asked. "Where is Drago?"

"You may use Julian's name now," Lara said. "It's over and done with. The man who wanted him dead can no longer hurt him."

Ramona stared deep into Lara's eyes, as if seeking answers to her questions. "What are you not telling me, Granddaughter?"

" 'Tis a long story, Grandmother, and I want both you and Grandfather to know what happened because it involves Rondo."

"Rondo!" Ramona and Pietro said in unison.

Pietro frowned. "Rondo has been banished for his misdeeds."

"I'm sure he'll be reinstated once everyone knows that he saved both my life and Julian's."

"Start at the beginning," Ramona urged. "I looked into my crystal ball and knew that danger stalked you. Did it find you in Scotland?"

"Aye. I was kidnapped and brought to London shortly after Julian and I were married by a preacher in Scotland."

Immediately Lara launched into a telling of the circumstances of her imprisonment and the outcome, leaving out nothing. In a hollow voice she repeated those confusing words spoken by Julian in the warehouse.

"Rondo has redeemed himself," Pietro declared. "He will be welcomed back when he returns. Let us hope he has learned a lesson from all this."

"What of your husband, little one? What do you intend to do?" Ramona asked.

Lara's gaze dropped to her hands, where they fidgeted nervously with the folds of her skirt. "If he loves me, he will come for me."

"Has he not proven that he loves you? Why are you punishing him?"

"I told you what he said. He'll never love me in the same way he loved Diana."

Ramona's wrinkled brow furrowed as she silently contemplated Lara.

After a lengthy pause, Ramona said, "Pietro, perhaps you should make sure Lara's coachman and outriders are fed and then sent on their way."

Taking the hint, Pietro rose immediately. "Aye, never let it be said Pietro's hospitality is lacking."

"My instincts tell me you are wrong about His Lordship," Ramona said quietly. "He loves you every bit as much as you love him."

"But Grandmother, I heard him say—"

"You heard what you wanted to hear, little one. You should have given your husband the opportunity to explain."

"Don't scold, Grandmother. Leaving Julian is the only way I can be absolutely certain he loves me for myself and not because he felt honor-bound to protect me. I need to know that he still wants me after the Jackal has been apprehended and Diana's death avenged."

"It may be a long time before he's able to leave his sickbed," Ramona reminded her.

"I know. Meanwhile, I'm where I want to be. I love Papa, but my real home has always been right here with you and Pietro and the others."

Ramona's probing gaze dropped to Lara's flat stomach. "When is your child due?"

Lara blanched. "How did you know?"

"I know many things," Ramona said cryptically. "Does His Lordship know?"

Lara hesitated a long moment. "No, he doesn't know. The babe won't be born until summer."

Ramona made a censorious sound deep in her throat. "The child is your husband's heir. You should have told him."

Lara sighed. She'd known this wasn't going to be easy. "I will. When he comes for me . . . if he comes for me," she quickly amended. "If you'll excuse me, I'd like to go to my wagon now, I'm exhausted."

"Go, little one. God and fate will determine your future."

Someone had lit the brazier in Lara's wagon, and she soaked up the warmth and sense of belonging like a needy sponge. Whatever happened, she cherished this time alone to come to grips with the knowledge that Julian might decide she wasn't worth the trouble and obtain a divorce as she'd suggested.

Lara felt little hunger when Ramona arrived with a bowl of savory stew and fresh bread but she ate anyway, just to please her grandmother. It began to snow that night. Lara crawled into bed, missing Julian dreadfully. It had been so long since he had made love to her . . . so very long. Would she ever feel his arms around her again? Would she ever feel the erotic power of his kisses or experience the glory of his lovemaking?

Pray God she would.

Julian cursed his weakness. He complained so arduously about the meager meals he'd been forced to endure that finally more substantial fare was provided. A man trying to regain his strength needed more than pap and liquids.

Julian had graduated from sitting up in bed to being held upright by the forthright Jeevers as he took his first tentative steps. Each day he pushed a little harder, until he was able to walk without help. A week after Lara left, Julian announced himself ready to ride to Kent to retrieve his wayward bride, return her to London, and introduce her to the *ton* as his countess.

His will proved stronger than his body. The first time he attempted to ride, his wound reopened and the doctor forbid him to mount a horse for at least three more weeks. It was a setback, but nothing Julian couldn't surmount. Unfortunately patience was something Julian lacked in abundance.

Then it started to snow. Seriously snow. The roads leading out of London were closed and traffic came to a standstill, prolonging Julian's departure. He was thankful he had been able to return to his own home before the snow began. Rondo had come with him.

Julian missed Lara. Missed her dreadfully. It seemed like forever since he'd held her lithe body in his arms, kissed her lush lips, felt her come apart when he made love to her. What had been in her mind when she'd left? he wondered. What had he said or done to send her fleeing back to her grandparents? He delved deeply into his brain and came up empty.

He knew he'd been a fool in more ways than one where Lara was concerned, but he'd hoped that was behind them. Didn't she know how much he loved her? Didn't she realize she was the only woman to penetrate the shield protecting his heart? He'd tried to tell her that he'd finally laid Diana to rest but feared he hadn't gotten through to her. He was prepared to tell her again and again, as often as needed, until she finally believed him.

During Julian's convalescence, Lord Randall came to call. He'd told Julian in no uncertain terms that his usefulness as a government agent had come to an end. Scorpion's identity was known to too many. Julian didn't regret retiring Scorpion. He'd lived on the edge of danger too long. What he wanted now was to sit back and enjoy a peaceful existence with his wife.

Lara spent much of the following weeks inside her wagon, cooking her own meals over her brazier and enjoying Ramona and Pietro's company. The blustery weather kept the small band of Gypsies from enjoying outside activities together, which suited Lara's dark mood.

Two weeks. Three weeks. Four weeks. Time passed slowly. Despair settled on her like a shroud. Ramona impressed upon her that travel was nearly impossible under such adverse conditions, and that Julian might not yet have recovered fully from his wounds. But Lara knew that had Julian wanted to find her, nothing would stop him. Surely he knew there was only one place she would go, so locating her shouldn't be a problem. Had he washed his hands of her? Had she gone too far this time?

Julian paced his study while Rondo lounged in a chair, watching him. "Sit down, Drago," Rondo said, using his Gypsy name from force of habit. "You're exhausting me. Pacing won't change the weather."

"I know pacing won't help, but it makes me feel better. I worry about Lara. She didn't look well the last time I saw her. I fear her recent ordeal was too much for her and she's not thinking straight. 'Tis the only explanation I can give for her sudden departure."

Unless she doesn't love me and never has, he silently lamented. But he wouldn't let himself think like that. That was something she'd have to tell him in person.

"Are you ready to ride, Rondo?" Julian asked suddenly. "If not, you can remain behind until the weather improves."

"I'm not quite as anxious as you to take off in the middle of winter," Rondo replied. "Your home is comfortable, Julian. I'd like to continue my convalescence here, if you have no objections."

"Of course, if that is your wish. I'll instruct Farthingale to see that your stay is made comfortable. I plan to leave at first light."

Julian strode from the study, his face set in determined lines. Bad weather or no, wound or no, he was going to find Lara and learn for himself what in bloody hell was going on with her. Then he'd wring her pretty neck. Or make love to her until she promised never to leave him again.

Julian headed out at first light. A fine snow was falling and the temperature had plummeted during the night. But that didn't stop him. The sooner he reached Lara, the quicker he could talk some sense into her.

Chapter 20

Four weeks had passed since Lara left her father's house in London, and she began to fear that Julian had indeed filed for divorce. It was a bitter blow, one from which she'd probably never recover. But she had only herself to blame. She could have remained in London and lived with Julian in a loveless marriage, for she knew he'd never suggest that their marriage be dissolved. Julian was too honorable a man. But that didn't mean he had to love her. And existing in a marriage without Julian's love wasn't an option.

No one forced love. It sneaked up when one least expected.

Suddenly another thought occurred to Lara. What if Julian's wound hadn't healed? What if something unforeseen had happened, like infection, or something equally as debilitating? Surely her father would have sent word if Julian wasn't recovering as expected, wouldn't he? But given the state of the roads these past weeks, Lara wasn't sure a messenger could get through, much less find their camp.

Her face set in determined lines, Lara decided she

couldn't go on another day without knowing what had happened to Julian. She wanted him to come to her, but she wasn't too proud to go to him. Especially if he needed her.

Her mind made up, Lara found a wrap and stepped outside into the frigid air. Trudging through two inches of new snow, she made her way to her grandparents' wagon. Her knock was answered immediately.

"Lara, what are you doing out so late?" Ramona asked. "Are you ill? Come inside and warm yourself."

Lara walked over to the glowing brazier and held out her hands.

"Sit, little one," Pietro urged. "Something is bothering you. Do you wish to tell us about it?"

"I've been a fool, Grandfather," Lara lamented. "I left Julian without positive proof that he was going to recover. Oh, he seemed well when I left, and all signs pointed to a quick recovery, but sometimes signs can be deceiving. What if he had a relapse? What if my leaving hindered his recovery?"

Ramona and Pietro exchanged speaking glances. Then Ramona said, "Julian will recover, little one. I have seen this. But it appears that you have come to a decision about your marriage. You wish to return to London, do you not?"

"You always know what I'm thinking, Grandmother," Lara said fondly. "Aye, I'm going to return to London, but I need your help getting there."

"I will take you myself," Pietro said. "As soon as the weather permits."

"I cannot wait that long," Lara protested. "The weather is better than it has been in recent weeks so I see no reason to delay. I wish to leave tomorrow morning."

"You are carrying a child," Pietro reminded her.

"I am strong and healthy. A short trip will cause me no harm."

Pietro looked at Ramona for direction.

Ramona stared into the glowing brazier for several long minutes, her eyes closed, her body still. Suddenly she opened her eyes and smiled.

"You will leave tomorrow, just as you wish, little one. Pietro will escort you and all will be well."

"Are you sure?" Pietro asked, obviously not convinced.

"Did I not say so?" Ramona chided gently.

Pietro stared at her a moment, then nodded his compliance.

"Dress warmly, granddaughter," Pietro admonished. "We will leave at first light."

Lara kissed both her grandparents soundly. "Thank you! Thank you!" she gushed. "I will be ready to leave in the morning when you are, Grandfather."

"Get a good night's sleep," Pietro advised.

Lara hurried through the biting wind to her wagon, happier than she'd been in a long time. At least she was doing something positive instead of sitting in her wagon waiting and wondering.

Lara undressed, donned her nightdress, and climbed into bed. She was no longer ill in the mornings and had actually begun to enjoy her food. Her stomach was still flat, but she imagined she could feel her babe beneath her heart, his or her little heart beating in time to her own.

With that pleasant thought, she closed her eyes and drifted off to sleep.

* * *

The weather showed little improvement the next day, but Lara wasn't about to let snow or cutting wind stop her. She dressed warmly in woolen petticoat, thick stockings, and boots, pulling her heaviest dress and a fur-lined cloak on last. When Pietro arrived leading two horses, she was ready.

Lara mounted with Pietro's help. Then Ramona came hurrying up with a sack of food, which Pietro stuffed into his saddlebags.

"If the weather holds, we'll reach London before nightfall," Pietro predicted as he bid Ramona farewell. "Don't look for my return until our granddaughter has been safely delivered to her husband."

"Thank you, Grandmother, for everything you've done for me," Lara said. "Perhaps we can visit before you leave for Scotland."

"Go with God," Ramona said, waving them off.

The first part of the day passed uneventfully. Then, after they had stopped to rest the horses and share the lunch Ramona had prepared, the skies lowered and snow began to fall at an alarming rate.

"We'll have to seek shelter soon," Pietro said, gazing at the threatening sky. "We will never reach London before nightfall in this weather, and riding in darkness, on dangerous roads, is too risky. I won't jeopardize your health, little one."

Though Lara wished it otherwise, she knew her grandfather spoke the truth. "What do you propose?"

"There is an inn not too far from here. We'll stop there for the night."

Lara remembered the inn well. She and Julian had

stayed at the Three Feathers after he spirited her away from London. In fact, she had fond memories of their stay there.

Lara was cold, hungry and exhausted by the time they reached the Three Feathers Inn. Drifting snow had almost obliterated the road, and the lights from the inn were barely visible through the dense, white haze. They turned into the yard and Pietro helped Lara to dismount.

"Wait inside for me while I find someone to tend our horses," Pietro said.

Lara didn't need to be told twice. She'd thought the trip to London would be easy, but being pregnant had taken its toll. She was grateful to her grandfather for stopping, for had it been left to her, she probably would have fallen from the saddle before suggesting that they stop short of London.

Lara warmed herself by the fire in the nearly empty common room. Obviously few travelers were brave enough to venture out on a night like this. Pietro arrived shortly afterward, and Lara heard him making arrangements for their accommodations.

"Ye can have yer pick tonight," the innkeeper said. "Not much business in this weather."

"A room for my granddaughter and another for myself," Pietro said.

"Aye, I'll send a lad up to lay a fire so yer rooms will be warm for ye and yer granddaughter. Will ye be wanting a meal?"

"Aye, something hot and filling. We'll take it down here before the fire. We'll have warmed mulled wine while we're waiting."

Pietro joined Lara while the innkeeper barked orders to his help.

"We'll have a hot meal soon, little one," Pietro said. "You look exhausted."

"I'm not very hungry, Grandfather. I'd rather go right up to bed."

"Ramona wouldn't forgive me if I let you go off to bed without your meal. You're eating for two now. Besides, the fires are being laid in our rooms as we speak and it will be a while before the chill leaves."

Lara didn't relish undressing in an icy cold room so she bided her time, drinking her mulled wine while their meal was being prepared. Once their meal arrived, it looked so appetizing that Lara dug in with surprising gusto. She *was* hungry, she realized as she chewed and swallowed a savory morsel of meat pie and washed it down with wine. She topped off the meal with an apple tart loaded with cinnamon and raisins, then sat back and sighed, her hunger appeased.

Pietro grinned at her. "I thought you weren't hungry?"

"I thought the same thing, but the smell of the food restored my appetite. Do you think our rooms are warm now?"

"Go on up, granddaughter. I'm going to sit here by the fire a while longer and finish my wine. Your room is up the stairs, the first door on the right. My room is the one beyond yours. Leave the door unlocked, I'll look in on you before I retire."

Lara kissed his cheek. "Good night, Grandfather."

Julian cursed the weather and the rotten luck that was keeping him from Lara. He had fully intended to reach the Gypsy camp tonight, but weather and fate had conspired against him. Pelted by the relentless fury of stinging snow, he could barely see the road for the drifts. Gritting his teeth in frustration, he feared there was no way he could go on tonight without risking limb and life.

Julian had traveled this road often enough to know that the Three Feathers Inn loomed somewhere ahead. He recalled the night he and Lara had stayed there and couldn't stop the smile that curved his lips. It seemed so long ago; so much had happened since then.

Julian's toes and fingers had gone numb by the time he spied the lights from the Three Feathers blinking in the distance. If not for the lights he would have passed it by and never known it was there, that's how thickly the snow was falling.

Julian turned into the yard and guided his horse to the stables behind the inn. No one was about so he tended his own horse, noting as he worked that only two other horses were stabled within.

Julian entered the inn and shook the snow off his cape. After greeting the innkeeper, he made directly for the roaring fire in the common room. He held out his hands to the flames and pushed back his hood. A movement from the corner of the room caught his attention and he turned slightly. He nearly lost the ability to speak when he saw Pietro. The two men stared at each other for several moments before Julian found his voice.

"Pietro! What in bloody hell are you doing here on a night fit for neither man nor beast?"

"I was about to ask you the same thing, my lord."

"I was on my way to your camp to claim my wife when bad weather forced me to seek a room for the night. How is Lara? She left me without a word of explanation." His eyes glittered. "She and I are going to have words when I catch up with her."

Pietro gave Julian a strange look. "This is incredible!"

Julian frowned. Had he missed something? "To what are you referring?" Then a terrible thought occurred to him and he asked anxiously, "Lara *is* at your camp, isn't she?"

"As a matter of fact, she isn't," Pietro replied.

A jolt of sheer panic kicked Julian in the gut. "What? Where could she have gone? My God, man, my wife is missing! I didn't worry excessively about her, believing she was with you and Ramona. Now I don't know what to think."

He began to pace.

Pietro must have taken pity on him for he said, "I know where you can find Lara."

Julian whirled, his face taut with anxiety. "Out with it, man! Where is my wife?"

"Upstairs, first door on the right. The door isn't locked."

Words failed Julian. His mouth worked noiselessly until the words began to flow. "Lara is here? In this weather? Is she mad?"

"Mad with love for you, I suspect," Pietro said with a chuckle. "Ramona must have known you and Lara would meet like this, else she wouldn't have let Lara start out in this weather. My wife is a wise woman."

"Granted," Julian allowed, "but Lara shouldn't be traveling in this weather. Where is she going that she couldn't wait until the weather clears?"

"Surely you know the answer to that question," Pietro chided. "Lara was coming to you in London.

She fretted endlessly and regretted leaving you before you had fully recovered. She feared you'd had a relapse. The weather interfered with our journey and we were forced to seek shelter." He chuckled. "Fate has a strange way of bringing people together."

"Fate or love," Julian muttered beneath his breath.

"Go to your wife, Julian. I'll explain to the innkeeper and arrange everything."

"Aye," Julian muttered hoarsely as he started up the stairs.

Julian found Lara's room and turned the knob. The door opened noiselessly and he slipped inside. The glow from a single candle sitting on the nightstand emitted enough light for Julian to make out Lara's form beneath the covers. She appeared to be sleeping soundly. He closed the door behind him and approached the bed. Bending close, he kissed her smooth forehead. She sighed but didn't awaken. Julian's love expanded as he stared at her. She looked innocent and waiflike in sleep, as if she hadn't a care in the world.

Julian wanted to devote the rest of his life to making Lara happy, keeping her safe, giving her children, and loving her forever. But experience had shown him that nothing valuable was easily obtained.

Waking Lara seemed such a shame, Julian decided as he watched her sleep. But leaving her wasn't an option, and the bed looked too inviting to resist. A smile stretched his lips as he began to undress.

Lara's dream seemed so real. She could almost feel Julian's arms around her, smell the pine forest on his hair and skin, as if he'd just come inside from the cold, frost-scented air. She sighed and cuddled closer, surrounding his cool body with her warmth.

Why was his skin so chilled?

Lara opened her eyes, stunned to discover that she wasn't dreaming. A flesh-and-blood Julian was in bed with her. She stiffened and whispered his name.

"Julian. You've come."

"Did you doubt it? I would have been here sooner had the weather cooperated."

Her hands flattened against his chest. "You're so cold."

" 'Twas a damn cold ride. Are you happy to see me?"

A weighted pause. "That depends. Why are you here? Did you file for divorce as I suggested?"

"Is that what you really want? Talk to me, love. Why did you leave London without consulting me? Did your ordeal unsettle your mind?"

"My mind is perfectly clear. 'Tis your mind I question. Or, rather, your feelings for me."

"What will it take to convince you that we belong together? I do love you, you know."

A huge sigh. "I . . . wasn't sure."

"Then let me convince you."

He raised up on his elbow. A beam of moonlight revealed the taut planes of his face, stark and intense in his need. She closed her eyes and waited for his kiss. His lips touched hers, and a surge of pleasure coursed through her, as sweet and heady as fine wine. His kisses were gentle at first, nibbling her mouth with a feather-light touch, but they didn't remain that way for long.

He licked the seam of her lips with the tip of his tongue, then drew on them with increasing passion, until she grew limp and boneless. Then his kiss became a deep, soul-searing invasion into her very soul, and she wanted to melt into him, to absorb him into her core. He angled his lips sideways against hers and tilted her chin, prodding her mouth open. She eagerly obliged. He stroked the sleek lining of her cheeks, playing wickedly with her tongue. Warmth and wetness flooded her body.

She moved her hands around his torso and up his back, stopping briefly to explore the fresh scar that had barely healed over. He lifted his head and stared down at her. She felt his hot breath fan her flushed cheeks and swollen lips.

"Do you truly love me, Julian?" she whispered. "You're not here because your honor demanded it, are you?"

"I'm here because you're my wife and I love you," Julian declared.

"You love me? What about Diana?"

"Diana is dead," Julian said flatly. "Diana is my past; you are my future."

"But in the warehouse you said—"

"I have no idea what I said, only what I *meant* to say. Obviously you misunderstood my words and came to a false conclusion. What did you hear me say?"

Lara thought back to that day Julian had burst into the warehouse to rescue her and was shot by the Jackal. His words were still fresh in her mind.

"You said you were sorry about our marriage. That you were a fool to think it would last, and that you couldn't forget Diana. Then you said," she nearly choked over the words, "what you felt for me wasn't love."

Julian's brow furrowed. "I remember wanting to tell you how I felt about you . . . about us . . . but I don't recall saying those words. What I wanted to say is that I was sorry for not accepting our marriage from the beginning, that I was a fool to think I'd never find love, that you showed me the error of my ways. What I felt for you then and now is the kind of love that will last forever."

"Oh, Julian," Lara cried happily. "I love you so very much."

"Forgive me. I should have come to my senses and told you long before now how much I love you."

"I needed to know that, Julian. I had to hear the words from you. I . . . I'm very fragile now."

"My wild Gypsy wench fragile? Never! Forget everything but here and now. Today begins the rest of our lives together, and I want to start out right by making love to you."

He kissed her again, and yet again. Her mouth, her nose, her chin. She trembled with pleasure. With an impatient motion he tugged at her nightdress. "Raise your arms. I want you naked." Her arms flew up and he lifted the cloth over her head and off. "That's much better."

She felt his breath bathe her breasts, felt the rough pad of his tongue against her nipple. She sucked in a shuddering sigh when he opened his mouth over the crest, taking the velvety tip deep in his mouth. He moved smoothly to the other breast, nipping gently, then soothing it with his tongue. Lara whimpered, arching up into him, wanting more. Abruptly Julian raised his head and stared deeply into her eyes. His smile was wickedly sensual as he slid down her body.

Her chest rose and fell erratically when he pressed his mouth to the soft flesh of her inner thigh and slowly nibbled higher. His mouth closed over her mound. Her hips surged upward, her back bowed backward. She whimpered softly, tangling her fists in his hair, bringing him closer. He eagerly obliged, sweeping his tongue deep within the velvety folds, grazing the nubbin hidden within, stealing her ability to think coherently.

He sucked and probed greedily, giving no quarter as his tongue and mouth drove her ruthlessly toward release. Lightning raced along her nerve endings, blinding light exploded behind her eyelids. Her whole body was caught in a crescendo of building need, until the crisis soared and broke inside her. Her cry rose in a keening wail. Convulsions engulfed her, and all sensation centered in that tender place where his mouth was working its magic.

Her wits returned slowly. She opened her eyes. Julian was leaning over her, his hard body sleek with perspiration. She grinned up at him. "My turn," she said, pushing him onto his back.

She felt him quivering, and carnal satisfaction made her feel omnipotent. The knowledge that this strong, powerful man trembled beneath her made her giddy with delight. Her ability to inspire his passion was more intoxicating than strong spirits.

A smile hovered on her lips as she scooted down his body. She heard him inhale sharply when she took his sex in her hands. She brought it to her mouth and placed a kiss on the thick tip. He made a sound, half agony, half pleasure, deep in his throat. She ran her tongue over the head. His fists twisted in her hair, his hands trembling against her temples. She could feel the tautly controlled passion building within him and reveled in it, savoring his salty essence, drawing him deeper . . . deeper . . .

She felt him stiffen. He gave a low, guttural roar, grabbed her about her waist, and hauled her upward. "No more. I need to be inside you."

Lara heartily agreed as she undulated her hips against his thick staff. Hot liquid seeped from between her thighs. He caught her nipple between his teeth and she cried out, desperate now to reach that place known only to lovers.

He came into her in one long, smooth thrust. She wriggled slightly, taking him deeper. Then he began to move. The pace he set was hard and fierce. She tilted her hips and met his thrusts, needing, wanting everything he had to give, and more.

Suddenly he reversed their positions, placing her beneath him. Her hands fluttered from his shoulders, sweeping down his muscular back to his taut buttocks. She felt him stiffen and dug her fingers into the rounded mounds. He lifted her legs and wrapped them around his grinding hips. He surged forward; she tightened her legs.

"Come to me, my love, come to me now."

His words inspired her, drove her up and over the crest as climax after climax shook her slender form, peaking and crushing like a tidal wave upon a storm-tossed shore, wild and tumultuous and exquisitely satisfying.

Julian covered her mouth with his, swallowing her cry of pleasure and shuddering as her hard spasms gripped him, intensifying in strength, squeezing his engorged staff until he could stand no more. He tensed and arched above her, potent, powerful, a sheen of sweat dampening his body. With a roar, he gave in to his wildness, his hips gyrating convulsively as he pushed hard and deep within her. He climaxed violently.

In the moment before he spilled his seed, Julian had the illogical thought that he and Lara were no longer two separate beings. A passion he'd never experienced with any other woman combined with a love he'd never envisioned made them one in body and soul.

When it was over Julian sank down on her, replete, drained of strength. Forcing himself to move, he rolled to one side, taking her with him, their bodies still tightly joined.

"I love you," Julian whispered. "Don't ever doubt me again."

"I love you, too, Julian. I'm sorry for doubting you."

"I'll never say anything to hurt you again."

" 'Tis already forgotten and forgiven. Today marks the true beginning of our marriage."

He nuzzled her neck. "I like the sound of that. I'm retiring from government service and intend to devote the rest of my life to you, our marriage, and our children, should God grant us sons or daughters."

He felt her sudden stillness and wondered what he had said this time to upset her.

"Do you want children, Julian?"

A weighty pause. "At one time, after Diana's death, I wanted neither a wife nor children. Sinjun's son was to be my heir. Life is so tenuous. Diana's death and the loss of the child I never knew nearly destroyed me. The knowledge that I was responsible for the death of a woman I cared about and a child I sired was so devastating that I swore never to marry or have children. Then you came along."

"You haven't answered my question. Do you want children?"

His arms tightened around her. "I want to give you children, Lara. As many as you want. Each one will be as dear to me as you are."

He felt a shudder go through her and wondered if she feared the birthing process. "I won't let anything hurt you, sweeting. If you fear childbirth, I won't demand that you produce an heir for me. Sinjun's son can still inherit."

Her trembling sigh brushed his cheek. "There's no need for you to name your brother's son your heir. Oh, Julian, my love, I'm already carrying your son and heir."

It took a few moments for Lara's words to register. When they did, an indescribable joy roared through him. "You're pregnant!"

"Aye, nearly four months gone."

Julian shuddered, his heart pounding furiously when he realized how close he'd come to losing his wife and child. "You were pregnant when you were kidnapped!" he exclaimed. His voice shook with repressed emotion. "You went through that horrifying ordeal while you were carrying my child. My God, how did you survive? Why didn't you tell me in Scotland that you were expecting?"

"I wanted to make sure before telling you. Besides, I wasn't sure how you felt about having a child with me."

Julian's stare delved deep. "Why didn't you tell me before you left London?"

"Don't be angry, Julian. Ramona has already scolded me for my reticence. I wanted you to want me for myself."

"What if I decided you weren't worth coming after? What if I had started divorce proceedings? Would you have told me about my child?"

"Your son, Julian. Ramona said I'm carrying your heir." She lowered her eyes. "Truthfully, I didn't think that far ahead. I hoped, I prayed you'd come for me and I'd never have to make that decision."

Julian heard little beyond Lara's first sentence. "You're carrying my heir? A son? Are you sure?"

Lara gave him an enigmatic smile. "Ramona is rarely wrong. But if by some remote chance she is, I'm sure at least one of our children will be a boy."

"Son or daughter, it matters not. I'll love him or her equally." Heaving a regretful sigh, he started to pull out of her. "Expectant mothers need their rest."

Lara's arms went around him. "I'm not tired and you're still hard inside me. Make love to me again, Julian, please."

"We have the rest of our lives, sweeting."

"Beginning with tonight," she teased, moving her hips enticingly.

Every nerve ending inside him suddenly came to life. He felt himself stretch and expand, held tightly within Lara's snug sheath. She was hot and wet and eager. He was hard and thick and ready. Together they reached for the stars.

Two days later the weather cleared enough for Lara and Julian to leave the private paradise their room had become. They bid a fond farewell to Pietro and promised to visit before Lara became too ungainly to travel.

"I'll always remember this inn," Lara said wistfully as they rode away from the Three Feathers. "I'll bet the innkeeper thought it strange that we didn't leave our room once in two days."

Julian sent her a wicked grin. "I wasn't going to let you out of my sight. Pietro told him we were newlyweds and arranged for our meals and baths to be sent up."

"If I wasn't anxious to see Papa I would have suggested that we linger another day or two," Lara said with a twinkle.

"We'll have plenty of private time together, love, I'll see to it. You, and our children, are now the focus of my life."

They reached London late that afternoon. The sky was a dull gray. Overhead a weak sun was trying to break through the clouds. But to Lara the day was bright and beautiful.

"Can we go see Papa first?" Lara asked hopefully. "He's probably worried about me."

"Aye. I spoke to him before I left and told him I was going to fetch you back to London. Are you sure you're not too tired? Maybe you should rest first."

"I'm pregnant, Julian, not ill. I'm fine."

A short time later they drew rein at the front door of Stanhope Hall and knocked on the door. Jeevers opened it immediately.

"Lady Lara! Welcome home. Your father is in the study. He's most anxious to see you."

"Thank you, Jeevers. Julian and I will announce ourselves."

Lara burst into the study without knocking. "Papa, I'm home!"

Stanhope leaped to his feet and held out his arms. Lara ran into them and they closed around her. "Lara! Thank God. I was so worried about you."

"I'm fine, Papa."

"Have you and Mansfield reconciled?"

Lara grinned at Julian. "Oh, yes. We're quite happy, actually. It turns out I misunderstood Julian. I should have listened to you. Julian loves me, Papa."

Stanhope beamed. "Of course, didn't I tell you as much? Mansfield, I'm glad all turned out well for you and my daughter. Now that your career as an agent is over, you can settle down and give me a grandchild or two."

Lara and Julian exchanged meaningful looks, then Lara giggled. "I'm already with child, Papa. I'm carrying Julian's heir."

Stanhope's mouth flew open. "His heir?" Then his brow cleared. "Ah, I understand. Your grandmother has already predicted a son for you and Julian."

Lara couldn't stop smiling. Her hand settled over her stomach. "Grandmother says my child will be a boy and she's rarely wrong."

Julian came up behind her, enfolded her in his arms, and pulled her against him. "Son or daughter, it matters not. There's time for both." He kissed the top of her head. "Now if you'll excuse us, I'm taking Lara home."

"Home," Lara repeated softly. "Oh, yes, let's go home."

Hand in hand they left Stanhope Hall to begin the first day of forever.

Epilogue

Scotland
1770

The sun was high in the cloudless sky and the scent of wildflowers wafted through the air on a balmy breeze. Glenmoor Castle stood like an ancient sentinel against a backdrop of mountains and heather-covered moors. The inner bailey rang with children's laughter and adult chatter. Clansmen wearing kilts and bonnets mingled with their English guests. The clansmen had gathered to celebrate the birthday of their laird, Christy Macdonald.

Lara placed a platter of roasted partridges on the long table set up in the inner bailey and exchanged a smile with Christy, who was arranging a basket of bread beside the meat.

"There's enough food here to feed an army," Lara quipped.

Christy rolled her eyes. "Have you ever seen a Highlander eat?"

Julian strolled over to join them, his small daughter perched on his shoulder.

"Have you seen Charlie?" Julian asked.

"Our son is probably charming one of his female cousins," Lara said. "The little scamp is such a rogue. I fear he'll be another Sinjun."

Julian raised his eyes heavenward. "God forbid."

"Sinjun has reformed," Christy reminded them. "I couldn't ask for a better husband for myself and father for my children."

"Put me down, Papa," the little girl on Julian's shoulders squealed. "I want to go play with Lizzy."

"Emma's Lizzy is an adorable little girl," Christy remarked. "And Lizzy's brother Trevor is every bit as mischievous as my Niall and your Charlie. I wonder how Gordie will turn out? He's still too young to get into trouble."

Julian lifted Serena, named for Lara's mother, off his shoulders. Before she scampered off, Lara admonished, "Try to keep your dress clean, Serena. I've already changed you once today."

Serena made a face. "Lizzy never stays clean."

"Serena is right," Christy chuckled. "Lizzy, Serena, and my own Althea are incorrigible tomboys. Sinjun says Althea reminds him of me when he first met me. Oh, speaking of Sinjun, there he is now. I need to speak to him about the bagpipes. Rory and Gavin want the pipers to play when the birthday cake is carried out, but playing bagpipes is against the law."

"I wouldn't worry," Julian said. "Kilts have been outlawed, too, but every clansman, including Sinjun, is wearing one."

"Nevertheless, I still feel that I should to remind Sinjun of the ban. Excuse me."

" 'Tis good to be back in Scotland," Lara said after

Christy left. " 'Tis like coming home again. I'm glad Father and your Aunt Amanda decided to join us."

Julian grinned. "It took some persuasion to convince Aunt Amanda to travel to the Highlands. She considers Highlanders barbarians, you know. But the prospect of seeing all the children together in one place convinced her that the trip was worth the discomfort of travel to this savage country."

"She looks happy enough now," Lara noted, gesturing to where Julian's venerable aunt was engaged in earnest conversation with Emma and Rudy. "Do you remember how angry you were when Emma married Rudy? You feared Rudy couldn't reform and be a good husband to Emma."

Julian nodded. "I was wrong to judge him so harshly. Thank God you set me straight. He's proved an exemplary husband." He held out his hand. "Walk with me. I feel an urgent need to kiss you without a crowd watching."

Lara grinned and placed her hand in his. "I'm a pregnant woman, my lord. Mind your manners."

"You're glowing," Julian replied, leading her away from the crush of people. "You're always beautiful, but when you're carrying my child you're especially lovely. This will be our last, love. Childbearing is no easy task. Too many children can ruin your health. Your life is too precious to be burdened with a child every year."

Lara thought she'd never loved Julian as much as she did at that moment. Which was saying a lot, for she loved him to distraction at all times.

"Sinjun has been trying forever to get us all together, and Christy's birthday was a perfect time,"

Julian remarked. " 'Twill be the best family reunion ever. I'm glad Emma, Rudy, and their children could join us."

"Aye. Ramona and Pietro are camped nearby, making everything perfect. 'Tis a good thing for the cousins to get to know one another. Sinjun and Christy's London visits are always so short. Our children barely know their kin."

Hand in hand they walked to the cliff overlooking the loch. Then Julian turned her into his arms and kissed her, pressing her as close as her stomach allowed.

"There," he said when he broke off the kiss. "I wanted to do that all day. I can't wait until we can make love again."

"Neither can I," Lara agreed, her eyes sparkling. "The worst part of being pregnant are those weeks of not being able to be as close as we'd like."

Julian sent her a mischievous grin. "Fear not, love, I'll make up for lost time as soon you've healed from childbirth."

He kissed her again, long and hard, until Lara broke it off, laughing at his eagerness. "I could stand here all day kissing you, Julian, but Christy needs me."

"Very well," Julian sighed, turning her back toward the castle. "Let's rejoin the party."

They returned to utter chaos. The children were running about like miniature whirlwinds, while the adults were trying to calm them. Julian and Lara laughed aloud at their exuberant antics.

"Look at them," Julian exclaimed. "There's not a handsomer brood anywhere in the world. Sinjun's Niall has dark hair like his father, and Althea is a red-headed hellion every bit as wild and undisciplined as her mother was at that age. And little Gordie already has Christy and Sinjun jumping through hoops."

"Emma and Rudy's pair of urchins are darling," Lara noted, "and no less mischievous than their cousins."

"Are you calling our two mischievous, sweeting?" Julian teased. "Charlie handles himself quite well for a five-year-old. He's already aware that he'll inherit the earldom."

Julian's gaze found his daughter. Serena looked as he suspected Lara might have looked at her age. A wild, unruly Gypsy lass with an abundance of curly dark hair, dark eyes slanted at the corners, and a beguiling smile. He feared his lively daughter would steal countless hearts before she settled down to marriage. But for now, he just wanted to sit back and enjoy his growing brood.

His gaze settled on Lara. Ramona predicted this third child would be another boy. As he'd told Lara a few minutes ago, this would be their last. He wanted to fill Lara's life with more than children. Sinjun was of the same mind, for he'd remarked that he was more than satisfied with the size of his family.

Lara must have noticed his intense look, for she smiled up at him. "What are you thinking?"

"I'm thinking I'm the luckiest man alive . . . and the happiest. You taught me how to relax and enjoy what God has given me. Honor and duty are fine, but they're not the stuff dreams are made of. You are my dream, my life, and my future, Lara. You and the children."

Lara beamed and planted a kiss on his lips. "That's for being the kind of man you are, the best husband

and father to your children a woman could hope for. You never cease to delight me, Julian."

"God willing I never will."

He never did.

Author's Note

I hope you enjoyed the irresistible Thornton brothers. Though their lives were very different, their loyalty to their family made them memorable.

My next book returns you to the Scottish Highlands several years after the battle at Culloden. The Maiden of Misterly, Elissa Fraser, is distantly related to Christy Macdonald, Sinjun Thornton's wife, and just as headstrong as her kinswoman. The English king fears that Elissa's proposed marriage to the Gordon laird will unite two powerful clans and threaten the tenuous peace in the Highlands.

A Touch So Wicked pits Elissa against Damian Stratton, a man knighted on the battlefield for bravery. After years of service to the king, Damian, otherwise known as the Demon Knight, is finally rewarded for his courage and fighting skills. He is given Misterly, a remote holding that has suddenly become very important to the crown. There are conditions, however. In order to keep the rich lands and ancient fortress, Damian must prevent the Maiden of Misterly from marrying the Gordon laird and banish Elissa to a convent.

The task proves more difficult than Damian expected. Elissa is not willing to let Damian dictate her life. Look for *A Touch So Wicked* early in 2002.

For a bookmark and newsletter, send a long, self-addressed stamped envelope to me at P.O. Box 3471, Holiday, Florida 34690. Or contact me by e-mail at *conmason@aol.com*. Visit my website *www.conniemason.com* to find out more about my past and future releases.

All My Romantic Best,

Connie Mason